"We could wager kisses."

Covering her mouth with her fingers, Janet turned scarlet. "Sir, you are brash."

"We've kissed before. I rather enjoyed it, and if I had to guess, you enjoyed kissing me as well."

"I'll not lie, but we mustn't."

He slid a finger along her forearm. "Whyever not?"

Her breath caught as those brilliant blue eyes met his gaze. He raised her chin with the crook of his finger. "A wee kiss never hurt a soul." His heart thrummed faster while he slowly savored her beauty, lowering his lips until he plied her mouth with a single peck. "See," he growled. "That was not so wicked."

"I beg to differ. I daresay even a simple kiss from you is unquestionably wicked." Her eyelids fluttered closed as she puckered her lips, clearly wanting more.

But she might be even more tempted if they played the game he planned—one he couldn't lose.

THE HIGHLAND COMMANDER

"Readers craving history entwined with their romance (à la *Outlander*) will find everything they desire in Jarecki's latest. Scottish romance fans rejoice."
—*RT Book Reviews*

"Sizzles with romance...Jarecki brings the novel to life with vivid historical detail."
—*Publishers Weekly*

THE HIGHLAND DUKE

RT Reviewers' Choice Award Winner

"Readers will admire plucky Akira, who, despite her poverty, is fiercely independent and is determined to be no man's mistress. The romance is scintillating and moving, enhanced by fast-paced suspense."
—*Publishers Weekly*

"This story was so much more than a romance, it was full of intrigue, excitement and drama...a fantastic read that I fully recommend."
—Buried Under Romance

THE
HIGHLAND
RENEGADE

ALSO BY AMY JARECKI

Lords of the Highlands series
The Highland Duke
The Highland Commander
The Highland Guardian
The Highland Chieftain

THE HIGHLAND RENEGADE

A Lords of the Highlands Novel

AMY JARECKI

FOREVER
New York Boston

Forever
Hachette Book Group
1290 Avenue of the Americas, New York, NY 10104
forever-romance.com
twitter.com/foreverromance

First Edition: January 2019

Forever is an imprint of Grand Central Publishing. The Forever name and logo are trademarks of Hachette Book Group, Inc.

The publisher is not responsible for websites (or their content) that are not owned by the publisher.

The Hachette Speakers Bureau provides a wide range of authors for speaking events. To find out more, go to www.hachettespeakersbureau.com or call (866) 376-6591.

ISBN: 978-1-5387-2961-8 (mass market), 978-1-5387-2962-5 (ebook)

Printed in the United States of America

OPM

10 9 8 7 6 5 4 3 2 1

I would like to dedicate this novel to my friends Barbara and Maria, who have faced the brave fight with cancer and, through it all, continue to be avid readers and reviewers. I love seeing your faces and posts on social media.

I'd also like to dedicate this book to every brave soul out there who must stare down adversity and continue to fight. You are my heroes.

Acknowledgments

To all the amazing people who have helped with this novel, I am truly grateful. To my agent, **Elaine Spencer**, who stands by me through thick and thin. To my fabulous editor, **Leah Hultenschmidt**; not only is she tactful, she is brilliant. To the Grand Central Publishing Art Department, especially **Craig White** and **Elizabeth Turner Stokes**, for their brilliance in creating smoldering Highlander covers that ooze masculinity and foreboding. To **Estelle Hallick** for donning her armor and guiding my books through the tempestuous marketing maze, and to **Mari Okuda** and **S. B. Kleinman** for their fastidious and diligent copyediting, without which all my typing faux pas would shamefully be on display.

Chapter One

---

*T*he Highlands, late October 1712

The sign on the alehouse door caught Janet's eye as Kennan carried her across the muddied street.

> *Samhain Gathering, 7 o'clock, Inverlochy Hall, Friday, 31st October.*
> *No spurs. Weapons must be checked at the door.*

Her stomach fluttered at the thrill. The best part of the fete was the gathering after the livestock auction. There'd be a feast of roast pork, music, and dancing.

A great deal of dancing.

Two drovers brushed past them, nearly knocking Janet's hat from her head. The enormous red plume adorning it batted her in the eye.

"Watch yourselves, ye maggots," Kennan growled as

the two men pushed inside. Her brother could be overly protective, though he was as lovable as a puppy. Strong, too. He didn't miss a step, not even when the drovers practically ran them over in their haste for a pint of ale. If Kennan felt any strain from Janet's weight, he showed no sign of discomfort. But she knew better. The wool of her riding habit alone most likely weighed a stone.

Janet straightened her tricorn bonnet, shifting the feather out of her line of sight while Kennan gently deposited her on the footpath. "Those men must have a terrible thirst," she said.

He glanced toward the door, busy with people entering and exiting. "Thirst or not, a month of droving is no reason for a man to be careless. What if I'd dropped you in the mud?"

"But you didn't."

Kennan took her hand and led her inside. Janet had attended the fete at Inverlochy during Samhain annually as far back as she could remember, but she'd never seen the town this crowded. "Every year there are more people at the harvest."

He scowled at another brash drover heading for the bar. "And more bloody scoundrels. Stay close to me."

Any other week, Inverlochy was a quaint and quiet town, but right before Samhain, clans and kin descended from the hills or sailed from the Hebrides to peddle their livestock and goods. It was only fourteen miles from the Clan Cameron seat at Achnacarry, and Janet and her kin visited two or three times a year to purchase supplies. Though not large, the town boasted a haberdasher, a modiste, and a tanner who made saddles as well as shoes.

At the center of town was the alehouse. The only establishment that served meals, it catered to all manner of fellows. A lady must never enter unaccompanied, lest she be mistaken for a harlot. Judging by the way her brother had clamped his fingers around her hand, Janet need not worry about being mistaken for a woman of easy virtue, though she wouldn't mind if Kennan weren't quite so protective. After all, she did have an ulterior motive for visiting the fete without her father. Da hadn't before missed the Samhain gathering, though much had changed since he'd taken a new bride.

Needless to say, Janet was relieved to enjoy a wee respite from Achnacarry and her imposing stepmother, awkward as things had become.

"I wonder where all these people will stay," she said as Kennan pulled her deeper into the crowd.

"Tents, the alehouse, the loft in the stables." He raised his voice to be heard.

Through the haze of pipe smoke, Janet looked to the rafters, doubting the wax had been cleaned from the chandeliers since her visit six months past. "Aye, Mrs. Mac-Nash couldn't possibly take in the half of them."

Kennan grasped Janet's elbow and led her to an area near the back where respectable-looking patrons gathered. "Fortunately, we have a long-standing booking at the boardinghouse."

"Thank heavens." She scanned the faces of the rugged Highlanders dressed in kilts with their plaids pinned at their shoulders. Gazes shifted her way. Interested gazes. Brows arched. A ruddy man winked. Janet's cheeks burned as she tried not to smile.

With luck, she might meet someone who struck her fancy. Her stepmother had already started mumbling about finding Janet a husband, and in no way did she want that woman meddling in her affairs. By the eel-eyed way the new Lady of Lochiel looked at Janet, dear Stepmother would hog-tie the first poor sop who happened past their lands and force her stepdaughter into a life of misery.

Please, Lord, help me to find someone I like. If there actually was a man out there with whom she could fall in love. At the age of two and twenty, she hadn't given up hope, but she had grown anxious. And unfortunately, according to Her Ladyship, Janet was unduly particular.

"If it's not the Camerons!" a familiar voice called from a table in the corner. "Och, I haven't seen the likes of you since we were wed. Come, share our table." Dunn MacRae, chieftain of his clan, stood and beckoned them.

Janet's heart soared. One of her dearest friends, Lady Mairi, daughter of the Earl of Cromartie and Dunn's lovely wife, waved. Returning the gesture, Janet hastened to follow her brother to the table. The two men shook hands while she slid onto the chair beside her friend. "I'm so happy to see you. I was afraid I would be following Kennan to and fro for the entire sennight."

"What about John and Alan? Did your younger brothers not come?"

"Nay, they are both away at university."

"Then I agree, spending all your time with one brother for a sennight would be miserable." Mairi grasped Janet's hand, grinning and stretching the splay of freckles across her nose. "I've ever so much to do. I would be delighted to have you accompany me."

"To the haberdasher?"

"Indeed, that will be our most important stop."

Janet nearly squealed. "We might need a whole day just for that shop."

"I agree."

"Oh, this will be fun. Though I must drop the woolens I've knitted at the Highland Benevolent Society first."

"Bless your heart, dearest. 'Tis very kind of you to always be thinking of the unfortunate."

Dunn flagged a barmaid. "Ale, bread, and pottage all around, if you please."

The woman, looking haggard, gave him an exasperated nod. "Aye, sir, but it will be some time. We expected half these numbers."

An icy chill crept over Janet's skin when the door opened with a whoosh. All eyes shifted to soldiers dressed in scarlet. Not a one smiled as they sauntered inside with muskets slung over their shoulders and daggers at their hips. The laughter transformed into intense silence.

People scuttled away while the officer leading the retinue turned full circle, his heels clomping against the floorboards. "I am Lieutenant Winfred Cummins, in charge of keeping the peace at this uncivilized, pagan gathering."

Low murmurs of dissent rumbled through the hall. Janet knew him, unfortunately. He oft called into Achnacarry when his regiment rode out on "peacekeeping sorties."

He stopped and glared directly at her. "All disturbers of the peace will be escorted to Fort William and face the magistrate. There will be no malicious maiming of cattle, no poaching, no begging without a license, and all persons caught with a blackened face after dark will promptly be led to the gallows."

Janet drew her hand to her chest, leaned toward her friend, and whispered, "I have no idea why he's looking our way. He should be speaking to the drovers at the bar."

Mairi opened her fan and held it over her mouth. "He's looking at you, lass."

Janet slipped lower in her chair. "Heavens, no. That man is a snake."

"You know him?" Mairi asked while the soldiers shouldered through the crowd.

"Aye, as does everyone who lives within twenty miles of Fort William. He's *notorious*."

"I do not doubt it." Her Ladyship snapped her fan shut. "When a dragoon dons a red coat, it seems his mind is instantly addled."

"You have a way with words, wife," Dunn said.

Again Janet's attention was drawn to the opening door. A wee gasp whispered through her lips while butterflies swarmed through her stomach just as they'd done when Robert Grant had ridden his enormous black horse into the stables earlier that day. She clenched her elbows to her sides, making the queasiness stop. The man was too unnerving. Especially today. He was unshorn and unkempt, and his hawkish eyes shifted across the scene as if assessing everything.

Janet brushed a hand over her curls. "That man is simply barbaric." *Barbaric and nerve racking.* Every time their gazes met, he made her too self-aware. Curses to his braw looks, Mr. Grant was diabolical. And why was it that the most handsome of men always behaved like complete brutes?

"Aye, Grant looks as though he's been mustering cattle in the Highlands for months," Her Ladyship agreed.

Kennan snorted. "That brigand is mad—looks it, as well. As we were arriving, he had the audacity to accuse my kin of thieving his cattle."

Dunn looked to the bar, where the big Highlander had

shouldered in beside the other drovers. "Grant is a mite mistrustful of neighboring clans. He has cause, after all. But he's a good man." When Kennan guffawed, MacRae clapped him on the shoulder. "Though he's wrong about the Camerons."

"What do you mean, sir?" Janet leaned in. "I do not believe Mr. Grant to be a good man at all."

"Och, you'll find a heart of gold under that rugged exterior, lassie." MacRae winked. "I'll tell ye true, there's no man I'd rather have fighting beside me in battle. Robert Grant's loyalty may be hard to win, but once earned, you will not find a man more steadfast and true."

Mairi gave Janet a nudge. "I thought you found him a wee bit braw."

She snatched her fan from her chatelaine and cooled her face. "Pleasing to the eye, mayhap, but I could *never* be on friendly terms with a Highlander who accuses my father of thievery."

"Thievery, did I hear?"

Her shoulders tensing, Janet hid her cringe behind the fan as Winfred Cummins moved to their table and blocked the view of Mr. Grant. Honestly, Janet liked nearly everyone, but today the alehouse seemed to be filled with the most churlish gentlemen she knew.

"It seems some of Laird Grant's cattle were stolen. Some of Clan Cameron's went missing as well," Kennan explained.

"Is that so?" Flicking a bit of lint from his doublet, the lieutenant appeared unimpressed and disinterested.

The barmaid pushed in and placed four tankards of ale in front of them. "Your pottage will be along shortly."

"My thanks." Dunn reached for a drink and sipped. "So, Lieutenant, what news?"

Cummins shifted his gaze to Janet while she clasped her hands in her lap and stared at her fan, heat spreading up her face. "Things have been quiet," he said. "Though I'm skeptical they'll remain so with so many miscreants in town." He didn't bother to look at Mr. MacRae, to whom he was speaking—the lieutenant continued to ogle Janet as if she were on display in a shop window.

"Miscreants? Hardly," said Mairi.

At last Lieutenant Cummins shifted his attention and arched an eyebrow at Her Ladyship. "Whenever large numbers of Highlanders gather, there's bound to be trouble."

Casting her inner revulsion aside, Janet squared her shoulders and inhaled. "I certainly hope not. I came to Inverlochy to enjoy the Samhain celebrations, not rue them."

"And that's where you err, miss," said Lieutenant Cummins. "You Highlanders refuse to cast away outdated and pagan fancies. This gathering ought to be called the harvest fete, or something more civilized."

"That would be quite dull, indeed," said Mairi.

"I agree." Emboldened by Her Ladyship's support, Janet nodded. "There's a certain tradition in our Celtic heritage I think should never be lost, no matter who is on the throne or what religion is in vogue."

The lieutenant shifted his leering eyes to her again. "Do you speak blasphemy?"

"Hardly." This time, Janet wasn't about to feign meekness and look at her lap. She narrowed her eyes and stared at him directly. "I speak the opposite. I speak of freedom."

Kennan pushed his chair back. "Pay no mind to my sister. She is a strong-willed lass, passionate in her convictions."

A wry grin played on the lieutenant's lips. Still wearing his tall grenadier hat, he was a man of average height and acceptable appearance with gray eyes and a big mole on his right cheek. He leaned across the table and lowered his voice. "I should like to observe such passion at the Samhain dance—it would certainly liven up a dreary evening."

"Aye, Lieutenant Cummins?" Janet continued to hold his stare, refusing to show any sign of the abhorrence roiling inside. "It is my opinion that the dancing at Samhain shall be the most vigorous in the Highlands."

"I hope you are right." He straightened before he bowed. "Good day."

Mairi leaned in. " 'Most vigorous'?" she whispered.

Janet sniffed, wildly fluttering her fan. "What should I have said? I could not sit idle and allow him to degrade our traditions."

"But *vigorous*?" Mairi giggled.

"Aye, Sister." Kennan gave a pointed look. "I agree with Her Ladyship. Keep mum when in the presence of that man—or any dragoons. They have a knack of turning anything you say against you."

Janet grasped the handle of her tankard. "I intend to stay away from all soldiers." *Cummins most of all.*

As she sipped, she watched Mr. Grant follow a barmaid out the back toward the bathhouse. Over his shoulder, the brawny Highlander cast a tortured look Janet's way. A look filled with hunger. Had Janet blinked, she would have missed the glance from her father's sworn enemy. Oddly, the shudder coursing through her far exceeded the brief duration of his glimpse. How could a man impart such heated intensity within a mere heartbeat? Good glory, she could scarcely breathe.

Oh, to be in the barmaid's shoes. Janet would douse

the laird under his bathwater until he admitted the
Camerons hadn't stolen his miserable beasts.

Bath?

Robert Grant without his clothing.

Janet gulped, her skin afire.

Perhaps she'd best confront him on the matter some
other time.

* * *

"'Tis sixpence for a bath and shave. The men's tubs are
behind the curtain," said the wench. "Would you like me
to launder your shirt and kilt?"

"Please." Robert set down his cup of whisky, opened the
thong on his sporran, and fished out a handful of coins.

"A penny for the shirt and two for your plaid."

He dropped the change into her palm. "Is the water
hot?"

"The lad is bringing a kettle from the kitchen anon."
She dropped the coins into a pocket hanging from her
apron. "Shall I help you disrobe, sir?"

"Nay, just ensure the lad hastes with the water."

"Very well. I'll return later with the shaving kit."

Normally Robert enjoyed having a female unwrap his
tartan. He liked the thrill of having a wench's eyes on
him—her tongue slipping to the corner of her mouth, her
cheeks growing rosy. Occasionally breasts would heave,
and the boldest lassies would pay a compliment, or make
a proposition—usually a welcome one. But Robert was
still annoyed by his confrontation in the stables with
Kennan Cameron. Worse, the man's sister had stood by,
glaring at him as if he were Lucifer, and now the lass was
dining in the next room. Blast her. He could feel Janet's

accusing eyes boring into his back as he'd left for the bathhouse. The heat from her gaze still lingered on his skin. Must his nemesis have a daughter sent from hell to torture him?

If only the Camerons hadn't come. And why do they not leave their womenfolk at home?

He shouldn't have been so forward with Cameron when he'd confronted him at the stables, but his shepherd had been positive about the cattle thieves. Cameron men had been spotted nearby and no one else. Of course, Kennan had denied his clan's guilt and Miss Janet had grown indignant at Robert's accusation, insistent upon her father's virtue. And she'd stood beside her brother like a Viking princess, her rich blue eyes intense and far too confident—as if she were accusing *him* of poaching. Further, she'd had the audacity to point out her kin had sustained hefty livestock losses as well.

But the yearlings hadn't disappeared on their own. Someone was responsible for poaching Robert's cattle, and he intended to find out who.

Hell, I ken who.

Camerons and Grants had feuded for centuries, and it would have been too bloody tempting for Lochiel's men to ride on without pinching a few of Robert's head. But they hadn't left it at a few. The bastards had poached six and sixty yearlings—enough for him to consider putting Achnacarry to fire and sword. But first he needed more proof. With all the redcoats swarming through the Highlands, gone were the days of reiving without first securing a testimony.

Robert retrieved his whisky and took a healthy swig, then pushed through the curtain. A pair of men reclined in tubs, smoking pipes. He gave them a nod, wishing tobacco were banned from the bathhouse. He didn't enjoy the smoke. To him it reeked, and the odor clung to his clothes. Which is why he set his satchel on a chair and left his only change of clean clothes inside.

After the lad came with the hot water, Robert lowered himself into the tub and sighed aloud. Weariness built up after a month traversing the Highlands, sleeping on rocky ground and freezing his arse most nights; the big wooden tub was akin to heaven. He took another sip of whisky and slid down farther, resting his head back and closing his eyes.

By the time he finished his drink, the lass had reappeared with razor, bowl, and brush. "Are you ready for your shave, sir?"

"Aye." He beckoned her forward, examining her form. She was of sturdy stock, full bodied, the way women ought to be. Then she smiled, revealing a missing tooth right in the front. Wisps of mousy-brown hair poked from beneath her coif, and when she bent over him with the brush and bowl, her breath smelled sour.

Robert wiped his hand down his face. "Be careful with that blade, lassie."

"I always am," she said, as if she'd shaved hundreds of faces—most likely she had.

He raised his chin and submitted to her choppy ministrations, feeling like a sheep in the shearing shed. She hummed pleasantly, but her hand was anything but gentle. Robert winced when she nicked the back of his jaw.

The lass snapped her hand away. "Och, forgive me, sir. I'm sorry."

He wiped the cut, then rinsed the blood off in the water. "Do you have some other place you need to be?"

"Nay, sir."

"Are you not satisfied with your wages?"

"My wages are adequate. Why do you ask?"

"You're nay cleaving a slab of mutton here. I suggest you relax. Shaving a man is easier if you're not tense."

"Sorry," she apologized again before taking another swipe along his jaw, slower this time. "Ah...would ye be needing some company this evening?" she asked, her voice unsure.

He opened one eye and looked her up and down. The woman had not a line on her face, making it impossible to determine if she'd reached her majority. In the dark the missing tooth might not matter, but Robert had no intention of bedding a novice.

Chapter Two

*W*rapped in her woolen cloak and carrying a satchel holding the mittens, scarves, and hats she had knitted for the unfortunate, Janet met Mairi in the entrance hall of the boardinghouse. "It is blowing a gale outside."

Stepping down the creaky stairs, Mairi pulled her hood low over her brow. "Always does this time of year. At least it is not raining."

"Thank heavens for small mercies." Janet's stomach gave a wee flutter. She'd been looking forward to doing a bit of shopping, and being able to catch up on the news with Mairi was an added boon. She held up her satchel. "It will only take a moment to drop these at the Benevolent Society."

"Aye, and it is on the way to the haberdasher's." Her Ladyship opened the door. "I need to purchase some silk thread for a receiving blanket I'm making."

"Oh, my word!" Janet skipped beside her newly married friend. "Tell me you're not expecting."

"We are."

"What wonderful news. When?"

"Spring. I think."

"Should you not be home at Eilean Donan and in your chamber with your feet propped on a stool?"

"Wheesht. I'd go mad being cooped up for so long. 'Tis bad enough as it is. Dunn says this is my last outing afore he insists upon my confinement."

"Well, I'm glad you're here...as long as you are feeling well."

"Never better. It seems pregnancy agrees with me."

"You are fortunate. I've heard tell of women who take to their beds ill as soon as they miss their courses." Janet clutched her cloak tighter against the wind. "Have you been to the seer?"

"Nay." Mairi slapped her hand through the air. "I'm not about to allow an old crone to tell me whether I'll live or die, or if the child will be lass or lad."

"Smart of you...though I'm not certain I'd be able to wait nine months to find out."

"I think seers are wrong half the time, nevertheless."

"Aye. The women in Achnacarry jest that if ours says the bairn will be a lad, then expect a lass."

Her Ladyship gave a pronounced nod. "See what I mean?"

A shingle hung outside the West Highland Benevolent Society's door, screeching and unreadable in the wind. Janet pushed inside to find the same crusty old man with a stooped spine who had manned the office since she was a child. "Hello, Mr. Andrews. I've brought you some woolens," she said, pulling the assortment of scarves, bonnets, and mittens from her bag and placing them on the table.

"Och, just in time, lass." He gave her a grin, revealing two black top teeth. "With the chill in the air, I believe winter will be early this year, and there are certainly plenty of unfortunate souls who will be grateful for these."

Mairi examined a mitten. "Your work is quite good, Janet."

"Thank you. Is there anything else the society needs, sir?"

Mr. Andrews scratched his chin. "A hall with about twenty rooms and blankets."

"Well, I might be able to help with the blankets."

"That would be much appreciated, miss," he said, gathering the woolens into his arms. "I'll expect to see you a few months hence."

"Indeed you will, sir." Janet turned to Mairi. "See, that didn't take long at all. Now to enjoy our shopping adventure."

Together they continued on their way. At the curb they were forced to walk single file in order to use a plank to cross the muddy street. On the other side, Mairi took Janet by the elbow. "We've talked enough about me. How are things now your father has remarried?"

"I'd rather not talk about things at Achnacarry." Janet rolled her eyes as they stepped inside the haberdasher's shop. A sign on the door indicated the tailor was visiting between the hours of ten and three and that all gentlemen should schedule an appointment with the clerk.

"Good morn," said the merchant from behind the counter.

The two women greeted him in unison.

"May I help you find something?" he asked.

"Silk and sewing needles, please," Mairi replied.

"Ah yes, we received a shipment with brilliant new colors just for Samhain. You'll find them and the needles just here." Beaming, he motioned to the silk display case with at least a dozen drawers along the far wall. "Needles are in the bottom drawer."

"Thank you." Janet gave him a nod as the bell rang and two more ladies stepped inside.

"I'll leave you to make your selections," he said, then greeted the newcomers.

Janet used the tiny wooden knob to pull open the top drawer and peek inside. "These are lovely. Do you like the blue?"

"I think yellow is more neutral." Mairi moved in beside her. "Your tone was a bit foreboding when you uttered 'Achnacarry.' Is all well?"

"Och, let us simply say it is a welcome diversion to spend a few days in Inverlochy."

"Oh dear, I sense some discord."

"I suppose. Honestly, I have no grounds upon which to complain. 'Tis just difficult to see one's own father acting like a lovesick chap."

"I can hardly imagine my father behaving so un-earl-like." Mairi covered her mouth and stifled a giggle. "And your stepmother. Is she treating you well?"

Janet pursed her lips and glanced over her shoulder to ensure no one was eavesdropping, then lowered her voice. "I suppose she's nice enough. Though she looks at me with leery eyes. And I strongly suspect she's planning to marry me off to the first man who happens past."

"Truly?" A crease formed between Mairi's eyebrows. "Your father ought to have something to say about that."

"Thank heavens, else I would have been peddled off to a traveling merchant who called in a fortnight ago."

"A merchant? You are the daughter of a knight and a laird. Has your father not begun to seek an alliance with your hand?"

"*Haud yer wheesht!*" Janet knew all about arranged marriages. Mairi had been promised to the Earl of Seaforth all her life, until the earl fell in love with an English lass. Thank heavens he did, else Mairi never would have been able to marry the man she was meant to. "You are my dearest friend, m'lady, but I must say you are the last person who should talk to me about making alliances via the marriage bed."

Mairi stared, agape. "Goodness, you are right. I cannot believe I uttered it." She shut the top drawer of the thread display and pulled open the next—not that she seemed to be paying any attention to the colors whatsoever. "Forgive me for prying, but are you planning to forge your own alliance—say during Samhain?"

"Not at all. I'm nowhere near as flamboyant as you, my dearest." Janet sighed, knowing she'd just told a tall tale. *If only I could be forward like Mairi—bat my eyelashes at a braw lad and have him swoon at my feet.* "However, I am browsing. I would like to find a suitable gentleman afore my stepmother starts to meddle—if she hasn't already."

"Is there a suitor you might have in mind?"

"Nay. Please keep my confidence, but I'll admit I did think, with so many clans coming to the Samhain celebrations, why, there might be *someone*."

"Hmm. How about Ciar MacDougall? He's next in line to be laird, and his lands are vast indeed."

"MacDougall?" Janet said, her voice trailing off. She had known Ciar all her life. He was as much her brother as Kennan. MacDougall lands were not as vast as Cameron

lands, though that didn't matter a lick to her. Her friendship with Ciar was unquestionable. Unfortunately, she'd
never felt much of a spark for him. *Isn't there supposed
to be some sort of spark, heart palpitations, swooning,
falling in love?* In addition, she was quite certain he felt
the same. Spark-less. In fact, they'd discussed their feelings at a gathering when she was eighteen. They'd agreed
to be fast allies for life and never sweethearts. "He's a
good friend, I suppose."

"Friendship is a place to start."

"No, Mairi. I am not *attracted* to Ciar." Janet opened
the drawer of needles and pulled out an assortment of four
pinned on a black piece of cloth. "You found love," she
whispered. "Is it wrong for me to want that as well?"

"Not at all. I am the last person in all of Christendom
to downplay the merits of a bond with love. To me it is
the difference between building a house of stone and one
of sticks." Mairi opened her fan and held it up to ensure
more privacy. "Do you want to know what I think?"

Janet kept the needles to purchase and closed the
drawer. "I'll wager you're about to tell me."

"At every gathering we have ever attended together,
you have not been able to avert your eyes from the laird
of Clan Grant."

Janet nearly spat out her teeth, she guffawed so loudly.
"Oh please. Mr. Grant?"

"I'm telling you true."

"If what you say is *actually* what you have observed,
then 'tis only on account of his vile nature and his in-
sistence on blaming my father for his own livestock
losses. I declare, that man is neglectful of his affairs,
an unmitigated brute, and a rogue of the worst order!"

The curtain behind them swished open. A tailor with

a measuring ribbon around his neck stepped through and gave the ladies a sideways glance. The problem? On his heels was the very man for whom Janet had professed her dislike so profoundly.

Her throat constricted as she drew her hand over her mouth.

"Grant," Mairi said behind her, far too chirpily. "'Tis good to see you this morn."

The man towered over them by a foot, glowering directly at Janet. "Is it? Or would you prefer I collect my horse and leave the profits on my remaining yearlings for your brother to collect?"

Janet's face grew hot. "I—"

"Oh please, Your Lairdship," said Mairi. "You cannot hold Miss Janet and her clan accountable. You ken they would never thieve your cattle."

"I can only go on the facts, m'lady. And the evidence points to Cameron lads."

Shaking off her mortification, Janet stepped forward and shifted her hands to her hips. "My father's men did not thieve your yearlings, sir." She might not be flirtatious like Mairi, but she would hold her own against this brigand. "Did you not hear Kennan yesterday? The Camerons suffered losses, too. Someone else poached your cattle as well as ours."

The laird's polished-steel eyes glared down at her, his jaw hard. Janet's knees wobbled. Good gracious, the man had shaved, and he wore a clean shirt and kilt, looking far too braw for a scoundrel. But Janet could not mistake the hate in his stare; he was glowering as if he might be about to strike. "Then you'd venture to add *daft* to your litany of dislikes, would you, miss?"

"I-I—"

"You are filled with your father's bile just like all of his spawn." Mr. Grant strode past the tailor. "I'll return for my suit of clothes afore the end of the week."

Janet cringed, watching him storm out the door, his shoulders so wide hardly any daylight shone between his form and the jamb. She clutched her hands over her heart, every fiber of her body taut. No matter how handsome she found Mr. Grant, she would never like him. "He's horrible."

"Misguided, I'd say." Mairi placed her arm across Janet's shoulders. "Perhaps I'll have a word with Dunn—see if he can reason with the laird."

"What use would that be? Robert Grant will always think what he likes, no matter how mistaken he is. I stand by everything I said about him, and if he doesn't like it, he can bite his own backside."

* * *

Robert cracked his knuckles as he made his way to the alehouse. While he'd stood for the tailor to take his measurements, he'd heard the ladies enter the shop. Their banter had been mildly interesting until Janet spat a line of defamatory untruths about him. What the devil did she know of Robert's character? He wasn't vile or neglectful, and he most certainly was no fop. Aye, he had a reputation to uphold for harboring a certain talent with the ladies, but rogue?

He splayed his fingers. *Mayhap rogue. But on every other count the woman was utterly wrong.*

It wasn't even the noon hour, yet he needed a tankard of ale. Women. He could do without them.

Inside the alehouse, Dunn MacRae rested his elbow on the bar, nursing a tankard himself.

"Got an early thirst, have you?" Robert said as he flagged the barman. "Two, please."

"You look flummoxed. What's ailing you?" Dunn finished his tankard and slid the empty to the back of the bar while the barman placed two brimming ales in front of them.

"Och, bloody Camerons."

"The Camerons again? Good God, they ought to be the least of your worries."

"I wish they were, but why would my men lie about what they saw?"

"Cameron's men were *seen* pinching your cattle?"

"Nay, but they were the only ones about."

"Aye, though Kennan tells me they lost livestock as well...and as I understand it, your men didn't return for two days. Anyone could have happened past in that time."

"Not among the hills of An Cruachan."

"Well, ye ken what I'm on about. You cannot point the finger at Cameron with certainty."

Heaving a long sigh, Robert picked up his tankard and drank. "Mayhap I wouldn't if I'd received a letter from Lochiel explaining his side. And mayhap I wouldn't if our clans were on good terms, but the bastards have been stealing livestock from the Grants for centuries."

"In the past, aye, and you repay in kind. Your feud makes no sense to me. You and your da, God rest his soul, are like kin to me. So are Sir Ewen and his sons."

"I wish I could be companionable with half the lot you are."

"Perhaps 'tis time to make amends with the Camerons."

"Daisies will be dancing over my grave afore that happens. You ken the legend. The chief of Clan Cameron defiled a Grant woman in a drunken rage and left her to die in the moors. Bloody savage heathen."

"I reckon the lot of you have paid for that man's crimes time and time over." Dunn swirled his tankard.

"What are you saying?"

"I'm not saying the doing of it was right, but I need to ask, how long ago was the Grant woman defiled?"

Robert rubbed his fingers over the nick on his jaw, the one from the wench's shave last eve. It hurt nearly as much as the one he'd received on his forearm from a Cameron dirk when the cowards had put his lands to fire and sword when he was but sixteen years of age. "Seven generations, I'd reckon. Mayhap more."

Dunn tapped his fingers against the MacRae brooch pinned at his left shoulder. "In light of the trouble coming from the crown, do you not think it is time to mend your differences? The time is nigh when the clans will need to stand together."

"Aye, but what if I did extend the hand of forgiveness? Lochiel and his sons would be more likely to chop it off."

"I could arrange a duel of swords between you and young Kennan."

"Then I'd be accused of murder." Robert snorted. "The Camerons would partner with the Campbells, burn my lands, and reive my cattle."

"The Campbells?" Dunn slapped his palm on the bar. "Now I ken you're daft, ye bull-brained boar. Camerons would sooner march through the gates of hell than take up arms with the Campbells."

Robert hid his grin behind his tankard. "So you think a wee duel will solve generations of feuding?"

"I do."

"To first blood?"

"Aye, that's usually the way of it." Dunn clapped him on the shoulder. "What do you say?"

"I'd rather give no quarter," he mumbled.

"That's because you're likely to win, and I reckon *the cause* cannot afford to lose either one of you."

Robert didn't give an answer straightaway. He drank his ale thoughtfully. On one hand, it would be a relief to be rid of threats to the southwest. Not that a duel would solve everything. However, if Kennan was willing, then Robert wouldn't be one to refuse. "Very well. If the Cameron heir is amenable, I will face him."

"Then I'll arrange it straightaway."

His tankard empty, Robert shook hands with Dunn. He wanted to buy some heifers, and there was no time like the present to inspect the yards in advance of the auction.

No sooner had he started for the stables than Miss Janet and Lady Mairi stepped out of the dress shop, their arms laden with parcels. Lieutenant Cummins hastened toward them, tipped his grenadier hat, and bowed.

Robert crossed the street, his fingers automatically sliding around the hilt of his dirk.

"Please allow me to help you with your packages, ladies," said Cummins in a syrupy English accent.

"Thank you, but we are perfectly able to manage." With a cursory nod, Janet started off.

"I insist," he said, reaching for her items and making them fall to the footpath.

"For heaven's sake." She bent down.

"I'll fetch them." The lieutenant's hat fell off and hit the lass in the shoulder as he bent down.

Robert snatched the parcels before the man could lay a finger on them. "I beg your pardon, sir, but the ladies said they did not require your assistance." He straightened, watching the officer, fully aware he'd just broken his rule to steer clear of the queen's dragoons.

Cummins collected his hat and glowered. "And some people wonder why we need change in the Highlands." He smacked the tall headpiece against his thigh to clear the dirt. "Thievery is rife. You ken. You've suffered at the hands of poachers."

"I have. And what actions are the queen's men taking to prevent these thieves from infesting our grazing lands?"

The lieutenant shifted his eyes to the ladies, a smirk playing on his lips. "You are arrogant to insinuate Her Majesty's army is anything but vigilant."

"I implied no such thing. I simply asked a reasonable question." Robert gave a curt bow of his head. "Good day, sir." He cut off the conversation, then watched the lieutenant march away before he turned his attention to the ladies.

Miss Janet regarded him with the most confounded expression on her face. She held out her hands as if she expected Robert to put the parcels in her arms and saunter off, but Lady Mairi pushed between them. "Would you be so kind as to carry those back to the boardinghouse for us, Grant?"

He looked from Mairi to Janet, then gave a nod.

"'Tis unfortunate there are so many government troops about," said Her Ladyship.

"Aye," Robert agreed, keenly aware of Miss Janet's gaze searing into his back. He plodded ahead, feeling like an oversize errand boy. The lass had expressed her opinion of him quite clearly. Lord knew what feminine wares were in the parcels in his arms. They even smelled flowery.

Worse, Kennan opened the door as they neared the boardinghouse. "Found some use for the Grant laird, did you, Lady Mairi?"

"Oh no, Grant is being a gentleman and carrying Janet's packages."

The women stepped inside while Robert followed and gave Kennan a questioning glance, wondering if Dunn had spoken to him about the duel.

"I'll take those." Kennan pulled the packages from Robert's hands to the sound of ripping parcels.

"Ah." Not many things could make Robert Grant uneasy, but when he looked down at the scarlet petticoat in his hands, heat rushed to his face. Gulping, he tossed the garment into Cameron's arms and hastened for the cattle yards where he'd been headed in the first place.

Chapter Three

"*W*here are you off to in such a rush?" Mairi asked the next day as Janet raced through the entry of the boarding-house, throwing her cloak about her shoulders.

"No time to explain!" Having dressed in a hurry, she burst out the door before Her Ladyship could ask another question. In no way could she tell a pregnant woman where she was going. Blast Kennan. Moments ago, before he'd marched out the door, he'd given her a kiss on the cheek and asked her to say a prayer.

A prayer, for goodness' sakes!

Only then did he tell her about the duel of swords arranged between him and Robert Grant. Janet had begged and pleaded for him to renege, but that didn't stop him. Dear Brother left her alone, wearing her shift and robe, knowing full well she couldn't chase after him undressed.

Curses to men and their pride.

Her brother was going to get himself killed while

Dunn MacRae and the Cameron clansmen stood by. *A gentlemen's duel? I think not.* Convinced she was the only person who could stop the fight, she ran to the stables and found the lad. "Please saddle my horse at once."

"Straightaway, miss."

Janet stood aside, wringing her hands, her heart racing. *What if I'm too late?*

A movement of something red flashed in the corner of her eye. Lieutenant Cummins and his dragoons sauntered inside as if they were snooping about for some poor fellow to lock in the stocks for the day.

Janet drew in a deep breath and painted on her most serene expression, praying her nervousness didn't show, praying the soldiers would pass through without paying her any mind. But she could feel the heat of the lieutenant's gaze before he stopped at her side.

"Miss Cameron, 'tis surprising to see you here unaccompanied."

"Is it? I thought I would exercise my mare whilst the rain is at bay."

"I daresay you should be chaperoned. There are a great many unsavory sorts about town. I wouldn't want anything untoward to happen to you."

"I do appreciate your concern for my safety, sir, but I assure you I will not be alone. I am meeting my brother...ah...just out of town." Pursing her lips, Janet glanced away. Goodness, she'd nearly mentioned the Old Inverlochy Castle ruins. If Lieutenant Cummins caught wind of Kennan's duel, the Highlanders would all end up in the stocks or marched to Fort William and locked away.

The lieutenant scratched the mole on his cheek and looked out the stable doors. "I do not see your brother about."

"You do not see him because he's not in town, sir."
Goodness, will he not let matters lie? The stable hand led
her horse to the mounting block. Relieved, Janet hastened
to climb aboard and situate her knee over the upper pommel of her sidesaddle.

"Perhaps my men should provide an escort until you
find him." Lieutenant Cummins grasped the mare's bridle
and smiled pleasantly, which did nothing to ease Janet's
nerves.

She jerked the reins from his fingers with one hand
and slapped her crop against the horse's hindquarter
with the other. "I assure you that is not necessary."
While her beloved mare picked up a trot, Janet turned
and called over her shoulder, "Thank you ever so much
for your concern, Lieutenant." *There, that ought to dissuade him.*

As soon as she reached the road, she cued the mare for
a canter. Janet hadn't a moment to lose, and she wasn't
about to wait for Lieutenant Cummins to saddle his horse.
The man had been too friendly since she'd arrived in Inverlochy. She leaned forward in the saddle, demanding
more speed. Right now she couldn't think about Cummins or anything but preventing her brother from being
killed by that Grant rogue.

She took the North Road at a gallop. The ruins of Old
Inverlochy Castle were on the River Lochy right near the
crossing the Camerons used to travel from Achnacarry.
The mare snorted out steady breaths as her hooves pummeled the packed dirt in a steady rhythm. "Haste!" Janet
urged.

She'd never seen a duel of swords before, but she'd
heard horrible things. Kennan had assured her the fight
would end at first cut, but what did that mean? What if

first cut resulted in a mortal wound? And her brother expected her to bide her time in the boardinghouse until he returned?

Not likely!

Especially not with Robert Grant as Kennan's opponent. The big laird was renowned throughout the Highlands for his skill with blades—dirks as well as swords—and few men could best him. Moreover, the blackguard was older than Kennan and taller by a hand.

The sound of swords clanged through the air as Janet reined her horse to a stop outside the crumbling stone walls. She'd been inside before, and nothing remained but the shell of a once-great medieval fortress. As fast as she could, she dismounted and secured the reins on the tie line beside a row of other horses.

At a run she dashed under the archway and pushed through a crowd of men while clanging filled the air.

Once the duelers came into sight, she gasped, clapping her hands over her mouth, running toward the fighting men. Deadly blades caught the sunlight, flickering as Kennan and Robert swung and blocked with lightning speed. Midstride, a hand clamped onto Janet's shoulder, stopping her abruptly. She jerked away, her head snapping toward Dunn MacRae.

"Ye shouldn't be here, lass," he growled.

"Och aye?" She jammed her fists into her hips. "And you had no business arranging this duel. 'Tis my brother's life you are wagering." Mr. MacRae caught her by the elbows as she started off. She fought him to no avail. "Leave me be!"

"Nay," he barked in her ear. "These men must face their hatred, else the feud between your clans will never end. Do you not understand? Kennan and Robert represent the future hope of our kin. Not just your clan, but for the Highland ways."

Janet stopped struggling, a tear stinging her eye as she watched, clenching her teeth, clenching her fists. Why did Mr. MacRae have to sound so convincing? And how could everyone just stand idle? "If anything happens to him, I shall deem you accountable."

"Your brother can hold his own. And I would trust Robert Grant with my very life."

"So say you," she growled. Duncan MacRae might trust the laird, but that was because their clans were allies. When it came to Grant versus Cameron, the contest would be fierce.

Kennan locked guards with the beast, nose to nose, their faces red. "Admit your crime!" Mr. Grant growled.

"I admit to nothing, you swine. You accuse the innocent when you have no proof."

Gnashing his teeth, Robert shoved Kennan to the ground. "I know when I have been wronged!"

The big man pounced on her brother's chest, leveling his sword against Kennan's throat. "It pains me not to end your life now."

"No!" Janet screamed.

Robert turned his head toward the sound.

Moving like a cat, Kennan snatched a dagger from his sleeve. With a vicious snarl, Janet's brother did the unthinkable and sliced open His Lairdship's cheek. "First cut, ye bastard. I win!"

Shocked, she gasped, drawing a hand over her mouth.

Mr. Grant pushed to his feet and shook his head, his eyes dark and filled with hatred. "This settles nothing. Ye ken daggers are not allowed. We agreed to swords." He pointed directly at Janet. "And bloody *women* aren't permitted at duels. You brought in your sister to save your cowardly arse."

"Och, lads. 'Tis over." Dunn marched between them before they could start fighting again. "The feud between your clans is done."

Mr. Grant shoved MacRae in the shoulder. "The feud will be over when I receive my due."

Crack! A musket fired, the reverberation deafening inside the enclosure.

All heads turned toward the sound.

"This is an unlawful gathering and you must disperse immediately or face charges," Lieutenant Cummins shouted with a musket poised on his shoulder. Fifty soldiers lined the crumbling battlements, their weapons ready to fire.

Dunn MacRae held up his palms. "Just settling a dispute between men. 'Tis ended now. We shall be on our way."

Cummins looked over the butt of his musket. "You know better than to cross me, MacRae, and if you're not careful, I'll march the lot of you through Fort William's gates before this week is over."

Kennan looked to Janet and gave a nod, but when he reached for his sword, a soldier fired.

"Run!" someone shouted as pandemonium unleashed.

"Kennan!" she screamed, the crowd swarming around her. Picking up her skirts, she fought, pushing through a sea of men, trying to catch sight of her brother.

A grip strong as iron stopped her. "You're going the wrong way, lass." Before she could protest, Robert Grant hefted her over his shoulder and barreled out the gate.

Hanging upside down, being carried in a most unladylike manner, Janet slapped her hands against the blackguard's backside. "My brother! He's still in there."

"The lad can handle himself." The beast tossed her over a horse's withers like a sack of grain and mounted behind her.

Janet arched up, looking back. Redcoats and kilted men swarmed everywhere. "My mare!"

"I reckon Kennan will bring her back." Mr. Grant's horse took off at a canter while the brute slid his arm under her waist and sat her upright.

"You boorish, b-beastly rogue!" She jabbed him with her elbow. "Will you stop manhandling me enough to listen?"

"I've heard every word you've said, miss."

She thrust her finger toward the castle ruins. "But Kennan is still in there. They shot at him!"

"Aye, but they missed."

"How do ye ken?"

"I saw the dirt fly up from the musket ball. Unlike the Camerons, I do not lie."

"Nor do I, sir, and I resent your insinuation that I do."

The man chuckled, the audacious beast. "Mayhap not *you*. Indeed, from what I've overheard in the past few days, you are harshly honest."

Janet stiffened, unable to think of a response. Good Lord, she vowed to keep her opinions in check from this day forward. She had spoken quite bluntly about him in the shop, though she harbored no regrets.

"Kennan will be fine," he added. "Cummins has no cause—the soldiers witnessed nothing."

True, the duel had ended by the time the soldiers appeared, and she'd heard no more musket fire as they'd dispersed.

She leaned back, only to find a warm, sturdy, masculine chest. Suddenly it dawned on her that she was seated upon a horse between two very solid male thighs. Sucking in a startled breath, she froze, wondering where to rest her hands. Mr. Grant's fingers were wrapped around the reins, bold, strong fingers, his nails clean and neatly trimmed. Lowering her hands, she opted to place them on the horse's withers. Without an upper pommel like the one on her sidesaddle, she slid a bit. Wavering, she shifted back.

The man groaned, the wall of his chest unmoving along her spine, his arms firm around her sides—hardly touching, though so secure there was no chance he would allow her to fall. But had her movement hurt him? Did he have more injuries than the cut on his face?

A drop of blood splashed onto her cloak. In fact, a stream of blood soaking into the wool. Twisting, she examined his face. Heavens, Kennan had cut him deeply. "Oh my, you're bleeding something awful."

His gaze shifted her way, filled not with hatred, as she would have expected, but with humor. Unable to help herself, she stared into complex, disarming eyes while she pulled a kerchief from her sleeve. Light in color, his eyes reminded her of a polished steel looking glass encircled by a darker shade of blue. "Your brother gave me a good cut, though swords were the chosen weapon, nay daggers or dirks." He said the latter with a growl.

Janet offered no reply, though she knew there was a strict code of conduct for duels and it was foul play to use anything other than the chosen weapons. Her brother had erred, further damaging the Cameron name in this man's eyes. For his blunder, she would have a word with Kennan at her earliest opportunity. She dabbed Robert's gash. It had to be two inches long or more. He hissed, and she jerked the cloth away. "Am I hurting you?"

"Not overmuch," he said gruffly.

Her tongue slipped to the corner of her mouth as she dabbed more carefully this time. "I believe we've established a concord of truthfulness, have we not?"

Those eyes shifted downward again and met her gaze. Good heavens, the intensity of his stare gave her pause. His Adam's apple bobbed. "Aye, then. Your ministration caused a wee modicum of pain—nothing worth mentioning."

Janet forced herself to shift her gaze lower and examine the wound. "This needs to be seen by a physician."

"Not likely."

"But it must be sewn, else you'll end up deformed."

"Have you a needle and thread?"

As a matter of fact, she had several, thanks to her trip to the haberdasher's. "I do."

"Then you will do the sewing."

"Me? Why—"

"You are the kin of the man who cut me. At least allow me to enjoy your feminine company whilst I submit to the unpleasantness of the needle."

Her skin suddenly grew overwarm. Robert Grant expected her to sew his wound...He trusted her with a needle and thread? Why her? Why not Lady Mairi or one of the serving wenches at the alehouse?

"Agreed?" he pressed.

She nodded, returning her attention to the road, not certain if she was glad or regretful to see the shops of Inverlochy come into sight.

Chapter Four

*H*olding his kerchief against his face, Robert followed Miss Janet into the boardinghouse.

"Mrs. MacNash!" the lass called. "I have a wounded Highlander to tend."

The matron stepped into the entry, wiping her hands on her apron. "My heavens, why on earth have you brought him through the front door? He'll drip blood all over my carpeting." She grabbed Robert by the elbow and wrangled him around the Oriental rug and through the hallway. "Why is it Highlanders turn into savages at these gatherings?"

"Can you sew him?" Janet asked of the matron, following.

"Aye."

"Nay," Robert barked. "Miss Cameron's brother cut me, she will be the one to stitch me."

The lass groaned from behind. "I'll fetch a needle and thread."

Mrs. MacNash gestured to a stool beside a long table and gave him an accusing glare. "What the devil happened? 'Tis not like Mr. Kennan to cause a row. What did you do to him?"

"I overpowered him in a duel of swords—'twas all aboveboard and gentlemanly."

The woman huffed. "There's nothing gentlemanly about a duel."

"So say you, but it has been the accepted method of solving disagreements between men for centuries."

Moving his hand aside, she leaned in and examined the wound. "Well, I hope your differences were settled."

Robert frowned. *Nothing is settled unless Cameron admits his foul.*

Miss Janet returned, needle and silk in her hand. "I daresay, Mr. Grant, Mrs. MacNash may have a bit more experience with these things than I—"

"You will do me the honor, Miss Cameron." He knit his brows. Bless it, she would own her brother's folly. "And I expect the work to be your finest."

"Very well." Pressing her lips together, she turned to the matron. "I'll need a bowl of water and a cloth, if you please."

"Straightaway." Mrs. MacNash collected the items and placed them on the table. "If you do not need my assistance, I've a few more beds to make above stairs."

The lass held out the needle as if attempting to shirk her duty once again. "It would be better if you—"

"I'm certain Miss Cameron is able," Robert interrupted. "Thank you, matron."

Once the woman left, Janet faced him. "I could have used her help."

"I think not. Four hands would be too many."

With a pursing of her lips, Janet picked up the cloth and doused it in the bowl, working with her left hand. Robert watched her as she cleansed away the blood.

"How does it look?" he asked, eying her.

"The bleeding has slowed." She leaned in—disarmingly close. He closed his eyes to block her from his mind, but that served only to strengthen her sweet bouquet. Riding the horse, he'd caught the drift of her essence, part lavender, part sugar, all delivered in a heady perfume that roared *woman*.

Clearing his throat, he opened his eyes and leaned away. "Good."

He watched while she threaded the fine bone needle. "I'll wager a cut of that size will cause a scar."

"Wonderful. Something to remember your dear brother by."

Her lips disappeared into a thin line. She was true to her kin, that was obvious. If only she weren't a Cameron, he might be tempted to court her. But that would never happen. However, he would enjoy making her nervous while she stitched. Nay, he didn't care a lick about a wee scar on his face. If anything, it would make him appear more menacing to his enemies.

"Are you ready?" she asked, holding the needle with a wee tremor, moreover with the wrong hand. *Didn't her governess insist she learn to use her right?*

"You intend to stich me up with your *left*?"

"Aye, sir . . . You wouldn't be much impressed if I tried to use my right."

He dipped his chin and gave her a half-cocked grin—perhaps he'd made his decision too hastily. Nonetheless, he wasn't about to make a retraction. "The question is, Are you ready, lass?"

She bit her bottom lip. "Best have it over with."

Robert endured the first two stitches stoically. Judging by the way Miss Janet trembled, she hadn't been wrong when she'd suggested Mrs. MacNash might have the steadier hand. "Breathe," he growled through clenched teeth.

A whoosh of air slipped through her lips. "I didn't realize I hadn't been."

"In my experience, breathing helps steady one's fingers."

"Hmm." She pushed in the needle, more gently this time. "Are you looking forward to the Samhain gathering?"

The lass takes in a bit of air and suddenly she has a yen to chat? "Aye."

"Is that why you purchased new clothes?" She pushed the needle through again.

Bugger all, that hurts.

"Nay," he growled curtly.

"Are you heading back to Glenmoriston afterwards?"

He knit his brows. "How many more bloody stitches must you make?"

Janet's mouth dropped open as Kennan stormed into the kitchen. "What the devil is *he* doing here? And why in God's name was your horse left tied at the old castle?"

Robert held up his palm to keep the lass from responding. "I'll answer. On the first count, since it was you who cheated and lashed out at me with a dagger—"

"Cheated?" Kennan bellowed. "If it weren't for your flagrant accusations—"

Janet straightened and threw a pointed finger at her brother. "Hear him out, bless it!"

"Thank you, miss." Leaning away from the needle, Robert spoke out of the side of his mouth. "Given the *circumstances*, I felt Miss Cameron was the best candidate to perform the surgery. On the second count, I saved your sister from possibly being arrested and thus humiliated by the queen's dragoons."

"She could have ridden back herself. My sister is an accomplished horsewoman."

"Is she?" Robert glanced aside, gritting his teeth while Janet started another stich. *Typical.* The lout opted to argue rather than offer thanks—or an apology, for that matter.

"Aye." Kennan refused to let it rest. "And you hightailed away whilst I was under fire. Ye hauled my sister off like a bloody barbarian."

Robert's lips thinned. He had been a bit savage with the lass, though there had been no time for pleasantries. "He did me no harm." Janet tied off a stitch and mercifully snipped the thread. "That should set you to rights, Mr. Grant." Crossing her arms, she turned her attention to her brother. "Kennan, we must speak. Come above stairs with me."

"Thank you, miss," Robert said while he watched Janet marshal her brother up the back staircase. One thing was for certain. The Camerons might be reivers, but Miss Janet had some decency, unlike her brother.

Such a pity she's embroiled with that clan.

* * *

Janet calmly set the needle and thread on the sideboard, but when Kennan shut the door, she whipped around and faced him. "How could you have attacked that man with a dagger? I saw the fight. Robert Grant had you on your back in an untenable situation."

Scowling, Kennan threw up his hands. "The scoundrel fights like a beast."

"That may be so, but you agreed to the duel, did you not?"

"I did."

"Good heavens, Brother, you're no cheat. Why did you do it? The Grant laird already hates us, believes us to be dastards. Using a dagger as you did only serves to confirm his poor opinion of our kin."

"Do you honestly believe Grant would forgive all and walk away? The man has falsely accused us. He's the dastard. If the roles had been reversed, he would not have hesitated to use a dagger on me. I have *no* doubt. He is a deceitful, scheming boar, and I cannot trust him."

"But he did not err. *You* did, and you must own to it."

Kennan's eyes grew dark as he stammered, his lips twitching until he finally shook his fists. "Damnation!"

Janet stepped forward. "I still cannot believe what I saw. Why? Why did you do it?"

Kennan's shoulders dropped as he groaned. "I snapped. That braggart was on top of me with his sword at my throat. For a moment I thought he might take my life. When his attention flickered I saw my chance."

Covering her mouth, Janet turned her back. It had been her shout that had distracted His Lairdship. But if what Kennan said was true, Mr. Grant might have killed him. She paced. On the one hand, it was a wave of relief that her shout had drawn the man's attention away from the fight. Had Kennan been killed, not only would Mr. Grant be a murderer, all of Clan Cameron would have put his lands to fire and sword. A feud of colossal proportions would have erupted until the hills between their lands turned red with the blood of innocent men.

But Kennan's actions cannot go unpunished. And the Cameron name must be exonerated.

"We are not cheaters and swindlers." She faced him. "You may be my elder brother, but I must insist you write a letter of apology to Mr. Grant forthwith. You must name him the victor of the duel."

Her brother's expression shifted from angry to enraged. "Good God, whose side are you on? I will do no such thing. In war there are no rules, and you'd best learn that, Sister." Kennan slammed his fist on the sideboard. "Do you have any idea what I felt when I saw you bent over that miscreant in the kitchen? I cannot believe you tended him."

"Och, so now you turn the blame to me! What should I have done? Shoved him to the gutter?"

"Hardly, he's tougher than an oak's trunk. But Mrs. MacNash could have sewn his ugly face. Not you."

Janet pursed her lips. It would be a waste of breath to say Mr. Grant had insisted she stitch him. If she did so, Kennan might act out yet again. She crossed her arms and took in a calming breath. "Do not veil the issue with your anger—or talk of rules. You ken you have brought dishonor onto our clan, and I expect you to write that letter. Furthermore, I expect it to be in Mr. Grant's hands afore he leaves for Glenmoriston on Saturday morn."

"Christ's bones, you're worse than Ma used to be." With a grumble Kennan raised his chin. "Is there anything else you demand, *m'lady*?"

"I need your word it will be done."

"Bloody hell," he spat. "Och, you have my oath." The look on his face was hard and icy as he marched out the door.

Pressing her palm to her forehead, Janet sighed. What

had Kennan been thinking? She knew her brother to be a man of honor, trusted by not only her father but also the esteemed Baronet of Sleat. And now she'd been forced to stand up to him. Nonetheless, never in all her days had she believed she would take the side of Robert Grant.

I'm not taking his side. I'm righting a wrong, and that will be the end of it.

Chapter Five

*F*riday came without another incident. Even the auction proceeded peaceably, and at last the evening of the Samhain dance had arrived. Janet perched on the stool in front of the mirror while Lena, her lady's maid, curled, pulled, and pinned her hair. Already dressed, Mairi sat on the settee near the hearth. "Was Kennan happy with the livestock sale?" asked Her Ladyship.

"I believe so. Afterward, he was grinning for the first time since before the duel."

"Good." Mairi fanned herself. "And the apology—has he delivered the missive?"

"He's written it, aye. I read the letter this morn. But he has decided to leave it with the barman to give Mr. Grant as he leaves town on the morrow."

"Unfortunate Kennan doesn't just give it to the man now and have done with it."

"Agreed. I told him the same myself." Janet winced as Lena pushed a pin into her scalp. "Ow."

"Apologies, miss. The ribbon doesn't want to stay put."

Janet turned her head to better see it in the mirror. The lass had done a fine job twisting her hair atop her head, but the pink ribbon sat a bit cockeyed.

"I think you should weave it through her tresses rather than pin it in place," said Her Ladyship.

"Yes, m'lady."

Janet sighed as the maid pulled off the ribbon and started anew.

"In this light I am even more certain your choice of the blue taffeta is perfect," Mairi said.

"Are you now?" Janet rather liked it as well. "Though I'm not certain about the pink bows."

Lena stood back, eyeing her attack. "I'm afraid 'tis a bit late to change your mind."

"Aye, but should I ever wear this gown again, I think I'll replace the pink with ivory."

"The pink makes your cheeks glow, miss," said the maid.

Mairi stood and moved closer with a discerning eye. "I believe she is right. You are a picture of a delicate flower."

Janet twisted her lips. *Delicate flower* wasn't exactly the image she had been hoping for. Enticing maid. Alluring lass. Something a wee bit more daring would suit.

Mairi plucked the rouge pot from the dressing table. "Tell me, have any braw Highlanders caught your fancy?" She lightly dabbed Janet's cheek with a puff.

"Let's see..." Janet hummed. She hadn't met a soul to whom she would consider pledging undying love. "There's a stable hand who has a pleasant smile."

"Stable hand?" Mairi tossed the pot on the table. "That simply will not do for a daughter of a laird."

"But you—"

"Don't say it." Her Ladyship thrust up her palm. "Aye, I agree you must marry for love, but I've been to Achnacarry. You are accustomed to a great deal of comfort, my dearest, and I daresay you would not be content living out your days raising a family in a one-room shieling where you have naught but a firepit where you must do the cooking yourself."

Janet's shoulders shook with her chuckle. "I do believe the lad from the stables is a bit young anyway, and shorter than me by a hand."

"Shorter than you?" asked Lena, who was tall and lean. "It sounds as if he's but a child."

"Aye—I'd guess him at no older than eleven."

Mairi smacked Janet's arm with her fan. "You are a jester."

"I am without hope, is more apt. My stepmother will have me wed to some crusty old baron by Easter for certain."

"What say you? This is Samhain." Mairi twirled her fan. "Anything can happen. Leave it to me."

"Oh no. I do not want you meddling, even if you are the daughter of an earl."

"I'm not meddling. I'll just have a word with Mr. MacRae and, by the time everyone has been introduced, all the eligible gentry will be queued up to ensure you do not miss a single opportunity to dance."

"Oh dear." Janet leaned her forehead into her palm.

"I ken of Lairds Chisholm and Stuart." Her Ladyship refused to let matters rest. "They are bachelors. And you must have a turn with Ciar MacDougall—"

"I'm certain all of those gentlemen are capable of inviting me to dance if they so choose." Janet shook her finger. "There is no need to goad them."

Mairi frowned pointedly. "Aye, but sometimes a lad needs a wee prod up the backside."

"Please. Let us simply enjoy the evening without broadcasting that I'm desperate to find a suitor."

Stuffing her fan up her sleeve, Her Ladyship huffed. "You are no fun at all."

"On the contrary. The eve will be fun even if I sit along the wall and watch. As you said, 'tis Samhain."

"Och, mark me, if I see you sitting along the wall, I will take things into my own hands. And I *will* meddle."

"All done," said Lena, giving her work a pat.

Relieved at the change in subject, Janet issued Mairi a stern frown before she inspected the ribbon. It laced through the base of the coiffure piled atop her head and tied in a tidy bow at the side. "I believe you were right, Lady Mairi. It does look better woven through."

"I am seldom wrong about such matters. You will be the belle of the ball."

Janet sighed. "'Tis but a Highland country dance, not a ball."

"'Tis what you make of it, my dearest."

* * *

"What do you say we head for the hall?" asked Lewis, Robert's henchman.

"In a hurry, are you?" Standing at the alehouse bar, Robert sipped his whisky. He was dressed in his finery for the Samhain celebration, but would rather stay put and bend his arm. He'd even considered heading for home, but by the time the livestock sale was over, it was too late to ride. Moreover, the weather had taken a turn for the worse, and a raging storm was making the ale-house timbers creak.

Lewis finished his dram and pushed his cup to the back of the bar. "I might be. Besides, the music's been playing for a good half hour."

"Have your eye on a woman, aye?"

"I'll admit, there's a lass I'd like to see."

"At least one of us has had a bit of luck this Samhain." Robert tossed back his whisky and slammed his cup on the bar. "Just remember we're leaving at dawn."

"Aye, sir."

"The men are ready?"

"Of course, though I reckon they're already kicking up their heels."

"Very well. Let us not tarry."

If it weren't Samhain, Robert might have avoided the gathering altogether, but there was something about the festival that always lowered people's inhibitions, especially the lassies, and that he couldn't miss.

Together the men walked across the road, wind and sleet stinging their faces. Lewis quickened his step. "I think we're in for an early snow."

"Mayhap in the mountains—it has most likely started to accumulate up there." Robert opened the door and gestured with an upturned palm. "After you."

The hall swarmed with activity and warmth. Unfortunately, it also swarmed with redcoats. Too many of them mingled with the local lassies. *Wolves in fancy doublets and breeches.*

On the tables, turnips had been carved into ghoulishno faces. The candles flickering inside the hollowed-out cores made them come alive. Dancers lined the center of the floor while drummers tapped a rhythm for the piper and fiddlers.

Lewis gave Robert's arm a nudge. "There she is." He pointed to a comely lass standing among a circle of females.

"Go on," said Robert. "Ask her to dance afore someone else stakes his claim."

He made his way to the refreshment table, where Ciar MacDougall held out his hand. With his black hair and dark eyes, the man looked like a pirate. "Good evening, Grant. Can I pour you a cup of mulled wine?"

"There's nothing stronger?"

Ciar produced a flask from his sporran. "I bring my own kick."

"Then I don't mind if I do."

The MacDougall heir charged the cups and handed one to Robert. "How's your face mending? It looks angry."

"Och." Robert held up his drink. "After a few of these, I'm hoping to not feel a thing."

"Has Kennan apologized?"

Robert snorted. "I don't expect him to. 'Tis the nature of the beast."

Ciar shook his head. "I ken the man, and his behavior baffles me."

"Mayhap his da's lifelong hatred of Clan Grant runs so deep the son cannot see reason. Nonetheless, he's proved his character, and I shall not forget." Robert sipped. Over the top of his cup he spotted Miss Janet dancing with Dunn MacRae. She threw back her head and laughed unabashedly as if the laird had said something incredibly funny. Odd, but it was refreshing to see a well-bred woman laugh as if she hadn't a care. Without realizing it, Robert took a step toward her. A picture of feminine beauty, the lady wore a pale-blue gown trimmed with pink that matched the color in her cheeks, accentuated the blue of her eyes, and made her tresses more golden. No other woman in the room compared to Janet. They might as well all go home, for every eye was fixed on the Cameron lass.

"I take it your opinion of Kennan's sister is a wee bit different." Ciar tipped a bit more spirit into their cups.

"Perhaps. She has some scruples—must have been inherited from her mother."

"Aye, though with three brothers, she can hold her own."

Robert tipped up his chin while his gut twisted. "You ken the lass well?"

"Our clans are close." Ciar shrugged. "She's never shown much interest in me, however."

"Oh? I cannot see why. I'd reckon you'd be at the top of Lochiel's list of suitors."

"Nay, we are like kin." He chuckled. "She once told me I was too much like a brother to her. And I must agree. No man needs to have his future bride look upon him with brotherly love."

Robert grinned behind his cup. He didn't know why, but the news lightened his mood. Perhaps Ciar's whisky was potent.

Ciar inclined his head toward the merrymakers. "Most of the women in the hall are dancing with miserable dragoons at the moment."

"Bastards. Who invited them, anyway?"

"Are you jesting? The bloody troops invited themselves."

Robert downed the rest of his fortified wine. "Then we'd best rescue the lassies for the next set."

"Agreed."

Robert's palms grew moist as he moved behind Miss Janet and tapped her on the shoulder. When she turned, a wee gasp slipped through her lips, her eyes changing from cornflower blue to midnight. He bowed. "My I have the pleasure of the next dance, miss?"

She curtsied, and a cool façade erased her initial surprise. "You may."

He took his place in the men's line across from her. Before the music started, she clasped her hands, looking anywhere but at him. Robert glanced down the line. With a daft grin, Ciar stood across from Miss MacDonald.

After a brief introduction, the dance began, demanding he take Janet's hands. He tightened his grip on her delicate fingers as if needing to protect the lass from all the wolves in the hall.

"How is your wound?" she asked, her curls bouncing with the reel's tempo.

""Tis fine. As long as I don't smile, it doesn't hurt overmuch."

She cringed. "I am sorry."

"You have nothing to apologize for." As they promenaded in a circle, her skirts skimmed his calves. The light brush combined with the rustle of taffeta charged his protective instincts all the more. With a turn, he regretted having to leave her in the women's line while he hooked the elbow of the next lassie. Robert glanced back to see the golden highlights of Janet's hair catch the flicker of the candlelight from the chandelier above. Were those curls as soft as they looked?

They joined hands and sashayed down the tunnel of dancers. "Will you be riding for home on the morrow?" she asked, seeming to enjoy chatting while dancing with the grace of a swan.

"I will. And you?"

"At first light." Her tongue slipped to the corner of her mouth while she met his gaze. "And you're staying at the alehouse?"

Good God, did she have any idea how alluring she looked? Och, that pink tongue licked the rose of her lips while she watched him. Her eyes—vibrant cornflower blue—made his heart melt again. "No reason to stay elsewhere, I suppose."

Her shoulder brushed his. Gooseflesh arose on his arms. "Do you find it comfortable?"

As she passed his side, he tilted his nose toward her hair and inhaled. Aye, lavender eau de toilette for certain. "My room has a bed and a hearth," he replied. "They offer three meals a day. I reckon I do not need much more than that."

"How did your coos fare at today's sale?"

"Sold the lot." *Though the profits could have been better.*

She nodded, looking away as if she were trying to think of more questions to ask. Robert did nothing to make it easy for her. He rather enjoyed watching and waiting to see what she might come up with next.

Unfortunately, the music ended.

"There you are," Kennan grumbled as he pushed through the crowd. Spotting Robert, he curled his lip in disgust as he grabbed his sister's wrist. "Your next dance will be with me."

A fierce rebuttal flashed in her eyes while she pulled away, turned to Robert, and curtsied. "Thank you, Mr. Grant."

He bowed respectfully. "'Twas my pleasure, miss."

"One you will not enjoy again," Kennan said.

While his fists clenched, Robert stared the brother in

the eye. No, he would not be the first to blows, though it wouldn't take much goading for him to snap and feed the man a fistful of knuckles. "Well then, safe travels home, Miss Janet. If your brother can manage it." Aye, he couldn't help but prod the backbiter a bit. One day he'd face off with Cameron again, but not tonight. Not with the place crawling with redcoats, and not on Samhain. Before the musicians started the next set, he turned to head for another cup of mulled wine.

"You should have given him the letter and it all would have been done." Janet's whisper was barely audible while Robert strolled away, turning his ear.

"Wheesht, Sister. I made my decision and I've had enough of your badgering."

Robert could only shake his head. He wouldn't bother asking the lass to dance again. There was no use baiting her bull-brained brother, no matter how bonny she looked. He'd been right on the first day of the gathering. Janet Cameron was not a woman with whom he wanted to grow friendly. Pulling his own flask from his sporran, he fortified one last cup of mulled wine with whisky. He'd come to Inverlochy to sell his cattle, and that's exactly what he'd done. Profits might not have been what he'd wished for, but they were enough. And aye, the lassies at the alehouse mightn't have looked as alluring as he'd once remembered. Perhaps the luck of the fairy folk hadn't favored him this trip.

Undaunted, he spotted his men and joined them. "Have any of you seen Lewis?"

"Slipped out with his new sweetheart," said Tormond, one of Clan Grant's finest.

"Aye, his latest conquest," said Jimmy, the youngest of the group.

"He'd best be ready to ride come dawn. I have a yen for home."

* * *

Janet finally got a chance to enjoy a cup of delicious mulled wine when the musicians took a recess. Her feet sore and feeling as if she'd been dancing for days, she swept her gaze across the faces, searching for Mairi.

Ciar MacDougall moved beside her. "Are you looking for someone, Miss Janet?"

"I'd hoped to have a chat with Lady Mairi."

"She and Dunn left ages ago."

"That's unfortunate. Her Ladyship is always so amusing."

"Aye, she is. Are you enjoying Samhain?"

"Indeed, though I think I, too, am ready to turn in for the night. Have you seen Kennan?"

"He's in the side room, embroiled in a game of cards."

"Cards? Oh dear, he could be at it for hours yet."

"MacDougall," someone hollered from the next room. "Bring your wee flask."

The future laird of Dunollie bowed his head. "I've been summoned—but I'll see if I cannot convince your brother to escort you to the guesthouse."

"Thank you." Janet sipped her wine and moved toward the wall.

Winfred Cummins caught her eye, and she sharply changed direction, looking for any familiar face among the crowd. Unfortunately, the only person she recognized was Robert Grant, and she wasn't about to slide in beside her father's nemesis for another bout of idle chat. Besides, she'd already exhausted her arsenal of pleasantries when they were dancing.

The lieutenant cleared his throat behind her. "Mizz Janet," he slurred. "The minstrels are 'bout to begin the next set and you havn' danced with me yet." The man's breath smelled pickled.

She turned her head away from the stench. "Are you on duty, sir?"

"Always on duty, more or less. Here to serve queen and country." He grasped her hand and pulled. "C'on."

Janet glanced over her shoulder toward the card room, praying Ciar MacDougall had returned, but the only face she saw was Laird Grant's. The lieutenant tightened his grip and pulled harder. She yanked her hand away as the musicians began an introduction to a strathspey—curses, it would be terribly impolite to refuse him, but he was in his cups. Was that not grounds enough to decline his request? *Mayhap if I put it succinctly?* "Sir, you have clearly had too much to drink. Perhaps it is time for you to retire for the eve."

He stopped and glared at her—his eyes menacing. "I beg y'pardon? Do you think to tell me I am ine-ine-inebriated? I am an officer in the queen's dragoons, an' will tole-rate no chiding from a maid."

No trollop to be ordered about, Janet stood by her conviction. "Please, sir. I'm tired and I wish to go home." There. She had not only refused, she had agreed to refrain from dancing for the rest of the eve.

"No. Dance with me." He again grabbed her wrist, his grip hard and bruising.

"I will not!" Janet dug in her heels and tried to jerk her arm free, but he held fast.

He rounded and jutted his face into hers. "The lot of you Highland folk think y're above soldiers?" His voice grew louder. "You live in a luxurious castle, sneerin' and lookin' down your noses at those poor sops who try to maintain order in these savage lands."

At each word Janet's face grew hotter, her hands shaking like willow leaves. Good heavens, not only was he in his cups, the lieutenant was the vilest man she had ever had the misfortune of encountering. Well, officer or not, she wasn't about to withstand any more of his abuse. "You, sir, are being obnoxious and rude, and I insist you apologize this instant."

"Rude, am I?" He grappled for her arms.

Backing away, Janet lashed out with a quick slap across his face.

The noise in the hall ebbed to a low hum.

The scoundrel's eyes narrowed as he snarled. "You dare strike an off-cer? You will pay for your impertinence." He whipped around. "Men! Take this wo—" Lieutenant Cummins's head snapped back, his words cut off by the fist of Robert Grant.

The big man lunged forward and followed with a jab to the jaw, making the lieutenant trip over his feet and fall onto his backside.

In a heartbeat the hall erupted into a tumult of swinging fists and shrieking women. Chairs scraped the floorboards and sailed through the air. Janet flung her arms over her head, peering toward the card room. If she could make it there, she might find Kennan.

A strong arm encircled her shoulders while a deep voice whispered in her ear. "Come. Your brother needs to spirit you away before the dragoons gain the upper hand."

Tingles skittered down her spine at the sound of the big laird's voice. "You would help me escape this mayhem?" she asked.

"I will yet again, miss." He shielded her with his body as he pushed through the throng. "Where's your cloak?" he demanded.

"On a peg with the others."

"Color?"

"Green. Sealskin collar."

A corporal stumbled out of the card room with Kennan on his heels. Her brother took one look at Janet and Mr. Grant before his face reddened with rage. "Get your bloody hands off my sister."

"With pleasure, ye spineless weasel." The laird grasped Janet's shoulders and backed her toward Kennan, shifting his focus to her face. "Green did you say?" he asked in a much pleasanter tone.

"Aye," she said as her brother grabbed her wrist and tugged her behind him.

Across the hall, Winfred Cummins bellowed like a fevered bull and was fighting his way toward them. "Stop that woman! She 'costed an officer of the queen. And I want Robert Grant's head!"

Mr. Grant snatched her cloak from a peg and held it up, giving Kennan a pointed stare—the meaning of which even the queen wouldn't doubt. "I tell ye true, Cameron, Miss Janet slapped the lieutenant. The man's in his cups and out for blood. Make haste and ride, else she'll be locked in the stocks come morn."

Janet slipped under her cloak, and Kennan reached for his. "Jesus Christ, what have you done?"

She shook her head. "I only—"

"No more talk. Go!" Mr. Grant escorted them out the door as he hollered for his men to follow.

* * *

Clan Grant men fell into step behind Robert as he sped toward the alehouse. "Jimmy, haste to the stables and saddle the horses. Tormond, find Lewis. Tell him we're leaving in two minutes." Before he reached for the latch, he watched the redcoats run for their horses, stabled at the south end of town. They had ten minutes tops, and Robert preferred not to cut things so close.

"Good God, the town's rife with havoc," said Mac-Dougall, shaking Robert's hand. "I saw it all, and I'll stand witness. The lieutenant was in his cups and pestering Miss Janet. You did what you must to keep the lady from harm."

"Aye?" MacDougall followed while Robert ran to his room and nabbed his gear. "I'm not about to stay around and let them haul me to the bowels of Fort William's prison, only to await a pardon."

Ciar stopped in the doorway. "Bloody bastards, I kent something like this would happen. And they've been licking their chops, waiting for it all week."

After grabbing his satchel, Robert shouldered past his friend. "And here I've been trying to behave. Mayhap I should have given Cummins a fist to the snout when I first arrived and had it over with."

Still following, MacDougall chuckled. "If you hadn't hit the bastard, I would have done the honors."

Robert's men were waiting near the alehouse door as he marched through. "We ride, men." Crossing the road at a jog, he glanced over his shoulder. "Will you come with us, Ciar? We could use your muscle if we run into trouble."

"I shall top that. My men and I will hamper the soldiers as they head out of town."

Robert stopped in his tracks and gave his friend a clap

on the back. "Thank you. I will nay forget this. Are you ready?"

"Ever ready. We'll be on your heels."

As MacDougall strode away, Robert mounted and signaled to his army of ten men. "Follow me. We're heading where no Sassenach will find us."

Chapter Six

$\mathcal{J}$anet clutched her cloak tight while her teeth chattered. The brisk wind chilled to the bone, so savage it made her taffeta gown feel like ice. Things had never been so miserable, so wretched. Why did she have to slap the lieutenant? Good heavens, no one traveled in a ball gown. Worse, the night was darker than coal, with brooding clouds looming overhead. Rain spat on and off as she followed Kennan up the North Road.

Shouts came from behind. "Halt in the name of Queen Anne!"

Janet slapped her riding crop harder, leaning forward. "Hurry, Kennan!"

Her brother reined his horse to a stop at the river's edge. "She's swollen. Her current is swift."

Janet cued her horse to step into the rushing water, but the mare backed and whinnied.

"I'll give it a test. Mayhap we can still cross," he said.

She looked upstream. "We could try the Lochaber bridge. 'Tis only another mile."

"No time." Kennan's horse waded partway, and he beckoned her. "'Tis only up to his barrel, come."

Cuing her mare to follow the gelding, Janet leaned forward and hunched her shoulders to block the wind whistling up the river. But when the icy water ran over Janet's feet, the mare stopped with a shake of her head. "Come on, lassie." Janet smacked her crop and kicked.

Snorting, the mare reared. Janet tightened her grip on the reins and clenched her knee around the upper pommel. Up and up the horse continued, beyond vertical. Screaming, Janet lost her grip as she was thrown, arms flailing, into the torrent.

Her back hit hard. Frigid water enveloped her like thousands of tiny knives. She opened her mouth to scream, only to be silenced by a flood. Choking, she shook her head and fought for the surface. Strong fingers grabbed her shoulders and dragged her, coughing and sputtering, to the shore.

"Bloody Christmas," Kennan growled as he crouched beside her on the bank.

Janet wheezed, gasping for air as she shook with the shock of the cold.

"That's far enough," said a menacing voice. Winfred Cummins sat a steed, looking down the muzzle of his flintlock. "Release her." And he sounded almost sober.

Kennan drew his dirk. "On what charges?"

"Striking an officer."

"Aye?" Kennan emitted a mocking laugh. "You cannot handle a wee slap from a lass?"

"You insolent blackguard. For that you will enjoy the comforts of Fort William as well." Cummins signaled with his pistol. "Bind their wrists."

Janet pushed to her feet as Kennan lunged in front of her, slicing through the air with his knife. "Not on your bloody life."

Five dragoons circled him while his dirk hissed in a constant X pattern. "Stay back. Leave us be."

They crept nearer until a redcoat dove for Kennan's blade. From the opposite side, another slammed a fist across his jaw.

"Stop!" Janet screamed, so cold she could barely move.

But no one listened. On and on the soldiers beat him, punches, kicks, every hit landing in a sickening thud.

"Stop, I said!" Shards of icy pain shot up from her feet as Janet ran to Cummins and grasped his horse's bridle. "Tell them to stop. Now!"

"Will you agree to come peaceably?"

"Aye. Anything, just order your men to stop hitting my brother afore they kill him."

"Mount your horse."

Her gown soaked and heavy, Janet did as the lieutenant bade.

Cummins gave his men a nod. "Enough. We ride."

She glanced back to Kennan, lying on his side in the thick grass and not moving. "You cannot leave him there."

"You, miss, are in no position to tell me what I can and cannot do. You're lucky he's still breathing."

* * *

Shortly after Robert and his men took a turn to head into the hills, a piercing scream carried on the wind. By the chill spreading across his nape, there was only one person who could have uttered it. He pulled on his left rein and spun his stallion. "Miss Janet's in trouble! We're going back."

"We're what?" asked Lewis, his voice shooting up, he and the others following at a canter.

As they rode down the hill, a retinue of seven riders turned onto the North Road, but in the dark it was impossible to make out who they were. Lead sank to the pit of his stomach as Robert urged his horse faster. When he arrived at the crossing near Old Inverlochy Castle, a riderless horse caught his eye. Dread gripped his chest while he reined his mount to a skidding halt. "Miss Cameron!" he bellowed.

"'Tis Kennan's gelding," said Lewis. "His initials are on the saddle."

"Cameron!" Robert yelled as he dismounted, turned full circle. A dark form curled near the brush caught his eye. "Jesus, they've beat him." He kneeled beside Janet's brother and tugged him into his arms. "Where is Miss Janet?"

But Kennan was out cold. Robert felt for a pulse. Thank God it was strong, his breathing deep as well, but there was no sign of his sister. "Blast it all to hell, she must have been with the riders back yonder."

"Aye," Lewis agreed. "I reckon it was Cummins's retinue we passed, and I reckon they're headed for Fort William."

"What the blazes happened here?" shouted Ciar MacDougall, reining his horse to a stop with four riders following his lead.

"It appears Cameron has been enjoying camaraderie with Her Majesty's dragoons." Robert peered at Kennan's face, but the man wasn't going to be of use to anyone until at least the morning. He shifted his attention to Ciar. "I thought you were going to stall them."

"I did. Told them I reckoned Kennan had taken Janet back to the boardinghouse."

"Not convincingly enough." Making a quick decision, Robert stood and hoisted Kennan across the Cameron horse, then handed MacDougall the reins. "Take him to safety. I'm riding after Miss Janet."

Ciar nodded his assent. "She'll be doomed if they take her inside the fort."

"Aye." Robert mounted his stallion. "That's why we'll be taking Black Parks Path. 'Tis the only chance we have of heading them off. Come, men."

Snow began to fall while Robert rode as if he were being chased by Satan, praying Cummins would be in no hurry now that he'd secured his quarry.

With a gnashing of his teeth, Robert berated himself for not heading for the hills as he'd planned. Janet Cameron meant nothing to him, though her family owed him a great deal—cattle and now recompense for a scar he must carry on his face for the rest of his days. A reminder that the Camerons were never to be trusted. But still he continued. He wouldn't leave any Highland lass with those horrible redcoats.

He'd witnessed the whole incident at the Samhain ceilidh. Cummins had been in his cups while Miss Janet tried to politely dismiss him, and the arse refused to stop. The lieutenant mightn't have struck her, but, nonetheless, he attacked first by grabbing her arms. Holy hellfire, Robert had itched to draw his sword and challenge the lout to a duel there on the spot.

But that would only have purchased a one-way ticket on a convict ship headed for hell.

Christ, I'm headed for hell one way or another.

They rounded the bend where Black Parks Path crossed the North Road, and Robert slowed his mount. Sure enough, hoofbeats came from the north—several riders by the sound of it. A quarter mile up, lantern light winked through the flurries. Aye, the retinue approached at a steady trot.

"Ready your weapons, men. But only kill if you are about to be killed." Clan Grant might make it through this without forfeiting hearth and home, unless some dragoon decided to be a hero and ended up dead.

Robert drew a flintlock pistol—one he always kept primed—and dropped in a musket ball. "Halt!" he cried.

Now twenty feet away, Cummins raised his hand and reined his horse to a stop. The men rode in a diamond formation, shielding Miss Janet in the center, blast it all. This wasn't going to be easy.

"Ah, Grant." Cummins peered from beneath his snow-covered tricorn, his face cadaverous in the dim light. "Now I shall have two felons to hand over to Fort William's colonel."

"If you should live so long." Robert steadied his pistol, aimed at the lieutenant's heart. "I never thought I'd live to see the day when the queen's dragoons saw fit to set upon helpless women during a public gathering."

"She struck me," Cummins whined like a spoiled youth.

"A wee lass?" The men behind Robert laughed. "Come now. Every man in the hall will attest that you provoked her." He glanced over his shoulder. "You're far outnumbered. Hand Miss Cameron's reins to me and I'll spare you."

Cummins inched his mount forward. "Sir, if you do

not lower your weapons, I will order my men to shoot you dead. And if perchance you happen to escape, I will hunt you to the corners of Christendom. You will have no rest. You will live in fear. And I will break your spirit."

Aye, the man had sobered enough all right.

The corners of Robert's mouth turned up in a sneer. "I'm certain a spirit will be broken, and it will not be mine." He shifted his aim slightly and shot the grenadier hat clean off Cummins's head. "Charge!"

Throwing his reins into his teeth, Robert shoved his pistol in his belt with one hand while drawing his sword with the other. At a gallop, Clan Grant attacked, barreling through the retinue of soldiers. Robert used the broad side of his blade to knock Cummins off his horse. On the recoil he slammed the pommel into the temple of another. As he rode past, he grabbed Miss Janet's reins and raced for the hills.

Chapter Seven

*R*obert didn't stop until they reached the Nevis lookout. On a clear day it gave a panoramic view of Inverlochy and Fort William below, but presently the low clouds blocked most of the moonlight. From the saddle he searched the shadows below for movement.

"There they are," said Lewis, pointing.

Robert squinted but could see nothing. "Are you certain?"

"I saw movement. They're after us, mark me."

"Then we continue until the horses are spent." He looked to his men. "Was anyone injured?"

No one said a word, but his gaze settled on Miss Janet, her hair hanging in strings with no sign of the lovely, curled coiffure from the ceilidh. Shaking like a leaf in a windstorm, she clutched her fists in front of her mouth and blew on them.

"We're free from danger, lass." When she didn't respond, he steered his mount beside her. "Are you well?"

"C-c-c—"

She couldn't manage to utter the word. He leaned closer to better see in the darkness. Was she...? He grasped her cloak and rubbed it between his fingers. "God's blood, you're soaked clean through."

Her head nodded. "Uhnn," she replied in a chilly pitch.

Robert looked to the sky as he removed his cloak. Snow spattered his face. "Take this. Wrap it tight around your shoulders," he said, swinging it around, then looking to Jimmy. "Tuck your blanket around the lady's lap."

"Straightaway, sir."

After Robert dismounted, he removed her wet slippers. "Your feet are like ice. I have a pair of hose in my saddle bags. May I have your permission to pull them on?"

"A-aye," she said, holding his cloak tightly, her teeth still chattering.

"There's nothing to warm her up here. 'Haps you should take her to the boardinghouse," said Lewis.

"If we do, she'll fall into Cummins's clutches for certain." Robert busied himself pulling the woolens over the lady's frozen toes and up her calves, trying to turn a blind eye to the long, slender, and delicate legs beneath his fingertips. He must think quickly. Miss Janet wouldn't last long in this weather, not wearing a wet gown. He double-checked the blanket Jimmy had tucked around her lap. "Do you think you will be able to ride a bit farther, miss? I need to take you to a place where we'll not be found."

Still shivering, she looked down toward town. "M-my brother. They beat him and left him for d-dead."

"That's where we started. Found him unconscious in the scrub."

"And you left him?" she asked, her voice turning shrill.

"Nay," he barked. "Ciar MacDougall has taken him to safety."

She looked up the mountain. "W-where?"

"I know not."

"We must haste, sir," said Tormond. "I saw the flicker of a lantern. I'm wagering they've started up the slope."

Robert mounted. "We ride until we reach the pass at Coire na Ciste." He signaled to Jimmy, praying the woman could make it that far. "Ride beside Miss Janet and keep a watchful eye. Lewis—we'll need kindling. When we reach the forest, take Willy, gather wood, and meet us at the pass."

"Aye, sir."

* * *

Robert's cloak and stockings and Jimmy's blanket initially helped Janet's teeth slow their chattering, but she'd never been so cold in all her days. As the night wore on, they steadily climbed higher and higher, up to where the temperatures were beyond bitter. She hadn't been to Coire na Ciste, though her brothers had talked about it—and not in a good way. The riding in the cliffs was treacherous. 'Twas why Mr. Grant was leading them up there now. Lowlanders and Englishmen wouldn't chance taking their horses up the Highlands, which made the mountains all the more alluring for clan men escaping from their enemies.

Janet curled her shoulders forward, hunching low over her horse's withers, trying to stay warm. Snow relentlessly piled atop her and atop the mare's coat, making it ghostly in the darkness. Her breath came in slow, shallow gasps. She blocked out her misery and focused on one thing—to keep going no matter the cost.

Thrice her beloved, fine-boned mare faltered and slipped, sidestepping to regain her balance. Janet knew better than to look down. She couldn't see much past the layers of wool even if she did. The horse's ears twitched at every noise. In the snowy darkness, it was impossible to see much farther than two feet in front of her nose. She could but trust the soft crunch of horses' hooves in front and behind.

With a whoosh they were hit by a fierce gale. It whisked the snow off her horse and cut straight through Janet's flesh. In minutes her teeth hurt from the chattering. No matter how hard she blew on her hands or how low she crouched over her mare, she could not stave off the violent shivers. Her lips were numb and her fingers ached, freezing and immobile as they gripped the leather reins.

Never had she known such cold. Every movement tortured her with pins and needles. Her eyelids grew so heavy it was agony to keep them open.

"Are we nearly there?" she whispered, only to have her words silenced by the howl of the wind. Onward they rode, through a narrow notch between two dark, looming, enormous cliffs. But Janet could take no more. Dropping the reins, she fell forward on the horse's neck, dangling her arms to either side.

"Robert, Miss Janet needs rest." She faintly heard Jimmy's holler, though she didn't hear a reply—if the Grant laird had spoken at all. It mattered not. She was too tired to open her eyes. Mercifully, sleep took away the bitter cold.

* * *

When Robert twisted around and saw Miss Janet unconscious and draped over her horse's neck, he could have spat out his eyeteeth. "Why did you not say something sooner, Jimmy?" He didn't wait for a reply. "There's shelter ahead. We'll stop there." He hastened to lead them beneath an overhang. It was crude, but it was dry and blocked the wind. Fearing the worst, he dismounted and rushed to Janet's side. "Lewis, use the wood you and Willy collected and start a fire. A big one." He pointed to the others. "You men, dig a shallow hole, five feet long. Jimmy, bring me the tarpaulin."

Having ridden without his cloak, Robert was chilled to the bone and shivering fiercely. He pulled the poor lass from the mare and carried her to the shelter. Sitting and balancing her on his lap, he removed his cloak from her shoulders and pulled it around then both. "I'll warm ye, Miss Janet. 'Tis necessary to keep you from succumbing to cold exposure." He didn't expect her to respond, but he needed to explain his actions nonetheless. He briskly rubbed his hands along her arms and her thighs. "Where's that bloody fire?" he bellowed, only able to see the shadows of the men as they worked.

"Setting flint to flax now, sir," Lewis said, his gruff brogue unmistakable.

"And the pit?"

"Still at it," said Tormond. "The ground's frozen and full of rocks."

Jimmy kneeled beside Robert. "Here's the tarpaulin."

Fumbling with the laces on Miss Janet's bodice, he eyed the lad. "Set it down and help me remove this damp gown. She'll never warm unless we can dry her."

"Ah...me?" Jimmy stood like a dumb mute.

Robert grasped Miss Janet by the shoulders. "Just hold her and I'll do it. And keep your bloody eyes averted. This is the daughter of one of the most powerful lairds in the Highlands, and she will have our respect. Ye ken?"

"Aye, sir." Cringing, the lad placed his hands on Janet's shoulders as if he were touching a hot stove.

Robert removed his gloves with his teeth, his fingers stiff and thick while he unlaced the lady's bodice and cast it aside, then untied her skirts. He began to untie her stays.

"You're not taking that off, are you?" Jimmy asked, his eyes bugging out.

"Just loosening them so the maid can breathe." Once Robert finished, he tugged Janet to his body. Her head lolled back against him with her moan. Was she coming to? Robert looked at her face, but her eyes were still closed. "Now drape the tarpaulin around us." It was nothing more than oiled leather but would provide a modicum of insulation.

Twenty minutes later, the fire was roaring, with coals beginning to radiate at its base. Robert stretched out his feet to warm them.

"Do you think Miss Janet will live?" asked Jimmy.

"Bloody oath, she had better, or the lot of us might as well give ourselves up and board a convict ship bound for the Americas." Not only did they have a mob of red-coats on their tails, if Sir Ewen and his sons learned the lassie had died in Robert's arms, they would not rest until Grant lands had been burned to ashes. "Spread half of the coals in the pit, then cover them with dirt—no rocks, mind you."

Robert continued rubbing Miss Janet's extremities

while the men worked to make up the heated bed by the light from the blaze. "One-hour watches," he ordered. "We'll ride at dawn."

"I reckon the dragoons have turned back by now," said Jimmy.

"I hope you're right. Cummins needs to sleep off the drink and realize he's the one who blundered—save the lot of us a bellyful of misery. But I'll nay take any chances."

Once the coals were covered by a good three inches of dirt, Robert gently patted Miss Janet's face. "Are you awake, lass?"

"Mm," she moaned, her body still limp.

"Och, 'tis most likely best if you're not awake." He looked to Jimmy. "Take the tarpaulin and lay it flat over the bed."

"She'll sleep nice and warm on that." Jimmy did as he was told.

"Aye." Robert stood and carried Janet to the bed, rewrapped his cloak around the lass, then lay down and pulled her beside him so her back molded to his front. He draped his arm around her waist and nestled his legs into her form. "Wrap the edges of the tarpaulin over us, then tuck it in good and tight. And make sure our feet are covered."

Jimmy didn't move. "You're not planning to stay there all night, are you, sir?"

"Where else am I going to sleep? I said this lassie will not die on my watch, and I stand by my word. She needs warmth and I have it aplenty. Now wrap that cloth over us, tuck it in, then go find your own place to bed down."

"Aye, sir."

The men chuckled as they went about their business.

"And I'll tolerate no snide remarks, you lot of miserable sops." The chuckles subsided, but no one needed to utter a word. And it didn't take a soothsayer to know their heads were filled with unchaste thoughts. Robert growled under his breath. *They can confess their sins on Sunday, the lot of them.*

He adjusted the position of his hips, carving out an indentation in the earth, and pulled Miss Janet closer. Warmth from the coals below soothed the tension in his shoulders. As he closed his eyes, the scent of woman mingled with lavender enveloped him, suddenly stirring potent male instincts akin to those his men had chuckled about.

Robert growled low in his throat. *This is not the place or the time, and 'tis definitely not the woman for me.*

Aye, Robert was as red-blooded as any Highlander, but that mattered not in the slightest. The woman in his arms needed his protection, and it must be given. Janet Cameron would be safe on his watch. He closed his eyes. *Nary a soul will touch her. I swear it.*

Chapter Eight

*J*anet's head throbbed while she dreamed of running. Warmth surrounded her, though her mind hovered beneath the threshold of consciousness. Daylight told her the morn had come and she must wake. But every time she began to stir, the pounding in her skull grew worse.

When something shifted against her back, her eyes blinked open for a moment, then lazily closed. She winced at the pain not only from the megrim, but because her entire body ached.

Dear Lord, please let me sleep for a few moments longer.

An arm was clamped around her waist, and a deep voice sighed. A very deep, masculine voice that in no way should be behind her when she was sleeping. Janet's eyes popped wide while her body stiffened. Not daring to take a breath, she slowly turned and looked back.

Holy snapdragons!

With a jolt she drew her fists beneath her chin. Of

all the people in Christendom who could be slumbering alongside her, it had to be Laird Grant. Deliciously handsome, rugged-looking Mr. Grant. The wound on his cheek oddly served to add to his allure while he breathed through slightly pursed lips. Soft, gentle, masculine lips. Were they as kissable as they looked? Her tongue tapped the top of her mouth as she considered how wickedly delicious he might taste.

No, no, no, no! This is an abominable state of affairs.

She inched up the stiff blanket and peered out. Good heavens, they weren't alone. Men covered with snow lay around the embers of a fire. Oddly, she was warm and dry, yet snow continued to fall. Shifting her gaze upward, she understood why. She'd been sleeping beneath a rock shelter—with Mr. Grant.

Lord have mercy, what if my father learns of this?

Suddenly panic seized her chest, making it impossible to breathe. If she didn't escape this very instant she might die of utter mortification. How had she ended up in such a precarious situation? Yes, Mr. Grant had ridden to her rescue. He'd given her his cloak when she was on the verge of freezing to death. Thank the stars for his kindness, but she hadn't given him leave to do…to do…*good glory*!

This disaster might ruin her for the rest of her days. She could ill afford to stay wrapped in a cocoon with Mr. Grant a moment longer.

Janet kicked her feet, but they wouldn't budge. She pushed against the blanket, but it was as stiff as oak bark. Had they bound her in this contraption? Had they taken advantage and accosted her while she was out of sorts?

Her megrim throbbed tenfold while she thrashed and kicked. "Let me out!" Gaining a bit of room, she jabbed her elbows into the big Highlander behind her. In her panic, Janet's chest tightened, making it harder and harder to breathe.

"God's blood, woman!" Mr. Grant bellowed. In a heartbeat the blanket released her.

She sucked in a gulp of precious air.

Sitting up, he threw the blanket aside and sprang to his feet. "Have you caught fire?" he demanded, grabbing her shoulders and looking her from head to toe, his eyes wild and filled with alarm.

Janet gave him a hearty push as she scooted away. "No, you brute!" Looking down, she froze. Her life was all but over. How could he have removed her clothing and left her wearing nothing but a shift and stays? She was practically bare, and now she had nearly a dozen men staring at her. In her undergarments of all things. Swiftly hopping to her feet, she grabbed the leather blanket they'd been wrapped in and clutched it beneath her chin, trying to shake away the miserable pounding in her skull. "I demand you tell me why I am in such a compromising state of undress."

His Lairdship spread his palms to his sides as if pleading innocence. "I beg your—"

She shook her finger. "You—you—you have taken advantage of a helpless maid. My brother was right. You are a scoundrel of the worst sort."

"I did no such thing! If I had not taken action and removed your damp garments, you would have succumbed to the cold."

She spotted her cloak and gown draped across a big rock under the shelf. Careful to ensure the blanket covered as much as possible, she scooted toward them.

"Beg your pardon, Miss Janet," said Jimmy, shaking the snow off as he stepped toward them. "But Robert speaks true. You were half-dead when we arrived last eve. And he bellowed at us all, telling us to mind our own affairs and leave ye be."

The lad's words only served to make her shudder. She snatched her cloak and threw it over her shoulders. Had they all stood by and gaped while the laird removed her outer garments? She reached for her gown, suddenly realizing her stays had been loosened as well.

How dare he?

"I bid you all turn your heads whilst I dress," she said in a commanding voice—at least she sounded as commanding as possible given her disgraceful state of dress.

Once all backs were turned, Janet pulled on her gown and tied the laces as best she could. Thank goodness her clothing was dry—even her shift and stays had dried, though they were as frigid as ice. When certain her cloak covered every possible loose string, she glanced to the laird's satchel. "May I have my shoes, please?"

"If Your Ladyship will allow me to turn."

"I am composed."

"Very well." He retrieved the shoes and gave them to her. "We have a bit of dried meat. We shall eat and be off."

She slipped her feet inside the shoes, the fit a bit snug with Mr. Grant's stockings. Janet looked down. *No, I'm not giving them back until I'm safely home.* "Are we heading for Achnacarry? My father will have a word with the colonel at Fort William. I'm certain he can set things to rights with the lieutenant."

A rider approached from the glen, the snow making him look fuzzy at first. "Redcoats spotted!"

"Blast. The bastard cannot let petty grievances lie," Mr. Grant said, marching toward the rider and jamming his fists onto his hips. "How far out?"

"Twenty minutes, mayhap more with the hackneys they're riding. Those English nags cannot negotiate the mountains like our Highland stock.

"Pack up your gear and mount your ponies, men." Grant handed Janet a stick of dried beef. "I'm sorry, miss. You must eat on the run."

"Are we not doubling back?"

"I do not recommend it. Not with the redcoats on our tail."

Holding the mare's reins, Jimmy walked Janet's horse up beside her, then bent down to give her a leg up. But she didn't step in the lad's threaded palms. Not yet. She wasn't about to ride off with Robert Grant while there was no end in sight to what had become a treacherous storm. "Then where are we to go? We'll all catch our deaths if we venture farther into the mountains while it keeps snowing like this."

"I've kept you alive this far, have I not?" A tic twitched in Mr. Grant's jaw as he tied his satchel behind his saddle. "I'll tell you true, lass. I could have ridden for Glenmoriston last eve. If I had, I'd be sitting before home's hearth about now, but I turned back. God only kens why."

Janet looked to the pass from which the rider had come. Her choices were dreadful no matter in what direction she went. And if the redcoats were on their trail, she wasn't about to head west. Groaning, she allowed Jimmy to help her mount while a tempest nearly as violent as the wind blowing through the cliffs swirled in her breast. She was extremely grateful to Mr. Grant for coming to her aid. If he hadn't, she would surely be in dire straits in the hands of Winfred Cummins.

But why had the big Highlander risked his life for her? He was her father's sworn enemy. And now she was in his care, what would the chieftain of Clan Grant do with her?

Can I trust him?

* * *

Bloody women. All of Christendom would be better off without them. Try to do the right thing by a lady, and her scorn was the thanks he got? And why the blazes had she awakened prior to Robert? He was a light sleeper. He'd planned all along to be up and about before Janet roused. She mightn't have even known he'd slept by her side all night. And it hadn't been easy to do so.

God save him, never in his life had Robert Grant slept with such a beautiful woman in his arms and behaved himself. And the woman had been unduly aghast— treated him with disdain. If anything, Miss Janet should be bubbling with appreciation.

Robert removed his feathered bonnet and combed his fingers through his hair. He'd thought something like this might happen. Damn it all, any woman of Janet's station would have reacted the same way. She was completely within her rights to be outraged and offended. And now he'd gone and made a mess of things. No matter how hard he tried, he'd never be a good man in that woman's eyes. He'd always be her father's enemy. There was no use trying to convince her otherwise; her hatred had been ingrained since birth.

And now they were venturing through the most treacherous mountains in Scotland. Aye, Robert and his men could weather the storm and the crags, but could Miss Janet? The lass had spent her entire life being cosseted in a castle nestled beside a picturesque river.

He glanced back at her face—pursed lips, a determined glint in her eyes.

We are not turning back. Not on my life. I have too many responsibilities to be rotting in the bowels of a gaol.

The lass might be uncomfortable traveling under Robert's protection for a time—at least until Winfred Cummins gave up his hunt and opted to pursue someone more deserving of his ire. But the lass couldn't dispute that enduring Robert's company was a great deal better than spending God knew how long in Fort William's hell awaiting a sham of a trial.

"Lewis." Robert signaled to a lookout point he'd used before. "Climb up Scout Rock and report back."

"Straightaway, sir."

The snow came harder and, with it, the wind. All the riders hunched low and clamped their cloaks and plaids tightly about their shoulders. Miss Janet rode up behind Robert. "The storm's growing worse."

"It is."

"Do you have a plan? What if we're stranded up here?"

"We'll not be stranded."

"So tell me you do have a plan," she insisted.

"One's coming together." Robert shrugged, trying to ease her trepidation. "When on the run, a man has no choice but to improvise a bit."

"Improvise? The snow is nearly to my mare's barrel. If it gets much deeper, she'll not be able to move at all."

"That's part of my plan."

"For us to be stuck in the snow, unable to move? Heavens, we shall *all* die of cold exposure."

"That's where you're wrong. Lieutenant Cummins and his wayward dragoons will falter afore we do." He pointed ahead to a peak in the distance. "Once we cross that ridge yonder, we'll be on a downward slope."

"And then turn for home?"

"Aye..." *More or less.* He wasn't about to tell her they wouldn't be seeing Achnacarry for a fortnight or more. He was a cautious man and could not take her home before he knew the troops had given up their search. They'd be safer at Glenmoriston, where Robert's kin kept watch for a twenty-mile radius. It was home, just not Miss Janet's home. No one came near his manse without Robert's knowledge.

He led them through the rugged high country for a few more hours before Lewis rejoined them.

"What did you see?" asked Robert.

"I caught a wee glimpse of red is all. Otherwise, there was nothing but white. She's coming in from the west like no storm I've ever seen."

Robert shook his head. Blasted Cummins hadn't turned back, the bull-brained mule. Not good news. On one hand, Janet was right. If they didn't start down the mountain now, they'd end up stuck. He'd set out to take her down through the glens, but if he turned north, they'd descend faster. That meant traversing the treacherous Finnach Ridge. "How is your mount faring, Miss Janet? Can she handle a bit of a challenge?"

"She's as sturdy as your stallion." That was a stretch, though thus far the lass had proved herself to be an accomplished horsewoman.

"'Tis settled, then." He circled his hand over his head. "We're heading down Finnach Ridge."

"Is that a good idea, Rob?" asked Jimmy.

"Have you a better one?"

Miss Janet looked to the lad. "I will be fine, if that concerns you."

"'Tis what I like to hear," said Robert before the naysayer could interject. "We'll stop after we cross the tree line to rest the horses and build a fire."

"That sounds wonderful. I wish I could warm my hands by a fire for the rest of my days."

"It'll take some digging to find dry wood," said Jimmy.

Tormond snorted. "Ever the cynic. Not to worry, Miss Janet. There are always dry bits. Ye just need to ken where to look."

Ten minutes later, Robert stopped his horse at the edge of the ridge. A narrow, snow-covered path with perilous braes sloping downward on both sides reminded him of the devil's spine. "We'll ride single file from here." He looked to Miss Janet. "Let the men traverse first. Once I'm confident the crossing is safe, I'll follow you."

She gave a nod, her face a bit white, whether from cold or fear, he didn't know. What he did know was that on a midsummer's day the path could be treacherous. Now it was the first of November, and the ice and snowdrifts made Robert's toes curl. One missed step, and horse and rider would end up at the bottom of the ravine and most likely dead.

Neither one of them said another word while they watched each of his men take a turn. The lady gasped when Tormond's mount slipped on a boulder. The horse foundered a bit while the rock hurtled down the slope, its noise muffled by freshly fallen snow.

Willy's pony stopped in the middle of the crossing as if considering whether it was a good idea to turn back. After a few nudges from Willy's heels, the beast started forward and made it without incident.

Once the last man had crossed, Robert gently patted the mare's neck. "Are you ready, Miss Janet?"

"Aye, may as well be off afore I lose my nerve."

"Your mount is surefooted, else I wouldn't let you ride." He kept his hand on her horse for a moment longer. "I am impressed with your fortitude, miss. You have weathered our misfortune far better than I ever would have guessed."

"My thanks...I think." Miss Janet tapped her riding crop along with her heel, commanding her sidesaddle with expert precision. The mare picked her way across with her head low, her steps sure.

When Janet had nearly made it to the other side, Robert looked skyward and thanked God the lass had been blessed with a Highlander's spirit. Most well-bred women would have swooned ten times over by now. As his gaze shifted back to horse and rider, snow and rock fell away beneath the horse's front hoof in a shower of debris.

The mare faltered. She backed. Janet tapped her crop. The horse shook her head and reached for another next step—a step that sent them both falling down the steep, snowy slope.

A shrill scream echoed across the mountains. Robert's gut turned to lead, and he watched helplessly as Janet and her mount tumbled down the hillside with clouds of snow in their wake. Shouting orders, he reined his mount down the treacherously sheer ridge. "I'm going after her!"

"Wha—" Lewis's voice echoed.

"Meet me at Glenmoriston!" Robert bellowed, leaning so far back in the saddle his back bounced against his horse's rump.

Chapter Nine

The stallion skidded to a halt at the bottom of the glen. Robert feared the worst as he leaped down into thigh-deep snow. But the sting of the icy crystals was nothing compared to the panic seizing his chest. Janet was some-where beneath the blanket of white.

With his gloved hands he attacked the snow, scooping and sweeping it away as fast as he could. Every breath, every heartbeat counted in a race against death. Finally he spotted a swath of blue taffeta.

"Miss Janet!" he yelled, the name clipped and rushed while he rapidly clawed away the snow until he found her shoulders. Heaving, he hoisted her from the snow.

"Ow!" she squealed, falling atop him.

He grinned so wide, tears stung his damned eyes. Her cry of pain had to be the most uplifting sound he'd heard in all his days. "You're alive."

"My arm." She curled forward, cradling it against her

stomach, her breath coming in short gasps. "I can't move my fingers. I-I think it is broken."

Robert reached for her blood-soaked sleeve. "May I have a look?"

With her nod, Janet's eyes filled with fear and pain. "What have I done?"

"'Twas nothing you did, lass. The snow gave way." He peered beneath the blue taffeta and lace that should never be worn in the midst of a snowstorm this high in the mountains. *Holy Christ.* Janet's forearm was broken, all right. The bone protruded from the flesh and needed setting for certain.

"I-is it bad?" she asked quietly, though her voice strained with the high pitch of pain.

Before he answered, Robert's gut twisted. He mustn't mollify his response, no matter how much he wished to. "Aye. You were right. 'Tis broke." Rocking back on his haunches, he scratched his head while snow continued to fall atop them. "I'm no bone setter. I need to take you to a healer."

She sucked back a gasp, blinking away tears. "Is there one nearby? Is there a village? A croft?"

There wasn't. "Nay."

The lass whimpered, cradling her arm tighter. "Oh dear, oh dear, oh dear. What a dreadful mess."

Robert had to agree; they were at the bottom of a ravine near the top of the highest mountain range in Scotland. "One thing's for certain, we cannot linger here."

"Dear Lord, my arm hurts to move." Janet rocked back and forth. "My horse? Where is she?"

Robert looked back to the mare, covered with snow and debris. She tossed her head, fighting to break free. He hastened to the filly's side and pulled away a log. As soon as the weight lifted, the horse sprang up and tried to run, but she was nearly too lame to walk.

Ballocks. "She's faltering—favoring her left hock." He reached for his flintlock pistol.

"No!" Janet shouted as if he were about to murder a bairn.

Grant pulled back the cock. "She's in pain."

"So am I, but you're not planning to shoot me, are you?"

He watched the horse, clearly in agony, blood dripping from her nose as she hobbled nearer his steed. "Bloody hell, you'll never be able to ride her again."

"I don't care. I love that mare. I trained her from a foal, and I'm not about to let you shoot her."

Against his better judgment, he sheathed his weapon. "Very well, but she'll have to keep pace. I'm not willing to risk our lives for a nag."

Still cradling her arm, Janet rocked to and fro. "She'll keep pace. I promise. She has the heart of a lion."

Robert removed his neckcloth. "We'll all die if we don't find shelter soon. I need you to hold your arm close to your body. I'll tie it in place."

"Then where to? You said there's nowhere close."

"One thing at a time. First we'll restrain your arm to keep it still." He looked her in the eye and held out the cloth. "I'll try not to jostle it overmuch."

Janet tensed and hissed while he slid the makeshift sling around her wrist. "That should be the worst of it," he said, tying the ends of the cloth at her nape.

Her shoulders shook. "This is a colossal muddle. A-and my poor mare."

"I ken, lass." Robert tried to sound consoling, though Miss Janet's horse was the least of their woes, especially if the storm didn't ease. "I need you to bear down and keep your arm still whilst I lift you onto my stallion. Can you do that for me?"

Cringing as if she wanted to cry but was forcing herself to be strong, she gave a nod. Robert stood, bent his knees, and gently pushed his hands into the snow and beneath her. "Ready?"

"Aye," she said, but her breathing sped while he lifted her from the snow and cradled her to his chest.

"Not much farther," he cooed, noticing a gash just below her hairline. *Most likely she has bumps and bruises everywhere.* As carefully as he could, Robert lifted her up to his saddle, then mounted behind. "We'll follow the burn. 'Tis cutting a path through the snow," he said aloud, though it was more of a thought than anything. At least the water hadn't frozen yet. He knew two things: they were heading northeast, which was away from Fort William, and, if his bearings were sound, they were riding toward MacDonnel's summer grazing lands. No one in their right mind would be camped up there on the first of November, especially not in the midst of a blizzard.

Moreover, the stallion was already spent from riding half the day and wouldn't make it till dark. The lass might be putting on a brave face, but she needed tending sooner rather than later.

Robert ground his molars while they picked their way through thick forest and snow, tugging the lame mare on a lead line behind. How the hell had he ended up in this mess? After the altercation at the gathering, he and his men were safely heading home. Why had he turned around? Christ, Miss Janet would have been better off imprisoned in Fort William for a sennight or two than stranded in the snowy mountains with a broken arm.

They rode in silence for a time while Robert continued to berate himself. A few miles on, the trees opened to a mountain lea. He sat taller, a whit of his burden easing from his shoulders.

God giveth.

Fifty feet away stood a shepherd's bothy. Hewn of stone with a crude thatched roof, it butted up against a small outcropping. "Do you see that, Miss Janet?"

She glanced up and gasped. "Is anyone living there?"

"I doubt it—the sheep and cattle have been taken to the saleyard, I'd reckon. But she'll give us shelter for the night." And that's all he would say. *No use adding to the poor gel's trepidation.*

Janet searched the horizon before giving a nod. Lord knew if there were any other option—any other comfort within miles—if the ground weren't covered with three feet of snow, he would rather take her elsewhere, too.

But right now, the wee bothy might as well be a palace.

Robert wanted to cue the stallion to a canter and race to the door, but his horse was spent. Instead he dismounted and led the beast through the drifts of snow. "I'll have a look inside afore I jostle your arm again."

"Hurry, please." The poor lass sounded in agony and breathless.

He didn't expect to find much. Inside was a crude hearth made without mortar, but it had a grill plate suspended from a rope and hook. Beside the hearth sat a cast-iron pot. He found pelts of deer and cowhide piled against one wall, and a small stack of firewood. Robert guessed the two upended logs were used as stools. He spotted an ax, utensils, and some wooden dishes. Not horrible for a bothy, and it would do in a pinch.

He took a few of the furs and fashioned a pallet, then

carried Miss Janet inside and rested her atop the makeshift bed. "We've no recourse but to weather the night here. With luck, this squall will pass. 'Tis still early in the season. I doubt the snow will last."

"I can only imagine what my father will say about this."

He rolled a rabbit pelt and slid it under her head. "If he's smart, he'll be grateful you're alive."

She pursed her lips and glanced away.

"I'll set to starting a fire." Robert used a bit of flax tow from his sporran. He struck his dirk to flint. Sparks ignited the wooly ball. Carefully he added kindling, then a small stick of wood. Once sure it had taken, he used a twig and lit a crude tallow lamp. "I'd best tend the horses," he said, excusing himself.

Outside, he loosely hobbled the stallion's rear legs so he could use his front to dig through the snow and find the mountain grass. The mare wouldn't wander. He preferred to focus on small tasks than think of the brutal chore ahead. Bile churned in Robert's gut as he looked to the bothy's door. If only there were another way. But putting it off was no option.

Using his dirk, he cut two green branches from a tree, ensuring they were both about the same width and length. Then he cut one more—this one a bit smaller and shorter.

Gulping, Robert stared at the rickety wooden door for a moment before he entered.

Janet glanced up from her pallet, perspiration beading her forehead. "Is there more of that dried meat?"

"Aye, and I'll fetch it in a moment." He doubted she'd have much of an appetite after. Not looking her way, he pulled his spare shirt out of his satchel and tore it into strips for bandages. Then, steeling his nerves, he faced the lass and presented his flask. "We've put off setting your arm long enough. You'd best have a few sips of this."

As she sat up, her face was ashen, even in the amber firelight. "Must you? It is not hurting quite as much now."

Robert's lips thinned. "Can you move your fingers?"

Her jaw twitched as she glanced downward with a look of determination, but those fingers didn't budge. "Och. I cannot even feel them."

"Then it must be done," he said gruffly, hoping she wouldn't cry. Good God, he could handle screaming and shouting, but weeping would tear his heart to shreds.

Defiance filled her gaze as she leaned away from him. "B-but mayhap tomorrow we'll find a healer."

"I will say this once." Robert shifted the flask under her nose. "If you ever want to use that arm again, you'd best drink."

She took the whisky and tossed back the tiniest of sips, then gagged and coughed as if he'd given her poison. "'Tis awful."

"The first sip burns the most. Again." He made her take a total of five tots before he kneeled and rolled up her sleeve. "Now lie flat."

Her lips quivered as she did as he asked.

He examined the arm, his stomach turning over. By the swelling, it was clear where the bone had been displaced. He had seen a man's shinbone set before—the poor bastard bucked harder than a bull in the castrating pen. But at least Robert had witnessed the surgery. That had to count for something. He held out the smallest of the three sticks. "Bite down on this."

"Dear Lord, have mercy." Taking the twig between her teeth, she closed her eyes and released a shaky breath.

Before he started, he put one of the bandages in his

teeth, wishing he had another pair of hands. "Steel yourself, Miss Janet."

Her face contorted, but she managed to nod.

He placed one of the splints on her arm and pushed hard and fast until the bone slipped into place.

Shrieking, Janet kicked, her head thrashing.

Robert bore down, holding her arm steady. He worked as fast as he could, wrapping the bandage around, then grabbing the second splint and applying it to the underside of her arm. He bound it tightly until he used all the bandages he'd made. Then he tied them off and tested the splint's soundness. Thank the stars, she wouldn't be moving that arm for days.

Pursing his lips, he made himself look at her face. A sheen of sweat moistened her forehead. She took one glance at him and gasped while her eyes rolled back.

"The worst is over," he whispered, cupping her cheek. "Ye are the bravest lass I've ever seen." Without another thought, he bent down and kissed her forehead.

Chapter Ten

*W*infred Cummins rubbed his gloved hands while his breath billowed around him. Every muscle clenched tight against the frigid cold. The corporal and pair of sentinels who had gone up the pass to scout hours ago were finally returning. Meanwhile, Cummins's troops had been useless. The meager fire they'd started popped and hissed and all but fizzled out while he waited.

He hated the Highlands. He hated bloody Scotland. And he'd never been so cold in his life. Earlier his feet had plagued him with pins and needles, and now the right had gone completely numb.

"The trail is impassable," said the corporal, reining his horse to a stop as the sentinels followed suit.

Winfred clenched his fists at his sides. "You mean to tell me you have allowed those blackguards to evade us?"

"With all due respect, sir, no one up there will survive this blizzard. The poor sops will be trapped for the winter."

"Dead within a sennight, I reckon," said another of the sentinels.

Winfred took a step forward and cried out as his leg collapsed beneath him. Flinging his arms forward, he caught the corporal's stirrup before he fell.

"Are you unwell, sir?"

Hanging on, the lieutenant pulled himself up, unable to keep his teeth from chattering. "If you lot would have shot Robert Grant before he escaped, I would be fine. We all would be fine—warm in our cots at the fort."

The corporal's lips thinned while he exchanged glances with the men. Winfred knew what they were thinking. He'd heard the murmurs. They thought he was overreacting.

They're soft, the lot of them.

None of this was his fault. Highlanders were the basest lowlifes in all of Christendom, and he'd been billeted to this God-forsaken outpost to keep order.

How does a soldier keep order in an icy hell where men vanish into the mist?

Moreover, Janet Cameron needed a lesson in manners. Winfred had watched her dance with enough kilted bastards on Samhain; it would have served her well to give the same attention to the officers in the queen's dragoons.

To hell with her and her bastard savior. They deserve a long and painful death.

"At least Britain will be rid of a few more trouble-makers," said the corporal.

"So say you." Gnashing his teeth, Winfred hobbled to his horse and managed to pull himself into the saddle. "But if I discover you have provided me with false information, you will face a court-martial. Hear me clear—all of you men will face consequences."

He picked up his reins and pointed his steed toward Fort William and a warm fire. Winfred planned to submit a complete report upon his return—as long as his foot didn't freeze solid in the interim.

* * *

Thrashing her head from side to side, Janet woke with a start. Heaven help her, she was freezing and in agony.

Can a person die from pain?

Her arm throbbed and ached as if she'd been branded with a white-hot poker. Sweat streamed from her brow while the inside of her skull pounded. She opened her mouth to cry out, but her tongue was dry and covered with sticky goo. "Water," she managed to croak.

Someone moved—followed by some rustling. Then Laird Grant kneeled over her, holding a wooden cup. "How are you faring, lass?"

Unable to answer, she cringed as he helped lift her head and lowered the cup to her mouth. She gulped down a sip and licked her lips. "More."

"You feel warm."

She forced down another swallow. "C-cold. Hurts."

He set the cup aside and uncorked his flask. "All I can offer to take the edge off your pain is a tot of this."

She gave a single nod.

"Can you move your fingers?"

Lord in heaven, the mere thought made her stomach squeamish. But she bore down and tapped her pointer finger twice. The movement brought on a violent shudder.

"Och, 'tis a good sign," he said, shifting the flask to her mouth.

Janet gulped greedily, then wiped her lips with the back of her hand, trying not to cough. "Whisky is awful."

"Mayhap when you're not accustomed to it. But this is a fine Highland spirit. I'd think any Cameron would appreciate whisky from the Duke of Gordon's still."

"My father may like it, but I'd rather a tincture of willow bark and chamomile."

"I pray I'll find some for you on the morrow."

"Is it still snowing?"

"Aye—at least when last I checked."

"Do you think we will be able to travel come morn?"

Shifting his gaze to the door, he ran his fingers over the stubble on his jaw, which had grown thicker. "We've no choice but to wait and see."

There was a sinking feeling in her stomach—one she'd managed to ignore until now. Janet might have been able to weather the scandal of running from the redcoats with Laird Grant and his army, but now she was alone with the man and trapped in a blizzard. When and if they ever made it back to civilization, she would be ruined. Lord knew what action her stepmother might take. But Janet harbored no illusions. Her situation was as precarious as it was grave. Her options would be few: find a man of decent repute who would marry her on the spot; become a governess and commit to a life of spinsterhood; or flee to France, join a convent, and pledge her life to God.

Why did this have to happen to me?

"You're worried," he said, brushing a wisp of hair away from her face. The sensation of his touch made gooseflesh rise across her shoulders.

Janet met his gaze. In the firelight he didn't look anywhere near as stern as he usually did. In fact, he appeared rather compassionate. "I am," she whispered.

His finger trailed to the top of her injured arm and rested there. "I'll wager in two to three months your arm will be as good as new. Your break was clean. I felt the bone slip into place and tied the splint firm."

"I thank you for your care, sir, but I am not as worried about my arm as I am about..." Her gaze shifted aside.

"A scandal," he finished, his voice grave.

"Aye."

With a deep sigh, he rocked back onto his haunches. "I will attest to your virtue. No one will doubt me. All ken when my word is given, it is true."

"All?"

He pursed his lips. "You are referring to your father."

"He and my kin. The feud between our families has run deep for generations. When my father hears the news..." Her mind raced. There was every chance her father would take up arms and put Laird Grant's lands to fire and sword.

"I will challenge any man who questions me." Mr. Grant uncorked his flask and drank. "My mother always said there was no use worrying about that which we cannot control."

"But I could be ruined."

"Have faith, lass. You fell down a ravine and broke your arm in the midst of a blizzard. Let people think what they may, but I will speak on your behalf." He was right. They were stuck alone in the bothy now, and not a soul could save her.

Janet nodded as he handed her the flask. This time she took a long swig, welcoming the burn and resultant swirling in her head. "This spirit won't last long."

He took it and pushed in the cork. "Ah well. We shall enjoy it whilst we can."

"Are you always so untroubled?"

He smiled—dimples, white teeth. It was an endearing smile, rather than the sinister sneer she would expect from a clan enemy. "Mayhap if I were, the Grants and the Camerons would be fast friends."

"Hmm." Janet couldn't pull her gaze away as she considered his words. When she'd first seen him in Inverlochy, he'd accused her kin of stealing his cattle. He'd been adamant about his accusation, regardless of the Cameron livestock losses. Aye, she'd seen him at Highland gatherings over the years, but he'd always kept his distance. For the most part, she'd considered him an arrogant mule until the day she sewed his cheek. He became a person then—akin to a friend or acquaintance.

"What are you thinking?" he asked.

She quickly dropped her gaze to her hands. "N-nothing. Ah..." *Good heavens, he must think me daft for staring.* "I was just wondering how your cheek is healing. I-it is difficult to tell beneath your stubble."

He rubbed his finger along the outside of the wound. "It itches more than anything. I'd like to pull the stitches out."

"But you mustn't do that. The healer always says to leave them be for a fortnight."

"The bloody sutures might drive me mad by then."

Her ears piqued at his vulgarity.

"Forgive me. I shouldn't speak so coarsely when in the presence of a lady."

Her shoulder twitched up. "I suppose Kennan wouldn't bother to apologize."

"That's different."

"Is it?" She chewed the corner of her lip.

He grasped her good hand and held it between his

warm palms. The pads of his fingers were rough and meaty. Her heartbeat quickened as he slowly raised it to his lips and kissed. "You must try to sleep."

The back of her hand tingled with the lingering essence of his kiss, and she drew her palm over her heart. "You as well, sir."

Those dimples teased her again as he threw his thumb over his shoulder. "If you need anything I'll be just there."

"Thank you."

"You will ask should you need assistance?"

"Aye." She smiled. "Good night, Your Lairdship."

* * *

Janet awoke with a start and no idea of the time. Everything ached as she forced herself to sit up. Daylight shone from a crack at the top of the door. The only other light was provided by embers glowing in the crude hearth, but Mr. Grant was nowhere to be seen. As she set her hand down, her fingers brushed the whisky flask. Beside it were a cup of water, a piece of dried meat, and a note that looked as if it had been written on a slip of vellum with nothing more than charcoal.

Starving, she bit into the meat while she read:

Miss Janet,

Gone to hunt. Warm water & soap by fire.

RG

Though moving caused enough pain to make her swoon, she couldn't wait any longer to step outside.

Careful to hold her arm close to her midriff to prevent it from jostling, she opened the door to thigh-deep snow as far as she could see. Mr. Grant had trampled a path toward the wood. Janet's feet turned to ice as she followed it with silent footsteps, quickly took care of business.

Once done, she clucked for her mare. At the edge of the wood, the horse nickered, standing akimbo to protect her hock.

"Good girl," she said. "We both need to heal quickly because we certainly cannot survive a winter in these mountains."

Content that the mare was settled, Janet hastened back inside.

"Brr." She shivered and blew on her good hand as she neared the fire. The pot of warm water looked tempting. Beside it were a wee bar of pine soap and a scrap of linen. Slipping out of the gown was easy because of the loose-fitting trumpet sleeves. It took some time, but she managed to loosen her stays enough to pull them around to the front and open the laces enough to push them off over her hips. Down went three petticoats, leaving only her shift.

Janet added a stick of wood to the fire, then stood very still and listened. Nothing. At Achnacarry hunting took an entire day; thus she figured she had plenty of time to bathe. Slowly she pulled the string at the neck of her shift while she looked longingly at the warm water. After her flight to the mountains and her tumble down the hill, she was covered with sweat and grime. Gritting her teeth, she gingerly slipped the garment away from her injured arm.

She crouched and soon realized washing with one hand was cumbersome at best. Unable to lather the cloth, she resorted to scrubbing herself with the soap, then dousing the cloth and running it over her body. The most tempting part? There was enough water remaining to wash her hair. She patted the tangled mass that had been styled by the maid three nights ago. Surprisingly, the decorative comb still held some of the coiffure in place, though strands hung on either side of her face.

She pulled out the comb, ribbon, and remaining pins, dunked her head in the water, did her best to work up a lather, rinsed, then wrung it out.

Now dripping wet, Janet realized her next challenge was finding a drying cloth. *Curses. I should have thought about that before I washed my hair.*

Coming up with nothing, she resorted to wringing out her hair again—not an easy accomplishment with one working hand. Then she crouched beside the fire and briskly rubbed her skin, the friction and warmth helping her to dry while she cradled her injured arm close to her body, trying to block the pain from her mind.

Her ears pricked up when a noise came from outside. Holding her breath, she stopped moving and listened.

'Twas nothing.

Nonetheless, she must dress straightaway. Removing her clothing had been difficult enough, but the mere thought of tugging her splinted arm through a sleeve made her skin crawl. Clumsily she grasped the neckline of her shift and gathered it until she could slip the whole underdress over her head. With it around her neck, she worked the armhole down to the fist clinched at her waist. Taking in a deep breath, she attempted to lift her arm and straighten it enough to pull the sleeve on.

A sharp, bone-jarring, torturous jab hit her so fiercely she cried out and fell to her backside. "Owwwwww!" Weeping hysterically, unable to catch her breath, she couldn't move.

Then, to her horror, the door burst open.

Chapter Eleven

*R*obert charged through the door at a run. He'd been outside cleaning rabbits when a shriek came from inside the bothy. He was halfway to her side when the woman's state of undress dawned on him. Aye. Not just undress, but near complete nudity.

Perfection.

"No!" she shouted, trying to tug the shift down from around her neck.

"Did you fall? Has the splint shifted?" he demanded, dropping to his knees beside her while his heart nearly pounded out of his chest.

"Go away!" She tried to curl into a ball, tears streaking down her face.

Robert forced himself to shift his gaze aside. "Clearly you need help."

"This is humiliating. P-please go," she sobbed.

"Nay." He'd already seen her. He had no choice but to block his mind to it and help the poor lass. Spotting the skirts of her gown, he whisked them from the floor. "I shall drape this over your lap for modesty."

"Noooooo..."

"Bear up your courage. 'Tis not the first time I've helped a woman dress."

Those words seemed to settle her—or shock the lass—because her weeping turned into staccato breathing. Robert's jaw twitched. Most likely she thought him a more hideous rake than before. With the brushing of taffeta, he covered her lap with the gown, but the sight of her creamy flesh disarmed him. Smooth and shapely thighs led to dark curls—curls that concealed a tempting treasure. Higher up, her arm crossed a perfectly rounded breast while Miss Janet's fingers tugged futilely on her twisted linen shift.

Gulping, he shifted his gaze to her face and brushed the tears from her cheeks. "Och, lass, I left the water for you to splash your face and hands, not for a full bath. No one, man or woman, who'd only just broken their arm could be expected to dress without assistance."

"But I felt so slovenly, and the water temperature was deliciously nice."

"I cannot say I blame you there. It has been a harrowing couple of days." Trying not to stare at the soft curve of her breast peeking from beneath her arm, he pointed to the shift. "That's twisted up tighter than a hemp rope."

"I'm afraid I bunched it up overmuch and then it twisted more due to my damp hair and...ah...Goodness gracious, this is so improper."

"Nonsense. You are in need of help and, since there is no one about for miles, I am the only person who can give it." He started untwisting the linen. "Tell me," he said, trying to calm her unease, "did it not hurt to remove your clothing?"

"It hurt a great deal, but not anywhere near as much as trying to put my things back on. I thought I would swoon from the pain."

"Hmm." The shift unfurled until he had it completely covering her torso. Now came the impossible part—pulling the sleeve up her splinted arm. He tugged the armhole downward, but the tie at the neckline prevented him from moving it far enough. "I'll need to release this bow."

"Must you?"

"Aye, unless you can raise your arm about five inches."

She met his gaze with a mixture of apprehension and trust. "Very well, untie it," she whispered, so softly it made his stomach stir—causing a great deal of stirring in inappropriate places.

He pulled on the bow and the collar dropped wide. So did Robert's mouth. Except for the arm hiding the tips of her breasts, he beheld the most exquisite feminine bosom he'd ever seen in all his days. Everywhere he looked, Janet's skin was as smooth as warm cream. On the curve of her breast, a tiny mole peeked above her hand—exactly where his lips wanted to be, worshiping, tasting, exploring her.

He licked those wayward lips, pretending to examine the widened hole. Most likely, if Janet had released the tie at the collar, she might have been able to slip her arm inside, though Robert could imagine the agony and pain she must be enduring. Carefully he fingered the sleeve. "I shall slip this over your hand now."

Janet sucked in a gasp, but he managed to quickly slip it over the splint and up to her shoulder. "Breathe," he whispered, his lips very near her ear.

She smiled with her stuttered inhalation, her eyes mesmerizing. They were flecked with shimmering shades of blue from turquoise to indigo. She glanced downward as if bashful.

"Don't," he said, wanting more.

With a mere flicker of her eyelids, those vivid blues again stared back. "What?" she asked, her voice breathless. Did she feel the connection, too?

Of course not. Her father is my sworn enemy.

Clearing his throat, Robert released his grip on the shift and stood. "I'll turn my back whilst you finish."

"Thank you."

After a great deal of grunting and rustling, silence filled the bothy.

"May I turn around now?"

"Mm…" It sounded as if she had her mouth full.

He glanced over his shoulder. One end of her shift's ribbon was in her teeth and the other was in her good hand. She was trying to tie a bow.

"Allow me to help."

She shirked away, as if he hadn't just helped her pull the damned thing up her broken arm. "Och, you won't be able to dress alone." He briskly tied the damned bow. "My guess is a lady's maid helped you tie your stays when you were dressing for Samhain. Am I right?"

She nodded, looking sheepish. At least she was covered, albeit with a single layer of holland cloth that left little to the imagination.

If only the good Lord would bring a heat wave on the morrow, my torture would be ended.

Offering his hand, Robert helped Janet to her feet, stopped staring, and picked up the taffeta skirt.

"Petticoats next," she said.

He straightened, keeping his back turned. "What do you need all those for?"

"The gown will look wilted without them."

"We're stranded miles from civilization and you're worried about having full skirts?"

"Well, we can't leave them here. A-and they help provide warmth."

He hadn't thought about that. So he sorted through the pile of India muslin and helped her tie three blasted petticoats in place, then again picked up her skirt.

She shook her head. "Stays next."

He held up the contraption. "How in the devil did you manage to remove this?"

"It wasn't easy. I nearly broke my good arm twisting it backward."

"'Tis a miracle you didn't. But why wear these now? You can put them on afore we ride."

"Are you serious? No proper woman would be seen outside her bedchamber without her stays."

"Right. Of course. How terribly unfeeling of me." He looked to the stays. "Would you prefer the laces in front or in back?"

She huffed. "I believe the front would be most practical."

Wrapping the stays around her midriff and then painstakingly tugging the laces through each eyelet until his fingers brushed the delicate softness of her breasts turned his knees boneless. And then she gasped. It was not a shocked gasp of horror, but a wee, barely audible gasp. A sound emitted by a female only when she was aroused.

Robert's hands stilled. She stared at him with desire in her eyes, her chest heaving with the same unsteady breaths he was experiencing. Her lips parted—heaven help him, he wanted to kiss her.

Nay, you will not kiss Sir Ewen Cameron's daughter, you clodpoll!

Finishing the job, he tied a bow, praying she didn't notice the slight tremor of his fingers.

"You are adept at this, Mr. Grant," she whispered. "Wherever did you acquire your skill?"

"Anyone can tie laces." That wasn't quite true, but he would never own to his many conquests, not to a maid as pure as Miss Janet. "Besides, I have a sister."

"You do?"

"Aye." He held up the bodice of her gown and carefully helped her slide into it, injured arm first.

"I do not recall ever seeing her before."

"I doubt you have. She keeps to Glenmoriston."

"How old is she?"

"Ten years my junior. She's only seventeen."

"Seventeen, and you do not take her to gatherings?"

"She hasn't wanted to go."

"Is she shy?"

"Yes." Robert grasped Janet's shoulders, turned her to face the wall, and started with yet another set of laces. "Pull your hair aside, please."

"'Tis wet and matted."

He glanced at the hand-painted comb on the floor. "I'll work out the knots for you after I've finished cleaning the rabbits."

"Oh, my goodness, you caught rabbits?"

"Four of them. I found some hazelnuts beneath a grove of trees where the snow wasn't as deep—gathered enough to fill my sporran. They'll make a tasty pottage."

"I daresay they will. I'm hungry."

Once she was put back together, Robert helped her sit atop her pallet of furs. "How's your arm?"

"It's the most painful injury I've ever had, but I have no alternative but to endure it."

"I wish I would have been the one to fall and not you." He pressed his lips to her forehead and kissed. "Please remain still and do not cause yourself injury whilst I fetch the rabbits."

Chapter Twelve

*J*anet watched the imposing Highlander stoop over the fire and use a wooden spoon to stir the pottage. "My, you are far more industrious than I ever imagined."

"Given your clan's bias, I doubt you ever imagined anything good about the likes of me."

She closed her eyes and sighed. Robert Grant had no idea how Janet had noticed him at every ceilidh she'd attended. Who wouldn't admire a man of his stature, even if he was the leader of a feuding clan? She'd always appreciated his brawn, though never entertained any illusions that his character might be anything more than menacing. Janet had once avowed the same sentiment to Lady Mairi—"Robert Grant might be a brawny Highlander, but he is a wolf in sheep's clothing." Now that she'd experienced his gentleness, his capacity for kindness, she was confused and muddled.

He raised the spoon to his lips and tasted. "Does the fact that I'm cooking surprise you?" he asked.

"Aye, and everything else. You managed quite well with my gown, you cleaned rabbits, set my arm, rescued me from certain death at the bottom of the glen." Again she sighed. "I suppose it should be of no consequence to watch you prepare a pottage."

He shrugged. "I suppose 'tis nothing I wouldn't expect from any other man. We all must dress ourselves, and when droving cattle for months on end, a man learns a bit about preparing food, else he starves." He tapped the spoon on the edge of the cast-iron pot, then set it down. "Don't expect this to taste like a Michaelmas feast. Without seasoning, it will keep us alive and that's about all."

"I'm hungry enough to eat tanned leather."

"Good." He grinned, those confounded dimples making her insides dance. "Camp food tastes better when you're starved."

"I shall remember that." Janet picked up her comb and started working through the knots at the ends of her tresses. Using one hand was all but hopeless. Her hair was too thick and too unruly.

"Let me help." Robert sat on the pallet beside her.

"You're busy. The least I can do is work a comb through these knots."

"Aye, though we've naught to do but wait and let the rabbits simmer for an hour or so." He slid his hand over her fingers and took the comb. "Please, allow me."

"Good luck to you. I'm afraid the tangle is beyond repair."

"I do not ken about that." He started at the ends, working the comb with quick flicks.

"My hair has always been difficult to manage. My lady's maid complains about it incessantly."

"Then I would venture to guess she is underworked."

Janet glanced over her shoulder just as he looked up. Goodness, her stays were hardly constricting, and yet her head swooned. Not only that, her entire body swooned, if such a thing could happen. "I daresay you have an arresting look about you." *Och, did I just utter those words aloud?*

He confirmed her dread when his gaze dipped downward and then back up while his tongue slipped over his lip. "I cannot say I have ever been thus accused. Mayhap 'tis on account of the stitches on my right cheek."

"Apologies." She winced. "Your wound looks a bit red around the edges. But you said earlier 'tisn't ailing you?"

"Not overmuch."

"As I mentioned afore, leave it sewn at least another sennight, else your scar will be worse."

"Hmm." He winked. "I doubt such a battle wound will add to my status as an arresting gentleman."

An unladylike chuckle pealed from her throat. "Agreed. The scar will be fearsome enough without it taking up half your cheek."

His gaze returned to her tresses, and he drew the comb through the length. "There. I say your locks are like silk thread. They might tangle easily, but I am convinced your maid hasn't worked a solid day in her life." He plucked a half-dry tress and drew it to his nose. "And the scent reminds me of a field of lavender."

She pulled away while her hair slowly slipped across his palm. The swooning of her insides grew tenfold. "Now I ken you tell tall tales."

"I beg to differ, miss. In this instance I have been reticent if anything."

As her gaze slipped from his intense silver-blue eyes to the fullness of his lips, Janet raised her chin slightly. For a moment when he was helping her dress, she'd thought he might kiss her, and now she craved for him to do so. She shivered with the unbridled strength of her longing. He needed only to dip his chin a few more inches and their lips would touch. They sat motionless for a lingering moment, staring, not moving, while Janet's heart pounded.

But rather than dip his chin, Robert swiped his knuckles across the thick stubble along his jaw. "So, Miss Cameron, how do you spend your days at the illustrious castle of Achnacarry?"

All thoughts of swooning turned to sinking lead. "I doubt my days would hold any interest for a great laird such as yourself." She looked to the rafters. Her father always paid far more attention to her brothers' pursuits.

"Humor me. What would a day in the life of Janet Cameron be like?"

"Boring."

"Nay, lass. I do not believe you."

"Very well. In the mornings, I like to visit the stable and work the fillies and colts."

"Colts? Honestly? Isn't that a bit dangerous for a wee—"

"A wee woman?" She squared her shoulders. "Do you not think I can train a horse?"

"As I have witnessed, you are quite a proficient rider, but young colts are skittish."

"They are." She leaned nearer—sideways, shoulder to shoulder, as she would with her brothers. There would be no more temptation. She could not allow it. "The key is patience."

"Patience? They're bloody beasts of burden."

Janet held up her finger. "So says every man I've ever met bar one."

"And who may that be?"

"The stable master at Achnacarry. He taught me everything I know."

"And is this stable master arresting?"

"Nay. *Crusty and old* is more apt—but he is endearing."

"And patient with young horses."

"Aye."

"If you show them patience you'll never manage to break them."

"True." Janet held up a finger. "The goal isn't to break a horse but to become their alpha mare."

The man snorted, a sarcastic grin making his dimples prominent. "That sounds like hogwash. Do you incant a spell and wave a magic wand as well?"

"Now you're mocking me."

Awkward silence swelled through the air.

"Forgive me." Mr. Grant scooted over and stirred the pottage. "I just have never witnessed such a thing."

"Then admit you cannot pass judgment until you've seen it with your own eyes. I think you owe me that, for I am not one to tell tall tales, either."

"Very well." He rolled his hand through the air. "You spend your mornings in the stables."

"Aye, when I can. I also spend the evenings knitting."

His eyebrows shot up. "Knitting," he said, as if it were the most interesting thing to come out of her mouth thus far.

"I make mittens, bonnets, scarves, and stockings for the West Highland Benevolent Society."

"A worthy cause."

"It is. I delivered a score of each before Samhain. 'Tis the reason Da allowed me to accompany Kennan, else I doubt he would have let me go."

Robert gestured to her arm. "I reckon you would have been better off had you stayed at Achnacarry."

"True."

"But Kennan is a responsible man. I do not see why your father would object to having him provide escort."

"It wasn't Kennan so much as Da likes to keep me under a watchful eye." She groaned. "That's what he says, though I'm never quite sure why. When I'm at home I hardly see him."

"Doesn't he pay you much mind?"

"Mind? He's a laird of a vast estate—just like you." Batting her hand through the air, she shook her head. "We chat at mealtimes, so he always kens what I'm up to. At least he thinks he does."

"Thinks? I hardly see you as surreptitious."

"True. Though every lass has her secrets."

He took up a lock of her hair and twirled it around his finger. "What kind of secrets?"

Her lips parted as she watched a curl form as he drew his hand away. "Och, do not tell me a braw Highland laird the likes of Robert Grant would have any interest in the things I choose not to tell."

"Hmm. I am very interested."

"Bah."

"Shall I guess?"

"I think we should change the subject. I'm sure your hopes and dreams are far more entertaining than mine."

He wagged his finger beneath her nose. "Not so fast. I like the guessing game better. I'll wager you have been kissed, but no one but the lad who kissed you kens."

Janet drew her hands over her mouth while her cheeks burned. "Kissing is not a proper topic to discuss, sir." She had kissed a lad once, though she never would own to it.

"It may not be proper, it's certainly very interesting," he chuckled.

"Sir! I assure you I am not about to discuss whom I have and whom I have not kissed. Especially with you. Goodness' sakes, you are the head of Clan Grant."

He dipped his chin, and intensity filled his eyes. That and unquestioning sincerity. "I would never reveal your secrets to anyone."

"Even though I am a Cameron?"

He gestured from wall to wall. "Here in this bothy, we are but two souls stranded in a snowstorm." He dug inside his sporran and presented her with a pair of dice. "Have you ever played hazard?"

"N-no. Is it not a gamer's sport?"

"Och, 'tis a simple game of main, nicks, outs, and chance. And I thought—"

Janet shook her head. "I have nothing with which to place a wager."

"If you would allow me to continue…I thought it might be amusing if the loser of each main revealed a secret about themselves."

She tapped her lip. It sounded innocent enough, and Janet would quite like to learn more about His Lairdship. "You have no qualms about telling me your secrets?"

"Not especially."

"Does the winner ask a question to which the loser must reply, or does the loser volunteer something?"

"What would you be most comfortable with?"

"Volunteering. Most definitely."

Chapter Thirteen

*R*obert stretched out his leg until his foot touched the wall. Odd, a stone about the size of a cannonball shifted.

"'Tis your turn," said Janet. The wee vixen had taken to the game of hazard like a bird to flight. Thus far Robert was the only one divulging any secrets.

"A moment." He crawled to the loose stone and examined it. Sure enough, the wall had been hollowed out and concealed a cranny. It took only a flick of his fingers to roll the stone away and peer inside.

"What is it?" Janet asked.

"Mayhap my luck has changed for the better." He chuckled. "It appears our shepherds have a taste for spirit." Wrapping his fingers around the neck of a bottle, he pulled it out. Indeed, it was a full flagon of whisky sealed with cork and wax. He handed it to Janet and, before he rolled the stone back into place, he slid a guinea into the cranny—more than double the price of a bottle of fine whisky, but well worth it.

"'Tis nice of you to pay."

"It is only fair. Though I venture to guess the man who left this will bring along a replacement." He uncorked the bottle and poured two cups—half for the lass and full for himself. "This will help ease your pain, but be careful not to overindulge, else you'll suffer from a sore head come morn."

She raised her cup. "Whisky is so potent, I doubt I could drink more than a wee dram, though it does help numb the awful throbbing."

Robert tapped her cup in toast, then sipped. It wasn't the smoothest drink he'd ever had, but it was a mite better than water. He picked up the dice. "My turn to call the main, did you say?"

"Mm-hmm."

"I'll call it five."

"Only five?" she asked as if she were an expert, following her words with a healthy drink. Evidently Janet was a quick learner at more than the game of hazard.

"Oh ye of little faith." He shook the dice in his hands and tossed them onto the floor. A two and a three.

"I'll be. Nicks on the first throw." Her cheeks turned a lovely shade of rose while her round eyes sparkled in the firelight.

Robert waggled his eyebrows teasingly. After a few sips of whisky, the game had suddenly grown more interesting. "Tell me a secret, lass."

The flutter of her lashes spoke of bashfulness and something else. Perhaps a bit of pride? "If you must know," she said with a flip of her hair, "I wear trews."

"You what?"

"Trews. On occasion…when Da and the lads are away, of course."

Why on earth would a lass as bonny as Janet Cameron think about donning a pair of breeches? The woman filled out a gown far more fetchingly than perhaps any in Christendom. Robert's jaw dropped. "Aaaand you enjoy the feel of them?"

She shrugged. "'Tis more for practicality."

"I suppose. If you are running a footrace."

"Or riding a horse astride."

"Ah." Now he understood. He wouldn't ride sidesaddle for his life. "You prefer to sit a horse like a man, do you?"

"When I'm trying to attain maximum speed, aye." Janet's words were spoken with such confidence, Robert had to purse his lips to stanch his laughter—not at her but at the picture he conjured in his mind. Miss Janet wearing a pair of plaid trews, standing in the stirrups with her heart-shaped behind in the air while her horse galloped around a racetrack. Now that would be a sight he'd love to witness.

He took another drink of whisky before he spoke. "I hope you will be able to give me a demonstration after your arm heals."

"In trews or riding astride?"

"Ha!" Och aye, hazard was growing more enjoyable by the moment. Unable to stop his grin, he replied, "Why, both, of course."

He lost the next roll of the dice. "I never wanted to inherit the lairdship," he confessed.

"Honestly? But you're such a commanding man, everyone respects you."

"Not everyone." He drummed his fingers. "Your father comes to mind."

"Hmm. What would you have done had you not inherited?"

"When I was a lad I wanted to be the master of my own ship—sail to the Americas and find my fortune."

"Sailing across the sea can lead to a man's end."

"True—though the lucky, I hear, find riches we only dream of in the Highlands."

"Now that you are a laird, do you ever dream of sailing off on an adventure?"

"Only when I face misfortune—such as losing half my herd of yearlings to tinkers and thieves. But I could never leave my clan and kin. They mean the world to me."

"My da would say the same."

"Your father wanted to be an adventurer?"

"I do not ken about that, but clan and kin come before queen and country."

"Well, I'll be damned. Cameron and I agree on something."

"If you'd sit down with him, you'd likely find you have more in common than you think." She held out her cup. "I believe I might withstand another dram…just a dollop, mind you."

"Very well, but after this I'm calling an end to your drinking."

"And yours, sir."

Though she was right, he scowled and gave her a slanted leer as he poured, helping himself to a bit extra. "Are you planning to roll the dice, or shall I have another go?" *No use having the mitten knitter think she can outdo me.*

Then he bloody lost the next round. He'd already told her everything he dared reveal to anyone, let alone the daughter of Sir Ewen Cameron.

The vixen sat taller, her eyes becoming heavy-lidded and a bit glazed. Now dry, her hair hung to her waist in waves like the mane of a lion. Moreover, the innocent lass had no idea how tempting she looked. She leaned closer, the motion giving him a delicious view of her cleavage as ample breasts strained against a bodice too frilly for a bothy in the wild.

"Do you have any more secrets, Mr. Grant?" Damn, her eyes met his with a moment of sizzling apprehension.

He took a lock of her hair and wound it around his finger. For all his days, he would never forget of the silken feel of it. "I enjoyed combing your tresses..." Drawing the lock to his nose, he inhaled her unique scent. "Ever so much," he whispered.

The intensity of their unwavering gazes grew tenfold. She seemed to be aware of the mounting awkwardness and dispelled it with a smile. "I do believe you are flirting with me."

"Never." He scooped up the dice. "But I need another secret from you, lass. I've revealed far too much."

"Very well. I call nines as main."

"Nines?"

"Nines." She threw the dice and rolled two fives.

"Outs." He grinned at her from behind his cup. "I'm listening."

"Ugh." Slapping her hand through the air, she huffed. "Two years ago, I kissed Malcolm MacGowan at the gathering in Inverness. There." She picked up the dice and pushed them into Robert's palm. "I've had enough of this game. It will end in nothing but trouble, I ken it right down to my bones."

He slipped the dice into his sporran. "I'll not utter a word, I give you my oath, as long as you pledge to keep my confidence."

"Of course I will." The lass raised her chin, looking innocent yet worldly, composed yet disheveled.

Without thinking of the consequence, he smoothed his fingers along her cheek. When her lips parted, his finger ventured to trace her bottom lip. "Satiny smooth."

He half expected her to slap him or at least shove him away, but instead she reached up and swirled her fingers around his uninjured cheek. Wonder glistened in her eyes. "Your beard is softer than I imagined."

He cleared his throat. "I should shave on the morrow."

A wee smile played on her lips as she studied him. "I think you are quite braw with a dark shadow. Perhaps you look like a sea captain."

His errant hand threaded through the hair at her nape. "Did you say braw?" he asked, his voice deep and gravelly.

"Mm-hmm." Those rosy lips turned up, bow shaped, pert, trembling a little, and looking exceedingly delicious.

Robert gulped while he lowered his chin. "And you kissed MacGowan two years ago?"

"I did."

"Anyone else since?"

"Nay."

"Then it has been far too long since a lass as bonny as you has been showered with such affection."

As their lips met, he ached to lift her onto his lap and explore her mouth with toe-curling determination. But this was no alehouse wench. This was a jewel as precious as a diamond. She needed a man who was gentle, understanding, and most of all patient. As Janet sighed against his lips, her breath shuddered. Unable to resist, he slipped his tongue into her mouth like a man who had been craving her taste for days. The lass stiffened, and Robert forced himself to ease away. Carefully he brushed her tongue with his, caressing it, showing her how sweet a kiss could actually be.

He hadn't asked, but by her response, he figured Mac-Gowan had been about as experienced as a mackerel. Cradling her in his arms, he plied her with light, teasing kisses, just enough to still her resistance. And when she slackened in his arms, he returned for more, holding her firmly yet reverently, and deepened his kiss, showing her the potency of the fire coursing through his blood.

* * *

Malcolm MacGowan turned out to have been a complete nincompoop when it came to kissing. There was no question of the validity of Janet's conviction. She turned to molten honey as Robert's kiss spilled through her. At first she startled at his forwardness, but as soon as he slowed the pace and showed her how to kiss open mouthed, he aroused an intense yearning in her core—and that was a secret she would carry to her grave.

Under no circumstances should she ever have such a carnal reaction, especially when kissing the forbidden lips of the chieftain of Clan Grant. But he was rugged and braw. Powerful and tender at the same time. His taste shocked her with an unexpected wildness. In a rush, recklessness and hunger thrummed thorough her blood. Without realizing what she was doing, she slid her hand up the wall of his chest and teased a nipple through his shirt.

The friction brought a moan rumbling from the recesses of his throat and renewed fervor to the swirling of his tongue. Janet threw her head back when he pushed her hair aside, bared her neck, and scattered delicious kisses along her throat.

Sighing, she arched her back and gave in to his wiles.

Until she leaned on her injured arm. Hot, searing pain made her jolt. "Owww!" She cradled the limb against her waist. "Goodness, goodness, goodness!"

"Jesus, I am a dolt. What can I do to help?"

She ran a hand across her lips, a combination of pain and guilt making her rue the kisses they'd just shared. "Perhaps we shouldn't imbibe whisky and play hazard in the future. 'Tis dangerous for what remains of my virtue."

With a shake of his head, the corners of his mouth drew downward. "Nay, 'tis my fault. I never should have allowed myself to lower my guard." He stood and began stirring the pottage with his back to her.

Janet stared at him. His guard? What did he mean? Had the kiss meant nothing to him? How on earth could he impart such passion without feeling?

Chapter Fourteen

*T*he morn of their third day in the bothy, Robert was on the verge of declaring himself mad and fit for an asylum. Either that, or he might prove his insanity by pledging undying love for Miss Janet. Already he'd conjured dozens of ways to convince her to accept him and claim her as his wife in the way of old Highland tradition, then promptly bed her...which he certainly, absolutely, and unequivocally must *not* do. This was the eighteenth century, and things had grown quite a bit more civilized since the medieval days when Highland chieftains ruled their lands with absolute power.

Robert liked to think he had absolute power. However, declaring Miss Janet his wife and bedding her, no matter how much he wanted to, would not be appropriate behavior for a man of his station. Not to mention that the lass must be amenable. And by the way she'd kept to herself since he'd kissed her, he assumed she was not.

Though she had melted in his arms and hadn't pushed

him away. The lass might be battling an attraction for
him, but she wasn't daft. She knew as well as he did that
there could be no possible future for them, given the generations of feuding between their families.

Grumbling under his breath, Robert saddled his horse,
but before he mounted, Janet's wounded mare nuzzled his
stallion's rump. He eyed the beast. "You stay here."

She snorted and tossed her head.

"I mean it. Else I'll have to hobble your front legs,
which could be uncomfortable given your bad hock."

The animal seemed to understand because she sauntered away and stood beneath an old tree.

Robert gathered the reins and climbed into his saddle.
"We'll return anon, ye wee filly."

The frigid air served its purpose to cool the heat in his
loins as he rode through the snow. At least the clouds had
cleared and, after having a few days to settle, the drifts
weren't quite as deep and had an icy crust. He took the
horse along the brae a good two miles until they reached
a vantage point. From there the hills opened and revealed
a view all the way down to the shimmering deep blues
of Loch Ossian on the eastern edge of Rannoch Moor.
With the snow, traveling down the mountains would be
challenging but not impossible with a lame horse in tow.
But if they could reach the loch, he could slip through the
glens to Loch Ness, and then it would only be a few miles
to the River Moriston and home.

Robert checked his pocket watch.

Quarter past seven.

Even if they left straightaway, it was unlikely they'd
reach home before the witching hour.

He glanced back in the direction of the bothy. If he
spent one more night trapped in that tiny space with

lovely Janet Cameron, his sanity would be lost forever. The mare had survived thus far. As long as he took it slow, she'd make the descent.

Chances are the snow has melted far more down below.

His decision made, he turned his horse and hastened back to the tiny hovel.

* * *

"You brought me to *Glenmoriston*?" Janet shouted, standing in the entry of Moriston Hall and thrusting her hands into her hips. They'd ridden hard all day and well into the night, barely stopping to rest while her arm had ached worse and worse not to mention her poor horse could barely keep pace. The only thing that had kept her spirits up was the thought of home—of sleeping in her own bed and stabling the mare where she'd be pampered and well cared for. But Moriston Hall? How dare he?

Mr. Grant spread his hands wide, looking completely aghast, as if he were an innocent bystander. "I said I was taking you home."

She shook her fists. "Aye, but you made me think you were taking me to *my* home, to Achnacarry." In truth, for the past ten miles or so, she hadn't had a clue where they were headed, but it was dark, and she'd trusted the man—the fiend.

"I did no such thing."

"You said, and I quote, ''Tis time to take you home, lass.'" She jabbed him in the chest with her pointer finger. "You deceived me."

He guffawed, throwing out his arms. "If that is what you think, then you are gravely mistaken. There is no chance on earth I would venture within twenty miles of Fort William without knowing what that snake Winfred Cummins is up to."

"Why did you not say so in the first place, blast you? My father's army is large enough to stand up to an attack by the lieutenant, or the *colonel* for that matter."

"So say you. However, I am laird, and thus the keeper of the peace in these parts, and I will decide when 'tis safe for you to rejoin your kin." He spun on his heel, marched to a narrow door, and opened it. "Mrs. Tweedie!" he bellowed like an overbearing bull.

"What is the scuffle about?" asked a soft, feminine voice from the stairs. Janet stepped around Robert to discover a tall lass standing on the landing. Dressed in a tartan arisaid and a green kirtle, her hair the color of cinnamon, she wasn't looking at them, but rather her face was tilted upward as if she was listening.

"Emma." Robert moved to the staircase and extended his hand while the woman descended. She didn't take his hand and seemed unperturbed when he grasped her elbow. "We have a visitor."

The lass's smile was so warm and welcoming, Janet's ire cooled a bit. "I love visitors."

Robert cleared his throat. "Miss Janet Cameron of Lochiel, this is my sister, Emma."

"Pleased to meet you." Janet curtsied and bowed her head. When she looked up, Emma was still smiling, but her eyes were closed. On closer inspection, her eyes were recessed a bit, with dark circles around them.

"Pleased to meet you as well," Emma replied, giving a hesitant curtsy. "We've been unbearably worried since Lewis and the men returned without you."

"We were caught in a snowstorm." Robert took his sister's hand and kissed it. "My dearest, would you be so kind as to show Miss Cameron to the rose bedchamber? She has broken her arm and is in sore need of rest."

The girl stared at the floor. Such odd behavior.

"I'd be delighted, but a broken arm? Goodness, miss, you must be in terrible pain."

Janet swept an errant strand of hair away from her face. "It has been none too comfortable."

Robert turned to Janet. "I shall summon a healer at once."

She arched her eyebrows. "And my father as well? I have no doubt he is worried half to death."

"Ah. I will dispatch a missive to him straightaway."

Janet gave him a firm shake of her finger. "And pray he doesn't come to put this extravagant house to fire and sword."

"He wouldn't dare," said Emma, her hands searching through the air until Robert took Janet's hand and placed it in his sister's fingertips. The lass smiled. "Come. I cannot wait to hear about your adventure. It must be quite a story."

"*A tragedy* is more apt." *Robert should have warned me about his sister's blindness.*

As Emma pulled her toward the stairs, Janet eyed Robert over her shoulder, but he'd shifted his attention to a woman who'd entered through the narrow door. "There you are, Mrs. Tweedie."

"Aye, sir." The woman, who was wearing a coif and apron, wrung her hands. "Thank the stars you're home at last."

"'Tis good to be here. Please see to it a lad sets a fire in the rose bedchamber, and summon the healer."

"At this hour?" Mrs. Tweedie shifted her gaze up the staircase. "Whatever is the matter?"

"Do it, I say, and tell her to bring proper arm splints."

"Straightaway, sir."

Emma gave Janet's hand a tug. "This way."

"You ken the way?" Janet asked.

"Of course I do, silly. This is my home."

"But you're *blind*, are you not?" she blurted, at a loss for how to state Emma's condition more delicately.

"Och, you are observant," the lass said with a tad of sarcasm.

"Apologies. I shouldn't have been so forward."

"I fail to see why not. 'Tisn't as if my blindness is a secret." After exiting onto the second floor, Emma ran her fingers along the wall, passed one door, stopped at the second, and turned the knob. "I love this bedchamber because it smells of rosewood."

Janet followed the lass inside. It did have a pleasant scent, but it was also decorated in a lovely shade of pink. It wasn't a large room, but large enough to sport a four-poster bed with pink bed-curtains with a floral design, an overstuffed chair, and a bedside table holding an ewer and bowl. The window was recessed in an embrasure with cushions on opposing seats—they were upholstered in pink, of course.

A lad came in carrying a pail of peat. "Come to set the fire, miss."

"Thank you."

Emma led Janet to the bed and sat—quite familiar of her. "No one ever tells me a thing, and all Lewis would say is Robert rescued you from the clutches of Fort William's dragoons and you fell down a ravine whilst escaping." She clutched her hands over her heart. "And the men all presumed you were dead!"

Tired and in pain, Janet practically collapsed beside the lass. "I daresay 'tis a miracle I am not."

"How did you fall?"

"My horse slipped on ice and the ground gave way."

"Good gracious, 'tis a miracle you escaped with merely a broken arm."

"I suppose it is. As I was falling, I thought I might perish before my lifeless body hit the bottom of the ravine, but my horse saved me. I'm convinced of it."

Emma's fingers slid over, brushing Janet's skirts. "You poor dear. Falling is one of my greatest fears."

"I can only imagine." Janet bit her tongue, wishing there were something witty she could say, but at a complete loss for words. She sat very still while the lass seemed curious about the texture of the taffeta.

"What I don't understand is how Robert came to rescue you from the redcoats in the first place. I thought Grants and Camerons were mortal enemies."

"That we are, and once my father discovers Laird Grant has brought me to Glenmoriston, the feud may grow worse."

Emma drew her fingers away and clasped her hands in her lap. "Then why did he do it?"

"Bring me here?"

"Aye."

Janet sighed. "I have no idea—though he says he thinks I'm safer at Moriston Hall."

"Hmm. If that is what Robert says, then 'tis fact."

"Oh?" *Or does it have more to do with the feud between our clans?*

"Aye. If nothing else, my brother is true to his word."

"Hmm." Well, Janet wasn't convinced, though she kept her opinion to herself. "Is he always so domineering?"

"Always—and protective to a fault."

"I'll say."

At the hearth a fire came to life with pops and crackles. The lad took the pail and slipped away without a word.

Emma clapped her hands. "We should plan an outing whilst you're here."

"'Tis a bit cold."

"Aye, but Robert can hitch up the team, and we'll bring along plenty of blankets. There's nothing more invigorating than a brisk ride along the river."

"That could be diverting," Janet said with a shrug. "Though I'm not certain my arm would like it."

"How thoughtless of me. I'm such a nitwit."

"I don't think you are, not in the least."

Emma sat for a moment and swayed. Janet was about to inquire as to her well-being when the lass's face brightened.

"At least we ought to have a feast in your honor." Emma began clapping again as if she were about to plan a gathering.

Janet wasn't sure she wanted to agree to any merry-making activities at the moment. She was still cross with His Lairdship, and no matter how much he professed that she'd misunderstood, in her mind he'd deceived her. She could see it now. All the Grants come to Moriston Hall to have a peek at the ruined Cameron lass who'd spent three days in a bothy with their chieftain.

"A feast? With clan folk?" Her voice cracked. "I doubt I will be here more than a day or two."

"Och, we do not need a gathering of people for a celebration. Truth be told, I'm not comfortable in the midst of crowds. Leave the planning to me."

Chapter Fifteen

*T*hough it was nearly midnight, the healer arrived in short order. Robert led her to the rose bedchamber and knocked on the door. "May we enter?"

Voices from behind the timbers grew quiet. "Aye," said Emma gleefully.

Amused and a bit relieved that his sister had taken to Janet so quickly, Robert ushered the elderly woman inside. "This is Mary Catherine, the best healer in Ross-shire."

Emma patted Janet's shoulder as if the pair had been friends for ages. "She's the only healer allowed under this roof."

"That's on account of I do not approve of blood-letting." Mary Catherine's serene and careworn face had a way of putting people at ease as well. She set her basket on the bed and bent over Janet's arm, carefully pulling back the sleeve, then opening a gap in the makeshift bandages for a closer examination. "By the looks of this, the break is not new."

"We were trapped in the snowstorm," Robert explained. He tugged his sister to her feet. "Emma, would you please go ask Cook to send up a tray? Neither Miss Janet nor I has eaten a substantial meal in days."

"But—"

He walked her through the door. "Thank you, dearest." No matter how much he loved his sister, the bedchamber was crowded enough, and giving Emma a task would keep her occupied and out of mischief.

"Let me see you move your fingers," said Mary Catherine.

Janet winced, but all five fingers twitched.

"'Tis a good sign, but we'll need to apply a proper splint. This one looks as if it has been through the wars."

"Proper?" Janet's voice shot up. "I think it would be awfully painful to change the dressing at this point."

The healer calmly patted the lass's hand. "It shouldn't cause too much pain as long as we keep your arm steady. Now lie flat, if you please."

The lass cradled her arm against her midriff and pursed her lips, casting a dubious glance at Robert.

But Mary Catherine had too many years of experience to let reluctance dissuade her. "Come, lass, the break will heal better, and your arm will be more comfortable with slats from a linden tree. I have them sanded smooth by the carpenter in Inverness."

Clasping his hands behind his back, Robert stepped nearer. "I think you'll feel much improved once the healer has set you to rights. I ken I will."

"Och, if you must." Janet grimaced as she swung her feet onto the bed. "But if you dare make me endure anything remotely like the pain of setting the bone, I shall never forgive you, Mr. Grant. I shall tell my father to—"

"Understood." He turned to the healer. "Would it be best if I left you alone?"

"Nay." Mary Catherine pulled two fresh slats out of her basket along with a roll of bandages. "I'll need your hands to ensure we do not jostle the arm any more than necessary."

"Do you have a stick for me to bite down upon?" asked Janet, perspiration already beading her forehead as she continued to cradle her arm against her body.

Mary Catherine returned the question with a serene smile, one that would absolve the sins of every tinker for a hundred miles. "That shouldn't be necessary. Now stretch your arm out flat."

Janet did as asked. After putting a small pillow under her palm, Mary Catherine cut the dirty bandages while Robert held a slat beneath the injured arm. Within two ticks of the mantel clock, the healer removed the old splints while he supported Janet's arm with the new slat. Aside from a few gasps, the brave lass remained calm.

But the healer didn't rewrap Janet's arm right away. Mary Catherine took a salve, doused a cloth, then lightly cleansed the injury. "You're healing well. Though you'll need to keep splinted for two more months."

"Two months?" Janet cried. "Why so long?"

"If you want full use of that arm and fingers, you'll do as I say. Earlier, you moved your fingers with a fair bit of pain, did you not?"

"Aye."

"Then 'tis settled."

While Mary Catherine applied the top splint and started wrapping a fresh bandage around the arm, Janet shifted her gaze to Robert. "The healer is as stubborn as you are."

"Me? I am not stubborn."

"Och," said Mary Catherine, tying off the bandage. "I believe that's the first tall tale I've ever heard you utter, Your Lairdship."

Janet grinned—at least she wasn't crying or howling from pain.

"Now, how does that feel?" asked the healer.

Janet raised her arm and slowly lowered it to the bed. "Like I have two boards bound to my arm."

"You'll grow accustomed to it. In the meantime I'll give you a tincture of mallow, valerian, and willow bark. It will help reduce the swelling as well as take the edge off the pain."

"Is it laced with whisky?" asked Janet, waggling her eyebrows—the wee vixen.

A stunned expression crossed the healer's face. "I beg your pardon?"

"Hmm." The Cameron lass smiled, feigning a picture of innocence. "It seems Mr. Grant swears by his whisky."

Mary Catherine turned to Robert, shifting a fist to her hip. "You mean to say you gave this poor lady whisky?"

He gave an exaggerated shrug. "Merely a tot or two, and 'twas the only thing available at the time."

Janet sniggered, clapping a hand over her mouth. "I'm not saying another word."

"Come here, young man, and sit in the chair. 'Tis your turn." Aye, the cut on his face was the first thing the healer noticed when she'd arrived.

"I'd be obliged if you would remove these stitches." He plopped onto the seat.

"Do they itch?" asked Mary Catherine.

"Aye."

"That is a good sign." She hovered over him with a

bottle of salve and a piece of cloth. "But the skin hasn't quite healed enough to remove them yet. Tell me, what happened?"

Robert hissed with the sting from the ointment. "Miss Janet's brother sliced open my face with a dagger."

"Is he still alive?" Stilling her hand, the woman glanced back to the bed.

"When last I saw him," he growled.

"A Cameron attacked you with a blade and has lived to tell about it? Heavens, I never thought I'd live to see the day." She swiped a bit more salve over the wound, and none too gently. "Unless..."

"What?" asked Janet.

Mary Catherine replaced the stopper on the bottle. "Unless a bonny lass altered his priorities." Smug satisfaction curled up the corners of her lips. "Och, are ye smitten, Your Lairdship?"

Groaning, Robert stood and chose to change the subject. "Did you say you had a tincture for Miss Janet?"

"I did. And those stitches can come out in another four or five days." She retrieved a vial from her basket and set it on the bedside table.

"Is there anything else you need, Miss Janet?" Robert asked.

"Nay, aside from a sturdy horse to take me home."

"It would be best if you remained at Glenmoriston. The roads are too hazardous for a coach this time of year, and you risk another fall if you ride horseback. In fact, Robert, you must send a missive to her kin telling them she mustn't ride a horse until the arm is completely healed."

Janet bolted upright, swinging her legs off the bed. "You cannot be serious. I rode down from the slopes of

Ben Nevis this very day and you expect me to remain here for two months?"

"Come, lass. Now that you're safely at Moriston Hall, there's no use tempting fate. What is two months when compared to a lifetime?"

"But my mare needs proper care. I cannot sit idle while she suffers the onset of winter."

"I'll see to it my stable master treats her like a royal filly. I do not want you to worry yourself. She's a strong-willed horse, that one. If anyone can set her to rights, it is my man."

"Excellent." Mary Catherine picked up her basket and swept out the door.

Robert followed, taking the woman by the elbow and hastening her below stairs before she blurted another word in front of Miss Janet. He still couldn't believe the woman's audacity—even if she had been the midwife at his own birth.

Smitten? I have never in my life been smitten.

"Would you like me to return in a few days to remove your stitches?"

He glowered. "I reckon I can do it myself. I'll send for you if need be."

"Very well. And I meant what I said. I've lived a great many years and have seen many things. I was your father's healer most of his life. So you must heed what I say: everyone in these parts kens Sir Ewen Cameron is ruthless. Dispatch a missive straightaway and tell him everything that happened—and make it sound grave—life and death for his daughter. Tell him you are solely responsible for keeping her alive."

"Och, mind yourself. I have matters in hand." Robert didn't care much to be lectured by a mere healer. "Truth be told, I was in the midst of setting quill to parchment before your arrival."

Lewis and Jimmy were waiting in the entry. "Jimmy," said Robert. "Please see Mary Catherine home."

He bowed, paid, and thanked her. Once she was on her way, he took Lewis by the shoulder. "As ye ken, the Camerons insist they have not stolen our cattle."

"And you bloody believe them?"

"Not certain, but I believe their claim that they've endured losses as well. Take what men you need and scour every alehouse between here and Achnacarry. Do not wear anything that ties you to Clan Grant. Say you're in the market for prime beef at a bargain. See what your inquiries turn up."

"All right, but the thieves aren't poaching a few head. I reckon they're organized."

"Aye. That's another reason we blamed the Camerons, is it not?" Robert clapped his henchman on the back. "I want proof one way or another. Someone in Scotland kens what happened to our yearlings. Hell, if you must ride all the way to Crieff, then do so."

"Very well. We'll leave at dawn." Lewis started for the door but stopped and looked over his shoulder. "Ah…what do you plan to do with Miss Cameron?"

"I'll dispatch a missive to her father come morn." Robert's jaw twitched—he'd already started the letter, making it clear his sister was dutifully overseeing Janet's convalescence. Thank the stars he had a sister, or else things would be even more difficult to explain.

"God's bones, Lochiel is likely to declare war."

"Perhaps. But he kens if he rides on Moriston Hall with the bloody Cameron army, I'll repay his actions tenfold." All this talk about his archrivals was making him tense. Robert rubbed the back of his neck. "Mary Catherine says 'tis too perilous to move the lass. Said to wait two months."

"Two bloody months? That's past Hogmanay. And she'll be here over Christmas."

"Christ." With a groan he hit his head with the heel of his hand. "I hadn't thought about the holidays."

Lewis gestured south with his palm. "You rode here from Rannoch Moor, did you not?"

"I did."

"I reckon you should bundle her up and—"

"*Haud yer wheesht.*" Robert sliced his hand through the air and cut him off. "I will decide when 'tis time to take the lass home. You have a task at hand and you'd best set your mind to it."

Chapter Sixteen

*J*anet stood in the center of the rose bedchamber while Mrs. Tweedie worked on the hem of one of Emma's kirtles. "It will only take a moment to tack this up. At least it will set you to rights until the seamstress returns."

Janet swiped a hand across her forehead. "Och, I do not ken why everyone is making such a fuss."

"I don't think it is a fuss," said Emma from her perch on the chair. "You need a change of clothes and loose sleeves for your arm."

Since the healer had replaced the splint, Janet felt more comfortable, though she couldn't discount the benefits of the tincture and the feather mattress. She'd slept better last eve than she had since her fall. This morn Robert had started the ado by summoning the dressmaker after the morning meal. The woman had taken measurements and left, saying she would return with new clothes a sennight hence. Next Emma had volunteered one of her kirtles for the interim. The problem was that Robert's sister was a good six inches taller than Janet.

"I thank you." Janet glanced at the heap of blue taffeta discarded in the corner. "I'm afraid my gown is ruined." It had suffered tears and snags during her tumble from the cliff, not to mention the dirt and grime from spending three days in the bothy. Her shift's condition was equally deplorable. Fortunately, Emma had found a spare that had been her mother's. It smelled of camphor, but Janet wasn't about to complain, because the length was perfect. And it felt wonderful to have fresh linen against her skin.

Emma stood and held out her hand, smiling expectantly. Guessing the lass wanted her to respond, Janet grasped the lass's fingertips. "Is all well?"

"Aye." Emma slowly moved her free hand to the sling and touched it lightly. "Does your injury pain you overmuch?"

"I'll not say 'tisn't uncomfortable, but I am certain the worst is past."

"You mustn't jostle it," said Mrs. Tweedie with a mouth full of pins.

"True," Janet agreed. "Any wee bump hurts so badly my head spins."

Emma moved her hand to Janet's shoulder. "May I see you?"

"Don't mind her." Mrs. Tweedie scooted around to the back. "She sees with her fingertips."

That's why she acts awfully familiar. Janet nodded—though, realizing the gel wouldn't be able to observe the gesture, she also replied, "Certainly."

Emma placed her cool palms on Janet's cheeks. "I ken our clans have feuded, but I hope you and I can be friends."

"I'd like that very much." Janet closed her eyes while curious fingertips skimmed across her lids.

"'Tis forever lonely at Moriston Hall." The fingers continued upward.

"Do you attend clan gatherings?"

"Aye, clan only, otherwise I must be kept hidden."

Janet knit her brows. "Why?"

"Robert says 'tis for my own good—as did our father afore he passed."

"That hardly seems fair."

"But it is the way of it. People outside of kin are afraid of the blind—they think us demons."

Janet knew how superstition pervaded the Highlands, and Emma was right. Being out in the public eye could be traumatizing. Nonetheless, the poor lass deserved happiness, just as did any living soul.

"Your hair is soft," said Emma, still smiling, even though Janet was trying to blink back tears. How awful it must be to grow up without sight, let alone be kept hidden.

Janet sniffed. "'Tis an unruly bird's-nest most of the time."

Laughter accompanied the fingers as they swooped over Janet's coiffure, breaking every rule about maintaining a respectable distance. "I think you're telling tall tales."

"Oh no," Janet said emphatically. "My lady's maid complains about the knots often enough. Though Robert..." Goodness, her face grew hot while she drew her hand over her mouth.

"Robert?" asked Emma and Mrs. Tweedie in chorus.

Why didn't I think before I blurted his name? Janet certainly couldn't mention a word about the bath—or being naked and soaking wet, for that matter. "W-well, I'm left-handed, and when we were trapped in the bothy, my hair was in a tangle...f-from the fall, and Mr. Grant used my comb to work through the knots. Believe it or not, he was a fair bit gentler than Lena, my maid."

"I believe it. Robert has a great capacity for tenderness—at least with people he deems worthy." Seeing with her hands, Emma made her way back to the chair and sat. "Hmm. I reckon my brother is fond of you."

"Heaven's stars." Janet gripped her midriff to quell the sudden fluttering. "I think His Lairdship acted out of chivalry and will be much relieved when I am no longer a thorn in his side."

"Hogwash," blurted Mrs. Tweedie, being quite free with her opinion. She lumbered to her feet. "I've known that lad since the day he was born, and I'll tell you right now, he's enamored with you."

"Oh no, I—"

"I think so as well." Emma bobbed her head. "He's never brought a lady to Moriston Hall."

"He hasn't. And he shouldn't have brought you here, either, you being Sir Ewen Cameron of Lochiel's daughter." Mrs. Tweedie fanned her face. "Lord kens what will happen now."

"Nothing. Mr. Grant will take me home as soon the roads clear, and that will be that." She highly doubted an entire sennight would pass before Robert ignored Mary Catherine's orders and decided to take her home. Janet moved to the looking glass and pretended to examine her hem while her heart raced. His Lairdship couldn't possibly harbor feelings for her...just as she should not have any feelings for him. She brushed her fingers across her lips. Too clear in her memory was the passionate kiss they'd shared. A forbidden, secret, and irresponsible act neither one of them could afford to repeat.

The problem was that she'd enjoyed it, wanted more, craved more every time she thought of him—his ruggedness, the scar forming on his cheek, the vivid intensity of his gaze. Lord knew she was in uncharted and dangerous waters. Worse, nothing good could come of an affair between them. She could not entertain the idea of a union with a Grant, even though he was a laird in possession of a great many acres of land and a fine manse. Her father would sooner lock her in her bedchamber for the rest of her days than consent to such a marriage—if Robert were so inclined, of course.

I'm daft and thinking like a brainless finch. Robert Grant has no more interest in me than he would in an alehouse tart. He said himself he was no stranger to women's garments. I mustn't forget that he is a rake and no better than his reputation.

"Och, you're full of doom and gloom, Mrs. Tweedie." Emma tapped her chin. "If Robert is smitten, then everything will work out for the best."

The housekeeper busied herself by putting away her shears, silk, and pins. "Aye, if you're living in a fairy tale."

"Whyever can they not?" asked Emma.

"Please, enough of this talk." Janet faced them. "My arm will heal quickly. I shall return home to my kin, and you'll most likely never see me again."

"But I thought you said we'd be friends." Emma folded her arms and frowned.

"We will be. You are welcome to visit me at Achnacarry anytime. I will make sure of it."

"That would be well and good, but I ken you're bonny—and affable. You'll be escorted down the wedding aisle soon," Emma ventured, growing meddlesome while Mrs. Tweedie looked on with an inquisitive stare. "Are you already promised?"

The door swung open.

"Ah—Rob—er—Mr. Grant," Janet said in far too high a pitch.

He stepped in and bowed. "Ladies."

She returned his bow with a hasty curtsy. "As you see, Mrs. Tweedie has kindly hemmed one of Emma's kirtles for me."

"It looks fine." His eyes flickered no farther than her bodice while he moved nearer. "The courier is here to take my missive to your father. Before he sets out, I thought you might like to write to him as well."

Janet glanced to her sling. "I would most definitely, but I'm afraid I am unable to hold a quill."

"Thought of that—if you dictate, I'll write on your behalf."

"See, Mrs. Tweedie," said Emma. "Everything will be set to rights. I feel it in my bones."

Robert's smile fell. "What's this? Are the pair of you conspiring?"

"Never." For a sightless lass, Emma had quite an expressive face. She was scheming all right. Though Mrs. Tweedie looked far less amused.

His Lairdship beckoned Janet with his fingers. "Come. I have parchment and quill waiting in the library." Offering his elbow, the Highlander escorted Janet away. Thank heavens. Things had grown far too intrusive in the rose bedchamber. If Robert hadn't come when he did, Mrs. Tweedie might have started mustering the Grant defenses, and Emma seemed apt to send for the local minster to administer hasty wedding vows.

"I hope my sister hasn't been too overbearing," he said.

"Not at all. She's charming."

"And a bit impractical. Woefully, I have had no choice but to keep her sheltered from society because of her...*blindness*." He whispered the word as if it pained him to think of his sister as imperfect—a demon, as many would believe. "She doesn't understand many things."

"Oh no, I venture to guess you underestimate Emma. She's perceptive as well as bonny."

"Perhaps you're right." He opened the library door and ushered her inside. The room was lined with shelves and great leather-bound volumes. It smelled of old parchment and the candle wax encrusting the chandelier above. On the floor, a woolen Persian rug with filigrees of red, ivory, and black muffled their footsteps.

He moved to a writing table, but Janet chose not to follow. "Have you considered when you will start searching for a husband for her?" She could do a bit of scheming of her own.

Robert's eyebrows drew together, darkening the rugged angles of his face. "Heavens no. The lass is only seventeen."

Janet tiptoed nearer. "But she will be ready to wed afore you know it, and her suitor will need to be a patient and affectionate man."

He eyed her. "Since when did you grow into such an expert? Besides, if my math is correct, you are five years her senior. It surprises me that a woman as bonny as you hasn't suitors lined up for miles."

Janet tensed, unable to form words for a moment, while her own circumstances filled her with foreboding. Truly, since she'd fallen, she had put her lack of prospects out of her mind. Now, not only did Emma remind her of the fact that she was unpromised, with no suitors, Robert saw fit to wave it in front of her face. Worse, once Janet returned home, there was every chance her stepmother would have at least one gentleman waiting to take her away to wedded misery. Shaking her head, she gulped, steeled her nerves, and searched for the right words. "But we are not discussing my prospects. We are discussing Emma's. A-and her situation is unusual— though not untenable."

"You may be right, but I'm not about to set out to find a suitor today."

"Of course not." Janet stepped beside the desk. "Has she always been sightless?"

"She has. Born prematurely. Truth be told, it is a miracle she survived, though our mother did not."

"So sad."

"Emma copes quite well, if you ask me. And she's no trouble, mind you." He picked up a chair and moved it next to the one already behind the writing table. "Will you sit?"

Janet slid into the chair while studying Robert in a new light. How many people outside his clan even knew he had a sister, let alone a disadvantaged one? It didn't seem as though he tried to hide the fact. That he loved her was not in question. Emma was happy and healthy and thriving.

Perhaps I shouldn't meddle.

Robert dipped the quill in the inkwell. "How would you like to begin?"

" 'Dearest Father.' "

He wrote the salutation in a bold hand while Janet looked on, tapping the corner of her lip. "What have you written to him already?"

"That you were abducted by Winfred Cummins and his dragoons and I intervened to prevent you from incarceration in Fort William. We fled up the slopes of Ben Nevis, your horse foundered whilst crossing Finnach Ridge in the midst of a blizzard. Then I went on to say that once I dug you out, we had no choice but to seek shelter in a bothy where I splinted your arm, and you are now under the care of my sister and the local healer."

"You explained everything, I see." Janet drummed her fingers, thankful it was clear he had completely forgotten about the bone-melting, divine kiss that never should have been. The mention of the bothy was dreadful enough. "Perhaps I should make it clear that you are writing on my behalf."

He nodded. "Just say it as you would in a letter. That would be best."

"Very well." She drew in a deep breath. " 'Due to the fact my broken arm prevents me from taking up the quill, Mr. Grant is graciously writing my dictation verbatim. I am happy to report that Mary Catherine, the healer, believes my arm was set nicely, and she expects me to fully recover as long as I remain in a splint and do not injure it again. Because of the likelihood of a fall, given our inclement weather, she recommends I remain in Glenmoriston until the roads are clear and my arm is healed." Again Janet drummed her fingers and watched until his eagle feather stilled.

Robert glanced up.

"New paragraph." She flicked her hand at the parchment. " 'I am quite concerned about Kennan. Lieutenant Cummins and his dragoons beat him mercilessly and I would be greatly reassured to receive news of him. As for me, I assure you that Mr. Grant and his sister have treated me like kin, and I want for nothing. I do, however, miss home and look forward to the day when I will again see my beloved Achnacarry . . . I remain your faithful and loving daughter, Janet.' "

He dipped the quill into the ink and continued writing. "Would you like to try to sign with your right hand?"

"My left, please."

"Are you certain?"

"I'd like to try."

"Very well." Once he'd finished, he slid the parchment over, then inked, blotted, and gave her the quill.

Raising her arm hurt far too much, so she stood and supported her left wrist with her right hand and managed to sign while gnashing her teeth. It took thrice as long to scrawl her name as it normally did.

After she finished, Robert sanded the letter and held it up as he stood. "With a signature as steady as this, you'll be writing entire missives in no time."

"I hope so." Janet leaned forward and replaced the quill in the holder, albeit with her right hand. Content with herself, she stepped back, her heel catching on her hem. "Ack!" she squealed, flinging her only good arm out, reaching for anything to break her fall. But topple she did. Time slowed as she closed her eyes and clutched her sling tight to her body, praying not to suffer another break.

Just as she was certain her backside was about to collide with the Persian rug, Robert scooped an arm behind her back. His face hovered above hers while he drew her upright with his muscular arm as if she were no heavier than a bairn. As her feet touched the floor, that same arm held her securely while he moved a hand to her shoulder, gently steadying her.

Flustered, Janet craned her neck and stared at his face. Eyes like ice pierced her heart. They were shadowy, yet crystalline and focused. Emotion flashed through those eyes: concern, urgency, a touch of humor, and something else—something more powerful. Before Janet could examine him more closely, his gaze flickered to her lips.

"Ah...my hem—" Only two words slipped out before he crushed his mouth to hers, growling soft and low in his throat. A shock of searing heat surged through her as she plunged her fingers into his hair, pulling the thick locks from the ribbon.

The world spun with bone-melting anticipation while he lifted her onto the table. He said not a word, those sharp eyes entrancing her as he carefully drew her sling and arm away from her midriff and rested it on his hip. She grew breathless as he stepped between her knees. Lord in heaven, she'd never experienced such passion in her life. His arms slid around her. His lips slowly lowered. "I need another kiss, lass."

With a thrilling rush of desire, she parted her lips and savored his taste while he tempted her with hot, deep glides of his tongue. His hips rubbed back and forth between her legs—stoking a forbidden desire—passion more potent than anything she had ever experienced. The world around them swam into oblivion, and she held on, never wanting his kisses to stop. Craving more, needing more, moving in tandem with the daring and primitive tempo Robert commanded with the rocking of his hips.

Chapter Seventeen

Somewhere in the back of Robert's mind a tickle annoyed him—told him to stop—but he paid it no mind. Ever since he'd kissed Janet in the bothy, he'd hungered to have her wrapped in his embrace again, and now that she was there, he was unable to step away. Bless the stars, the lass took to kissing like a goddess. Everything about her was soft. Soft hair, soft skin, soft hips, soft...mmm...soft breasts.

He swirled his tongue deeper, imagining entering her. God save him, with a tug of her skirts he'd slip between those creamy thighs he'd admired in the bothy. Moving his lips to the mounds of her breasts peeking above her neckline, he grasped her kirtle and inched it higher.

"Robert?" Emma's call came from the doorway.

Moving with lightning speed, he released his hold on Miss Janet. After taking a deep breath, he spun around, clasping his hands behind his back, his eyes wide. "Ah...Emma." Dear Lord, he sounded as guilty as sin.

She moved inside, turning her ear as she oft did. "Is all well? I thought I heard a moan of pain. Is Miss Janet still here?"

"I'm here and quite well," the lass responded, also sounding a bit flustered—Good God, her appearance alone broadcast what they'd been up to. Janet's hair had come undone on one side and hung draped over her shoulder, making a glaring announcement that she'd just been ravished...which she might have been had Emma not interrupted. For the first time in Robert's life, his sister's blindness proved a blessing.

"Thank heavens," Emma said, smiling and clapping her hands. "I just had the most wonderful idea."

Janet's gaze flickered with guilt before she quickly averted her eyes and wiped a hand across her swollen lips. Was she wiping away the sensation of their kiss? *I hope not.* "What is it?" he asked, trying to sound unperturbed.

"It will be the Sabbath three days hence, and after services I thought we might take the pony cart along the river. Miss Janet hasn't been to Moriston Falls, and Jimmy says the snow on the path has melted—if the outing will not be too taxing for Miss Janet."

Robert glanced at the Cameron lass, wishing he could have a word with her without his sister's prying ears. "Ah—"

Janet recovered her wits and smiled graciously. "'Tis a fine idea, and shouldn't pain my arm overmuch. Would your cook be able to pack a basket for our midday meal?"

"Indeed, I'll speak to him straightaway." He retrieved the missives from the writing table. "I left the courier in the kitchen. May as well take these to him whilst I'm at it." He bowed to Janet, watching her expression, but she remained a picture of good form and returned his gesture with a polite curtsy.

* * *

While he strode out of the library, Janet watched the hem of Robert's kilt slap the backs of his knees, his well-formed calves flexing beneath his woolen hose. Good heavens, that man had turned her wanton. Her fingers still trembled. His Lairdship had rendered her completely senseless. Drawing her hands to her lips, she recalled the thrill of Robert's kisses. Then she clutched her palms to her stomach—how she'd come undone when he'd urged open her knees and brushed himself against her most private place.

I shall be accursed for the rest of my days.

"Truly, are you well, Miss Janet?" asked Emma, as if she could sense her unease.

Snapping from her reverie, she faced the lass. "Quite well, thank you. 'Tis very thoughtful of you to suggest an outing to the falls. I think it is exactly what I need to refresh my sensibilities."

"Och, your arm must be bothering you terribly. I thought a diversion would be just the thing to help."

To be honest, since Robert brought Janet into the library, she'd experienced many sensations, though physical pain was not one of them. "I'm certain with this new splint I will heal faster by the day." She hastened over to the shelves and pulled out a couple of books, jostling them in her hand. "Shall I read to you? I love stories—they're so entertaining."

"I'd like that. Robert rarely has time to read anymore. And he's forever away." Emma touched her way to the door. "Let us retire to the parlor. There's nothing more comfortable than the overstuffed couch—and there's even a French-made ottoman to prop our feet upon."

Janet let out a long breath, her nerves finally settling. She certainly didn't want to be in the library when Robert returned. "How do you fill your days, Emma?"

Robert's sister ran her fingers along the wall, though she was very sure of where she was headed. "Every morning I meet with Mrs. Tweedie and Cook and discuss the day's menu and housekeeping duties, as well as approve purchases of supplies for the house."

"Oh my, you are gaining such valuable experience running the entire household."

"I suppose I am."

"But what do you do for enjoyment?"

"I love music."

"Do you sing?"

"I do. And play the harp." Emma opened the parlor door. "Are you musical?"

"I sing a little, though I can't claim any proficiency with an instrument."

"Perhaps we can practice a duet."

"That might be diverting." Janet followed the lass inside, and they both sat in the downy comfort of the couch while a question needled the back of her mind. Biting her lip, she decided to ask, "You said Robert is oft away. Do you ken if he has plans to travel anytime soon?"

Chapter Eighteen

*T*he answer to Janet's question came three days later.

Though first, when Robert met them in the entry hall for Sunday services, his stitches were missing, the pink scar prominent just behind his dimple. Janet couldn't help but stare at it curiously during the sermon. "Why did you not ask me to remove them?"

He gave her a look. "'Twas no bother. Wheesht."

Still, since Janet had been the one to sew him, she felt she should have been asked to remove the sutures. The service continued with nothing further said, and, afterward, Robert dutifully helped the ladies aboard his new, shiny pony cart. Though the bench looked as if two people might ride comfortably, Emma insisted there was ample room for three, and the Grant heirs bookended Janet, squeezing her in the middle.

She cradled her arm against her stomach while the cart rolled over the rocky path, making all three of them jounce to and fro like a boat sailing through heavy swells.

It hurt, but the pain wasn't unbearable. Emma chatted continuously while Robert manned the reins, his thigh firmly wedged against Janet's. If she moved to the left, she shifted into Emma. Afraid a jolt might make her knock the lass off her perch, Janet opted to accept the close quarters and lean in to Robert. Sturdy as a stone wall, he seemed not to notice, driving the team of two garron ponies at a lazy walk—any faster and the little cart might lose its wheels on account of the holes and rocks while they rode beneath a canopy of brown trees, their spindly limbs dormant until spring.

"Do you visit the falls often?" Janet asked.

"Mostly in summer," Emma responded. "But it is so nice to be out and about after enduring such inclement weather."

"'Tis only November." Robert looked to the clouds overhead. "There's plenty of snow and rain yet to come afore springtime."

"Och, 'tis always raining." Janet took advantage of the cart's sway and slipped her hand into the crook of Robert's elbow—for balance, of course. "My da says if Scots waited until the sun shone, they'd have no fun at all."

"Well spoken." Emma beamed. Though she was bundled in her cloak and bonnet, the happiness in her expression was as if she kept a treasure of sunshine in her heart.

Janet smiled in response. "I do believe you have the most positive outlook of any soul I've ever met."

"I agree," said Robert.

"Why should I not? Things are ever so miserable if one broods about, always filled with melancholy."

The roar of the water neared until the trees parted and they crossed a narrow bridge. Robert stopped the team and pointed. "The falls start at those rocks."

"I love the sound," said Emma.

Janet leaned forward. All around them, hills spotted with patches of snow sloped down to the river and its white swells. The banks were lined with trees thick with green moss. "This place must be magical in summer—I'd like to see it then."

Robert slapped the reins. "I hope you can, though I venture you'll be completely healed and reunited with your kin well before."

A hollowness took up residence in Janet's chest. Only a few weeks past, she had considered Robert Grant one of the vilest miscreants who stalked the Highlands. Just because she had an affinity to the man didn't negate the timeworn feud between their clans.

Out of the corner of her eye, she observed him—tawny locks clubbed back, though a wave of hair skimmed his cheek right where his stitches had been. In truth, the scar added to his allure, that and the hint of stubble along his angled jaw. The fullness of his lips, a mouth she had kissed fervently more than once—a mouth she'd like to kiss again. *Forbidden temptation.*

With a sharp inhalation, she forced herself to look straight ahead and change her train of thought. *What am I doing?*

They arrived at a stone bower that might have served for a medieval watchtower had there been anything to guard aside from the rushing falls. "What is this place?"

"An old shelter built by our great-grandfather." Robert secured the reins.

"'Tis a magical place where fairies make mischief." Emma gave her a playful nudge.

The big laird hopped down from the cart and offered

his hand. "I sent Jimmy ahead to light a fire in the brazier. The bower ought to be toasty warm for our luncheon."

Janet placed her fingers in his palm. But when she looked to the ground, she hesitated. Goodness, it seemed a long hop down. Before she uttered a word, Robert's big hands closed around her waist. Strong fingers gripped her securely, but not so tight as to leave a bruise. Without thinking, she placed her hand on his shoulder as he lifted. But he didn't just set her on her feet. Oh no, he drew her against his hard chest, his heartbeat thrumming through the folds of his cloak. His lips parting. Janet watched his eyes turn from ice blue to midnight as he gradually lowered her until her toes touched the earth. Powerless, she remained captive to his spell, expecting and wanting him to dip his chin and kiss her.

"Excuse me," Emma piped from behind. "I'm waiting, mind you."

The magic broke when Robert shifted his gaze. "Forgive me, Sister."

Janet bumbled aside while he helped Emma alight, lifting the lass and setting her on her feet, much as he'd done for Janet. Except it wasn't the same. Robert didn't take his time or gaze upon his sister's face or hold her aloft.

He gestured to the bower. "Go on inside and warm your hands. I'll fetch the basket."

* * *

Robert's mind cleared when Janet took Emma's arm and led her into the bower. Good God, it was all he could do to keep his hands on the reins while the lass sat beside him, the supple curve of her thigh pressing against his. He thought he'd grown impervious to her scent, but she smelled as tempting as whisky laced with lavender. How the hell did she manage to discombobulate him every time she was in his presence? Had he gone completely senseless? Christ, he'd nearly kissed her when he helped her down. Thank God Emma was there, lest he completely lose control and ravish the forbidden Janet Cameron.

He toted the basket inside the old ruin and took it to the bench across the brazier from Janet. Sitting beside her was as dangerous as boarding a sinking ship. *I never should have brought her to Moriston Hall. She was right, dammit. I should have set a course for Achnacarry and taken my chances.*

"What's in the basket?" Janet asked. Smoke lingered in the air, making her appear surreal.

"Ham, pickles, and bread," Emma replied.

Robert pulled away the cloth and looked inside. "And a flagon of watered wine with wooden cups and plates."

"That is practical. Allow me to help serve," Janet said, joining him. She reached for the plates, her fingers sliding over the back of Robert's hand. His breath caught. The softness of her touch made gooseflesh rise across his skin. Aye, he. The great Grant laird tingled at the caress of a wee maid—a woman he had no business lusting after. He reached out to pat her shoulder but stilled his hand in midair.

I would be a cad to encourage her affection.

He busied himself pouring the wine while watching the lass out of the corner of his eye. Even with one hand, she efficiently portioned the plates, first giving one to Emma, then offering him one. "I hope you are hungry. There's enough food here to feed ten men."

Robert couldn't help but meet her gaze. Her

cornflower-blue eyes were kind, and blonde curls framed her face beneath her tartan bonnet.

"My thanks," he said hoarsely, taking the plate and giving her a goblet in return.

Once everyone was served, Janet ventured back to her place across the fire. Though the bower was only ten feet wide, she seemed too far away. A hollowness spread through Robert's chest. He ached to touch her as she nibbled a bit of ham, the heat from the brazier making her face waver. In the future all his dreams would be filled with this vision of grace.

She smiled and looked down, blushing. "You said your great-grandfather built this place. What was its purpose?"

"He built it for his wife...ah..." Robert stopped himself before he blurted the story. God, he was daft.

"They once came here for the magic," Emma broke in. "Great-Grandmamma said the water from the falls makes wives fertile and men..." She laughed and shook her head. Thankfully Emma didn't say "hard," but judging by the O forming on Janet's lips, she understood the idea.

Uncomfortable silence filled the air.

Janet fanned her face. "So," she said in a very high pitch, "That's why 'tis magical."

"Aye," Emma agreed, "and to add testament to it, Great-Grandmamma birthed seven sons and four daughters."

The poor lass's jaw dropped, though she refused to look Robert's way. Instead her cheeks grew scarlet while she turned to stare out the window.

He took a long swig of watered wine, wishing it were something stronger. "Now the bower is just used for clan gatherings. In summer we oft turn a pig on a spit whilst the wee ones wade in the pool down below."

"Hmm." Janet returned her attention to her plate. "That sounds lovely. Our gatherings at Achnacarry are usually on the banks of the River Arkaig."

"Is there a waterfall?" asked Emma, growing oddly still.

"Not like Moriston Falls. The river is wide, though in places it moves swiftly with white water, especially when the floods come."

"A rider's coming," said Emma.

Robert's spine went rigid as he turned his ear, but he heard only the rush of the falls. Still, it wasn't wise to ignore his sister's warning. Emma could hear a whisper two rooms away. "I'll see what it is about." Standing, he picked up his musket and headed to a vantage point where he had a clear view of the bridge.

No sooner had he raised the butt of his rifle to his cheek than Jimmy rode out onto the bridge at a canter, leaning over his horse's withers as if he was on a mission of grave import. Robert lowered his weapon and met the lad at the bend. "What's afoot?"

"Lewis has returned with news. Word is there's a band of thieves holed up in the caves of Creag Ard."

Robert scratched his chin—Creag Ard was no more than thirty miles away. "Bloody hell, that's practically near enough to spit."

"Aye, and I'll reckon the bastards poached our yearlings, altered their brands, and drove them thorough the glens. Sold them at Crieff market—clear the other side of the mountains from Inverlochy."

"Blast. Why are we only finding these thieves out now?"

"You've found the cattle thieves?" Janet asked, dashing from the bower.

"It looks as if we may have. And there's no time to waste. Quickly, pack the basket. Jimmy, go on ahead and tell the men we ride in an hour. I'll be there shortly, and I'll want a full account of these miscreants from Lewis straightaway."

Chapter Nineteen

*R*obert and his men crawled on their bellies until they peered over the crag and across to the caves of Creag Ard. The sun had disappeared on the western horizon, and what little remained of the daylight was dim at best. But he saw clearly enough.

"That lot is nothing but a mob of ragged tinkers." He raised a spyglass to his eye. "Six of them."

"Their fire's burning like a beacon," said Jimmy. "And I can smell the beef from here."

Robert scanned the lands below and saw not a single beast. "Bloody hell, Lewis, who told you these scoundrels stole my yearlings?"

"Met an old crofter in the alehouse down by Laggan. Said he'd run them off his land with a pack of dogs and a musket."

"They're thieving. I've no doubt." Robert closed his spyglass. "But I do not think they're the maggots who made off with our yearlings. They're too sloppy."

Jimmy stared along the sights of his musket, though his finger wasn't on the trigger. "Mayhap they ken who did."

Pushing back to his knees, Robert started back down the hill. "That's why I aim to pay them a visit."

"Now?" asked Lewis.

"At dawn."

* * *

Janet put a candle on the table beside the settee and sat. Though it was nearly midnight, she couldn't sleep. So many things weighed on her mind. A new shift, a set of stays, and three day gowns had arrived from the seamstress—they were practical woolen kirtles much like Emma's, and Janet had accepted them with a mixture of gratitude and trepidation. On the one hand, she needed clothes. On the other, three gowns signified the expected length of her stay. With Robert away, the servants had acted more reserved and less friendly toward Janet, though Emma maintained her good-natured demeanor. Still, things were not as comfortable without the laird's presence.

Janet prayed for Robert and his men to find the reivers and return safely. She also prayed the thieves confessed. If the mystery of the missing yearlings was resolved, it might help end the feud between Clan Grant and her kin. Eons had passed since the Grants accused the old Cameron laird of debauchery, after which they'd burned her ancestor's house and stolen his cattle. That alone should have been the end of it. But no, both sides carried on like a mob of warring enemies from the Dark Ages, with nary a one having spine enough to attempt to make amends.

What if her father did make amends with Robert? What then? Would the braw Highlander ask permission to court her? Twice now they'd shared kisses sizzling with a passion she'd never dreamed could be so moving. But was she the only one so moved? Janet was inexperienced with these things, and His Lairdship's reputation alone told her he was not.

Whom am I fooling?

Though Robert kissed like a man enraptured, his behavior otherwise was unpredictable. Throughout the pony cart ride their thighs and shoulders had touched. And then when he lifted her down, there'd been a heated moment between them. But that was the end of it. In the bower he sat across the brazier as if he had an oak board up his backside.

Was it Emma?

No, silly. 'Tis the same reason I cannot think of him as anything more than an acquaintance. Goodness, I'm daft.

Robert Grant could no more look fondly on her than she could upon him. That was the unpleasant reality of their predicament, and she'd best hold firm to her conviction, lest a scandal erupt. Yes, the laird had extended the undisputed hand of Highland hospitality, welcoming her as his guest under the watchful eye of Mrs. Tweedie and his sister, but if Da suspected foul play, there'd be no stopping the Camerons from staging an all-out war against the Grants.

A chill snaked up Janet's spine. What if Da misunderstood Robert's good intentions? What if Da declared her ruined? Would he force Robert to marry her? Worse?

Good glory, all this worry made her nervous. Her father wasn't an unreasonable man. Robert had saved her from a grisly death at the bottom of the ravine. He'd acted heroically, and Da had no choice but to own to it. Janet needed something to while away the time while she healed and stop her confounded worrying. If only she could start knitting again, making mittens and scarves would busy her—calm her nerves as well. She wiggled her left fingers to mild pain. Perhaps crocheting might be a better option.

I wonder if Emma knits...Hmm.

Not a bit tired, she reached for one of the books she'd taken from the library and opened it. Shockingly, two dice and a cup fell onto her lap. On closer inspection, she saw that a square had been cut out of the inside pages. She gave the book a shake and two gold guineas dropped out as well. Hmm, The coins made more sense than a pair of dice. She pushed the pages aside to the title page. "Property of John Grant, remove at your peril" was written in a bold hand just below the title, *The Faithful Lovers*. Evidently Robert's father did not appreciate romantic novels.

Does Robert know this book was his da's hiding place?

She chuckled, remembering their game of hazard in the bothy. At the time she'd thought the kiss she'd received from Malcolm MacGowan had been something special. Well, now she knew differently.

Janet ran her fingers over her lips, unable to quell the sensation of Robert's mouth on hers. When she closed her eyes she was there again, in the library, on the writing table, in his arms. If only she could be there now. If only he were a man with whom she could fall in love.

But he is not.

Why had he done this to her? In all her days, she would never believe any other man could kiss her so thoroughly, so possessively. No other man would make her feel so unbridled, so daring.

What if Da arranged her marriage with a man whose kisses were no more impassioned than Malcolm Mac-Gowan's? What if her heart didn't thunder every time their gazes met? What if she felt nothing?

Am I doomed to a marriage of mediocrity?

Her head swimming with more questions than answers, Janet replaced the items in the treasure book and blew out the candle.

Perhaps I'll not marry at all.

* * *

Five Grant clansmen stood behind Robert with their muskets at the ready while he crouched and angled his dirk against the neck of the guard sleeping at the cave entrance. "If I were a sheep-swiving tinker, I'd not slumber so soundly."

The man's eyes flew open as he startled. "Friggin' hell!" He reached for his dirk, but Robert pressed his knife against the throbbing vein on the bastard's throat.

"If you want to live, you'd best not move. One twitch and you'll bleed out faster than ye can draw your blade." Robert raised his voice and projected it toward the cave. "Up, up, the lot of you. We have you outnumbered."

"Throw down or we'll shoot," brayed an ugly voice from inside the blackness.

"With what?" Robert ventured. "You're nothing but a mob of beggared tinkers, and I'll wager you've not got an ounce of dry powder between you. Come out now, and I'll spare ye. Fight, and every last one of you will be roasting in the fires of hell afore the sun peeks over Creag Ard."

"Ye swear you'll nay harm us?" said the voice, not so deep this time.

"I'm Robert Grant of Glenmoriston, and when I give my word, it is sincere." Robert beckoned them. "You're fortunate it is I who found ye and not the queen's dragoons, else you'd be hanging from Fort William's gallows on the morrow."

After a pause, footsteps crunched from inside the cave, and in no time four grimy faces appeared from the dim shadows. Robert recognized one of them—Leith Whyte, their leader for certain.

Jimmy shifted his musket. "There were six of them."

"Call out the last," Robert demanded, holding his dirk steady. "I'll tolerate no skulduggery."

"Come, Mor," Leith hollered over his shoulder. "Let us hear what Laird Grant has to say." The man turned back and gave Robert a sideways leer. "And it had best be good."

"I wouldn't be so cocksure." Releasing his grip on the guard, Robert inclined his head to the firepit where he'd first seen the tinkers. "We'll talk there." Three and twenty more Grant clansmen surrounded them, just to keep things amiable.

"We've committed no crime," Leith said.

"I doubt that." Robert sauntered to the fire, his dirk secured in his fist. "Starting with the steer you ate last eve."

The shift of Leith's eyes proved his guilt.

"I do not give a rat's arse from where you stole the beast, but I am very interested in what happened to my steers—six and sixty of them went missing during the grazing season."

"What makes you think the lot of us thieved over sixty head of cattle? We've no horses for driving. No dogs, either."

"That's why we're talking at the moment and you're

not dead." Robert eyed the man, planning his interrogation. "How long have you been up in these hills?"

"A time now. Though 'tis dangerous to stay in one place overlong."

"A man like you who moves around ought to have heard rumblings about poachers and thieves."

Leith scratched his wiry beard. "Can't say that I have."

Lies. "Where do they sell them?"

"I haven't a clue."

"Hmm. 'Tis a shame." Robert signaled his men with a nod. "You might have walked free if you'd spoken true." With his nod, the Grant men seized the backbiters and bound their wrists. "A fortnight or two in the Glenmoriston gaol ought to help your memories."

Chapter Twenty

*H*e was weary from sleeping in the drizzly mountains with nothing to keep him dry but an oiled tarpaulin. Robert's shoulders sagged when he finally walked in the front door of Moriston Hall. They'd marched the tinkers down the slopes of the Highlands and around the banks of Loch Ness at a snail's pace. Thankfully the blighters were now tucked away in the wee gaol built out the back of the stables by his grandfather. The chieftain of Clan Grant's word was law throughout the district, though it had oft been encroached upon by government dragoons of late.

We'd all be better off if Parliament returned to Edinburgh. Nary a Scotsman was in favor of the queen's abolishment of the Scottish assembly seven years past. Worse, the aristocracy was forced to travel to London whenever the houses were called to session. England upped the taxes on Scottish goods and took her landowners away from their homes far too many months of the year.

As he passed the drawing room, the mantel clock

chimed midnight. He removed his sword belt and climbed the stairs, his every footfall echoing as if the house were empty.

In the corridor he paused for a moment outside Janet's door, his hand itching to turn the knob. And then his jaw dropped when the door opened of its own volition.

"Robert? You've returned." Janet's eyes glistened like sapphires in the shadows.

"I have." His gaze dipped lower. She wore only a linen shift with an arisaid draped about her shoulders and clutched at her long, slender neck—he pictured his lips tasting her there. And the picture was made only more enticing by the waves of golden tresses cascading clear down to her waist. "But you should be abed," he said. "'Tis late."

"I couldn't sleep."

Suddenly Robert didn't feel like sleeping, either. He leaned on the doorjamb. "Is it your arm?"

"Actually, it has been feeling better of late." Her gaze meandered down his chest and back up. "I'm surprised you've returned so soon. Did you find the thieves?"

"We found a mob of a half-dozen tinkers, but I doubt they had the wherewithal to steal six and sixty head of cattle."

"Do they know who the culprits were?"

"Said they didn't, though I tossed them in a cell to help jog their memory."

"They're here?"

"Locked up out back."

"Are they cold? Hungry? Do they need blankets?"

"Och, they're prisoners, lass, not bloody guests."

"Well, I'd like to visit them on the morrow. No one should suffer the cold, no matter how lowly born."

"Or how far he's fallen." Sighing, Robert snatched a lock of her hair and twirled it around his finger. If only he were on a bed with her silken locks spread across his bare chest.

"I want to show you something." She ducked inside and retrieved a book from the table, then handed it to him. "I thought I'd do some reading and found this in the library."

He opened the cover and chuckled. "Look at that. I'd forgotten about Da's hazard dice."

"He added an inscription to the book—remove at your peril."

"Aye, to dissuade any sticky fingers from helping themselves."

"Is that why he hid them?"

"Nay. He kept them hidden from my mother."

"She didn't approve of gambling, I take it."

"Nor should you."

"Then I blame you for your scandalous influence."

He winced. "Apologies."

"No apology needed." Biting her bottom lip, she tapped the book with her finger. "So, what do you say? Shall we partake in a few wicked rolls of the dice afore we retire?"

Robert's knees wobbled but he cleared his throat and squared his shoulders. Bugger the dice; God save him, he wanted to roll with the lass.

He started moving inside her chamber, but she placed her hand on his chest—a very warm, inviting hand. "Might we venture to the library?"

Damnation. "Ah...how about the parlor? The furniture is far more comfortable." Especially the settee, where he could sit alongside the lady, perhaps with their thighs touching. *More if I'm lucky.*

"Very well. Give me a moment to don a proper dress."

His shoulder twitched up. "Och, no one will see you at this hour."

Leaning forward, she peered up and down the corridor. "Are you certain?"

"Positive." He offered his elbow, and to his astonishment she placed her dainty fingers around it without another objection. Together they walked side by side down the stairs.

"What shall we wager this time?" she asked.

He opened the door to the parlor, led her inside, closed it, and set to lighting the candles. "I have an idea."

She sat on the settee, exactly where he wanted her. "Yes?"

"You are quite talented at kissing." He slipped into the seat beside her . . . his thigh snug against hers. "We could wager kisses."

Covering her mouth with her fingers, Janet turned scarlet. "Sir, you are brash."

"We've kissed before. I rather enjoyed it, and if I had to guess, you enjoyed kissing me as well."

"I'll not lie, but we mustn't."

He slid a finger along her forearm. "Whyever not?"

Her breath caught as those brilliant blue eyes met his gaze. He raised her chin with the crook of his finger. "A wee kiss never hurt a soul." His heart thrummed faster while he slowly savored her beauty, lowering his lips until he plied her mouth with a single peck. "See," he growled. "That was not so wicked."

"I beg to differ. I daresay even a simple kiss from you is unquestionably wicked." Her eyelids fluttered closed as she puckered her lips, clearly wanting more.

But she might be even more tempted if they played the

game he planned—one he couldn't lose. Taking the book, he removed the cup, plunked in the dice, and rolled them. "I call six for the main."

She leaned forward and examined the dice. "Twelve."

"Nicks."

"I have a feeling luck is with you this night."

He shifted a hand to her waist. "I do believe you are right."

Her lips parted, making her look more tempting than an apple tart fresh from the oven. Powerless to resist, Robert captured her mouth in a searing kiss, hot enough to melt his very bones. With a wee moan, she slid lithe fingers up his chest. Och aye, she wanted him as much as he wanted her.

Growing more daring, he trailed kisses to her neck. Janet's back arched as she leaned in to him. The arisaid slipped from her shoulders, revealing ample breasts hiding beneath the thin linen shift. A shadow of dark circles enticed him, the buds of her nipples straining against the cloth and begged to be suckled. His lips traveled lower, and he tugged the tiny ribbon at the shift's scooped neckline.

"Good Lord," she said breathlessly. "You mustn't... 'Tis my turn."

Bugger the game. "I'm not yet finished claiming my prize," he growled, spreading open the linen and beholding pure perfection. "My God, you are divine."

"But—" He lapped her nipple with his tongue. "I-I may swoon."

His cock stood at attention, already leaking seed as he kneaded and kissed her breasts. Breasts that should be worshiped and loved morning and night. Breasts that were too perfect for words. Breasts he needed to kiss and suckle over and over again.

"Please, Robert."

Relenting, he gave each breast one last kiss and sat back.

"You push me too far," she said, closing her shift but not tying it. "I call fives," she declared, while Robert's cock throbbed beneath the folds of his kilt. He was surprised she hadn't decided against playing, slapped him across the face, and marched up the stairs.

It took her two rolls to make nicks—her turn. Arching her eyebrows, she faced him, her gaze meandering to his shirt. "Are a man's nipples as sensitive as a woman's?"

Again a pulse of desire thrummed through his member. "Why don't you kiss me there and find out?" He untied his lace and pulled the shirt out from under his waistband and over his head. His nipples hardened at the mere sound of her gasp.

A primitive growl caught in his throat as her silken finger caressed him. Her touch brought his flesh alive, tingling with the slightest contact as she drew him into her spellbinding web. She drew a line from the center of his chest down below his navel and toyed with the tuft of hair leading beneath his kilt. "You have more hair than I imagined."

"And there's even more where that wee line leads."

By the way her eyes grew dark, she was curious, but she snapped her finger away, leaned forward, and kissed his nipple as if she were kissing a bairn on the forehead. "Och, is that all?" he asked. For the love of God, he'd led her to the fountain, the least she could do was drink.

She gave him a sober look, though a wee bit of mischief twinkled in her eye. "I'm just starting out…planning my mode of attack, if you will."

Then, like a woman accustomed to the wiles of the boudoir, she took his nipple in her mouth and teased him with tongue and gently nipping teeth. By the time she came up for air, Robert was leaning back on the settee and panting as if he were the one being seduced, his cock as hard as the steel hilt of his sword. Given Janet's present state of undress, all it would take was a few flicks of his fingers and she'd be naked. He could take her right there in the parlor.

But I cannot.

I must not take her innocence. Doing so will incite a bloody war against Glenmoriston lands, and I will not risk the lives of my clan no matter how much I want her.

Still, he picked up the dice and rolled again. Janet won the next two rounds, and by the time she finished kissing him like a conquering lover, Robert was as hard as marble and on the verge of throwing caution to the wind. When he finally won again, he crawled over her like a fox stalking its prey. "There's one more place that needs to be kissed, lass."

He slid to his knees and wedged his shoulders between her legs.

Janet shoved her hands downward. "Oh no."

"Oh aye." He tugged up the linen, exposing her calves. "'Tis my turn to drive you mad. Deliciously, rapturously, stark raving mad."

* * *

Janet couldn't remember how she'd ended up on the settee with Robert's face between her knees, her bottom half naked and utterly prone to him.

Heaven help her, his tongue turned her wanton as he swirled it along her thighs.

"Och, ye smell like heaven," he growled.

"But—"

"Wheesht."

Janet grabbed the armrest as her back sank into the settee. Robert watched her while his tongue worked magic. With a devilish chuckle, he lapped his tongue right over the most secret part of her body. She gave a wee gasp as her thighs shuddered. "Mercy," she cried, arching her back.

But the rogue was ruthless in his attack. His fingers swirled in tandem with his wicked tongue. Janet gasped again when his finger slid inside her. Her core was wet and slick, and he worked his finger back and forth as he continued his merciless kissing.

Her eyes rolled back, and her hips began rocking in tandem with the escalation of desire—a craving low in her belly demanding more, threatening to send her to the brink of insanity if he dared to stop. His finger worked faster. Stars darted through her vision. Her breath came in short gasps, the mounting tension making her buck.

"No more," she whimpered, afraid his promise to drive her mad had not been in jest. As the words slipped past her lips, the rumble of his chuckle reverberated in her flesh. He swirled his tongue faster, matching the rhythm of his relentless finger. Unable to utter a coherent word, Janet gasped and tossed her head from side to side as he drove her body's need higher and higher, making her crave more and more. "Don't stop! Please!"

Then, all at once, her eyes flew open, and a cry caught her throat as her body shattered. Stars shot through her vision while she tried to catch her breath. Her breasts heaved as if she'd just run a footrace. Finally she gained enough control to gaze down at Robert's face, the predatory look in his eyes unmistakable.

"What happened? Have I gone mad?"

"Nay. You've experienced a sampling of what it is like to lie with a man."

"A sampling?" She glanced down to his loins, knowing full well what lay beneath—wanting more, but knowing such an act would ruin her for the rest of her days.

"Aye, but I reckon we've played enough hazard for one night." Sliding beside Janet, he wrapped her in his embrace and kissed her temple. "I could hold ye here forever."

Chapter Twenty-One

"*A*re you in here?"

Janet jolted awake as the door to the parlor opened and Emma moved inside. "Robert?" she called.

The big Highlander shifted Janet off his chest and stretched. "Aye," he replied, sounding as if he had gravel in his voice.

"Oh, thank heavens you're here. 'Tis time to break our fast, and I cannot find Miss Janet anywhere."

"Ah . . ." Robert's gaze shot to the woman in his arms.

Cringing, she straightened her shift, slid the arisaid over her shoulders, and held a finger to her lips to keep him silent. If he took his sister to the dining hall, she just might elude a scandal.

Emma sniffed. "Oh, there you are, Miss Janet. Did you ken there's a whole band of outlaws in the gaol? Cook is ranting about having a mob of underserving mouths to feed."

Curses. "I did. A-as a matter of fact, I was just discussing the prisoners with Mr. Grant. Emma, do you ken where I can find old blankets—mayhap some castoff cloaks and hats?"

"It seems the lass wants to shower the tinkers with kindness," said His Lairdship.

"I'll wager Mrs. Tweedie can help us there," Emma agreed, nodding.

Robert rolled his eyes. "Afore we go off making the miscreants all cozy, let us retire to the dining hall to break our fast."

Janet glanced down at her state of undress, including her bare toes. "Goodness, I'm afraid I've forgotten my shoes—silly me."

"No shoes?" asked Emma. "Then you'd best sit close to the hearth."

Janet wasn't about to be seen in the dining hall wearing little else but her shift. The servants would be agog with gossip—if they weren't already. "You pair go on. I won't be but a moment."

Robert stood, offered his hand, and pulled Janet dangerously close. "We'll wait in the hall. Haste ye, for I do not care for cold porridge."

Janet gave him a pointed look, wedging her fists between them. "V-very well." she said, twisting away and shaking her finger to tell him to behave. They were no longer alone. Moreover, the servants would be milling about, and if he persisted, a scandal was sure to erupt—assuming it hadn't already.

She met Mrs. Tweedie on the landing as she dashed up the stairs—speaking of servants. Regrettably, the matron had proved the nosiest of the lot. "My heavens, it is awfully drafty to be so scantily clad."

"My thoughts exactly." Not stopping, Janet dashed for

the rose bedchamber and closed the door. She clapped a hand to her chest to steady her breathing. *What on earth was I thinking? And why did Robert let me fall asleep in the parlor? I'll wager every servant in the house kens what we were up to by now. Blast it.*

Janet nearly leaped out of her skin when a knock came at the door. "Do you need help with your laces, miss?"

Why must she be an invalid at a time like this? "I do," Janet sighed, opening the door and stepping aside for the housekeeper to enter.

Mrs. Tweedie passed with a knowing glint in her eye and picked up a pair of stays. "You seem out of sorts this morn."

"I couldn't sleep...," Janet explained, her mind racing as she turned her back, letting the woman tie the laces.

"I take it neither you nor the laird slept overmuch." The nosy shrew was fishing, and Janet wasn't about to fall into her trap.

Janet stood straight while Mrs. Tweedie slipped a kirtle over her head. "Mr. Grant has a great deal on his mind."

"I'll say he does," the woman agreed.

Pursing her lips, Janet refused to say another word.

Mrs. Tweedie stepped around to fasten the front laces of the gown. "Your arm will be healed in no time, and then the laird will take you back to your kin."

"He will."

"In the interim, I would be remiss if I didn't offer you a word of warning."

"Oh?" *Why will you not let it lie?*

"I ken I am but a housekeeper, but I have been a servant in this house most of my life, and I have only the best intentions—for you and for His Lairdship." She drew an enormous breath through her nostrils. "I have seen the way the pair of you look at each other, and nothing good can come of it. Remember that you are a Cameron. I've kent of your da my whole life, and even if Robert lost his mind and fell in love, your father will not approve of such a union. Watch yourself, for you do not want any illegitimate bairns to come nine months hence."

"Mrs. Tweedie, you misspeak. I would never—"

"Do not go off believing you can pull the wool over my eyes. I am far older, and from my viewpoint you need the wisdom of a mother. In her absence it is my duty to speak firmly with you. The walls of this house have ears and eyes, and I kent you slept in the parlor in Robert's arms—with hardly a thread hanging from your bones, mind you."

"I—" Janet coughed out a groan. No, she couldn't deny what she'd done. But she wasn't about to apologize to the housekeeper for it. "Nothing untoward happened."

"Thank the fairies." Mrs. Tweedie patted the bow she'd tied. "And you'd best ensure you don your shoes, else Miss Emma will ken something's amiss."

"I will. And you had best mind your duties." She wasn't about to let the woman think she could completely run roughshod over her.

"I always do." Before Janet could issue any further reprimand, Mrs. Tweedie headed for the door. "And I'll collect those blankets you're looking for."

"Thank you." The door closed while Janet slipped her feet into her shoes. *Blast her meddling. How could I have been so careless? And why did it feel so utterly marvelous?*

Once she arrived in the dining hall, Robert and Emma were deep in conversation, bowls of untouched porridge in front of them. Janet slid into her chair and picked up her spoon. "Forgive me. Mrs. Tweedie wanted a word."

Robert's eyebrows arched. "Did she?"

"Aye, she's gathering blankets for the prisoners." She took a bite. "Emma, do you knit or crochet?"

"Nay, I've never tried it."

"Well, to knit, one needs two hands."

"I have those."

"Then I shall teach you. Together we ought to be able to turn out a half-dozen scarves and hats in no time."

"You're serious?" asked Robert.

"I am—that is, if you want to find out who the real thieves are. What have your prisoners eaten this morn?"

"Cook gave them porridge."

"And hot cider?" Janet asked, her hands still trembling from her altercation above stairs.

"Cider?" Robert looked up, aghast.

"Emma, we shall take them some when we give them the blankets."

"No, you will not," Robert objected. "You will not approach the gaol without a Grant man accompanying you. Those varlets are ruthless tinkers."

"I would have thought no less." Janet reached over and almost patted his arm, as she might do to one of her brothers at home, but if the walls had eyes and ears, she'd best start checking her every move. She snatched her spoon instead. "My, the porridge tastes exceptionally delicious this morn."

Chapter Twenty-Two

As he did every Tuesday when he was in residence, Robert sat in the great hall and listened to supplications from clansmen and women. "Who's next?" he asked his factor, Mr. Wallis, who kept the Grant books of accounts in order.

Wallis ran his pointer finger down his ledger. "Tavis and Shane have a wee dispute."

"When do they not?" Robert flicked his wrist. "Bring them in."

The two crofters sauntered forward with their bonnets in hand.

Robert sat forward in his velvet-upholstered chair. "What's the issue this time, gentlemen?"

Shane gave his neighbor a snort, then spread his hands to his sides. "Tavis's ram keeps jumping the fence. I scarcely have enough hay to feed my own sheep, let alone that rogue beast."

"The ram again, is it?" Robert asked. "What say you, Tavis?"

"The wee beastie only has a hankering for the ewes on the other side. He's doin' more swivin' than eatin'."

Robert scratched his chin and looked to the other. "If that's the case, I'd reckon you're building your herd. Tavis's ram is a fine specimen. Much stockier than that spindly beast you keep."

Tavis grinned.

As expected, Shane's frown grew deeper. "Och, all my ewes are already pregnant."

"Is that so?" Tavis asked, crossing his arms.

"Aye."

"Most are impregnated by my ram, mind you."

"Tell you what." Robert held up his palm to stop their bickering. "Tavis, I charge you with building a higher fence. And Shane, to show your appreciation for the service of your neighbor's ram, you'll grant him your largest lamb come fall."

"My largest, sir?"

Robert looked the man in the eye. "Or allow Tavis to have his pick. Now off with you both. I've better things to do with my time than listen to frivolous squabbles."

Neither man was smiling when they left, but Miss Janet's grin was enough to warm the chill out of winter when she came inside. "I have some news."

He beckoned her closer while shifting his gaze to his factor. "Is there anyone else waiting?"

Wallis checked his ledger. "Not unless someone has arrived whilst we've been in session."

"Go check, please. I need a word with Miss Janet." After Mr. Wallis left, Robert turned his attention to the lass, his fingers itching to grab her hand and pull her onto his lap. Fresh in his mind was the memory of the wee hours of last eve, her warm thighs either side of his face. "What is your news?"

She waggled her shoulders as if very proud of herself. "The tinkers do not ken the name of the person who paid them to poach your cattle, but they ken what he looks like."

Robert's jaw dropped. "They admitted to poaching my cattle?"

"They had a hand in it—and the thefts occurred over several weeks—whenever the shepherd was elsewhere. And the tinkers were paid poorly, if you ask me."

"How much?

"One penny per head."

"That is ridiculous, considering each man could swing from the gallows for reiving cattle." He tapped his lips. "You said a person hired them. What does this vagrant look like?"

Janet's shoulders danced again. "He's plain, brown hair, stands about seventeen hands, and has a dark mark on the side of his right cheek...and he has beady eyes. Do you ken anyone of that description?"

"About half the men in Ross-shire."

"I'll wager the mark will help us. They said it was prominent." She smiled. "And I cannot think of a single one of my father's men thusly described."

That still doesn't mean Lochiel is innocent. "Didn't they ask his name? Where is the man from? Where did he plan to sell *my* beasts? Was he dressed like a tinker or a gentleman?"

"They said the stranger wore Highland dress, but—" She tapped her lips.

"Yes?"

"He didn't sound as if he hailed from these parts and definitely wasn't a Gaelic speaker—they thought he might be a Lowlander."

"The plot thickens. And all from a gift of a few blankets."

"I reckon the hot cider made up their minds for the most part."

Robert could resist no longer. He snatched Janet's hand and pulled her onto his lap. Careful not to jostle her arm, he nuzzled her ear. "What else did you learn about my prisoners?"

Giggling, she leaned away. "They're poor, broken men who are down on their luck, for the most part."

He brushed an errant curl away from her face. "Men who turned to thievery. They cannot be trusted. How do you know any of what they told you is true?"

"The leader says he marched to Edinburgh with the Grant regiment in 1708 when the true king sailed to the Firth of Forth from France." Janet examined Robert's scar, drawing her finger down the length of it.

"He did." He enjoyed having her eyes on him. "Leith is from Inverness, had a taste for drink and an aversion to hard work. It didn't surprise me to see he'd taken up with that mob of tinkers."

Her gaze shifted to his mouth. "Half of them are young lads from the crofts. They have no trade and no work."

Robert moistened his lips. "If offered a day's work for fair wages, I doubt they'd finish the job afore they tired—or pilfered something."

"Mayhap you could give them a try." She dipped her chin.

"And have my silver go missing?" He guided her face closer with the crook of his finger.

"Is silver more important than souls?" she asked, her voice soft and dreamy.

Swallowing, he yearned to kiss her. "Perhaps I can find them a task where temptation will not whet their appetites."

"Now there's a thought." Finally their lips joined. Warm, delicious, stirring. Robert's insides turned molten.

But no sooner had he coaxed her lips to join with his than Mr. Wallis appeared and cleared his throat.

Janet flew off Robert's lap as if she'd been jabbed by a poker. "My heavens, you are brash, sir," she said, as if acting out a part in a Shakespearean play.

Robert gave her a wolfish grin and played along. "Och, there's no harm in a wee kiss."

"So say you." Clutching her splinted arm against her midriff, she shook her finger, though her eyes twinkled with playfulness. "Just remember that Emma expects you to be dressed in your finest tomorrow evening. She has something grand planned."

"Bless my sister, and thank you for humoring her. Things are not easy for the lass."

"No, they are not, though I commend her for her decorum. She sets an example for us all."

* * *

Janet soon found Emma an ideal student when it came to knitting, and Janet tasked her with making scarves while she focused on mittens, holding one needle stationary in her left hand while working the other with her right. It was arduous, but in two days they'd made sufficient progress.

Stopping only to prepare for dinner, Janet checked

her hair in the mirror, recognizing Mrs. Tweedie's robust knock at the door. "I have something for you."

"Enter."

Janet clasped her hands, preparing for another chiding, but the woman smiled, a gown of blue taffeta draped across her arm. "I've cleaned and mended this. It would mean ever so much to Miss Emma if you would wear it."

"My gown?" Janet crossed the floor as Mrs. Tweedie held it up. "Good heavens, it looks new, though I doubt that Emma will mind what I wear one way or the other."

"She may not see, but Emma senses things you and I would never dream of." *Hmm.* There seemed to be many facets to Mrs. Tweedie. And just when Janet was thinking the servants had begun acting aloof, the matron turned about with an unexpected kindness.

"I'm sure that's true. Every day I grow more astonished by her. And if it will make her happy, I will certainly comply." Janet released the bow on her kirtle. "We must hurry."

"Indeed." Mrs. Tweedie set the gown over the chair and helped Janet slip her arm out of the sling. "How is your arm faring?"

"I think it is healing well, though it itches terribly."

"I'm sure you will be happy when you no longer have to wear the splint."

"I most certainly will be. I think Emma is making more progress knitting scarves than I am with mittens."

After donning her third petticoat, Janet stepped into the gown. "So much has happened since the Samhain gathering it makes my head spin to think on it."

"It must be difficult to be away from your kin for so long."

"I do miss home, I suppose." To be honest, Janet hadn't

thought much of Achnacarry in the past weeks. She'd traveled to Inverlochy with Kennan to escape her stepmother and to secretly observe the gentlemen for a possible suitor. Nonetheless, after Mrs. Tweedie had been so outspoken, Janet hadn't been inclined to discuss anything of a personal nature. The fact that the woman had taken it upon herself to clean and repair the gown was a surprise—and the work hadn't been done hastily.

Mrs. Tweedie threaded the bodice laces in the back. "This is such a fine color on you. It enhances your eyes."

"How very nice of you to say." Over her shoulder, Janet looked at the woman pointedly. "I beg your pardon, but yesterday I believed you would prefer to have me return to Achnacarry as soon as practicable. What has changed?"

"I want to see Miss Emma happy." The woman pursed her lips as her gaze shifted away.

Janet tapped her lips with her pointer finger. It didn't take a seer to realize Mrs. Tweedie was either fabricating her response altogether or hiding something. "Mr. Grant asked you to repair the gown, did he not?"

"Aye."

"And he also asked you to help me dress, I imagine."

Though she didn't respond, by the scarlet infusing the woman's cheeks, Janet had guessed right.

Janet inhaled deeply. "Well, I think Mr. Grant is a remarkable man, and when I do return to my kin, my father will certainly hear of it."

"Yes, miss."

"Wouldn't it be nice if the feud between our clans were no more? Heaven's stars, we have enough to worry about with that imposter on the throne and her brother living in exile."

"Yes, miss." Now this was more like the Mrs. Tweedie she'd come to know. The woman hadn't taken it upon herself to mend the gown. And for some reason she'd now decided it best to hold her tongue.

What if Robert tried to resolve the feud between their clans? What then? Would they have a chance at everlasting happiness? Might he ask her to marry him?

Janet's insides swirled with bubbles of joy...until she thought about her father.

Would the great chieftain of Clan Cameron pay heed to a Grant laird and agree to start anew, or would he take up his sword?

Chapter Twenty-Three

*J*anet hastened below stairs but stopped before opening the door to the dining hall. She took a deep breath, patted her hair to ensure all the pins and curls were still in the right places, then proceeded inside to find Robert and Emma dancing.

"One, two, three, four, five, six. That's right," he said with a sweet gentleness. "If you ken the steps, your partner will lead you and prevent you from bumping into the other dancers."

Emma giggled as her brother began a circular promenade. The lass followed well and efficiently executed the steps, though instead of carrying herself rigid as girls were taught to do by being made to balance books on their heads, Emma swayed and flitted gaily as if there were actually music playing. Wearing an ivory damask gown, she made a picture of a bonny Highland lass, though she may have been overshadowed by the magnificence of her brother. He was bold and imposing in his kilt, waistcoat, and short black doublet, and his neckcloth was perfectly tied at his throat. The hem of his kilt swished in time to the dance steps, accentuating his stockings, tied with plaid flashes—or was the accent made more alluring by the flexing calf muscles beneath? Whatever the reason, Janet wouldn't have been able to hide her smile for a hundred guineas.

When the dance ended, she applauded. "You pair are marvelous."

"Miss Janet!" Emma spun toward the sound. "Did you see us? I didn't hear you come in."

"Then you must have been having a great deal of fun, because you have the best hearing of any soul I have ever met."

Robert led his sister forward. "I agree."

Grinning, Emma sashayed. "I wish I could go to a real ball."

"I think your brother ought to take you." Janet looked at Robert pointedly. They'd had this conversation. "Perhaps to a smaller affair at least. I'll have to set my mind to finding the ideal occasion."

"Then I will await your recommendation." Robert took Janet's hand, bowed deeply, and kissed it. "You look especially radiant this eve."

"As do you—most handsome, that is." She took Emma's elbow and led her to the table. "But you, my dear, are bonny enough to steal the heart of any gentlemen within forty miles."

"You jest."

"I never jest about beauty."

"Take heed, Sister. Miss Janet kens what she's on about." His Lairdship strolled along behind them. "As I recall, at the ceilidh in Inverlochy, every man in the hall queued all night just for a chance to dance with her."

Emma clasped her hands. "Och, I dream of such a night."

"Then you must have it." Janet arched her eyebrow at Robert. He alone must see to his sister's prospects.

Robert held a chair for each of the ladies before taking his own. The table was set with fine china depicting pastoral scenes in pastels. There were crystal goblets, polished silver, and two footmen to serve the meal.

"My, this is as lavish as a royal feast," Janet said while a footman poured the wine.

"Have you been to a royal feast?" asked Emma.

"Only one—held by the Duke of Gordon in Glasgow. His Grace hosts a grand ball every year."

Robert raised his goblet to his lips. "Do you go there often?"

"Occasionally—when Da has business to conduct. I always plead with him to bring me along for the shopping." Janet admired the china plate in front of her, which depicted a couple enjoying a meal beneath a sycamore with roses encircling the edge. "Dearest Emma, what wonderful dishes have you planned for the menu this eve?"

"I'm afraid I didn't plan twelve dishes per course like there should be at a real ball."

"That was very smart and prudent of you." Picking up her goblet, Janet swirled her wine. "I daresay the three of us will have difficulty finishing off one dish."

The door from the kitchen opened, and in walked a footman carrying a tureen of soup from which wafted a delicious aroma.

Emma clasped her hands and inhaled deeply. "The first

course is beef broth with leek. The main course is roast goose and cabbage, bread of course, and then we will need to save room for apple tart with honey."

"My favorite." Robert licked his lips.

"And 'tis the last of the apples from the cellar."

Emma had done as lovely a job as the hostess as if she'd been born to it, and everything proceeded like a king's feast.

During the second course, Janet delicately cut a bite of goose. "This is the finest supper I've had in all my days."

"Even the one served by the duke?" Emma asked.

"Absolutely, and as tasty, for certain."

Robert reached for the saltcellar and used a wee spoon to season his food. "It is very good. We must ensure we compliment Cook come morn."

"Aye, we must."

After the footmen had cleared the second course, just as Emma promised, an apple tart baked in individual crockery was set in front of each of them. "Och, I believe I could live on the final course alone," said Emma, spoon in hand.

Janet closed her eyes while a bite of the tart melted on her tongue. "This has been a meal I shall never forget."

"To make the evening perfect, I believe a bit of entertainment is in order." Robert tapped Emma's arm. "Would you play for us?"

"Oh, yes." Janet clapped. "You promised to play your harp for me."

"I did, and Jimmy moved it to the hall just for this eve." Emma pushed back her chair and stood. "This is exactly why I have been practicing all these years."

Robert stood and took his sister's hand. "I'm certain there will be many more performances to come."

While Robert helped Emma situate her harp, the footmen moved two chairs in place. Taking her cue, Janet shifted to one of them. Once Robert joined her, Emma looked up expectantly—though not at them, at the far wall. "Are you ready?"

"I'm always ready to listen to your music," Robert said.

A mesmerizing cascade of notes began the performance. The hall came alive with sound as Emma's fingers expertly plucked the strings.

Janet leaned in to Robert. Covering her mouth, she whispered, "Where did she learn to play? She is a virtuoso."

"The vicar's wife comes once a fortnight. It began as an act of charity, but I'd say the student has become the master in this instance."

"'Tis such a shame not more people are able to hear her play."

"It is."

"You could invite the locals for a recital—you said she is accepted by the clan."

"Perhaps I will. She has played at gatherings, but a recital would be something she could plan for—something that is entirely her own."

The tune ended with a magical scale of notes and the two of them applauded animatedly, Janet making as much noise as she could by holding her injured arm against her ribs and clapping with her right. "That was the most delightful, stunning, flawless Celtic harp I have ever heard."

A furrow formed in Emma's brow. "But you pair were chatting all the while. I heard your whispers."

"We were discussing how practiced you are," said Robert.

"And I think you should plan a recital," Janet said.

Robert gave her a stern look.

But Emma beamed. "Truly?"

"Ah..." Robert waffled. "You should think on it. Select your best." Why wasn't he ready to commit?

Janet believed Emma far too talented to let the issue pass without some sort of commitment. "I would plan something for this winter when everyone is home and the work is minimal. Mayhap after Christmas and Hogmanay have passed. What say you, Robert?"

"I think—"

"Oh please, Brother. My mind is already running rampant with the repertoire."

"In the new year, then." Robert gave a thin-lipped nod. He knew it was time to face the facts that his sister was coming of age and he could no longer cosset her. Surely there was a man out there for her. She was too endearing to keep hidden. "But." Robert held up his finger. "I would like you to play a minuet, for I haven't had the honor of dancing with Miss Janet yet this eve."

"I'll play you a dozen minuets. I'll play all night if you'd like." Smiling, Emma began to play again.

Robert stood, bowed, and offered his hand.

Janet placed her palm in his and allowed him to lead her to the dance floor. "That went rather well," she whispered.

"Aye, though I would have liked to have some time to ponder the idea first."

"What's to ponder? She's magnificent. Such talent should not be hidden."

"But..."

"What?"

"I do not want to see her hurt."

"Something tells me you will ensure she will not be."

"True. I'd challenge anyone who would dare."

"I expect no less. Though..."

"Hmm?"

"Everyone experiences setbacks. 'Tis part of life."

"Believe me, my sister has endured enough setbacks."
Instead of taking Janet's hand for the promenade, Robert
pulled her into his arms and dipped his chin, pressing his
lips to her ear. "But I do not want to talk about recitals
this eve. I want to kiss you *everywhere*."

Forming an O with her lips, Janet pulled back while
he shushed her with his finger. A grin played on his
lips while that same wicked finger turned downward and
traced the exposed swells of her bosom. Gooseflesh rose
over Janet's skin. She shook her head, mouthing, "We
mustn't."

The scoundrel waggled his eyebrows and slipped his
finger directly inside her cleavage before he resumed the
dance. "Come to my chamber this eve," he whispered.

"Why not mine?" she asked.

He inclined his head toward his sister. "Mine is in the
quiet wing of the house not frequented by some."

Janet arched her eyebrow. She hadn't ventured past the
rose bedchamber, though she'd noticed the bend at the
end of the corridor where Robert disappeared at night.
That was the laird's wing and his alone.

* * *

In his chamber, Robert paced in front of the hearth.
What in God's name was he doing? It was no harlot
he'd invited to his private rooms. Miss Janet was the
daughter of Sir Ewen Cameron, a knight and, as chief
of Lochiel, one of the most powerful chieftains in the

Highlands. Again he berated himself for not taking her home rather than bringing her to Moriston Hall. The woman was too tempting. He awoke every morn thinking about Janet. Every time he entered a room he looked to see if she was there. He longed to see her in the blue taffeta gown again, because no woman would ever again look the same in such a color. She was more beautiful than roses and sweeter than water from a mountain spring.

He would do anything for her, yet she could never truly be his.

Groaning, he marched to the sideboard and poured himself a dram of whisky. *I should not have been so brash. Dammit, I need to take her home. Bugger the healer's recommendations and bugger my bloody feud with her father.*

He tossed back the drink and poured another.

A soft tap sounded on the door.

After two steps he opened it.

There she stood, eyes mesmerizing, hair of gold and a broken arm she never should have had to endure. She took a hasty glance over her shoulder. "I-I came to say what we did last night is wrong. I never should have—"

He pulled her inside and smothered her excuse with a kiss. A kiss that told her exactly how mad she had driven him. A kiss that showed her exactly how deep his passion ran—how much she had bewitched him, mind, body, and soul. He kicked the door shut and backed her toward the bed, his hands untying the laces of her gown while she sighed into his mouth.

When the backs of her legs hit the mattress, she toppled to her bum, her lips swollen, her eyes heavy-lidded. "No, Robert. We mustn't."

"You want it as much as I," he said, removing the kilt pin from his shoulder.

"It doesn't matter what I want. We can never be wed, and I will not become a fallen woman, birthing an illegitimate bairn. Things between us have grown precarious enough. Please, you tempt me far too much."

He sat beside her and brushed a curl away from her face. "Och, *mo cridhe*." Never in his life had he used the Gaelic endearment, "my heart," but it flowed over his tongue as surely as if it demanded to be uttered. "I ken 'tis hazardous for you to be here. I have a sister, and if anyone misbehaved toward her, I would challenge him to a duel of swords and give no quarter." He took her hand and kissed it. "You have turned me into a man driven by insatiable want, yet I give you my oath I will not take your innocence."

"Even with that promise, I fear I am already ruined. Merely by staying here I am compromised."

"I will testify that you are not. Every servant in this house will do so as well. And I have already explained to your father that you are under the care of my sister and my housekeeper."

"Yet here I sit in your bedchamber at midnight." She looked him in the eye and whispered, "Wanting you."

Chapter Twenty-Four

*J*anet released a trembling sigh as Robert nuzzled into her neck, praying she wouldn't flee. "Please stay," he whispered back...he pleaded.

"I am powerless to go. Your touch draws me, entices me, stirs my blood. But—"

"Do not think about what may come. Tonight there is only you and me. This night is ours and no one else's."

"And you will not get me with child?"

I have been with a great many women in my day and have not sired a bastard in all that time. "I swear it on my honor."

"I do not want to think of you with anyone but me."

"Nor do I."

Her gaze raked down his body until she reached his groin. All he needed was her eyes on him to make his cock lengthen. "Will you show me?" she asked, her voice breathless.

No words had ever sounded so divine. "Aye," he rasped.

Standing, he led her before the hearth. "Let us proceed slowly." He brushed her lips with a light kiss. "I want to strip you bare, one layer at a time."

She drew in a quick breath. "And you? It is only fair, if you are to see me unclothed, that I am granted the same favor by you."

"'Tis far more enjoyable if we're both nude."

"Again, I must have your word. You will not get me with child."

"I promise I will not."

He started by tugging free the laces of her bodice. "What I like most about undressing you is that with each layer removed, the anticipation of things to come mounts."

"Simply saying that makes gooseflesh rise across my skin."

Robert pushed the bodice from her shoulders and loosed the ribbon on her shift enough to bare her shoulder, made more tantalizing by the flicker of firelight. "This"—he kissed her flesh, warm and delicious—"is perfection."

Sighing, Janet dropped her head back. "You flatter me."

"I worship you." With every layer Robert found a new place on her body upon which to shower his adoration. And finally, as her shift sailed to the floor, he held her hand and stood back while his eyes drank her in. "By God, there are no words to express your magnificence."

A blush sprang to her cheeks, but she didn't try to cover her nudity. Instead she stepped toward him and unfastened his neckerchief. "I do believe we will witness true magnificence when you, sir, are shed of your clothes."

She tried to unclasp his belt, but with only one hand, she fumbled. "Let me help." He slid his hand to his buckle and released it with a flick. The wool whooshed to the floor. He grabbed the hem of his shirt and whisked it over his head. He stood before her, his manhood harder than a poleax and pointing straight at her.

"Oh my." She stepped into him, swirling her hand through the locks on his chest, the gesture making a bead of seed leak from the tip of his cock. "Men's clothing is so much simpler than women's."

"I reckon men are altogether simpler than women. Feed us and love us and we will be happy anywhere."

"Are you happy now?"

"My heart is racing with joy." He drew her against his body, his balls on fire. "And you, lass. How does this make you feel?"

"Like we are the only two people in all of Christendom."

"Then believe it."

He swept her into his arms and carried her to the bed. His lips fused with her lips as he tasted her sweetness; then he slid to her neck and buried his face between the mounds of her breasts. Aye, he wanted to explore every inch of Janet's flesh, and wanted it all in this very moment.

"Mirror me," Robert growled as he rolled beside her.

He slid his fingers down her abdomen and slipped between her thighs, finding her hot, slick, and ready for him. "You are wet—that's how a woman's body prepares to accept a man."

Following his lead, Janet wrapped her hand around his member. "When a man puts this inside her?"

Eyes rolling back, Robert clenched his bum cheeks and forced himself not to come. "Aye. 'Tis what I want to do right now."

She bit her lip. "But cannot."

"Mm."

"Show me how to pleasure you—like you did to me last eve."

"Touching me sends me wild. But if you hold it gently and slide your hand up and down, it is almost like being inside you." Robert's head dropped with his rumbling moan as she milked him.

"What about kissing it?" Her tongue tapped her upper lip, wet, shiny, seductive as sin.

"Kissing is extraordinary—akin to the epitome of intimacy between a man and a woman. But only if you desire to pleasure me with your mouth. Never in this life do I want you to feel you are lowering yourself when you are with me."

Without another word she scooted down and licked him, her eyes shifting to watch his face. "Like this."

"Aye," he croaked, unable to keep his hips from thrusting.

"Can I hurt you?"

"'Tis the most sensitive place on a man. If you grip too hard or use your teeth, I will be in agony."

She giggled, toying with him, licking, kissing, and milking, but it wasn't until she took him fully into her mouth that he arched his back and bellowed a groan.

"Am I hurting you?"

"Don't stop!"

Her sultry laugh rumbled through him as she slid her lips over his tip, wiggling her saucy bottom. Holy everlasting mother, the woman was Jezebel incarnate. Robert bucked and thrust as she pleasured him, picturing Janet on her back with her knees wide and exposed, picturing himself inside her while he plundered deeper and deeper, his desire mounting in a crescendo until he leaped over the edge into ecstasy. All at once his cock erupted in a pulsating fountain of seed.

Janet looked up, smiling as if she'd just witnessed a miracle. "That was astounding."

"You are astounding—and what's better?"

"I cannot imagine."

"'Tis your turn."

Chapter Twenty-Five

*J*anet's eyes flashed wide when the door to Robert's chamber burst open. Her breath stopped and her palms grew sweaty as she inched her head beneath the bedclothes. For the second time, someone had caught her sleeping in Robert's arms. *I am doomed for utter ruination.*

How could she be so daft as to allow herself to fall asleep in his bed? Hadn't things been bad enough when Emma found them in the parlor? And after Mrs. Tweedie's reprimand, the entire serving staff was rife with gossip.

"Robert." It was Lewis. Blast it, his footsteps clomped nearer.

Janet cringed while beside her the laird rolled to his back.

Please don't notice me.

"Sir Ewen Cameron of Lochiel and his army are camped on the southern shore of Loch Ness. I reckon they'll be here by noon."

"Och, Christ. My missive explained things plainly enough. I didn't expect the man to make a show of aggression, especially on the verge of winter." Robert sat up while Janet slunk lower.

Da? Holy help! I'll be imprisoned in my chamber for the rest of my days if he discovers us here.

"I'm surprised we haven't seen him sooner. The weather has been fine the past few days, though it looks as if another storm's brewing."

"Grand. What are their numbers?"

"A retinue of twenty."

"It could be worse. Mayhap he'll be open for discussion. Alert the guard, but tell them not to fire their muskets unless fired upon. I want the Grant men to do everything to ensure a peaceful meeting. And tell Cook we're expecting another twenty or so mouths to feed."

"Feed, sir?"

"You heard me, now off with you."

"Straightaway."

As the bedclothes lifted, Janet peered at the man responsible for her compromising situation. "Is he gone?" she whispered.

"Aye."

She could only shake her head. "I shouldn't be here."

"It seems it is a calamitous habit we're forming of drifting off to sleep in each other's arms." He urged her up. "Though I must admit I've enjoyed it."

Janet had as well. Too much so. She pulled the plaid from the end of the bed and covered herself. "I must haste to the rose bedchamber and dress. Curses. Why did my father not send a messenger ahead? 'Tis only proper."

"Proper if you are paying a call. Which I doubt he's planning."

"Good heavens, he can't be thinking to put Moriston Hall to fire and sword."

"I fear that is exactly what he'll do if he doubts my motives."

Holding the corner of the plaid against her midriff with her left hand, Janet threw the wool about her shoulders and hopped out of bed. "Then I must speak to him afore he tries to break down your door."

Stark naked, Robert began collecting her clothing, which lay scattered across the floor. Gracious, even if Lewis didn't recognize her form under the comforter, he would have known she was there by the stays and blue taffeta strewn about. "Nay. I will be the one talking," he said.

"He will not listen to you." She shoved a foot into her shoe. "Unless he sees that I am in good health, he will behave like a raging bull."

"Then we shall greet him together. However, I shall speak to the man, clan chief to clan chief."

"Very well, but first I must ensure I do not look like a ravished harlot." She marched toward the door. "How am I to make it all the way to the rose bedchamber without being seen?"

Robert set her things on a chair. "Give me a moment to dress, then I'll help you with these."

"Don the blue taffeta?"

"'Tis better than traipsing through the passageway wrapped in my tartan blanket—the very one woven by my ma."

"Ugh." Janet hid her face in the palm of her hand. "And you'd best have a word with Lewis and tell him to hold his tongue."

"You needn't worry there. He's my most trusted man. He'd sooner ride into battle than divulge my confidences."

* * *

Robert stood in the grounds before Moriston Hall while snow accumulated on his shoulders. There was already a good inch on the ground, and by the looks of the sky, there would be several more before this storm came to an end.

Lewis waited beside him, as did twoscore Grant men. Janet had insisted on being present, though she was securely under the portico with Jimmy bearing arms beside her. Robert didn't expect a bloody battle to erupt, especially with Sir Ewen's daughter behind a barrier of Grant men, but he wasn't leaving anything to chance.

When the dark figures of the retinue appeared at the end of the drive, he checked his pocket watch—seven minutes to twelve. Lochiel was arriving exactly when expected, even with the accumulating snow.

As they neared, the great clan chief rode at the head of his men, his gray beard full, his head topped by a red feathered bonnet. He wore a heavy woolen cloak that hung over his horse's back clear down to the man's spurs. Broad shouldered and scowling, Robert's nemesis was fearsome to behold.

Though much older and not as skilled with a blade by half.

Interestingly, Kennan Cameron was not riding beside his father, though Janet's younger brothers John and Alan were.

Once Lochiel led his retinue up to the inner gate, he held up his hand and stopped his men. "I received your missive, Mr. Grant."

"I gathered." Robert spoke loud enough to be heard. "Will you not come in out of the weather, sir?"

"What assurances do I have that your men will not attack mine? I see you outnumber us two to one."

"I give you my word. I offer you and your army Highland hospitality whilst you are on Grant lands. Your men are welcome to stable their horses and take their nooning in the servants' quarters."

Sir Ewen leaned forward in his saddle. "You offer this after accusing me of stealing your cattle? Why is it I cannot trust your word, sir?"

Robert's fists clenched. "My word is always true. You of all people must ken that. And on the count of my accusations, I have centuries of feuds between Clan Grant and Clan Cameron on which I formed my supposition. Your men were seen in the vicinity of Grant summer grazing lands. Circumstances suggested they were guilty."

"Guilty with no proof?" Lochiel shook his riding crop. "And what say you about *my* missing beasts? I reckon your claim against me is a sham to cover up your own thievery."

Robert strode forward while his eyes narrowed. "The Grants have never been cattle reivers—"

"Och, your great-grandfather spent a year in the Montrose tolbooth for raiding."

"And he was pardoned."

The Cameron laird sniffed, raising his haughty chin. "Pardoned by a purse of coin."

"Stop this!" Janet dashed down the steps and straight past Robert. "I do not believe either of you is guilty. Both Camerons and Grants lost livestock, and Mr. Grant has a half-dozen tinkers incarcerated on the premises who might lead us to the true culprits." She thrust her finger at Robert. "Why did you not say so in the first place?"

Tapping his heels, Sir Ewen walked his horse forward and stopped beside his daughter. "Aye? What is this skulduggery? Why keep silent about such information?"

"Because I'm not as convinced of it as the wee lass."

"Robert!" Janet whipped around with her fists on her hips.

"But it is a possibility." Uttering those words nearly killed him, but not as much as the injured look in her eye, which was exactly why he'd wanted to meet with Sir Ewen man-to-man in the first instance. *I will apologize later.* Robert beckoned Lochiel. "Come, sir. I would have a word with you."

"Oh aye? Afore I've inquired as to my daughter's health?" He shifted his attention to Janet. "I see Grant's claim that your arm is broken was no lie."

She nodded. "I wrote you myself and said it was true."

"But how would I deduce if you'd been coerced into doing so?" Sir Ewen dismounted and looked her from head to toe. "You have disgraced the name of Cameron by remaining in this man's house, broken arm or nay."

"I—" Peering at her father with eyes wide and nostrils flared, the lass turned as red as a blood rose. "But he rescued me from Lieutenant Cummins and those vile dragoons. Without Mr. Grant's assistance, I would have been imprisoned or worse."

"Aye, and if you'd spent a few days in Fort William, the colonel would have released you into my care—"

"I do not agree," said Robert. "Cummins might have ravished—"

"Of course you do not agree, you buffoon! You are smitten with my daughter and always have been in your own perverse way. Do not deny it. More than once I saw you gawking at her during your sham of a gathering at Urquhart Castle nearly two years past." Lochiel signaled to his men. "Bring the horse. I trust you can ride with one arm, Daughter. If anyone is an accomplished horsewoman, it is you. And on that point, how the devil did you fall? What did Grant do, push you off the cliff?"

Janet took a bold step forward. "He did not, nor would he ever contemplate such a thing. My mare slipped and broke her leg—she's still lame. I would have died had it not been for Mr. Grant."

"Hmm."

Robert's every muscle clenched. Good God, he'd heard enough of her father's drivel. "This is madness. Sir, if you will cease your baseless accusations, I bid you come inside and fill your belly with a warm meal and a dram of Highland whisky."

"My *baseless* accusations? Everything I have uttered is the unadulterated truth. You, sir, are the brigand who implicates innocents."

"Forgive me." Robert practically swallowed his tongue along with the bile burning his throat. "Please come inside. There is something of import I would like to discuss."

"I doubt there is any more to be said between us. Come, Janet. Alan will help you mount. We mustn't tarry, and God willing, the snow will cease as soon as we ride off Grant lands."

"But, Father, Robert—"

"Do as I say, or you will be responsible for the spilling of your kin's blood this very day. By the word of the Almighty, I thirst to take up my sword for your honor. You ken I will."

Robert's hand slipped to his hilt while Lewis raised his musket to his shoulder, their gazes connecting in an unspoken understanding. Never in his life had he wanted to order his men to attack as much as he did in this moment. But if they battled, Janet would be caught in the crossfire. If he fought for her, Sir Ewen would certainly attack. The lass could be hurt, even killed.

I cannot risk her safety.

He shook his head at Lewis and released his grip. With this one hateful act, Lochiel reached inside Robert's chest and ripped his heart clean away. While he watched the woman he adored mount the horse, every fiber in his body screamed at him to fight for her, to shout that he loved her. Yes, he would even admit that he had yearned for her for years and years, just as Lochiel accused. Janet had caught Robert's eye at every gathering they'd ever attended.

As she took up the reins, her eyes reflected the same searing pain burning his chest. This was not how he wanted to part from her. He never wanted to part from her. He would have asked Lochiel for her hand if Lochiel hadn't accused him of being a lecherous cur.

"Don't go," Robert pleaded through clenched teeth.

"I'll not let her suffer your presence a moment longer." Sir Ewen turned his horse to go. "We ride."

"I can't go without my mare." Janet pointed toward the stables while her father grabbed her bridle and started off.

"We leave her."

"You have my word I'll see to the filly's care!" Robert shouted, shoving his hand into his sporran and sprinting to Janet's side. He kept pace while he slipped the hazard dice into her palm. "I shall never forget you, *mo cridhe*."

She looked to the dice, then back at his face as he continued to run. "Is what my father says true?"

Before he could answer, Lochiel dug in his heels and led his daughter away at a canter. Robert stood in the snow watching her leave until nothing remained but a blanket of white.

"Ye had to have kent it wasn't meant to be," said Lewis. "She's a bloody Cameron."

The rage inside him boiled over. With a roar he balled his fist and slammed it across his henchman's jaw, sending him careening to the dirt. "Don't ever speak ill of her. She is an angel. Better than all of us!"

Lewis rubbed his jaw and sat up. "Och, everyone cared for Miss Janet. 'Tis her kin who are questionable."

"That's right, and I'll have you and every other Grant man own to it."

Chapter Twenty-Six

𝒥anet managed to arrive at Achnacarry without falling.
Her spirits had sunk to the depths of despair while her
arm ached terribly from hours upon hours of being
jounced. They'd spent a miserable night camped in the
snow, and the next day Father only stopped twice to
rest the horses. By the time they rode into the courtyard
the snow had ebbed, but the temperature was bitter. The
moment she dismounted, her father ordered her to bed,
and, despite the late hour, he called for the physician to
examine and resplint her arm. Complaining of a megrim,
she lay abed for two days, though it was nothing short of
melancholy that sapped her spirits.

Midmorning of the third day, Lena, Janet's maid, came
in carrying a tankard. "This is a tea of willow bark and
St. John's wort prepared by your stepmother's own hand.
She vows there is nothing better to cure both megrim and
low spirits."

Janet draped an arm over her eyes. "Must I?"

"Och aye, and that is only half of it. Your father expects you in the library in an hour. He said, ''Tis time our wee Janet returns to her usual self.'" Lena lowered her voice, trying to sound old and manly, and her impression of Sir Ewen wasn't far off the mark. In most circumstances Janet would laugh, but not today.

She sat up and wriggled her back against the down pillows, seeking exactly the right spot, while Lena handed her the tankard. "How is my stepmother?" Come to think of it, the woman had stopped in to check on her when she'd first arrived home, and Janet hadn't seen her since. *Hmm.* She blew on the steamy tea and sipped.

"Not well. She has the morning sickness."

Janet nearly spewed her mouthful across the coverlet. "You're not serious."

"'Tis the way of marriage." Lena headed for the garderobe.

"Aye, but my father is five and sixty. It is disgusting to think of him acting like a young stag."

"All men act like stags, no matter their age." The lass came out with a woolen kirtle and arisaid. "Drink the lot of your tea. I say you'll need it."

Janet again sipped the awful brew. "What I need is a holiday."

"Did you not just have one?"

She set the tankard on the bedside table. "Aye, what a holiday indeed. Complete with a broken arm and..."

"Oh heavens!" Lena clapped her hands to her cheeks. "Apologies, I didn't mean to be unfeeling. I hope that vile Grant treated you respectfully."

"He's not vile."

"I wouldn't utter those words too loudly. When the missive first arrived, your da stormed about the castle, ranting about how he aimed to call out Grant and put his lands to fire and sword."

"It's fortunate Da came to his senses." *At least deciding not to attack. Men so often behave like complete mutton-heads.*

Once she was dressed and had finished her tea, Janet made her way to the library and rapped on the door.

"Come."

She popped her head inside. "You wanted to see me, Father?"

"Aye." From his chair beside the hearth, Da beckoned her, looking both annoyed and impatient. "Sit." He inclined his head toward the chair across from his—a place where Janet oft sat and read aloud, though not since his latest wedding.

Swallowing her misgivings, she did as told, folded her hands, and tried to look pleasant. "I hear I'm to have a new brother or sister soon."

"Aye, God willing."

"Felicitations to you and Stepmother."

"Save your well wishes for when a healthy bairn is born. Too many things can go wrong at this stage, especially if one celebrates too soon."

So much for pleasantries. Da appeared to be in one of his moods, which meant the less Janet said, the better.

He reached for a letter on his side table and unfolded it. "I trust you didn't read the missive Robert Grant wrote to me."

"No, I did not, though he explained its contents."

"I gathered. The swine is as devious as a fox among sheep." Handing her the letter, he gave a nod. "Read it."

Tilting the missive toward the candlelight, she cleared her throat. " 'Dear Lochiel.' "

"No need to read it aloud."

"Very well." The letter began plainly enough. Robert first explained what had happened at the Samhain gathering and the events that had caused Janet to strike Winfred Cummins. Robert went on to say that as he was leaving Inverlochy, Janet's scream made him turn his retinue around; his men cut the lieutenant off on the North Road, rescued her, and fled into the mountains in the midst of a blizzard. He described the conditions and Janet's fall, then glossed over the time in the bothy and ended the paragraph with a report of the healer's recommendations and adding the fact that his sister and the housekeeper were overseeing Janet's convalescence.

All seems as Robert explained thus far.

But then she read on:

I chose to bring Miss Cameron to Moriston Hall because I need an explanation from you, sir, which I have yet to receive, regarding my missing yearlings. Furthermore, after swords were agreed upon in a gentleman's duel, your eldest son lashed out with a dagger and sliced open my cheek, thus attesting to the devious nature of you and your kinsmen. Miss Janet has proved to be the exception to the Cameron treachery, and I hereby declare she is welcome in my household and remains at Moriston Hall of her own free will. My sister and I will continue to provide your daughter with Highland hospitality until she is well enough to return to Achnacarry.

Allow me to reiterate: I am not holding your daughter for ransom. She is free to come and go when she is able. However, I would like your honesty, sir, in the matter of my missing yearlings. I

*need recompense for my losses. Own up to your
thievery, and let us cease the bloody feuding between our clans.*

By the time Janet finished reading, she was hunched
over and shaking her head. How could Robert be so arrogant? So self-righteous? Did he think by calling her kin
underhanded he would gain her father's accord and end
the feud between their clans? *He never listened to a word
I said about the Cameron losses or the fact that my father
would never steal Robert's useless beasts.*

She lowered the parchment and met her father's gaze,
unable to speak.

"Now I need the truth, Daughter, for I do not trust that
miscreant Robert Grant to tell me the time of day without
lying through his ill-bred teeth. Has. Your. Virtue been
compromised?"

Heat rushed to Janet's face as if it were a burning brazier. The parchment trembled between her fingers, and
she released it as if it were afire. The first, most embar-
rassing, and worst possible things flashing through her
mind were the image of Robert's member in her hand,
and then that of her mouth on him while he took his
pleasure.

By the saints, what have I done?

Had His Lairdship known all along her father would
come? Had he planned her ruination? Before the rescue,
before the duel, Janet had always kept her distance from
Mr. Grant. Everyone knew his reputation was that of a
rogue. She'd put out of her mind seeing him with a serving wench at the alehouse, but now the sickening image
was as clear as her face in a looking glass.

She gulped. *Still, he did not take my maidenhead.*

Though he'd sworn he wouldn't, he had taken her innocence. Never again would she wonder what it was like to
be with a man. She might still be a virgin, but now she
had a very clear idea of the wiles of the boudoir. Worse,
she doubted she would ever again be with a lad as virile
and potent as Robert Grant.

*Did he seduce me? Were his words but empty
promises?*

"Janet, your silence makes me suspect—"

"Nay," she spat. "He treated me as a gentleman
ought. His sister, Emma, was particularly friendly and
hospitable."

"Surprising." Da drummed his fingers on his thigh.

Janet swallowed down her revulsion. "I ken you must
think the worst, but Mr. Grant's healer was most concerned about me traveling home with a broken arm."

Da's nostrils flared. "Did Grant give you the option
of going to Moriston Hall or Achnacarry? He could
have easily brought you home from the moors of Ben
Nevis."

"He did not." Janet chewed the inside of her cheek.
Aye, she'd been upset when she realized where Robert
had brought her. "When he said he would take me home,
I believed he meant *my* home until we arrived at Moriston
Hall."

Her father crossed his arms. "And yet you think he
acted honorably."

Again she gulped. If she mentioned anything about
their liaisons, she would be ruined and Da most definitely
would ship her to France to join a convent. "Toward me
he did. Clearly he is obsessed with the loss of his yearlings. Even when you arrived, he was trying to seek out
the culprits—I-I think that may have been why he was so

anxious to talk to you. A-and he'd learned a great deal more about the mystery *after* he dispatched his missive to Achnacarry."

"Well, this whole debacle has me flummoxed." Da crossed his knees. "What am I to do with you?"

"As soon as my arm heals, I'll be able to resume my duties and continue knitting and raising funds for the foundlings and unfortunate—no need to concern yourself."

"Och, do not skirt the issues, dear gel. According to your stepmother, 'tis past time for you to marry."

Janet looked to the ceiling. "That may be so, but I am not ready. Please do not act hastily and arrange my marriage to a stranger. It would be diabolical."

"I am well aware of your wishes, but the time to act is anon. I've sent word to your mother's brother, Sir Broden MacLean. Kennan has returned to Glasgow to captain his new three-masted barque, and I'm sure you're aware he lets a room in your aunt and uncle's town house when he's ashore."

"Aye."

"After I receive word that Sir Broden is amenable to the terms I've suggested, I will send you to them. Uncle Broden and your brother can escort you to the balls and all manner of theater—and I have no doubt your Auntie Dallis will be over the moon to introduce you to Glasgow society. If all proceeds as planned, I'll expect to receive a letter from you every fortnight describing whom you have met. Once you find an eligible bachelor who strikes your fancy, I will commence the appropriate negotiations. You have a healthy dowry. You're as bonny as a rose. It shouldn't take long, given the right introductions."

The walls began to crumble around her as Janet stared at her hands. "When do you expect I'll sail?"

"Your arm first needs time to heal. And there's no use sending you in winter." Da stood. "But mind you, if you haven't found someone you fancy by the end of August, your stepmother will be all too happy to play matchmaker."

"No, please."

"I ken this is not what you want, but I am at my wits' end. You went to Inverlochy with Kennan to look for a husband, and you found a bloody scoundrel."

"I told you I was off to Inverlochy to do some shopping, which I did. I imagine Mrs. MacNash is still holding my parcels for me."

"I ken why you went, and I thought it was wise until I received Grant's missive."

"You didn't know I was rescued by Rob—ah, Mr. Grant until you received his letter?"

"I did not. And I was worried half out of my mind. I had no idea what happened to you or your brother. Kennan lost his memory for an entire sennight—and he still doesn't remember anything from the night of Samhain. Good Lord, he was convalescing in a crofter's cottage whilst I was visiting the colonel at Fort William and scouring the countryside looking for you both—mind you, in the worst blizzard we've had since the winter of 1687."

"I kent you would have been worried, but what of Lieutenant Cummins? He followed us into the mountains—at least at first. Did you see him at Fort William?"

"I did not at the time, though later word came that he and his men were trapped at Càrn Dearg. Cummins suffered frostbite, and his leg has been amputated from the knee down."

"Oh-oh, how awful." Even if Janet didn't like the man, she hated to see anyone fall prey to the surgeon's saw. The idea was gut-wrenching.

"The woeful part is the lieutenant's men reported that he was in his cups and acting with behavior unfitting a gentleman. I received an apology from the colonel telling me Cummins had no cause to chase after you in the first instance."

"My word." She shook her head, the melancholy stretching her chest until she could hardly bear it. "My broken arm, fleeing through the Highlands, my stay at Moriston Hall were all for naught?"

"Aye. That seems the way of it."

* * *

Robert sat in the dark, sipping whisky in the library. He'd played Janet's retreat over and over in his head, doubting his every word, his every action, hating himself for not fighting, but knowing full well that if he'd drawn his sword against Lochiel, he only would have made things worse.

Most likely the cur has already turned her against me.

God save him, he'd behaved like a fool the entire time Miss Janet had been in Glenmoriston. For a moment he'd almost lost his heart to the lass.

Robert drank again, though the whisky wasn't the only thing burning as it slid down his gullet. He'd lived seven and twenty years, and the only time he'd ever fallen for a woman, it had to be a Cameron lass—a woman he could never marry. He rubbed the scar on his cheek. Jesus, the wound alone should be a testament to the dishonor of Janet's kin. What if he had asked for her hand? What if Lochiel had accepted? *Then I'd have those miserable blackguards for in-laws.*

The door opened and Emma stepped inside. "Robert?"

"By the hearth." At least his sister couldn't see he was brooding, drinking alone without a lamp or candle lit.

She moved toward him, her fingers brushing the furniture to guide her progress. "You've been awfully quiet the past few days."

"Aye."

"I miss her as well."

"I do not ken what you are on about," he said, taking a gulp of whisky.

"Do not tell me you've taken to telling tall tales."

He shook his head. "I never should have brought her here."

"I disagree." Emma slid into the chair across from him. "I enjoyed Miss Janet immensely. And now I have no one with whom to knit. Knitting is very industrious, and I was just starting to become proficient."

"You can knit with Mrs. Tweedie."

"Goodness, Robert, Mrs. Tweedie is not half as interesting as Miss Janet."

God's bones, he'd heard enough. Launching himself to his feet, he shook his finger. "There's no use brooding. The lass is gone, and that's the end of it. If you want to continue with your knitting lessons, Mrs. Tweedie is your best option."

Clenching his fists, he stormed out of the parlor and marched for the gaol. Damn it all, he never had spoken harshly to Emma, and he'd just bellowed at the poor gel. This whole mess had him wound so tight, he wanted to hit something—hit a great many things. His woes had begun with the theft of his cattle. Well, the best way to solve a mystery was to attack it relentlessly until he revealed the truth.

He shoved through the gaol door and glared at the men wrapped in bloody blankets behind the bars. His gaze settled on Leith's pair of predatory eyes. "Do you want out of this shite hole?"

Chapter Twenty-Seven

Cold and miserable, winter passed, reflecting the melancholy weighing upon Robert's heart. Throughout the season Moriston Hall brooded in the midst of spidery, dormant trees and incessant rain. Like a caged animal, Robert paced through the corridors with one thing on his mind—vengeance. He would bide his time, but when he discovered the culprit, he would strike quickly and ruthlessly.

His only happiness had come when the vicar's wife had helped him organize a small recital for Emma at Moriston Hall. A few local affluent families had attended, and Emma's music had been breathtaking.

Janet's mare had grown saucy. She nipped and played with the other horses, though she would limp for the rest of her days. Still, watching the filly in the paddock reminded Robert that his time with Janet had not been a dream. The horse also reminded him how much he'd lost the day her father took the lass away.

Otherwise there was little to do aside from tend the livestock and build his army. Since he'd taken a leaf from Miss Janet's book of kindness and employed Leith's half-dozen miscreants, he needed the time to turn them into men worthy of riding with Clan Grant. Rough as crags, the men started out slow, but as the days progressed, their interest in belonging grew, as did their skill. Robert offered them shelter, food, and a fair wage, which none of them had ever enjoyed all at once. He made them attend Sunday services for their souls while teaching them how to fight with a blade and fire a musket from the back of a pony.

True, Lewis strode through the grounds scowling and mumbling under his breath about how bad things had grown, but Robert saw his henchman's disquiet as a good sign. By employing the tinkers, Robert showed his men how serious he was about stopping livestock losses at all costs, and six wayward souls were learning they had a purpose beyond reiving.

Acting upon what was most likely the last of Janet's influence, he gave each tinker a sturdy garron pony. And on the first of April, when the grasses on the slopes were beginning to turn a vibrant green, Robert rode out with Lewis, Jimmy, and Leith's men and drove his herd to the Highland grazing leas.

A crisp breeze blew down from the icy snowcaps, and Robert flared his nostrils and took in a reviving breath. "Bloody oath, it feels good to be in the saddle behind a mob of beasts."

"I cannot dispute that," said Lewis. "But when the time comes to drive them to market, we mightn't have a single head left with that band of ne'er-do-wells you hired."

Robert arched an eyebrow, giving his henchman a

sideways glance. "Do you think once a man has gone bad there's no hope for his reform?"

"I think a man's choices are a testament to his character. Once he has gone bad, he must prove his commitment to being virtuous tenfold. Those tinkers taking up the flanks haven't won my good graces. Not by half."

Robert couldn't argue. If it hadn't been for Janet, those men might have already swung from the gallows. "I have no intention of leaving them alone with my beasts. I'll be staying through the calving at least, and you'd best make yourself comfortable in the bothy, 'cause you'll not be seeing Glenmoriston until summer's end."

"I wouldn't have it any other way. Nary a reiver in all of Scotland will dare pilfer a single one of our beasts this year."

"'Tis good to hear your conviction is the same as mine, friend."

Robert tapped his spurs and headed for a cow and calf that had strayed for a clump of grass. "There'll be plenty more feed where you're heading."

"And they'll be nice and fat for market," Jimmy hollered over his shoulder.

"That they will." Robert almost smiled. He'd needed to spirit himself away from Moriston Hall and the memories that still lingered in the rose bedchamber. He needed to put Janet Cameron out of his mind and set himself to task. Aye, by the end of summer the lass would be forgotten, and he would be back to his old self again.

'Tis time. 'Tis past time.

* * *

Janet's arm had long healed, and she'd knitted many pairs of mittens and scarves, by the time Kennan sailed the three-masted barque up through Loch Linnhe and into Loch Eil, mooring off the coast of Corpach. During her idle time, she'd also written at least two dozen letters to Emma, which were stowed in the bottom of her trunk, since Da forbade her to dispatch a single word to Glenmoriston.

It was already May when Kennan dropped anchor in the Firth of Clyde off the coast of Newport Glasgow, Scotland's modern harbor facilities for shipbuilding and shipping. After a winch lowered her and Lena to a skiff, Janet took a seat on a rowing bench between her brother and her maid, then looked toward the shore. Coaches and wagons ambled along. Laborers in breeches and shirtsleeves pushed barrows, and gentlemen wearing tricorn hats and gold-piped doublets conducted business with their arms flailing. Seabirds squawked overhead, some diving into the water for a tasty morsel. The nearer the skiff came to the pier, the more pungent the odor of rotten fish and seaweed.

Kennan gave her a nudge. "You look as if you're in the midst of a funeral procession."

"I feel as though I am." Janet hadn't felt herself since the day Da arrived at Moriston Hall. Perhaps she'd grown up and taken on a mantle of seriousness bordering on misery. After all, it was time she ceased acting like a foolish maid and accepted the harsh reality of circumstances. Life was not intended to be an unending ceilidh full of merriment. Life was difficult for most, and merely passable for the fortunate.

"Miss Janet hasn't been in good humor of late," Lena said, not helping matters in the least.

A crease formed between Kennan's brows. "It isn't like you to be melancholy. Is your mood on account of that Grant scoundrel? By my oath, if he—"

"Nay!" Janet jabbed her brother with her elbow. "Why must you continually speak ill of His Lairdship?"

"Because he's a colossal clodpoll of the highest order."

"How can you say that...and after he saved you?"

"Saved *me*? What the devil are you on about?"

"He was there with Ciar MacDougall the night we were chased by Lieutenant Cummins. He arrived first—when Ciar arrived Mr. Grant told him to take you to safety. Only after did he stop the dragoons from taking me to Fort William. Think on it."

"MacDougall took me to the crofter's cottage?"

"Aye, and he must have left you there, because Da said you'd been abed in the cottage for a sennight when he found you—said you couldn't remember a thing."

"MacDougall, aye? The crofters told our father some-one knocked on the door and when they opened it I was unconscious on their stoop." Kennan rubbed his head. "Da spoke true. I can recall nothing from Samhain. It took a fortnight for me to come around. I wouldn't even re-member the kind folk who took me in if our father hadn't told me about them."

"I remember everything, and it is as I said. Ciar took you to safety whilst Robert rode ahead and kept me from the stocks or worse at Fort William."

"I had no idea. I must thank MacDougall as soon as I see him next."

"You ought to thank him *and* Laird Grant."

"Now you're stretching things too far. That man nearly got you killed."

"He most certainly did not." Janet slapped her hand on

the bench. "Gracious, Brother, Robert Grant is the reason I am still breathing. No matter what Da says, if Winfred Cummins had taken me inside the fort's walls, I might still be in chains."

"And Cummins might still have a leg."

"Oh, so you heard about that, did you?"

"I've heard rumblings here and there. He's blaming me, Grant, you, and anyone else he can think of."

"He has only himself to blame. None of this would have happened if he'd acted like a gentleman in the first place."

"Perhaps not, though I still think you'd be paying a visit to Glasgow."

Janet groaned as the seaman hopped out of the skiff and tied it to the pier. "I feel like a heifer being escorted to the auction block."

"I do not see why you're so averse." Kennan helped her alight. "Your options for finding a suitable husband are far better here in town than in Achnacarry—or Inverlochy, for that matter."

Except I've sailed in the wrong direction. The man I want to see is more likely to be in Inverness than Glasgow.

Together they strode to the end of the pier with Lena following closely. Kennan hailed a coach and instructed the driver of a wagon to follow them and deliver Janet's trunks to an address on Salt Market Street. Once the trunks were loaded and all was settled, Kennan helped Lena up to the driver's bench, then climbed inside the coach with Janet. "'Tis an eighteen-mile ride up the River Clyde into the city, but the roads are quite good."

Janet settled into the upholstered seat and opened the

shutter. At least the day was fine. "How long will you be in town afore you have to sail again?"

"I'll need to meet with the baronet on the morrow to discuss the schedule. But I expect I'll be in port for a time. The barque is scheduled for repairs, which I must oversee."

"My, the baronet gives you a great deal of responsibility."

Kennan shrugged. "No more than being a laird."

Janet chewed her bottom lip and turned her attention out the window. Of course Kennan would be laird when the time came. Being master and commander of a merchant ship was good training for certain.

They rode in silence for a long while. Kennan hadn't lied about the roads being good. The team was able to maintain a fast trot the entire distance, and within a few hours they stopped outside Auntie Dallis and Uncle Broden's town house. Janet had stayed there on two previous occasions, though in those instances her father had sailed up the Clyde in a smaller sea galley with no chance of running aground, and there had been no need to moor in the firth and take a coach all the way from the recently named village of Newport Glasgow.

Janet and Lena went ahead to ring the bell while Kennan supervised the unloading of the trunks. The door was opened by a well-dressed, tall, gaunt man looking more English than Scottish, though Janet knew the butler to be a Lowland Scot. "Well, have a look at this. 'Tis Miss Janet come all the way from Achnacarry."

Janet curtsied. "Good day, Lionel. I've brought Kennan with me. And this is Lena, my lady's maid."

The lass curtsied as well. "Pleased to meet you, sir."

"Your aunt and uncle have been expecting you for two

days. Thank heavens you're here, I do believe your presence will prevent Her Ladyship from having one of her spells." Giving one of his barely noticeable, sly winks, the butler beckoned Lena. "I'll take you to the housekeeper, and she'll help you find your way about the place. Miss Janet, please make yourself at home in the parlor whilst I notify Lady MacLean and Sir Broden of your arrival. I'm sure Mr. Kennan will find his way. He's been doing so now and again for the past two years."

"My thanks." Janet covered her urge to laugh with the tips of her fingers. The older gentleman had a way of being charming and saucy at the same time. He'd been Uncle Broden's butler forever, and he never seemed to age. He'd been old and gaunt since Janet first met him when she was a wee child.

As Lena and Lionel retreated through the servants' door, Kennan marched up the front steps with four porters in his wake. "Leave the trunks in the entry, if you please." He gave each a coin and shut the door while Janet ambled into the parlor.

Bathed in light beaming from the west-facing window, the room welcomed everyone who entered. Auntie had an eye for décor. Every chair was upholstered with a circle of flowers framing a fashionable scene of lords and ladies. On the walls were portraits of Janet's kin on her mother's side, most of whom she'd never met, though she was drawn to one portrait. The ache in her heart came back with force as she stepped in front of the painting of her mother. "I wish you were still here." She reached out and touched the edge of the frame so as not to spoil the canvas.

"I do as well," Kennan said, coming up behind her. "She always saw things in a way no one else did."

"And gave the best hugs."

"She did."

"There you are!" Auntie Dallis dashed from the doorway, a grin stretching her round rose-colored cheeks. In three steps the woman wrapped Janet in a smothering embrace.

"Och, 'tis good to see you," Janet squeaked, peeking over the woman's shoulder at her uncle.

Auntie held her at arm's length. "My, my, you grow bonnier every time I see you."

"That she does." Uncle Broden squeezed in and gave Janet a far less crushing welcome. "How was your journey, my dear?"

"Kennan sailed the ship as if the surf were smooth as glass."

"I believe the weather had a fair bit to do with it." The lad greeted them with a hug for Auntie and a handshake for Uncle.

"The servants are taking your things above stairs. I've ordered coffee and biscuits—have you tried coffee, dear? 'Tis all the rage in London."

"I cannot say I have."

"Then do not drink too much, else your fingers will set to trembling." Uncle Broden led them to the settee and chairs situated before the hearth.

Before Janet could sit in one of the chairs, Auntie pulled her onto the settee. "I am thrilled you have arrived. You must accompany me to the soldiers' hospital. Queen Anne's war in the Americas has taken a dreadful toll on the Glaswegian young men."

"That it has," agreed Uncle, flipping up his coattails and sitting.

Kennan opted to stand near the fire and rest his elbow

on the mantel. "I hear they're shipping the wounded home."

"Straight home to Glasgow, mind you. They arrive with limbs amputated, the ague, scurvy, and all manner of vile diseases." The lace on Auntie Dallis's coif shook with her forcible nod. "Dearest Janet, the men would be terribly grateful to have you sing for them—or read."

"Of course." Janet rubbed her hand over the hazard dice in her pocket. "I brought along a collection of Scottish folktales." *Though they most likely would prefer a bit of fun and a harmless wager or two.*

"That would be ideal."

Janet brushed aside her wayward thoughts and opted for a more charitable tack. "We must buy some wool, and I'll set to knitting scarves and mittens as well."

"Aye, colder weather will be upon us afore we know it." Auntie looked up and beckoned Lionel. "Ah, here's our refreshment. Janet, would you do us the honor and pour?"

Chapter Twenty-Eight

"'Oh dear, oh dear! The auld wife's brogues must have been shod with iron spikes,'" Janet read aloud. Was the soldier in the bed listening? He hadn't opened his eyes or even moved since she began. As she paused, a cold chill spread across her nape, so eerie she shuddered and glanced over her shoulder—finding nothing but a door that opened into the hallway.

Sighing, she straightened and smoothed her hand over the page she'd just read. The sentinel lay in the bed nearest the door, the outline of one arm clear beneath the bedclothes, but the white blanket was smooth and flat where his right should be. It was a long, narrow room with seven beds, a soldier upon each one. Some coughed, some breathed heavily, but this man lay silent and unmoving.

She glanced at his face to find he'd opened his lids and was staring—with brown eyes as intense as those of a starved deerhound. "Please don't stop, miss."

"You were listening?"

"Aye. Who wouldn't listen to a lass with a voice as bonny as a willow warbler?"

She smiled thoughtfully. "Where are you from?"

"Renfrewshire. Not far from here."

"Have you seen your kin since you've been home?"

His lips formed a thin line as he looked away. "They are not aware that I'm here."

"I could write to them on your behalf if you'd li—"

"Nay. I do not want them to see me half a man."

"Hmm." Janet pretended to look out the door again while she wiped her eyes. What could she say? This man's problems seemed so much worse than her own. And trying to commiserate with him would only invite his scorn. "In this bed I see a man," she said, placing her hand on the mattress and sitting taller. "A brave soldier for whom I have only respect. Tell me, were you conscripted?"

"Aye, of course. The bloody English always look to Scottish men to fight their battles."

"I thought no less." She moved her hand to his shoulder. "I hope you do go home once you are able."

"And be nothing but a burden to Ma and Da?"

"Not at all. I know a blind woman who learned to see with her fingertips and ears."

"I don't believe that."

"Well, she used touch to help her negotiate her way around any room. She plays a harp like one of God's angels, and I taught her to knit...and now she is better than I." That was a stretch, but Emma had potential. "I believe that when faced with adversity, lads and lasses adapt in the most marvelous ways. They just need to believe in their ability to do so."

An orderly stepped into the room and cleared his throat. "Your coach is waiting, Miss Cameron."

Janet closed her book. "Already?"

"Will you come back?" asked the sentinel.

"I will, if you promise to think on what I've said."

"If you wish it."

"I do." She gave his shoulder a final pat. "Everyone deserves happiness."

Rising to her feet, Janet followed the orderly out to the drive. With all her heart she longed to believe the words she'd just uttered. Wouldn't it be astonishing if she found happiness? *I just cannot imagine how.*

Uncle Broden's coachman opened the door and offered his hand. "How are the wounded, miss?"

"In sore need of a good game of hazard."

The man chuckled as she climbed inside. But once she looked at the bench, she froze, staring at what appeared to be a white dog rose. Its petals had been plucked and arranged around a stem with two thorns. Before the man could shut the door, Janet turned and popped her head outside. "Did you put the flower there?"

The man looked stunned. "Beg your pardon?"

"Have you been here beside the coach the whole time?"

"Aye, aside from taking a wee moment to visit the privy."

Janet tucked her head back inside while an icy chill streaked down her arms. In the Highlands a white rose was a secret symbol of the exiled King James. Jacobites wore the rose when there was news from the true king—and usually there would be a secret gathering of James's ardent supporters.

"What is it?" asked the coachman.

Janet swept the petals off the seat. "Just a remnant of a flower. I just didn't recall it being there earlier this day."

The man frowned. "I did not notice it, either, but I reckon it wouldn't be the first time something slipped past my inspection." He shut the door, climbed up to his bench, and pointed the team down the drive.

Opening the shutter, Janet scanned the grounds as the carriage bumped over the cobblestones. Her gaze darted to every shrub, searching for a villain hiding in the shadows. When the coach hit a bump, she tottered on the seat with a startled squeal. Clapping a hand over her mouth, she prayed the coachman hadn't heard.

I'm behaving like a mutton-head. 'Twas but a silly dog rose, nothing more.

* * *

Auntie Dallis didn't waste any time filling Janet's calendar. Mornings were harrowing with appointments for fittings—the modiste, the milliner, the cobbler. With Lochiel's coin they purchased fans and lace, new stays, new shifts, new stockings—according to Her Ladyship, Janet must have a fresh supply of all a young lass needed to immerse herself in Glasgow society. "It might not be London, but with the new port, every important gentleman in Scotland can be seen walking Laigh Green along the Clyde."

Afternoons spent reading and singing for the soldiers at the hospital proved quieter, especially since her aunt always had a reason not to accompany Janet.

This evening, she was looking forward to exhibiting one of her new gowns—a pink silk with all the matching accouterments, including a hand-painted fan trimmed with lace. Ciar MacDougall had come to accompany her and Kennan to the High Kirk of Glasgow for an organ recital of modern music, including two fugues by an acclaimed new composer from Germany, Johann Sebastian Bach. The organist performing the pieces was to be Scotland's own George Douglas, esteemed music principal employed by the kirk.

"Ciar!" Janet dashed down the town house stairs and into the entry to find her friend standing beside her brother. "It is such a delight to see you."

The MacDougall laird grasped her hands and kissed them. "Och, Miss Janet, you grow more radiant by the day."

"You exaggerate. But I don't mind one wee bit." She turned in a circle, showing off her new gown. "Auntie Dallis ordered the pink silk from London."

"Aye, and with the way our dear aunt is spending my father's coin, my sister will need two more trunks when she returns home." Kennan ushered the party out the front door. "We must make haste, for the Baronet of Sleat has the best seats in the kirk reserved for us."

Ciar offered Janet his elbow. "What have you been up to whilst you've been in Glasgow?"

"Aside from following my aunt to every shop in town, I've been visiting the soldiers' hospital."

"I kent you wouldn't have been in town for a sennight before you found a charity that needs you desperately." He offered his hand and helped her into the coach.

"Auntie Dallis isn't one to sit idle. Not when there's a well-bred maid to parade about," said Kennan, following his sister and taking the seat opposite.

Janet preferred to avoid talking about her true reason

for visiting her aunt and uncle and opted to ignore her brother. "Those poor soldiers are lonely and in pain, and some are heartbroken."

"And I'll wager you want to help them all." Ciar's broad shoulders filled the space beside Kennan as he knocked on the roof of the coach.

Janet rocked forward when the team got underway. "What brings you to Glasgow, Ciar? I'm surprised you're not preparing to take your sheep to Inverlochy."

"Things are busy, I cannot deny. I'll be sailing home on the morrow. I only ventured down to attend a meeting with a handful of Highland chieftains."

"Organized by Donald MacDonald," Kennan added.

"The Baronet of Sleat?" Janet asked.

"Aye."

"A meeting of the Defenders?" she persisted.

"Wheesht, Janet." Kennan gestured toward the coachman driving the team outside, though there was no way he could possibly discern a word with the racket of the horses' shod hooves, the wheels churning over the cobblestones, and the coach's frame creaking.

Ciar gave her brother a nudge. "A few of us met to discuss trade in Glasgow—things you shouldn't concern yourself with, lass."

"Like the queen putting English exports ahead of Scottish?" Janet shook her head. "I am the daughter of Sir Ewen Cameron of Lochiel. I ken all about the sanctions enforced by the crown."

Ciar glanced up to the ceiling. "Just be mindful of the company whom you are among afore you express your opinion. Doing so could be very bad for your well-being."

"Agreed," said Kennan.

"I see." Janet opened and closed her fan. Obviously

they weren't about to engage in a lively discussion about the details of the meeting or, most importantly, those who had been in attendance. *Just out with it.* "Did you see Robert Grant at your gathering with the baronet?"

Kennan groaned. "Bless it, Sister. Do not tell me you're still thinking about that backbiting varlet."

Ciar knit his brows as he gave Kennan another nudge. "The depth of your hatred stuns me."

This time her brother jabbed with his elbow in return. "Do not tell me MacDougalls have made amends with the Campbells."

"Hardly likely—and hardly the same thing." Ciar shook his head. "Besides, the Campbells are staunch government supporters. Grant sides with us."

After the coach rolled to a stop, the door opened and a footman peered inside. "Welcome to the high kirk."

Before Janet took the man's hand, she eyed her brother. "I, for one, agree with Ciar."

Kennan presented their tickets to the doorman, then led them through the maze of people gathered in the vestibule and straight to a couple dressed in such finely tailored clothes, they could be none other than the Baronet of Sleat and his wife.

Kennan bowed deeply. "May I present my sister, Miss Cameron." He gestured to the couple. "You may remember Sir Donald and Lady MacDonald from the gathering at Urquhart Castle."

"I do." Janet curtsied. "Pleased to see you again, m'lord, m'lady."

"Welcome," said Sir Donald.

"How good to see you again." Lady Mary, as she was known to her friends, grasped both of Janet's hands. "I must say, every time I see you, you are bonnier than the last."

"You are too kind." Janet admired Her Ladyship's gown. "And what a lovely shade of green. It is an ideal color for red hair."

Ciar stepped in and exchanged pleasantries, and then the baronet escorted them down the long nave while Janet's heels echoed all the way up to the vaulted ceiling. He stopped at the front row of seats. "From here you'll have an unobstructed view of Mr. Douglas."

"It will be marvelous," Lady Mary said, taking Janet's hand and leading her to a seat right in the middle of the row. "This kirk was made for music."

And it was. As soon as the maestro's fingers began to strike the organ's keys, Janet was surrounded by a vortex of fast-moving harmonies. Music spilled through her soul, more uplifting than anything she'd ever heard. Indeed, both organist and composer were nothing short of brilliant. When the performance stopped for intermission, Janet patted her chest, breathing as if she'd just run a footrace. "My, that was glorious."

"Outstanding," Ciar agreed, fanning his face.

During intermission, Janet followed the entourage to the west end of the nave for refreshments. "Are you enjoying the recital?" asked Lady Mary.

"Ever so much. I cannot believe how the pipes make this enormous building shake to the timbers."

"I believe Mr. Douglas is Scotland's very best organist." Lady Mary took two glasses of champagne from a passing footman and gave one to Janet. "Today we received word the Duke of Gordon is coming to town. He holds the most engaging royal balls this side of London. Have you met him?"

"No, I have not had the pleasure."

"Well, then, 'tis a good thing you happen to be in Glasgow at the moment."

Janet smiled and sipped, but with the taste of champagne came the eerie prickling across the back of her neck. She'd sensed it at the hospital twice now. Quickly she glanced over her shoulder to see a man hobbling out to the cloisters. "Who is that?" she asked, craning her neck, the crowd blocking her view.

"Who?" Her Ladyship searched, but the man was gone.

"Mary, there you are." The baronet stepped beside his wife and offered his elbow. "Forgive me, Miss Cameron, but we've been summoned to meet the artist of the evening."

"Of course." Janet curtsied and moved beside her brother. "Have you seen Winfred Cummins in Glasgow?" she whispered in his ear.

"That venomous, sheep-biting asp? I hope never to see him again." He turned to Ciar. "That reminds me, Mac-Dougall. Janet tells me I owe you a debt of gratitude for hauling me out of the mire on Samhain."

"Aye?" Ciar grinned, looking pleased. "I was wondering when you would remember that night."

"I still do not recall a damned thing."

"Kennan, language. This is a church." While Janet chided her brother, an idea came to mind. Was this her chance to finally prove to her brother that Robert wasn't an evil villain? She pulled the two men aside. "Ciar, you must tell us exactly what happened that night. The last thing I saw was a mob of dragoons knock Kennan from his mount and beat him senseless afore I pled with the lieutenant to make them stop. Cummins left Kennan half-dead while his men took me away."

Ciar nodded, his gaze shifting between them. "When I arrived, Robert Grant had Kennan cradled in his arms. When he saw me, he hefted Kennan over my horse's withers, asked me to take him to safety. Then Grant and his men hastened to ride after you, Miss Janet."

"Why did you take me to the croft?" Kennan asked. "Why not to Achnacarry?"

"I took you to the first cottage with a light flickering in the window. We all thought the worst. I had no idea how badly you were injured. Moreover, the castle is the first place the soldiers would have searched for you."

Kennan scratched his head. "And what say you? Grant tended to me first?"

"He did. And I'll tell you true, when he and I parted company in Inverlochy, he was headed for home. 'Twas Miss Janet's scream that made him turn his men around and ride back. He saved your life, I reckon."

"Why would Grant do anything to help me?"

"Mayhap because you're a Defender—just as he is, just as I am. When it comes to redcoats invading the Highlands, all clan feuds become but wee squabbles." Ciar scratched his chin. "Though I do not ken why he did it, especially after you brandished your dagger in the duel and sliced his face. Hell, I'm surprised he did not finish the beating started by the dragoons."

Janet cleared her throat. "He doesn't want to feud with us."

"Oh aye?" Kennan shook his head, though his expression was unsure. "He continually blames the Camerons for his own losses."

Since he was wavering, Janet stepped nearer and squared her shoulders. "That is only because he's trying to find the real culprits."

Kennan snorted. "Now you're making as much sense as a magpie."

"I'm making perfect sense." Janet shook her fan under her brother's nose. "Perhaps if the Grants and Camerons joined forces, something might actually be done about the poachers."

"Did you tell that to Grant?" he asked.

A bell rang, indicating it was time to return to their seats.

Kennan took her hand. "Come."

"I did. And he agreed." *For the most part...*

Kennan and Ciar stood aside, allowing Janet to sidle to her seat.

Dear Lord. Waiting on her chair was another white rose. This one looked as though it had been hastily placed, with only two petals plucked, though the bloom had four thorns. Janet drew her hand to her chest and gasped.

Ciar picked up the rose and twirled it in his fingers. "It seems we have a joker in our midst."

"Or a troublemaker," Kennan said, turning full circle. "That's not the first—"

"Sh," resounded through the audience as the organist took his place.

Janet took her seat, but once the music began she leaned in to her brother and cupped her hand over her mouth. "Someone left a similar gift in my coach a few days past."

"Why the blazes didn't you say something then?" Kennan didn't bother to whisper.

"I did not think much of it at the time."

From behind, a man tapped on Janet's shoulder with a resounding "Shush."

Kennan grasped her elbow and turned his lips to her ear. "From now on you *will* have an escort at all times."

Janet crossed her arms. As if things weren't stifling enough with Auntie Dallis running her affairs, now her every move was to be supervised. An icy shudder made her glance over her shoulder. What if someone was truly stalking her?

Chapter Twenty-Nine

14 July 1713

*T*he midsummer crowd at the Inverlochy alehouse wasn't as boisterous as in previous years. Robert didn't care overmuch, as long as the buyers were in town. He took a long draw of his ale. After three months in the mountains, the brew tasted like mead from heaven.

"God's bones, Grant, is that you? Ye look like a lion with all that hair sprouting from your face."

Robert turned away from the bar and laughed. "Mac-Dougall!" He thrust out his hand. "Och, 'tis good to see you, old friend."

Ciar gave a firm handshake. "Och, I hardly recognized you."

"I've been in the mountains for months. Haven't had a chance to shave as yet." Robert signaled to the barman. "Another over here, please."

"I'm surprised you're not in Glasgow."

"Why the blazes would I go down there? I've brought my vealers down for sale, and then I'm heading back up to the herd. Mind you, no one will be poaching my beasties this year."

"If anyone can stop the thieves, 'tis you." The barman placed a frothing tankard in front of Ciar and he held it aloft. "*Sláinte.*"

"*Sláinte.*" Robert tapped his cup in toast and drank. "Now what's this you say about Glasgow?"

"I just returned from there two fortnights ago. The new saleyards are booming."

"Bloody hell, I've gone without news for too long. When did this happen?"

"The Baronet of Sleat has been petitioning for proper livestock saleyards for ages, and now that the shipyards are open for business in Newport Glasgow, everything else is falling into place. You ought to drive your vealers south. I saw them in the paddock, and they look better than any coos I've seen in ages."

"Aye? Fat wee beasties, are they not?"

"They are, and it would only take a few days to drive them to Glasgow."

Robert wasn't convinced. Besides, there was a warm bath waiting for him out the back. "What about the coin? Same as Inverlochy?"

"I wouldn't have suggested it if you wouldn't double what you'd receive here."

"Double?"

"Mark me."

"Then why are you here and not driving your livestock to market?"

"I plan to." Ciar patted his sporran. "I'm in Inverlochy by chance—had a meeting with my banker."

"I hope all is well."

"It is, and I'll be driving my cattle to Glasgow come autumn."

"I must give it some thought, especially for the harvest." Robert signaled for another two ales. "What other news? It seems I've missed a great deal."

"Not overmuch. The Baronet of Sleat had some correspondence with the Duke of Gordon. Evidently..." Ciar looked over his shoulders, then leaned in and lowered his voice. "There's been a communication from the king."

"James?"

"Aye."

"A rising?"

"Nay, not yet anyway. His message to us is to be at the ready. He will not attack whilst his sister is on the throne, but the succession is paramount. We must repeal this beastly Occasional Conformity Act."

"With the Tories in power, that ought to be easy enough."

"One would think, but the Earl of Mar has earned the moniker Bobbing John. As the leader of the party, one day he's with us and the next he's not."

"Bloody oath, at times I reckon the peerage ought to be sequestered to their castles and allow levelheaded lawmen to run the country."

"I wouldn't go spouting such radical opinions about, my friend. You're likely to be escorted on a short walk up Fort William's gallows steps."

"I ken. But what of the Defenders? Will there be a gathering soon?"

"Aye, in Glasgow. You haven't heard word about that, either?"

"Clearly not. I haven't been amongst civilization for ages."

"The Duke of Gordon is having a ball—and has made it clear all Highland lairds are welcome to attend."

"Pardon? A ball?" Robert made a sour face. "What about a Highland ceilidh? What about games? I'd like to beat Dunn MacRae at the caber toss afore this year's out."

"Aye, perhaps you'll have your chance another time. A royal ball will allay all suspicion. The idea's brilliant if you ask me."

"When is it?"

"Three weeks away—August third."

Robert scratched his beard. "In that case, perhaps I should rethink driving my vealers to Glasgow—see what the new saleyards are about."

Ciar slapped the bar. "Mind if I ride with you? I wouldn't miss Gordon's invitation for a purse of guineas."

"Nay, but I thought you had just returned from there."

"I did, and now I've set my financial obligations to rights, I'm free to return."

* * *

Auntie Dallis bustled into Janet's chamber with Lena on her heels. "My dear, you must make haste and don your riding habit at once."

Janet set her knitting aside while her maid skipped to the garderobe. "What about the fitting at ten o'clock?"

"The seamstress can wait. Besides, the gown is already made. I'll send word you'll attend her on the morrow."

"Very well, but why a riding habit? Does Mr. Ellis have a penchant for riding today?" After the white rose incident at the kirk, Mr. Ellis, a behemoth of a man who looked and acted as if his prior occupation had been that of a headsman, had been assigned the role of her guardian. The man spoke little, if at all, which was for the best given his limited vocabulary. With him sauntering behind her every afternoon, Janet oft wondered if she was truly safe—perhaps the white rose phantom mightn't attack, but Mr. Ellis...She shuddered.

"Nay. Can you believe it? Ciar MacDougall is waiting below stairs and has asked to take you to the cattle sale." Auntie clapped her hands and plucked the plumed tricorn from Lena's hands. "Isn't it wonderful? I've always liked Ciar very much. Very much!"

Janet turned her back for Lena to untie her bodice, all too aware August was but a sennight away and she had yet to find a man who appealed to her remotely as much as Laird Grant. Time was not in her favor. "Aye, Mr. MacDougall is one of Kennan's closest friends and a staunch ally of Clan Cameron."

"And an ideal match for you, sweeting. After all, that is why you are here, and I cannot allow you to return to Achnacarry without a suitor head over heels in love with you."

With a roll of her eyes, Janet chuckled. "I assure you, Ciar shall not be my future husband."

"How can you say that?"

"Because he is more like a brother to me, and we—" Janet bit her tongue. It would be best not to tell Auntie Dallis they had spoken about a mutual lack of attraction. However, Janet drummed her fingers against her lips; if Her Ladyship believed her to be slightly smitten with the MacDougall laird, she might stop her overbearing meddling. Perhaps Janet might even delay the inevitable by pretending to be interested in Ciar.

"Yes, my dear?" Her Ladyship pressed.

"Well, I must admit he is a dear friend and I am fond of him." Janet stepped into the skirt, donned the shirt and jacket, then held her arms outstretched while Lena picked up the hook and began fastening the doublet's brass buttons—fifty of them.

"And so you should, lass. A man of property like Ciar MacDougall is a good catch for any woman in Scotland."

"I agree." Janet gave a smooth smile, checking it in the mirror to ensure she appeared genuine.

"Splendid." Her Ladyship shook her finger at poor Lena. "Boots—haste ye!"

"Lena needn't rush," said Janet. "I'm sure MacDougall has made himself comfortable below stairs."

"Aye, but the sale is about to begin. And the laird has an interest in the livestock. I hope you do as well, Janet, living up there in that drafty castle with nothing but sheep and coos milling about."

"We have horses as well."

Boots in hand, Lena kneeled with a snort, clearly finding their hostess exasperating.

Janet gave the maid's coif a pat. "Come along with us."

"Nay, she will not!" Auntie objected. "Mr. Ellis has been doing quite nicely, and I have instructed him to remain at a generous distance."

Not about to let it lie, Janet shifted her hands to her hips. "Och, then I promise to take ye for a stroll along the Clyde on the morrow, how would that be?"

Lena patted the bow she'd just tied. "I'd enjoy that very much, miss."

"After your fitting, mind you." Her Ladyship sidled toward the door.

In record time Janet had donned her riding habit. She

reached for her hat and pushed it over her curls. Had she more time, she would have asked Lena to lower her chignon, but Auntie might end up having one of her spells.

In the entry Ciar greeted her with a smile, offered his elbow, and they were off. Once on horseback and out of earshot of any member of the MacLean household, including Mr. Ellis, who was at least fifty paces behind, Janet threw back her head and laughed.

"What the devil is so funny?" Ciar asked.

"Dear Auntie Dallis practically has us walking down the aisle."

"Oh dear. Have you not told her about our pact?"

"Absolutely not. Until I find a suitor with whom I fall madly in love, I am afraid you will have to be the object of my affection."

"Not an entirely bad guise for me—at least until I find my match—if one exists."

"I am certain you will have no trouble finding the woman of your dreams once you set your mind to it."

"Perhaps, though I think I prefer bachelorhood. I've watched too many of my friends succumb to the iron branks of marriage."

"Iron branks? What a horrible thing to say. Besides, 'tis a torture device for women, is it not?"

Ciar shrugged. "I was speaking metaphorically. Wed a woman and you may as well have one of those contraptions holding your tongue."

"Oh please...Now tell me, why are you taking me to this livestock auction, of all places?"

"I thought you needed a new horse."

She grinned, loving his idea. "See? I ken why you are such a good friend."

"Someone else told me about what happened to your horse on Finnach Ridge. That's what gave me the idea."

Janet nodded, assuming she knew of whom Ciar was speaking. "Kennan may have mentioned it in passing, but nonetheless, you are very thoughtful to think of me."

* * *

A tent had been erected over the auction block, and Winfred Cummins sat at the rear of the benches with his hat pulled low over his brow. Due to the loss of his leg, pickings had been slim this year, not to mention that he'd lost some of his sources. In hindsight, he'd been smart to move the cattle he'd culled from the Highland herds to a Lowland croft. His man had altered the brands, and the beasts had grown fatter grazing on meadow grass for an entire year. If he'd been greedy, he would have sold the lot of the herd in Crieff last autumn, but then odds were he would have been caught, and thus he'd only sold twenty or so. But now there was little chance of anyone figuring out from where his beasts had originated. Even better, Glasgow was a new market, where no one knew of him.

At least that's what he'd thought. Winfred's spine shot ramrod straight when Ciar MacDougall escorted Janet Cameron to one of the benches in the front. The Highlander slavered over her hand, planted a kiss, and left her alone, the imbecile.

Licking his lips, Winfred leaned on his cane and pushed himself up. The harness on his wooden leg pinched. He grunted and adjusted the leather straps before he started for the woman. It wasn't easy to walk soundlessly with a peg leg, but the grass underfoot helped, as well as the relentless work he'd done to master the prosthesis. He resisted the urge to laugh as he came up behind her. Though she wore a tricorn, her hair was pinned up, revealing a long slender neck. His fingers itched to close around it and choke the life from the selfish wench responsible for the loss of his leg.

She remained unaware of his presence while he pondered all the ways he could kill her. A dagger to the kidney? A quick slash across the throat? His fingers caressed the handle of the pistol in his belt. *No, no, a lead ball to the skull would be far too quick. She needs to suffer as I have.*

Beneath his brim, Winfred's gaze shifted across the growing crowd. If he killed her now, there would be too many witnesses.

As if his thoughts had brushed the back of her neck, Janet shuddered and whipped around. "L-Lieutenant Cummins!" Her eyes flashed wide, betraying her fear. "I did not expect to see you here."

"I'll wager you did not, Miss Cameron." He removed his hat and bowed deeply with a mocking flourish.

"How long have you been in Glasgow?" she asked, regaining her composure, though her gaze dropped to his stump.

"On and off for a time now." No use telling her he'd been relegated to the lowly position of keeper of the records for the soldiers' hospital. Neither was there any point in telling her he'd watched her alight from her carriage many an afternoon. He smiled, trying his damnedest not to sneer.

"You have an interest in livestock?" she asked.

"Overseeing my family's affairs," he lied, "since I am no longer required in Her Majesty's service."

The woman's eyes narrowed while her lips pursed. "I am regretful for your suffering."

"Not half as much as I."

"That's him!" a man yelled from the entrance to the yards.

Winfred's gut dropped to his toes like lead. Leith Whyte pointed directly his way, the piss-swilling clodpoll. Worse, Robert Grant stepped out from behind the bastard. In a heartbeat Cummins fled, knocking over a bench as he stumbled toward his waiting horse.

* * *

Robert's heart lodged in his throat when Leith pointed to Winfred Cummins. Moreover, the bastard had been standing beside Miss Janet, chatting as if they were best of friends. As soon as the cur looked up, he spun on his peg and scurried for a horse waiting just outside the tent.

"Halt, ye maggot tinker!" Robert shouted, sprinting across the sale arena and leaping over benches. Janet called his name, her voice high pitched and filled with surprise. His heart squeezed, tormenting him, begging him to stop and grovel, but he did not. Not when the phantom he'd been chasing for a year was within his grasp.

He reached the tent's exit as Cummins spun his horse. Robert launched himself forward in a flying leap, and his fingers caught the edge of the bastard's stirrup and latched on. His feet pummeled the ground as he fought to match the horse's retreating gait.

"Let go, you dog!" Cummins threw a backhand with his cane.

Robert ducked, but the stick caught him in the shoulder. "I want my bloody beasts, ye pirate!" The next strike smacked him atop the knuckles. Unable to keep pace, he let go and plummeted to the ground, rolling over and over until he stopped on his back.

Damnation, I'll kill that miserable excuse for a man.

"Robert!" Janet cried, running up with Leith in her wake.

God's bones, why must she be here when I've been made a fool of by a cripple? With a grunt he pushed himself to his feet. "Miss Janet. What are you doing in Glasgow?" He thrust his finger in the direction of Winfred Cummins's retreat. "Do not tell me you are colluding with that onion-eyed knave."

"I beg your pardon?" Her eyes narrowed as she threw her shoulders back, heaving chest and all. "I do *not* hear one word from you in months, and in the blink of an eye you accuse me of siding with such an unsavory blackguard? How quickly you forget who is responsible for all that transpired after Samhain."

Robert jammed the heel of his hand against his forehead. "Forgive me. I am out of sorts. You may recall Leith?" He caught his breath while he gestured to the man.

Janet curtsied, as any proper, polite lady would. "I do. 'Tis good to see you, sir."

The man tipped his bonnet. "Good day, miss."

"I take it you are now in Mr. Grant's employ?" she asked.

"He is," Robert answered. "And he just identified our cattle thief."

"The lieutenant?" Janet's eyes grew round, lovely blue eyes that made his heart twist. "Oh, my word." Her lovely mouth formed an O. "Lieutenant Cummins has a prominent mole on his right cheek."

"Aye." Robert sighed. "And now he's at large."

"Before you entered the tent, the lieutenant came up behind me, startled me something awful. He said he had an interest in the cattle sale—on behalf of his family."

"Not this side of the border. The man's from Newcastle." Robert brushed the dirt off his doublet. "Did he say where he's staying?"

"There wasn't much time. He had hardly started a conversation when Leith spotted him. But..." Janet's brow furrowed while she rubbed the outsides of her arms.

"What is it? Did he threaten you?"

"Not exactly. I-I just felt very uneasy, and he seemed to revel in my discomfort."

"I'll wager he did." Robert offered his elbow. "Come, I'll escort you back to the tent. The sale is about to begin."

"Thank you—I'm here to purchase a new mount." A delicate gloved hand slid onto his elbow.

God save him, he hadn't been prepared for the bone-melting rush of emotion that came with the light touch of her fingers on his arm. But he wouldn't linger. He'd see the lady to her seat and stand at the arena's edge with his men. Nay, he hadn't come to the sale to trifle with Cameron's daughter, no matter how much he wished to.

"How is my mare?" she asked.

Robert shifted his gaze to her eyes—cornflower blues that had been etched on his heart forever. "She's happy. Growing fat on lush Glenmoriston grass."

"I cannot tell you how wonderful it is to hear such news."

"Miss Janet?" A tall, gaunt man strode toward them. "Are you in need of assistance?"

She snapped her hand away from Robert's arm. "Ah, Mr. Ellis, had you been here a moment ago, I might have." Appearing none too pleased, she gestured between the men. "Allow me to introduce Grant of Glenmoriston."

Chapter Thirty

*W*aiting for the hunting party outside the Duke of Gordon's enormous Renfrewshire manse, Robert lowered his reins and reined his horse to a stop while Ciar did the same beside him. "I do not want to pretend that murderous thief isn't at large and ask Miss Janet to go riding as if she were my only care. Why the blazes do you not take her, MacDougall?"

"Because she likes you."

Robert's heart skipped a beat, but he wouldn't give it a second thought. "What about her pernicious brother?"

"He's gone to Edinburgh—checking on a ship for Sleat." Ciar thwacked his riding crop against his thigh. "Come, just take Miss Janet riding. She needs to exercise the mount she purchased at the auction."

Robert ground his molars. It had nearly undone him to see her at the auction. He'd not soon forget how her father had snubbed his offer of hospitality. Hell, even if he still wanted to marry Janet, her father would never give his blessing. "I'm beginning to think you brought me to Glasgow for reasons other than the live-stock sale."

Ciar shrugged, admitting nothing. "You profited well, did you not?"

"I suppose, though not a great deal more than I would have in Inverlochy." Robert wasn't about to be swayed by whether he'd profited from the venture or not. "Tell me true, did she put you up to this?"

"Good Lord, if you think that, then you do not deserve her."

A weight lifted from his shoulders. With his reprimand Ciar had allayed the doubt clawing at Robert's gut, though he chose not to admit his relief to his friend. "Forgive me. I am irked that Cummins has gone into hiding and here we sit waiting for His Grace to take us on a hunting excursion. I'd rather be manhunting at the moment."

"The magistrate has taken your statement. The bastard will be ferreted out. Now there's naught to do but enjoy the morning—mayhap fell a deer."

The duke rode out of the stable in his finery, and a footman handed him a musket. "Good morn, gentlemen. Are you ready for a wee ride?"

"Aye." Robert took inventory of the party—Sleat, MacLean, MacDougall, Chisholm, and MacRae were all staunch Jacobites. Tapping his heels, he rode beside Ciar. "At least the duke keeps good company."

"That he does."

The Gordon setters ran ahead, yelping loudly enough to ensure every deer within fifty miles knew the hunting party was in pursuit. But Robert rode along, the cool breeze in his face bringing on a sense of calm—something he hadn't realized how much he needed.

Once they were well away from town, the duke shot his deer and the men all dismounted and gathered around with their flasks in hand for a toast.

"Thank you all for coming," said His Grace, or Geordie, as he was called by his closest allies. "The hunt was invigorating, aside from being the only way I can bring you together without suspicion."

"Do you have news from the king?" asked Ciar.

"I do." His Grace looked over his shoulders and stepped in as if the trees could hear him whisper. "The king will attend my ball a sennight hence. He will be in disguise."

"Does he want to speak to us?"

"Are we to stage another rising at long last?"

"He asks his followers to wear Highland dress."

"Aye, but—"

The duke held up his hand to silence the mounting questions from his guests. "Allow me to continue." He pulled a handful of red-and-black tartan ribbons from his sporran. "Tie your hose with these and insert your *sgian-dubh* on the left. With these he will recognize you as his ally."

"Will we have a chance to meet with him and plan the next rising?" asked Robert.

"Nay. You will greet him as an aristocrat from France. But make no bones about it, this visit stands as proof that he is committed to ascending to the throne. We in turn must do everything we can to subvert the Act of Succession. James is the true king, and once his sister is laid to rest, we cannot allow another imposter's arse to corrupt the throne."

"Aye, aye," the men chanted together.

Robert took his ribbons, carefully rolled them, and put

them in his sporran. It was a risk for James to visit Scotland, but it was reassuring as well. Perhaps in the future the sovereign would not need to appear incognito.

Ciar walked with him to their horses. "So, are you still planning to be in Glasgow for the ball?"

"If James Francis Edward Stuart is making an appearance, I wouldn't miss it for all the gold in Scotland, even if he will be in disguise. Besides, I aim to be in bloody Glasgow until Winfred Cummins is led to the gallows."

* * *

Again dressed in her riding habit, Janet thrust her fists on her hips while Auntie Dallis paced the floor. But this time the woman huffed as if on the verge of a spell. "Why is Grant, of all eligible bachelors in the kingdom, taking you riding?"

She absolutely must go riding with him, if only to prove that she would never collude with Lieutenant Cummins. At Moriston Hall they had parted too abruptly. Her father hadn't even allowed a proper farewell—or a thank-you, for that matter. Janet threw up her hands. "His missive asked—"

"But where is Mr. MacDougall? You said you liked him—and he's so *amiable*."

"I do like Ciar, but it wasn't he who offered to—"

"Good heavens, if your father hears about this, he'll sail for town in a heartbeat, take you away...and all of Glasgow will think ill of me."

Wound tighter than a spring, Janet inched toward the door. *Blast Her Ladyship. All she is worried about is how she would look to society. Absurd!* "Mr. Grant has been an acquaintance nearly as long as Mr. MacDougall. And I'll have you know the Grant laird saved me from being incarcerated in Fort William." She bit her lip. The details of her adventure had been kept under strict secrecy, and her father had been very clear that she was not to reveal anything about her time at Moriston Hall...or in the bothy.

Reaching the door, Janet made her escape.

Unfortunately, Auntie followed. "Heavens, I wish your brother were here. If you insist on going, I will ensure Mr. Ellis follows *very* closely. I will instruct him not to let you out of his sight."

Curses. "Fine," Janet said over her shoulder as she continued down the stairs.

When she rounded the landing, she nearly swooned. Robert Grant, the man she had dreamed about every night for the past nine months, stood with his back to her, watching out the window. Janet's heartbeat raced. Powerful, imposing, Highlander to his core, His Lairdship was magnificent. He wore a blue-and-green kilt belted low around his hips, with a length of tartan pulled over and pinned at his shoulder. His tawny hair was clubbed back and tied with a red ribbon. The thick muscles in his calves bulged beneath his hose as he turned around and grinned.

Dimples. I adore those dimples.

His smile was only made more alluring by the prominent scar on his cheek—straight white teeth, bold chin, and eyes of polished steel—hawkish, intelligent eyes that missed nothing and expressed everything.

Somehow Janet arrived at the bottom of the stairs without once feeling her feet touch the ground. Rapture washed over her as she opened her arms, then quickly snapped them back. "Mr. Grant, how lovely to see you." Her voice shot up awkwardly, as if she were an adolescent greeting for the first time a lad she'd worshiped from afar.

He stepped forward, every bit the confident laird. Grasping her hand, he bowed over it, moving slowly, languidly, reminding her of another time, days gone by existing only in her memory. His lips kissed her flesh, soft, gentle, breath as warm as a summer's breeze. He straightened and met her gaze with an intensity that made her breath catch.

"I must apologize for my brevity at the livestock sale." His eyes shifted aside.

"Not to worry. You were there to conduct business. I trust your auction was successful."

"It was." His lips twisted when he glanced to Auntie Dallis, but relaxed when those silvery eyes shifted back to Janet. "And you're happy with your new gelding, are you?"

"Aye, I'm eager to put him through his paces." She pointed to Robert's scar, almost touching it. "Your knife wound has faded a great deal. It makes you look a bit dangerous."

He chuckled. "I hope not too dangerous."

A fire rose in her cheeks, and she looked to her hands. "Nay."

"And your arm, miss? Is it still paining you?" His finger brushed the outside of her forearm as softly as the caress of a feather.

Janet drew in a stuttered breath. "I hardly ken it was broken. The physician said whoever set it kent what he was on about." She called on her inner strength and met his gaze again. "I owe you a debt of gratitude."

"I—"

"Mr. Ellis will chaperone," said Auntie Dallis, with the man skulking behind her. "And you mustn't forget your duty to the hospital, my dear. The soldiers will be disappointed if you are late."

Robert offered his elbow. "Then we must make the best of what little time we have. That gelding of yours needs far more than an hour for his paces."

* * *

The weather was windy with clouds overhead, but at least it wasn't raining as Robert trotted beside Janet down the Salt Market Street. With the man gaunt enough to be the image of the Angel of Death ambling behind them on a garron nag, neither Robert nor Janet had said much aside from the exchange of pleasantries. Damnation, there was so much he wanted to share with the lass, yet so many things he didn't dare.

He shouldn't have sent her a missive this morn. He shouldn't have invited her to go riding. But after hearing Ciar's words of encouragement, Robert could think of nothing else but seeing Janet again. Even riding alongside her and saying nothing was better than brooding in the alehouse waiting for news of Cummins.

When they turned onto the path leading to Laigh Green, he looked ahead to check for passersby. Only a single coach ambled along the river, but the lea to the west was wide open and inviting. "Is your mount ready to stretch his legs?"

Janet glanced at him with a mischievous glint in her eyes. "I thought you'd never ask." Leaning forward and striking her crop, she cued the gelding into a canter.

Robert dug in his heels and barreled past her at a gallop.

"You devil!" she shouted, gaining speed behind him.

He looked over his shoulder and chuckled. Just as he'd thought, Mr. Ellis fell farther and farther behind. Though lanky, he was a large man and oversize for the pony carrying him. Robert slowed enough for Janet to catch up. "When we reach the top of the hill, turn left and ride for the copse of trees. That ought to buy us a moment's respite."

Janet followed, giggling all the way, and when they pulled their horses to a stop, she fanned her face. "My, that was fun!"

Oh, how he'd missed her smile. "How is the gelding?"

The horse stood snorting in air and shaking his head. "I think he liked the run as well."

"Let us continue into the wood. Ellis will be on our heels soon enough." Only a moment ago, there had been so many things he wanted to say, and now Robert couldn't think of a one, or how to start. *Might as well begin where we left off.* "How is your father?"

"Well, I suppose. We recently received word that I have a new brother." She bowed her head with a heavy sigh. "Father sent me here to find—"

"Find a husband?" Robert ventured to guess. After all, she was three and twenty now.

"Aye," she whispered.

"Have you had much success?"

"None."

Robert's stomach flipped over. If only he could reach across and pull her onto his lap, ask her to be his bride, kiss her, show her how much he'd missed her, and tell her she'd best not think of any man but him.

"How is Emma?" she asked.

"She misses you." *So do I.*

"I miss her as well. I've oft written to her, though all the letters are still in my trunk."

"Why not dispatch them?"

Janet's cheeks flushed red. "Da forbade it."

"I see." Pursing his lips, Robert looked up through the trees and watched the clouds sail overhead. No use pursuing that line of conversation further.

"Were you able to arrange a recital for her to play her harp?"

"I did."

"Och, I wish I could have been there."

"You would have enjoyed it. She was marvelous." During the entire performance, Robert had pined to have Janet beside him. "Ah…how have you enjoyed Glasgow?" he asked, changing the subject.

"It has been diverting. My aunt means well, but she's a bit suffocating. The only reprieve I can manage from her meddling is the time I spend reading to the patients at the soldiers' hospital."

"Oh, aye. The hospital." Robert gestured over his shoulder. "Does Satan incarnate accompany you there as well?"

"Unfortunately, he does—ever since the Jacobi…ah…I mean the white rose incident."

"You mean the Stuart symbol?" he asked, being clear but not obvious in case anyone was lurking.

"Aye."

"What happened?"

"Och, that is right, you couldn't have kent what happened." Janet drew the reins through her gloved fingertips. "I found one with the petals plucked in my coach, and then another on my seat at the organ recital."

"Petals plucked?"

"Mm-hmm."

"That's odd—menacing, even."

"Kennan and Ciar think so—and Auntie Dallis had one of her spells when she found out." Janet glanced back, inclining her head toward Ellis, who had crested the hill. "Hence my own personal guard."

But this news of petals plucked from a white dog rose troubled Robert. "Where was your coach when you found the first rose?"

"At the hospital. And the driver said he didn't see a soul."

"'Tis odd. Have Ciar and Kennan checked into it?"

"Not exactly. They have no description, no witnesses. Even if we found the culprit, what are we to do? Arrest him for disfiguring roses?" She smiled, that same flash of mischief twinkling in her eye. "I do believe Mr. Ellis is about forty paces away from joining us. Shall we give him another wee run?"

Chapter Thirty-One

*T*he measly hour with Janet didn't last long. When she and Robert arrived at the town house, Lady MacLean hastened outside, giving him dagger eyes as if he were a barbarian about to throw the lass over his shoulder and carry her off to his Viking ship. Obviously he wasn't invited in for refreshment. Downtrodden, he headed for the alehouse. Why the devil did he insist on pursuing a woman he couldn't have? Before arriving in Glasgow, he'd nearly stopped thinking of Janet every other minute of the day. For the love of God, he was a masochist. If he was serious about courtship, all he need do was stroll up Salt Market Street. Affluent young heiresses idled their time away shopping while their fathers conducted business.

I am not in the market for a bloody wife.

He would do his duty and show his support for *the cause* at the ball and head for home. There was work to do, yearlings to fatten for the autumn sales. He hadn't seen Emma in four months. Robert grew more irritated with every step until he was met by Lewis at the door to the alehouse. Judging by the look on his face, the man had news. "What is it?"

"I found where Cummins has been, but not where he is now."

"Bloody hell, I want the bastard. He was in my grasp only three days past. How hard can it be to locate a man with a peg leg?" Robert signaled for two ales, then slid into the chair at the table with his men. "Tell me your news."

"After his surgery, Cummins was sent here to the soldiers' hospital for convalescence."

Robert's jaw twitched—the very place where Janet spent her afternoons. "How long was he there?"

"Well, once he recovered, they kept him on as a records keeper."

"God's blood, why didn't you say so before I sat?" Robert shoved to his feet, pointing his finger northward. "Miss Janet is reading to those soldiers every single day."

Lewis spread his hands to his sides. "What does that have to do with the lieutenant?"

"A great deal. She's been receiving disfigured white dog roses—and I think I ken the culprit."

Shoving his chair back, Lewis groaned. "But Cummins hasn't shown up for work in the past three days. He's not there."

"Are you positive?"

"I've just returned from the hospital. The orderlies said they haven't seen Cummins—I reckon not since you drove him away from the saleyards."

"I've heard enough." Robert grabbed his feathered bonnet and headed for the door.

"Where are you off to now?" asked Lewis.

"To do some sleuthing of my own."

Rather than head for the public stables, Robert hastened up the road and took a right on Gallowgate. The soldiers' hospital wasn't more than a mile west, an easy walk.

A brass placard on the wrought iron gate informed him that he'd arrived at the hospital. Standing in the shadows of a giant sycamore, he scanned the hedge-lined grounds. A coach waited in the drive. Six steps led to the arched entrance of the sandstone building—which, at two stories, looked as if it could have been a country residence at one time.

Unfortunately, Mr. Ellis was nowhere to be seen. Nonetheless, chances were the coach belonged to Sir Broden MacLean and was waiting for Janet.

Robert skirted the hedge to the rear of the property and slipped through a back door leading to a narrow corridor. To the right he heard the familiar sounds of a bustling kitchen. He pulled on his cuffs and affected an air of importance while he strode with purpose until he found a woman folding linens. "Good afternoon, could you please point me in the direction of the records office?"

She gave him a curt once-over. "Lost, are ye?"

He feigned a wee bit of discomfiture. "I'm afraid I am."

She pointed. "Well, you're not far off course. Two doors down on the right."

"My thanks," he said with a bow.

Just as the matron had said, Robert found the office. He turned the knob and peeked inside. The place was a shambles—parchment everywhere, half-opened drawers, ink blotches on the writing table, no fewer than five quills lying askew, and not a one in the holder.

"May I help you?" asked an elderly officer, hastening through the door.

"Can you tell me where I might find Lieutenant Cummins, sir?"

"Seems everyone is looking for that fellow, including me." He held out his hand. "I'm the officer in charge here. Captain Wainwright at your service."

"Pleased to make your acquaintance. Grant here." Robert shook the man's hand.

"What is the nature of your affiliation with Lieutenant Cummins?"

"I have reason to believe he was involved in the theft of some of my cattle a year past. My investigations have led me here."

"Cummins? A year ago, you say?" Wainwright tapped a finger to his lips while his graying, bramble-inspired eyebrows drew together.

"Aye."

"That's preposterous. Winfred had not yet lost his leg a year past."

"You are correct. I saw him myself in Inverlochy the week of Samhain, directly before the incident that claimed his limb."

"Well then, your thief couldn't be he. The lieutenant was still in uniform."

"He may have been, but I have a witness who has positively identified him as the culprit behind not only my missing cattle, but the missing beasts of several other clans who graze their herds in the mountains in summer."

"This is most disturbing. I cannot believe Lieutenant

Cummins would do such a thing—not a lieutenant in the queen's dragoons."

"Well, if you should see him, please send me word at the Caledonia Alehouse on Bridgegate. I'm Grant. *Laird* Robert Grant. I expect to be there for at least another sennight."

"I most certainly will." The captain tapped Robert's elbow. "Please allow me to see you out."

Stepping away, Robert shifted his arm aside. "I understand a dear friend of the family is reading to the fallen. Would you please direct me to where I can find Miss Cameron?"

"Ah, yes. She's upstairs. Last door on the west side."

Robert bowed. "Thank you, sir."

Before reaching the top of the stairs, he peered down the corridor. Blast it all, Mr. Ellis was lurking outside the damned door. Doubling back, he found the matron who had been folding the linens. "If I were to ask very nicely and offer you a crown, would you do me a favor?"

"What kind of favor?"

For the second time, he feigned a wee bit of embarrassment. "Och, you see, there is a wee lassie above stairs with whom I would dearly love to have a word—a wee word, mind you...Mayhap ply her hand with a kiss as well. But she has a hulking henchman following her about, and I cannot reveal my heart with him hovering behind the scenes."

She grinned. "Aye, so that is why you slipped in through the rear door? You want to make Miss Cameron swoon?"

"Mayhap a winsome sigh would do quite well." He gave the lass a wink for added benefit. "Will you help me? Tell the old lurker the coachman needs his assistance for a moment."

She held out her palm. "For a crown?"

He dug in his sporran and dropped a coin in her palm. "My thanks."

"'Tis I who should be thanking you." She slipped the crown into a pouch tied around her waist. "This coin will buy shoes for my bairns."

"A very good cause indeed." Robert waited in a window embrasure midway down the corridor while the maid told Mr. Ellis he was needed in the courtyard, bless her.

Once Ellis headed down the stairs, Robert stepped into the chamber. "Miss Janet, I need a word at once."

"Mr. Grant? Whyever are you here?"

"Never mind that, please. I haven't much time."

She closed her book and gave a nod. Hastening to take her elbow, he led her into a storage cupboard and closed the door.

"What is—"

"Wheesht." He held up his finger. Good God, she smelled sweeter than a vat of simmering lavender. His head spun, but now he had her alone, he needed to impart his findings before the bloody knave returned. "Did you ken Winfred Cummins has been working here at the soldiers' hospital all along?"

"Here?"

"Aye. How long has that mongrel been following you?"

"He's been following me?"

"I reckon so—and I also reckon he's behind your ruined white roses."

"My heavens." She covered her mouth, her eyes filling with shock. "I remember now. I even asked Kennan if he'd seen Lieutenant Cummins at the recital."

"Where you received the second rose?"

"Aye—I thought I saw him hobbling away during intermission—and then I found the rose on my seat directly after."

"'Twas he. Make no bones about it."

"Have you confronted him?"

"Nay. He's not here—hasn't shown his face since the sale." Robert grasped her shoulders. "You must be vigilant. I do not want you to venture outside without an escort—your brother or Mr. Ellis or..."

"Or you?" she asked, her gaze meeting his.

Robert's heart stuttered out of rhythm. "A-aye...and I must have a word with your uncle straightaway."

"But Sir Broden mightn't agree to see you." Her hands moved to Robert's waist as she stepped nearer.

He licked his lips, fighting the desire to pull her into his arms. "He'll see me, all right," Robert growled. "And I'll make damned sure he does."

Footsteps pounded in the corridor. "Miss Janet!" Mr. Ellis's muffled shout rumbled through the timbers.

The lass started to draw away, her mouth opening, her head turning as if she were about to give away their hiding place. But Robert wasn't ready for this moment to end. Giving in to his yearning, he drew her into his embrace and covered her mouth, stealing a kiss. His hand slid up her back, slipped over the softness of her throat, and cupped the silken warmth of her cheeks. His knees turned molten as he dared to thread his fingers into her hair—

"Miss Janet?" The man's voice grew nearer and more frenzied.

With Robert's next breath, the lass pulled away and turned. "I'm here." She slipped out the door, leaving him alone.

"Why the devil were you in there?" Ellis brayed.

"I needed a moment of respite," she replied in the smoothest tone Robert had ever heard. "That poor sentinel is facing such hardship."

The silence filling the corridor stilled the air. Robert dared not breathe—frozen in place—not a finger twitched.

"I see," Ellis finally said. "Where is your hat, Miss Janet?"

Robert glanced downward. Damnation, he held her blasted feathery bonnet between his fingers.

"Heavens, it must have fallen off," Janet said, her voice filled with wonderment.

The latch clicked. Robert stood out of sight behind the door. When Janet stepped inside, the backlighting emphasized the mess he'd made of her hair, with tendrils spiking in every direction. The lass looked as if she'd been ravished for certain. Robert held the hat up where only she could see.

"Here it is. How daft of me!" She snatched it away and slammed the door. "Shall we be off?"

* * *

The next morn, Janet sat in the drawing room with Uncle Broden, which had become their custom for the morning meal. Auntie Dallis never came below stairs before ten o'clock and always broke her fast in her chamber as she dressed for the day. Quiet morns were welcome, and Janet ate her porridge while her uncle read the gazette, oblivious to her presence.

Lionel, the butler, stepped into the chamber. "You have a caller, sir."

"'Tis a bit early." Sir Broden lowered his paper. "Who is it?"

"Laird Grant."

Janet coughed, spewing her oatmeal back into her bowl. Taking in a gasp, she hastened to cover her mouth while erupting in a cacophony.

"Are you all right, dear?"

Unable to stop coughing, Janet nodded and waved her hand.

Sir Broden looked to Lionel. "What the devil does His Lairdship want? Wasn't he here just a few days past?"

"He didn't say, sir. And aye, he took Miss Janet out to exercise her new hackney in Laigh Green."

Sir Broden heaved a sigh. "Have him leave his weapons with you and show him to the parlor. I'll be along after I've read my gazette." Once again Uncle disappeared behind his paper. "Fie, I believe it is time for Glasgow to stop growing, lest we see more vile characters knocking on my door at an indecent hour."

Janet glanced at the pocket watch attached to her chatelaine. Quarter past nine. "'Tisn't all that early."

He lowered the paper a fraction and gave her a dour look. "If I say it is too early, then it is so."

"Of course." Janet busied herself spooning another bite of porridge. Should she tell Sir Broden about Robert's suspicion of Lieutenant Cummins? She'd thought about it last eve, but then Auntie Dallis might have made a scene. She'd already made her disapproval quite clear where Laird Grant was concerned. *Cursed clan feuds.*

Janet lifted the spoon to her lips but couldn't eat. She glanced at her uncle, still reading the gazette. *For the love of God, the thing is two measly pages. I could have read it twice by now.*

When he finally set the blasted paper aside, Janet's gaze darted to her bowl.

"You'd best go above stairs and check on Her Ladyship. Doubtless she'll have your day completely planned by now."

"I will after I finish breaking my fast." Janet's reply didn't say anything about when that would be or the detours she might take along the way.

As soon as he left the drawing room, she sprang to her feet and followed on tiptoe. Down the corridor, the double doors to the parlor were closed. If only they had left them slightly ajar, it would have been far easier to eavesdrop.

"It is bold of you to come to my home." Uncle's muffled voice resonated through the timbers. "Have you forgotten the MacLeans are staunch allies of the Camerons? My sister, God rest her soul, was Sir Ewen's first wife."

Janet moved closer, pressing her ear to the door.

"I understand I may not be exactly welcome—"

"That is an understatement."

"Nonetheless, I must inform you that I have spent the greater part of a year investigating the theft of my cattle—"

"Your cattle again, is it? Aye, we've all heard about how you accused Lochiel and Kennan of thievery."

"I admit I may have jumped to conclusions, but in my defense—"

"Of course you misjudged us. Clan Grant always—"

"I beg your pardon, Sir Broden." Robert's voice boomed loudly enough to shake the door. "But if you continue to interrupt me, I will never say what needs to be said, and the matter is of grave import."

Uncle cleared his throat while Janet stifled a snort.

She could picture the dour man staring at Robert with a pinched brow. "Go on."

At least he hasn't shown him the door.

"I have not ignored the fact that the Camerons suffered losses last season as well, and I believe I have found the culprit who robbed us both." Uncle remained silent while Robert told him about Winfred Cummins, starting with Samhain, including meeting and hiring Leith Whyte, how the lieutenant lost his leg and ended up working at the hospital, the white rose incidents, and the incident at the saleyard, and finishing up with the fact that the lieutenant was at large.

She clapped a hand over her heart. She'd die if he mentioned any number of things from Glenmoriston—the parlor, the bedchamber. *Lord help me.*

She jolted when the front door opened, and in walked Kennan. Stepping away from the parlor, Janet clasped her hands behind her back. "Kennan. I didn't know you were returning this day."

"Kennan, is that you?" Of course, Auntie Dallis chose that very moment to venture below stairs.

"It is." He offered his hand and helped his aunt waddle down the last few steps.

With perspiration on her brow, she looked very annoyed, as if on the verge of a spell. "Lionel just advised that Mr. Robert Grant is in the parlor with your uncle."

"What the devil?" Anger stretched Kennan's handsome features. "Why did you not say something as soon as I walked in?" He reached for the parlor's doorknob.

"Stop!" Janet grasped his elbow. "He has uncovered the mystery of the missing cattle."

"Mystery, my arse." Kennan flung the door wide and

marched inside. "Laird Grant, you are trespassing, and I must ask you to leave at once."

Robert stood and whipped around, his fingers sliding to his dirk but grasping air.

Lionel took his weapons.

"Listen to what he has to say afore you haul off and accuse him," Janet yelled, rushing between the two men before they came to blows. "I swear on our mother's grave, I ken how feuds are started. 'Tis on account of bull-brained men jumping to conclusions afore they hear the whole story!"

Kennan threw out his hands. "Damnation, I'm beginning to think you're taking his side."

"Aye, dearest, the way you are carrying on is simply not ladylike," Auntie scolded from the doorway.

Groaning, Janet chose to ignore Her Ladyship and focused on her brother. "And I'm beginning to think that when it comes to this man, you behave like a complete and total Whig!" She thrust her fingers at the two opposing chairs. "Now both of you sit down while I relate the story once again."

Robert immediately took a seat, while Kennan waited for a nod from Uncle Broden before he sauntered to his chair. The two men crossed their arms as well as their legs and gave each other dead-eyed stares while Janet did her best to sum up recent events, much as Robert had just done.

Once she finished, Kennan tipped up his chin. "So, you are no longer blaming Camerons for your livestock losses?"

Janet held her breath while Robert unfolded his arms. "As much as I'd like to believe in *your* guilt, Miss Janet has spoken true."

Kennan snorted. "I never thought I'd hear such an admission come from a Grant's mouth."

"I would not grow accustomed to it," Robert said, straight faced. "And there is still the issue of the white roses. After all that has transpired, I fear your sister is in grave danger."

"Well then, 'tis a good thing I returned early from Edinburgh. You needn't worry about Miss Janet. I will see to her safety. I always do."

Robert eyed him. "Aye, just like you did at the Inverlochy crossing."

"There were six of them, ye bloody maggot—or would you prefer another duel?"

"Kennan!" Janet chided.

Robert placed both feet on the floor and leaned forward. "I'm ready to face you again at any time. But only if you agree to be searched. I'll tolerate no concealed weapons, and you've proved you cannot be trusted."

Kennan sat back and smirked. "I reckon I did you a favor. My wee bit of work makes your bonny face actually look like a man's."

"You're full of shite." Robert pushed to his feet but bowed his head to Janet. "Beg your pardon, miss."

"My brother doesn't behave so poorly unless you are about. I thank heavens he's otherwise a good man, though you haven't enjoyed the pleasure of observing his good-naturedness."

"Enough," Kennan barked.

Robert turned to Uncle Broden, who had taken a seat behind the writing table. "It is not safe for Miss Janet to venture out alone. If anyone sees or hears of Cummins's whereabouts, I want to hear about it straightaway." Again he bowed. "Thank you for your time. I shall take my leave."

Janet hastened to accompany Robert to the door. "Will you be attending the Duke of Gordon's ball?" she whispered.

Resting his hand on the latch, he stopped and faced her. "I will." He winked, taking her hand, and plied it with a brief peck. "I trust you will save a dance for me?"

"Most certainly. And thank you for your concern." Sighing, Janet clutched her hands over her heart as she watched him leave.

"I'd like you to stay away from him at the ball," Kennan said, leaning against the doorjamb.

Auntie Dallis nodded rapidly. "Aye, and there will be so many eligible gentlemen there. You mustn't give Grant a second thought."

Kennan draped an arm around Janet's shoulders and gave her a squeeze—a loving squeeze, albeit untimely. "Are you worried about the dragoon?"

"Concerned, aye."

"Do not be. Cummins is no longer a threat, though I cannot say the same for the Grant laird." Kennan kissed her forehead. "And I'm not certain I like the way he looks at you."

Janet pushed her brother away. "I must fetch my bonnet. Auntie and I are off to the cobbler." Tenser than the head of a snare drum, she clenched her fists and started up the stairs but stopped before the landing.

Enough is enough.

Unable to allow her brother's remark to pass, she grasped the banister and faced him. "I'll have you know, Mr. Grant has behaved with nothing but kindness toward me, and, moreover, I happen to like him." Not waiting for any of her opinionated kin to provide a retort, she dashed for her chamber.

Chapter Thirty-Two

"*I*'ve never seen such a beautiful gown in all my days," said Lena as she fastened the back of Janet's bodice, the last piece of eight layers...or was it nine?

Janet smoothed her hands down the gold silk. "I cannot say I have, either, unless a painting of Queen Anne counts."

"It does not."

The ivory virago sleeves alone were a work of art. In two pieces, they puffed at the shoulder and gathered above the elbow and again at the forearm. The top piece had been slashed vertically to allow the gold to shine through beneath. The ivory silk tapered off at the elbow, with the gold extending to three quarters. But her favorite part of the gown was the peplum skirt made voluminous by rows of gossamer ruffles, muted slightly by a short overskirt of satin in the same ivory as the upper sleeves.

Facing the looking glass, Janet ran the tips of her fingers over the delicate lace around her plunging neckline, so low it scarcely covered her nipples. "I feel a wee bit bare. Perhaps you should tuck in a modesty panel."

"Absolutely not," Auntie Dallis insisted as she flung the door wide, carrying a velvet box. Her ladyship wore a lavender gown, her flamboyant tresses piled even higher than Janet's curls and adorned with at least five purple ostrich feathers. "Now, let me have a look."

Janet covered her cleavage with both hands. "We still have the hat to pin in place." Though the collection of silk roses and feathers was more of an embellishment than a hat.

Her Ladyship stamped her foot. "Never mind the hat. I want to see this masterpiece!"

Releasing a long exhalation, Janet opened her arms and turned. "What do you think?"

"Oh, my heavens, you are stunning. I do not believe I've ever beheld a gown so lovely or a lass so bonny. What say you, Lena?"

"Aye, m'lady. I was just telling Miss Janet the very same."

Auntie Dallis pattered forward like a clucky hen. "Show us a minuet, dearest. I want to see how well the skirt holds up to vigorous movement."

"Subdued movement, I say. Minuets are stately and sloooow." Janet complied, pretending she had a partner, stepping and executing a turn with grace and precision, just as her dance master had drilled into her since the age of ten.

"Lena, retie the bodice. It needs to be tighter." Her Ladyship pointed. "See? There's a bit of a buckle on the right."

"Straightaway."

Janet moved to her place in front of the looking glass

and placed her palms firmly on her waist. "I'm already laced so tight I can hardly breathe."

"Not to worry." Auntie Dallis snorted, making every inch of her person jiggle. "If you swoon, a dashing gentleman will hasten to your aid, and that's what we want, is it not?"

If the gentleman happens to be the chieftain of Clan Grant. "I certainly hope that will not happen." Janet flashed an appropriate smile, though thinking about how dreamy it would be to swoon into Robert's arms and have him whisk her away—yet she knew her brother, her uncle, and even Auntie Dallis would muster an army before they'd allow her braw hero to kiss her hand in public, let alone ride off to the land of Happily Ever After with her in his arms.

"Pin the hat, Lena, and then I have a surprise."

Janet had learned not to relish the anticipation of her aunt's surprises. Once her hat was pinned in place, she was ready—wrapped in lace, silk, gossamer, and feathers to prance before Scotland's noblest in the hopes of catching a suitor's eye. *Saints preserve me.*

Grinning, Auntie opened a velvet box and pulled out a string of pearls holding a gold locket engraved with the profile of a beautiful lady. She opened it to reveal a miniature of the profile of a young woman. "This was my mother's, and since the Lord did not bless me with a daughter, it will go to you when I pass."

"And the miniature, is it you?"

"Aye."

With a gasp, Janet ran her finger around the circumference of the frame. "Heavens, 'tis exquisite."

Her Ladyship held it up. "And I would like you to wear it this night."

"I am honored." Janet turned to allow her aunt to fasten the necklace.

"Always remember you are the descendant of an ancient clan, a clan that has nurtured the land and fought to hold our place in the kingdom. You will make a fine wife, and you are bonny enough to marry a king."

"You will make me vain with your flattery."

"A wee bit of flattery never hurt a soul."

Janet grasped her maid's hands. "What say you, Lena? Am I ready for the ball?"

The lass smiled. "I do not see how you could be more so."

"Then we must go." Auntie gestured for Janet to proceed, and together they descended the stairs. By the time they arrived at the bottom, Uncle Broden and Kennan were waiting in the entry, both wearing formal attire—velvet doublets with gold trim and kilts in the Highland style, plaids secured at their shoulders with their clan brooches.

"God save us," Kennan said, gaping at Janet's bosom.

She threw a panicked grimace at her aunt. "See, perhaps I do need a modesty panel."

"You most certainly do not. Kennan, stop your gawking."

Flustered, he shook his head. "Where's the blue gown I brought from Edinburgh?"

"The one I wore to Samhain?" Janet asked.

"Aye."

"It was ruined after I fell down a cliff and tore it, escaping with a broken arm and, thankfully, my life. Sorry to disappoint."

"You look ravishing," said Sir Broden.

"See, that's what I'm afraid of," said Kennan, offering his elbow. "Honestly, Sister, you are too bonny to behold.

Every gentleman will be slavering to dance with you, and they'll be thinking about doing a whole lot more than dancing."

"A lass as bonny as our Janet is not about to find the suitor of her dreams wearing a smock," chided Her Ladyship. "Now stop your critiquing and lead the way to the coach."

Janet teetered and nearly swooned into her brother. What would she do if some unfortunate gentleman did fancy her? Someone other than the one man she wanted?

* * *

Wearing their Jacobite garters and holding glasses of champagne, Robert stood beside Ciar, doing his best to appear genteel, though the starch in his new neck-cloth was enough to make him wish for the Highlands and a simple life in a bothy...with Miss Janet disrobed and bathing. The two men chatted while the guests proceeded through the welcoming line. Young MacDougall leaned in and cupped his hand over his mouth. "The king is in line beside the duke. I'm surprised to see him greeting the guests."

Robert raised his glass high enough to conceal his lips. "Aye, but he looks like French nobility and sounds like one, too, especially since he's being introduced with the newly created title of the Duke of Touraine."

"What did you expect? His father was forced into exile when he was a bairn. Doubtless he *sounds* French. But he's a Stuart king, of the pure royal line, we mustn't forget."

"Thank the good Lord for small mercies."

As the words left Robert's lips, the steward boomed, "Sir Broden, Knight of the Order of the Thistle and his wife, Lady MacLean, their nephew, Kennan Cameron, heir to the Lochiel chieftainship, and their niece, Miss Janet Cameron of Lochiel."

"Interesting the steward added the heir part. Is that new protocol?" asked Ciar.

"I doubt it." Robert leaned to the side, trying to catch a glimpse of Janet. "The added information is for the edification of Gordon's esteemed guest."

"Oh aye."

On the arm of her brother, the object of Robert's affection moved into the hall. Truth be told, the woman all but floated. In that moment, the crowd disappeared into oblivion while he beheld the most absorbing vision he'd ever seen. Janet Cameron had always been bonny, but tonight she looked more radiant than a sunset, more stunning than a queen, and more precious than a diamond.

"Careful there, Grant." MacDougall nudged him. "You'd best collect your chin from the floor afore someone treads on it."

Straightening, Robert gave his friend a leer and guzzled the dregs of his champagne. "If anyone dares look twice at her, I'll invite him out back and give him a royal hiding."

"Royal is right. It seems the Duke of Touraine has already taken a fancy to her." Ciar inclined his head toward the king, who was plying Janet's hand with a languid kiss, then clutching her fingers over his heart, the devil.

"Ballocks and bloody pig's sweat," Robert spat under his breath. "The man is married."

"He is, though it seems the higher up in the aristocracy a man climbs, the freer he is with his—ah—*sword*."

"You are baiting me, ye bastard." Damnation, his jaw began twitching.

"Perhaps, but I do not believe I've had more fun than I have watching your face in the past half minute."

Robert pulled Ciar behind one of the ballroom's enormous pillars. "I'm more worried about Janet's brother interfering than I am about *His Grace*—we all ken the Duke of Touraine has more important affairs to attend to this night. But I have a plan: Cameron cannot stay away from the cards—I need you to keep him in his cups and at the tables in the card room whilst I—"

"Dance all evening with the bonniest lass at the ball?" Ciar shoved Robert's shoulder. "I reckon a host of other gentlemen will want to dance with Miss Janet, including myself."

Robert took a backward step, barely believing his ears. "What are you saying? Are you smitten with her?"

"Of course not."

"Why are you not?"

"I just may be fishing in someone else's loch."

"You dog, a woman is pregnant by you?"

"Of course not. Good God, when it comes to riddles, you have no imagination. If you must know, I have my sights on someone else."

"Whom?" Robert demanded.

"Ah...I-I'm not prepared to discuss the matter as yet. I'm still at large, if you will." Ciar glanced aside and ran his hand over his hair. "So, as you were saying, you desire for me to deter Kennan for a time, aye?"

"All bloody night if you can. I'll be in your debt."

"And believe me, I may have cause to call upon it someday soon."

After Ciar left to find more champagne and chat with Kennan, Robert mingled on the fringes of the crowd, keeping his distance from Janet and her kin, but watching her out of the corner of his eye. Not long after, the first dance was announced.

It was no surprise that the guest of honor chose Miss Cameron for his partner and led her to the floor. Robert's jaw continued to twitch as he folded his arms. *Patience, the evening has only begun.*

As a minuet began, Sir Broden bowed to his wife across the aisle in the women's queue. Leading the dance at the head of the two lines were the Duke of Gordon and his wife. With raven hair and skin like amber, the woman was a beauty in her own right. They looked happy dancing together, exchanging intimate touches—a sly glance here, a wee smile there. Robert longed to know that kind of love someday, though he could hardly admit the fact to himself, let alone anyone else. If he couldn't find a way to lure Janet away from her family, there might be no hope for him ever to find happiness.

Down the hall, Ciar and Kennan were laughing like the old friends they were. So many of his allies held forth about the Cameron heir's strength of character, but Robert didn't see it. He moved toward them, stopping behind a pillar where he could eavesdrop.

"I hear the duke is serving his finest whisky in the card room," Ciar said, bless him.

"Aye?" Kennan asked. "Gordon spirit is the best in Christendom if you ask me. We'll need to slip inside and sample a dram or two. Though after Samhain last October, I'm inclined to keep better watch over my sister."

"She looks bonny tonight for certain, but I'd reckon your auntie will ensure she stays out of mischief. Her Ladyship told me she already has a host of potential suitors lined up to dance with Miss Janet."

"That she does. In the coach ride here, Auntie recited the name of every available gentleman within fifty miles...Come, then. The whisky's calling our names; besides, I hate dancing."

Robert chuckled to himself as he plucked another glass of champagne from a passing steward's tray. Kennan Cameron was well known for his prowess with a blade and his aptitude as a ship's master, but every lass north of Fort William could protest sore toes from his clumsy dancing.

Robert's gaze meandered back to the dancers and stopped when met with a wide and enticing blue-eyes. Her white teeth slowly scraped her bottom lip, and his loins stirred to life.

The dance demanded a glissade to the right and she stutter-stepped—it was the first time he'd seen her misstep when dancing, and it made him grin. To hell with the king. Miss Janet's attentions were elsewhere. Robert didn't give a rat's arse about Her Ladyship's list of potential suitors, he intended to dominate the bonny lass's time.

To his chagrin, Lord Hamilton—a bloody royalist—claimed Janet for the next dance. The lass curtsied politely before casting a forlorn glance Robert's way. He gave her a wee shrug while Auntie Dallis returned his gesture with an evil eye, blast her meddling.

It wasn't until the musicians took their first recess that Robert found an opportunity to pull the lass aside. "Quickly, let us adjourn to the terrace whilst your aunt is engaged in conversation with His Grace."

Giggling, Janet latched on to his arm and grasped her skirts with one hand for a hasty retreat. "She has been suffocating and incorrigible all evening."

"And it has only begun." He opened one of the French doors, glancing over his shoulder to ensure they were unseen. Fortunately, the guests were either crowded around Gordon and the king or heading for refreshments. Ciar and Kennan were nowhere in sight, thanks to cards and whisky.

Outside, the night was clear, and more than one couple had opted to enjoy the pleasant temperature—this time of year, the days were exceedingly long, and the grounds of the manse were shadowed in impending dusk. Improvising, Robert led Janet down the steps and out to the maze of hedges. By the time they were completely alone, they were running and laughing. His heart soared as he pulled her into his arms. "Och, it has pained me to watch those overdressed peacocks dancing with you."

She rose up and kissed him, her hands sliding up his back. "Does it give you respite to ken I loathed dancing with each one of them?"

"Even the Duke of Touraine?"

"Especially the Duke of Touraine."

"Why?"

"Because he's not you, and I truly wanted you to be my first dance partner."

"You have no idea how much your words warm my heart." Cupping her cheek, he kissed her. "Och, you are the bonniest woman at the ball. You are the bonniest woman I've ever seen in all my days, and in the past nine months I have not taken a breath without thinking of you."

"Oh, Robert, I have not been able to stop dreaming of you, either."

"I cannot tell you how much your words warm my heart." He plied her forehead with a tender kiss. "Dearest

Janet, I have decided to court you properly." As long as he was improvising, he might as well dive in headfirst. He'd intended to speak to her father man-to-man when he came to Glenmoriston, but he'd not controlled the situation as he should have. Nay, Robert had allowed old feuds and posturing to mar his judgment, and he'd stood there like a wounded stag watching Janet's father take her away.

"But how can you?" she asked. "My brother—my aunt and uncle for that matter—will not agree, and we cannot forget the wrath of my father."

"I let them stand in my way afore, but never again. I love you. I loved you when I first saw you in the Inverlochy stables. I loved you when I danced across from you at the Samhain ceilidh. You ripped my heart from my very chest when you plummeted down that hill. Ever since I have been a slave to my love for you, and I give you my solemn oath, I will let no man tell me I am not worthy of your love."

"Of course you are worthy; if anything it is I who am not worthy. It is my family standing between us." Clasping his cheeks between her palms, she rose on her toes and kissed him. "Take me away from here right now. I will go to the ends of the earth with you."

"As much as I want to, I shall not. The man who runs from his adversaries is a coward. I have my clan to protect and provide for."

"And Emma."

"Especially Emma." He took her hand between his and held it over his heart. "Our charade ends tonight, and I aim to begin by having a word with your Auntie Dallis."

"Oh, goodness, you might have more luck facing Uncle Broden. At least he's not as fanatical as Her Ladyship."

"That's why I will start with her. Once I win her favor, then I'm sure to win your uncles's."

"You are braver than I am. But if you're bent on this, we'd best return to the hall. I imagine we've already been missing long enough for Auntie Dallis to work up to one of her spells."

"Does she have spells often?"

"Daily."

And Janet wasn't far off the mark. When Robert opened the French door, Her Ladyship was hastening toward them with Sir Broden in her wake. "Where have you been?" she shouted in a heated whisper.

Hmm. Clearly the woman knew better than to make a scene in front of Scotland's gentry and spoil her niece's chances at landing a worthy catch. Robert smiled and bowed deeper than necessary. "M'lady, you are just the person I am looking for." He walked inside, leading the party to an unoccupied antechamber off the main room. "Lady MacLean, I must say how bonny you look this night. Lavender suits you."

"Oh…" She patted her hair and chuckled. "Thank you, though we mustn't skirt the issue. Grant, your behavior—"

"Forgive me. You are right. I was brash in stepping just beyond the doors so as to have a brief word with Miss Janet. You have my oath it will not happen again."

Her Ladyship smacked his shoulder with her fan. "That is right, it will never happen again, because I will not—"

"In the future, I will seek your approval ahead of time…" No matter how much he wanted to relieve the woman of her fan, Robert remained composed. "Because I fully intend to see Miss Janet often."

"But you—"

"Aye, and I intend to stay in Glasgow and prove to you that I am willing to cast all my differences with Clan Cameron aside and start anew, if you will."

Her Ladyship whipped around to her husband. "Broden, you must do something!"

Robert grasped Her Ladyship's hand and plied it with a polite kiss. "It is most excellent to make your acquaintance, Lady MacLean. I do hope we can become staunch allies." He bowed to Sir Broden. "And you, sir, I am your indebted servant. Please do not hesitate to call upon me as you see fit."

The knight bowed. "Grant, would you be prepared to sign a writ declaring your change of heart toward Clan Cameron and her allies?"

"That is a wonderful idea. When can you have papers drawn?"

Sir Broden stuttered, looking a bit flustered. "I'll need have a word with my advocate first."

"Of course." Robert bowed again. "With that settled, please allow me the honor of dancing with Miss Janet for the duration of the evening."

Her Ladyship vehemently shook her head. "Absolutely not."

"The next set then?"

Janet stepped beside Robert, clasping her hands. "Please, Auntie. I want to dance with him."

"Go on, let her have her fun," said Sir Broden.

Auntie Dallis again wielded her fan, smacking her husband's arm as if he were a traitor. "Broden!"

The man gave her a frown, and Robert could have sworn he heard him growl. "Grant is a well-established and propertied member of the gentry. Half the fops you have lined up to dance with our poor niece may have titles, but they are paupers. This Highlander has made clear his intentions and, more importantly, has cast aside his animosity and centuries-long blood feud with our kin. I reckon he's entitled to a few turns on the ballroom floor."

Robert thrust out his hand. "I say, sir. You are a good man."

Sir Broden glanced toward his wife, his face flushed. "At least someone thinks so."

* * *

The next set passed in a blur. The fever in Robert's every touch, the intensity in his glances made Janet feel as if she were floating on a cloud. Being so close to him, yet unable to wrap her arms around him, to hold him, caress him, and say how much she'd admired him as he boldly faced her kin, was like sitting before a sugared plum yet being unable to eat it.

Nonetheless, Janet was in heaven. Topping off her euphoria was that Uncle Broden had finally shown Her Ladyship her place. It was a story to go down in history.

When the musicians stopped for their second recess, the hall grew oddly silent. Kennan staggered from the card room, his hair disheveled, his eyes droopy.

"Grant. There are a great many lassies in attendance. Why must ye tarry wi' me sistah?" Kennan garbled.

Ciar draped his arm over her brother's shoulders. "Pay no mind to him. He's tipped the bottle back a few too many times."

Robert tugged Janet behind him. "Ciar and Kennan, dear friends. I'm certain His Grace's honored guest, the

Duke of Touraine, will be interested to see how well we put old clan feuds behind us."

"Ol'?" Kennan's face grew red. "Wha' the blazes are ye yammerin' abou' ...?"

Robert shook hands with Ciar. "Ye see? This man I call my friend. You do as well, do you not, Cameron?"

"Aye."

"As I told your uncle earlier this eve, I say the same to you: From this day forward, I am forgiving and forgetting all past feuds between our clans." He extended his palm toward Janet's brother. "Will you shake hands with me, friend?"

Janet pressed praying fingers to her lips. *Please take it, Kennan, please.*

Her brother eyed the man who'd just pledged his love for her. "Is this one of yer tricks?"

Robert spread his arms to his sides. "In front of our betters? And before so many members of Scotland's gentry?"

Appearing to sober a bit, Kennan gave a cautious nod. "I will take your hand, and this had best not be a ploy to woo my sister under your spell."

Janet released a breath she hadn't realized she'd been holding as the two men joined hands. Robert stepped in and whispered something in Kennan's ear—something that made her brother's eyes pop. For a moment she thought Kennan might take a swing, but Ciar pulled him away. "Come, I reckon 'tis time to switch to a beverage less potent."

As they headed back to the card room, Auntie Dallis stepped in and insisted she had experienced one of her spells and thus decided it was time to take Miss Janet home.

Chapter Thirty-Three

$\mathcal{J}$ust after dusk, Winfred sat on his horse, stopped on the fringe of the Duke of Gordon's lands while he watched the glow of the candlelight as the royal ball took place, all too aware that none of Her Majesty's highest-ranking officers were in attendance. To the depths of his soul he knew this was an unlawful Jacobite gathering, but since he'd lost his leg, no one listened to him. Once he'd been an officer, a leader of men, and now he was mocked and pitied.

And now he'd been forced into hiding by that meddler Robert Grant. When the faint sound of music floated on the cool evening's breeze, Winfred turned his horse. This was the chance for which he'd been waiting.

* * *

After bidding good night to Janet, Robert stepped into the smoke-filled card room. Through the haze he spotted Ciar at one of the round tables. MacDougall sat beside Kennan, and in front of each was a pile of coins and a tankard of ale. When Ciar glanced over, Robert gave a bow and a clipped salute to tell his friend he was leaving. With Janet gone, he had no reason to tarry.

Then he found the Duke of Gordon and the king surrounded by admirers. He managed to sidle in to pay his respects. "My compliments, Your Grace. I believe this is the finest ball I have ever attended—and that includes those presented by the crown in London."

"Thank you, sir. It was fortunate you were able to come and meet our esteemed guest." The duke gestured to King James.

Robert bowed. "Your Grace, I am honored to have met you. Please accept my sincerest wishes for your health. I look forward to our next meeting."

The king glanced to his garters and clapped Robert's arm. "I do as well, Grant. I've heard favorable things about you and your army."

"Indeed. My clansmen have supported Scottish kings since afore the time of the Bruce."

"I am heartened to hear it." The king placed his bejeweled hand on Robert's shoulder. "I have every confidence that your loyalty will be rewarded."

Robert again bowed, deeper this time. "Thank you, Your Graces."

Having imparted an appropriate farewell, he took a coach back to the alehouse, where he found his men.

Lewis beckoned Robert to their table, the air thicker with smoke than the card room had been. "You're back a fair bit earlier than I thought you might be. Did everything go well?" Lewis gave him a once-over. "I see no blood."

Chuckling, Robert reached for an empty tankard and poured from a ewer of ale. "Pull yer miserable head in. I end up bloodied once in my life and you think the worst every time I venture out."

"Mayhap when there are Camerons about. But I'm glad you did not ruin your finery."

"I am also." Robert raised his tankard. "Listen well, men. I have called a truce with Clan Cameron. And I expect every one of you to honor it."

"What if they provoke us?" asked Jimmy.

"Then I must have word of it afore anyone takes up arms against them."

"What if they take up arms afore we can talk to ye?" As always, Jimmy was persistent.

"Do what you must to defend yourself. No more. Let no Cameron accuse a Grant of malice."

Lewis shook his head. "I never thought I'd live to see the day."

"Och, I kent the end of the feud was near as soon as we rode into the hills with Miss Janet," said Tormond. "That or else we'd be attacking Achnacarry this very moment."

"There are many battles to be fought, though I reckon the days of clan feuds are numbered." Had they been in Glenmoriston, Robert would have said more about the need for all Highlanders to stand together and support James in the succession but eavesdroppers might consider such talk treasonous, especially in the Lowlands.

He held his tankard high. "To Clan Grant, stand fast, stand sure!"

"Stand fast, stand sure." They boomed the clan motto, then raised their tankards and drank.

"The stale smoke in this place is not agreeing with

me." Robert gave Lewis a nudge. "I'm stepping out for some air."

"I'll go with you."

"Nay, stay and enjoy yourself. I have a great deal on my mind."

"All right, then. Keep clear of Trongate. Word is some poor sop was dirked there last eve."

"Dirked, aye?" Robert snorted. "Soon Glasgow will be as bad as London."

Straightening his sword belt, he opted to head northwest, walking through the closes and alleyways until he arrived at the MacLean town house.

As his gaze swept up to the third-floor windows, ice shot through his blood.

* * *

When Janet arrived home, she hummed and danced all the way up the stairs.

Lena was waiting in her chamber with a broad smile. "It sounds as if you had a lovely time."

"It was glorious." Janet swayed, still hearing the music, while the maid unlaced her gown and placed it in her trunk.

"All the gentry in their finery," Lena said as she closed the lid. "I would love to attend a ball one day."

"It was a night I shall never forget." Janet sashayed through the chamber and sat on the dressing table stool.

Lena started the task of removing hairpins. "Did you dance all night?"

"I did."

"Forgive me for asking, but I'm curious. Did any gentleman strike your fancy?"

Janet flipped open her fan and covered her face—all but her eyes. "There may have been one."

"Och, 'tis exciting. Have you met the gentleman afore?" Pins removed, Lena picked up the brush.

"Aye, I ken the gentleman well."

Lena's hand stilled. "If you already ken him well, then why are we in Glasgow to find you a husband?"

"Because the gentleman isn't exactly on good terms with my father."

Covering her mouth, Lena gasped. "Do not tell me ye are speaking of the Grant laird."

Janet gave the lass a wee backhand with her fan. "Since when did you become so opinionated?"

"Forgive me. I spoke out of turn."

"Nay." Janet sighed. "But Mr. Grant made it clear he was prepared to cast aside all differences between our clans because he intended to court me." Janet's insides leaped.

"Intended? My, it sounds as if he behaved quite boldly."

"Aye, you should have seen him, and he rendered Auntie Dallis speechless."

"He didn't!"

"He did."

"Och, I would give an entire month's pay to see such a sight."

Janet stood and shook out her shift. "I never would have believed it if I hadn't seen it for myself."

"So what now? Will we be seeing more of Grant?"

"I suspect we will. Though we've yet to win over Kennan."

"And your da."

The mention of her father made her stomach squeeze.

"That will be the tricky part. Perhaps I can enlist Uncle's help on that account." Janet twirled in place. "I have no idea how I'll sleep."

"But you must. Shall I turn down the bedclothes for you?"

Janet plucked a book from the dressing table and sat on the chair in front of the hearth. "I think I'll read for a bit. You go on and go to bed."

Lena curtsied. "Thank you, miss."

"Nay, thank you, lass."

Try as she might, Janet couldn't concentrate on reading, either. Setting the book aside, she yawned. *Perhaps I am tired.* Still dancing, she blew out the candles, leaving only the oil lamp burning near the bed.

Then she turned down the bedclothes.

In the blink of an eye, a cold chill slithered across the back of her neck.

Clutching her hands to her stomach, she drew in a sharp gasp. Elation turned to terror gripping her stomach, making her every muscle freeze.

A plucked white dog rose lay atop the mattress, a dagger through the center, pinning it to the bed. Before Janet could think, a figure lurched from behind the bed-curtains. Clutching her chest, she ran toward the door, but a hand clamped over her mouth and jerked her back, knocking the oil lamp to the floorboards.

Chapter Thirty-Four

$\mathcal{J}$anet screamed, though her cries were muffled by the brutal hand over her mouth. She thrashed and kicked, desperate to free herself from the beast's iron grip, her mind frenzied, every nerve spun taut with fear. But when the man thrust the point of a dagger at her throat, she froze. Panting, unable to control her breath, Janet shifted her eyes from side to side as she searched for an escape.

"Shut your bloody gob," he growled, pulling her away from the flames creeping from the fallen oil lamp. Janet's blood ran cold at the sound of Lieutenant Cummins's voice. "You ruined my life, and now we will burn together in the fires of hell."

She shied away from the knife, her head pushing into him. "Noooo," she garbled through his fingers. A bead of sweat bled from her forehead as the flames climbed up the coverlet and ignited the bed-curtains. Dear God, she was going to die at the hand of this madman. Smoke billowed around them. Her eyes burned and watered as she panicked, pressing her body against the devil. In a rush of courage, she stomped on his instep.

"Bitch!" Cummins staggered and shoved her to the floor.

Janet's head hit the chair leg hard. She winced. "Ow!"

"Whine all you want, wench. I prefer a woman who moans." Tottering toward her, he began to loosen his falls. "I will take my plunder whilst we burn."

"Stop!" she shrieked, scooting away and dragging her feet beneath her.

"Yes, it pleases me to see the terror in your eyes. Fear me, wench!" He dropped to his knee, his peg leg scraping the wood behind while he grabbed for her shoulders.

Janet ducked away from his hands. She sprang to her feet and dashed toward the door. "Help!" she cried, lunging for the latch. Cummins caught the hem of her shift and yanked so hard Janet's head whipped back. As she thudded to the floor, the blackguard launched himself atop her. "You will be mine!" He yanked up her hem, the smoke choking her while the flames leaped from the canopy to the ceiling.

"Help!" Janet screamed, praying for a miracle, fighting to slide out from under the madman. Tears flooded her eyes. She sputtered and coughed while struggling with all her strength.

An ember fell beside her head. "Help!" she yelled over and over, while she wrenched a hand free and slammed her fist against the lieutenant's temple.

"You shrew!" he bellowed, swinging his arm back with an open hand.

Janet winced, protecting her head with her arm.

The door flew open. She sucked in a whoosh of air while the fire behind them leaped.

Lunging inside, Robert stopped Cummins's hand in midstrike and dragged the brute off her. "I'll kill you for this, you ragged-arsed fiend." The silver of His Lairdship's eyes gleaming with rage, his voice low and deadly, he swung at the scoundrel's jaw.

The dragoon ducked, wrenching his arm way and skittering toward the flames. "You! Just the man I wanted to see." Cummins cackled like a madman. "The pair of you will die here this very night!" Gnashing his teeth, he drew a flintlock from his holster. The blaze leaped behind the viper as if he were Satan incarnate.

Robert kicked the pistol as it fired. Still coughing, Janet scooted toward the door, gasping for air while Robert drew his dirk. "Come at me."

"No!" Cummins's eyes were wide and crazed. "We burn!"

Bless the saints, Lionel and the servants barreled inside with buckets and blankets, racing for the flames. Hissing filled the air as the men emptied their pails.

The lieutenant lunged to the floor, reaching for his dagger. "You're traitors, the lot of you!"

"Watch out!" Janet warned as Cummins slashed the blade through the air, hobbling toward the servants. As he raised the weapon over his head, Robert grabbed the brute's wrist and stopped the attack as he wedged himself between Winfred and the men battling the fire with blankets.

The two men faced each other, snarling in a bout of strength while the razor-sharp blade shook between them. Scowling, Robert gained the upper hand, shifting the point of the dagger toward the madman. Slowly, torturously, the knife inched toward the weaker man until, in a heartbeat, Robert overpowered him, striking the blade straight across Winfred's gullet. The evil man dropped to his face, the water from the buckets mingling with his blood and pooling red.

"Miss Janet!" Robert dashed to her side and wrapped his powerful arms around her. "Did he hurt you?"

"I-I-I—" Heaven help her, she curled into his warmth, his strength, his security while she caught her breath. "Nothing but a bruise or two."

Lionel and the others doused the remaining flames with blankets, snuffing the fire.

On a sigh she threaded her fingers around Robert's neck. "I thought I would die for certain."

"Not this night, lass. Not until you're old, with great-grandchildren playing about your feet." He tightened his grip and stood. "I'll take you below stairs and away from this gruesome sight."

"Thank you," she said, then stretched a hand to Lionel. "I will ensure you and the men are rewarded for your gallantry."

"Bless you, Miss Janet," said Lionel, walking with them to the chamber door. "The men will indeed be indebted to you for your kindness."

She rested her head on Robert's chest as he started down the steps. "I am grateful to you most of all, my love."

"I only thank God I arrived when I did."

"The man was insane. I fought as hard as I could. But he overpowered me."

"Aye. And now he's headed for Hades." Robert stopped at the landing and looked her in the eye. "I am amazed by your bravery, your strength. With your fighting spirit, you purchased valuable time. And now you are free of him."

"I am." She raised her chin and kissed his lips. "Let us think on him no more."

"Agreed, though your aunt and uncle are waiting below. They're worried to death. Are you ready to face them?"

"In your arms I can face an army."

He kissed her forehead. "That's my lass."

She cupped his cheek, the scar making him look all the more gallant. "How did you know I was in peril?"

"I was restless and took a stroll. Somehow I ended up across from this house." A furrow formed in his brow. "Thank God I did."

"Oh, thank the heavenly stars! Janet, my dearest," Auntie Dallis called out as soon as they started down the final flight of stairs. A tear splashed on her cheek as she drew her hands over her mouth. "Are you injured, my poor sweeting? What happened up there?"

"She needs fresh air." Robert did not set her down as he stepped into the entry. "The smoke had all but overcome her."

"I'm coming good," Janet said, coughing. "Thanks to Mr. Grant's heroism."

Uncle's gaze trailed upward. "Is the fire snuffed?"

"Aye, and Winfred Cummins dead."

"So it was he?" Sir Broden shook his head.

"It was. I'm afraid the bedchamber is badly burned. I recommend all rooms above and below be vacated until reconstruction is completed."

"I've already sent a runner to Sir Donald requesting his hospitality for the night. The liveryman is hitching the horses as we speak."

Robert nodded. "With your consent, I would like to accompany you to assist Miss Janet. She has had a terrible ordeal. And—"

Before he could utter another word, Kennan bounded through the door with Ciar right behind. "What is the meaning of this? Unhand my sister this instant!"

Auntie blocked his path. "Just one moment, young whelp."

"Not until Grant sets Janet on her feet. Then I need an explanation for this untoward state of affairs." He blinked. "Are...are you wearing nothing but a shift?" Sniffing, Kennan turned full circle as he swept a hand across his bloodshot eyes. "Something's afire."

"Was afire," said Uncle. "Miss Janet had a stowaway in her bedchamber, and—"

"You bloody bastard!"

"Kennan," Janet chided, keeping her fingers firmly laced around His Lairdship's neck.

Both Sir Broden and Ciar blocked Kennan's path to Robert, who managed to smile even though her brother was behaving like a boor. He gave her a wink. "Are you well enough to stand on your own, miss?"

"I believe so." She coughed for added effect.

"Everyone's tired," he continued after setting her down. "Let us retire to the parlor, where we can explain the whole ordeal whilst we wait for the coach to come around."

Once Janet had a cloak secured about her shoulders, Robert sat on the settee beside her while she related exactly what had happened. Kennan stood at the hearth with his arms crossed, frowning and glaring at Robert throughout the soliloquy. Ciar looked on from beside Kennan as if he'd planted himself there to intercede if necessary.

By the time Janet finished, Kennan had resorted to pacing back and forth. "I didn't think Cummins had it in him to steal into my uncle's house—up to the third floor with a peg leg, no less. Good God, had I known, I never would have allowed you out of my sight, Sister." He kneeled before her and grasped her hands. "Can you ever forgive me?"

"Perhaps." It was her turn to smile as she glanced to Robert's handsome mien. "As long as you agree to a truce with Mr. Grant."

Kennan took in a deep breath as he rose. Then his gaze shifted to Robert, a bit heated at first. His lips thinned, then he bowed his head. "I owe you a debt of gratitude for rushing to my sister's aid. Please tell me, how did you come to be in such proximity to the town house?"

"I couldn't sleep and stepped out for a bit of air. I was across the street when I saw the flicker of fire from a third-floor window—honestly, I had no idea it was hers until I heard Miss Janet's scream. And I'll tell you true, the only other time I've heard such a chilling shriek of terror was when she plummeted down the ravine at Finnach Ridge."

"Thank heavens he was there. After our sweeting shrieked, Broden and I had only just opened the door to our bedchamber, and I'd never seen such a sight," said Auntie Dallis. "I do not even think Grant's toes touched the stairs, he was moving so fast."

Kennan folded his arms, his expression softening. "The words you whispered in my ear this night. Did you speak true?"

"I am an honest man—"

"I'll vouch for that," said Ciar.

Robert cleared his throat and stood. "And to further

prove my sincerity, if I have ever spoken truer words I know not what they are."

Kennan gave a resolute nod. "Then we must make haste to Achnacarry afore word of this night reaches my father."

"So soon?" asked Auntie Dallis.

"A moment." Janet shoved herself to her feet, swooning a bit. But Robert immediately steadied her. "If it concerns me, I must know what you said to my brother, Robert."

"Very well, if you insist." His Adam's apple bobbed as he squared his shoulders. "I said, and I quote, 'I aim to marry Miss Janet. When she is mine, I vow on my life I will spend my days making her happy. Is that not what you want for your sister?'" He took her hand in his and dropped to one knee. "*Mo cridhe*, I planned to propose marriage in a more intimate setting, but I can no longer wait. Will you marry me?"

Kennan placed his hand on Robert's shoulder. "If our father grants his consent."

Janet's heart soared. She'd gone from facing certain death to being the happiest woman in all of Scotland all in one evening. Tears welled in her eyes. "I will marry you, Mr. Grant. And God save my father if he does not agree."

His smile filled the room with happiness, and as he plied her hand with a kiss, Janet did not care if all of Glasgow witnessed this moment.

Kennan squeezed his fingers into Robert's shoulder. "The two of you may have made a pact for now, but nothing is settled until my father gives his blessing."

Robert eyed him. "If I must, I will wait."

Though the night had gone from terrifying to rapturous, there was still something Janet had to settle. And it couldn't wait. "Kennan, I need to hear you apologize to Robert for using your dagger against him at the duel. You're no backbiter, and I shall not tolerate any further jibes against His Lairdship."

Kennan gaped as if smacked between the eyes. "Ah..." His astonished gaze shifted to Robert, who stood rigid and unsmiling. Without a word the big laird turned his cheek and pointed to the puckered scar. "Jesus," Kennan cursed, gulping.

"Well?" Janet grasped one of the chairs and sank her fingers into the upholstery.

"It was a rather vicious attack." Ciar clapped her brother on the nape. "And that's not like you, even considering the rift between your kin."

Dropping his shoulders, Kennan gave a nod. "I was wrong. Just couldn't admit it, is all." He thrust out his hand. "Truth be told, ye fight like Goliath, and I'd be honored to have you by my side in any battle."

Robert seized the offering, clamping his fingers around Kennan's forearm—a Highlander's grasp, which meant far more than a mere shaking of the hands. "And you, sir. You're faster than a wildcat. Next time I, too, would prefer to have you on my side."

"Och, I'm glad that's settled." Broden joined them. "I will write a letter to Lochiel and explain the goodwill Laird Grant has shown us."

Janet clapped her hands together. "Oh, Uncle, that will help us immensely. Thank you."

"Excellent," Kennan agreed. He turned to Robert. "Now, sir, I bid you good eve. The repairs to the barque are complete. We will sail for Achnacarry on the morrow, and I aim to ensure you do not take liberties with my sister again until and *if* you are properly wed."

"I, ah…Of course." Robert reached for Janet's hands. "Will you feel safe with your brother?"

If only she could say no, but they'd just managed to win Kennan over, and to disagree would be unwise. Moreover, she desperately needed her brother as an ally when they faced Lochiel. "Until the morrow."

Chapter Thirty-Five

*R*obert was all too happy to spend the fine day on deck with Janet. With her brother manning the helm of the three-masted barque, there was little more they could do than chat and stare into each other's eyes. But they were together, and Robert was content. Later they moored in the saltwater Loch Eil and offloaded the horses, with a half-dozen Cameron men riding at their flanks. At the confluence with the River Lochy, Kennan pulled his horse to a stop. "This is where we part company."

Robert nearly spat out his teeth. "I beg your pardon?" Had he given Cameron his trust only to be stabbed in the back?

But Kennan raised his palms. "During the voyage I thought long and hard about how to broach the subject of a union between Grant and Cameron with Da. You ken as well as I that my father will not welcome you straightaway. I bid you stay at the alehouse in Inverlochy until I've had a chance to explain matters."

"I'd rather do that myself. I let your father take Janet away once before, and I'll not sit idle while you do it again."

The lady drew her reins through her fingers. "Surely we can speak to Da and then he'll understand. Why insist he stay away?"

Kennan shook his head. "I won't be swayed on this. I ken what is best, and I bid you stay the night in Inverlochy, and I promise I'll send word on the morrow."

"I do not like it. What if you are not convincing enough? I should be the one to speak with Lochiel man-to-man, laird to laird." Robert's hackles stood on end. Only Lewis had sailed with them; his other men were riding north and wouldn't arrive for another two days. *Two days and I'll have the men to take Janet by force if I must.* Weighing his odds, Robert dragged his fingers through his hair. On the one hand, Kennan made sense. Doubtless Lochiel would be irate at first. The old man needed time to mull over the idea.

Still, years of feuding made him doubt the young heir's motives, even after his apology. "What say you, Janet? Is your brother speaking true, or is he about to strike me across the face?"

Kennan threw back his shoulders. "I said I was wrong. What more—"

"I. Will. Answer!" Janet boomed in a tone so commanding, every man in their party sat up and took notice. She turned her attention to Robert. "Kennan speaks true. Da has a temper like a tempest, but once it hits shore, it ebbs, and eventually the thunder and lightning are replaced by rays of sunshine."

"Do you think he will listen to *your* reason, *mo cridhe*?"

Frowning, she tapped her lip. "Perhaps if Kennan is steadfastly backing me." She thrust her finger at her brother. "Steadfastly! And with the letter written by Sir Broden, I think he might just be swayed."

"This is not agreed." Robert clenched his fingers around his reins. "I must speak to him directly."

"Understood." Kennan held up his palms—at least the man hadn't drawn a weapon. He even sounded sincere. "Let us make a wee truce."

"What say you? I turn my back so you can take a swing at me again while you plot against me with Lochiel?"

"Bloody oath, Grant, you make it difficult for me to like you. But my sister loves you. You have sworn to me you will make her the happiest woman in Christendom, and I damn well aim to hold you to it." Kennan thrust his finger northward. "Janet and I will ride on and meet with our father. If I have not sent a messenger to Inverlochy by the noon hour on the morrow, you come to Achnacarry."

"While your da places a sniper on the battlement walls, ready to shoot as soon as ye see my bonnet," Robert growled, growing angrier by the moment.

"You have my word. Clan Cameron will grant you safe passage."

"You have my word as well," said Janet.

Christ. Robert groaned. "I'll wait, but only if Janet thinks it best."

She gave him a nod. "I do, until midday tomorrow."

* * *

Janet wrung her hands, her eyes growing wide as Kennan opened the door to the library. "Is Da amenable?"

He gestured to his person with both hands. "I'm still breathing, am I not?"

"You're hardly convincing."

"I'd be lying if I said he was dancing a reel." Kennan threw his thumb over his shoulder. "'Tis your turn. Hold your head high and stick to your convictions. He'll cut ye to the quick if you do not."

She grasped his hand and kissed his knuckles. "Thank you. Now wish me luck."

He cupped her cheek. "Godspeed, Sister. You have survived his wrath before, as you will this once."

She gulped as she stepped inside the library. Da was seated at his writing table, his fingers steepled against his lips. "Ah, my wayward daughter. It seems I send you to Glasgow to find a husband and you encounter Robert Grant. Tell me, does that man follow you everywhere you venture?"

Janet looked to the missive from Uncle Broden open on his table. Surely from that and Kennan's testament, Da knew all the details of what had transpired. "I assure you my meeting Mr. Grant in Glasgow was purely by chance."

"Likely story."

"But fortuitous all the same."

"Why him? He all but kidnapped you. The man is a dastard of the highest order."

"He *rescued* me, Da. I'm certain you have already heard of his heroism regarding the fire."

"Aye, but any man can fight a cripple."

"Very well, if in your eyes Mr. Grant can do nothing heroic, then let me tell you I love him. I want to marry—"

"Ewen." Lady Jean, Janet's stepmother, entered. She

shut the door behind her. "Before this goes any further, I believe I should have my say…"

* * *

Robert sat in the alehouse with his back to the wall. He clicked open his pocket watch for the hundredth time that morn.

"Still read quarter to twelve?" asked Lewis.

"'Tis fourteen minutes to twelve, ye wastrel."

The man snorted. "Father Time enjoys playing tricks. There's never enough of it when you're working your fingers to the bone, and when you're waiting, the clock seems to bloody stop."

Robert looked to the bar, tempted to order a bottle of whisky. Unfortunately, doing so would be folly. Imagine showing up at Achnacarry in his cups, tripping over his feet, slurring his words, and most likely ending up with Kennan's boot up his arse.

He pushed back his chair and paced…until he looked out the window. "Boar's ballocks, the rascal is here." In two strides he sat, tipped the chair back, and started cleaning his fingernails with a dagger. When the door opened, Robert feigned nonchalance, though his gut was spinning like a wheel.

As footsteps approached the table, he gradually shifted his gaze until he met Kennan's blue-eyed stare. Interestingly, this was the first time he'd noticed the lad had his sister's eyes.

They look bonnier on Janet. "I was beginning to think you weren't coming," he said with a growl in his voice.

Kennan smirked. "Anxious? That's not like you."

"Aye? I reckon you might be as well if circumstances

were reversed." Robert looked to Lewis. "Give us a moment, please." Then he signaled to the barman. "Two ales over here."

Kennan slipped into the chair opposite. "Over the past month or so, I have had discussions about you with Ciar as well as my sister."

"Have you now?"

When the barman placed two tankards on the table, Robert wrapped his fingers around the handle of one, Kennan the other. Watching each other's eyes, they both drank.

"It boggles my mind," Kennan continued, "but they both reckon you walk on water."

"I doubt that."

"Hmm. What perplexes me most was Ciar told me you had my unconscious body in your arms when he arrived at the bank of the River Lochy. Is that true?"

"It is."

"Why would you ride to my aid when I cut your face only days prior?"

"Several reasons."

Kennan arched his eyebrows in question before he took another drink. "Go on then. Unless it is a secret."

Robert sat back and sighed. "First of all, I returned because I heard your sister scream. I didn't care to admit it at the time, but I've always harbored a fondness for Miss Janet and I would never turn my back on her. Never." He paused to ensure Kennan understood the depth of his sincerity. "Secondly, no matter how deeply the rift runs between our clans, in the face of another rising I would take up arms and fight beside you notwithstanding."

A furrow formed between the man's brows as he tapped his finger on his cup. "I misjudged you."

The churning in Robert's gut eased. "It has been known to happen."

"I owe you another apology. In your eyes, I imagine I've behaved like a toad."

Shifting his gaze aside, Robert gave a single nod. "'Tis difficult to cast aside centuries of feuding."

"It is. And I tell you true, last night I spoke to my da. Janet, too. He's not happy, but he has agreed to talk to you."

"My thanks. That is all I ask."

"Och, you'd best thank my stepmother. In truth, I believe she had more sway with the old man than either me or Janet."

"Stepmother?" Robert couldn't picture the woman. Janet hadn't said much about her other than to indicate there was no love lost between them—though Lady Cameron was rather anxious to see her stepdaughter married.

"Aye, if anything she seemed overjoyed with the news."

Robert shoved his chair away from the table and stood. "Then let us away."

At a steady trot, it still took two hours to reach the castle. Robert had never been inside the grand manse, but he'd seen Achnacarry from afar, and it was nothing short of palatial. In truth, one of the reasons he had gone along with his father's prejudices toward the Camerons was their lavish wealth. As with many Highland clans, their reputation was fierce; it held that when they were raided, they repaid with vengeance, burning and pillaging like savages. Now he rode beside the heir to the Lochiel lairdship straight up to the prominent double oak doors.

As they dismounted, Miss Janet cantered from the stables as if she were chasing a fox.

"What are you doing here?" Kennan scolded.

She ignored him and skidded to a stop alongside Robert. Her eyes flashed with mischief as she leaned toward him. "I've been warned not to speak to *Mr. Grant* when he arrives, but I will have him know I will be working my new gelding in the round pen for the duration of the afternoon."

He grinned. "I hope to find you there. Soon."

She gave him a wink as she rode away.

Kennan rolled his eyes. "Come, afore anything else happens. She's supposed to be in her chamber."

Robert couldn't help his chuckle. Janet wasn't one to obey orders, especially when they made no sense. Perhaps that's what had attracted him to her in the first place.

The interior of the home was as magnificent as the exterior. The walls of the entry were trimmed with mahogany paneling and festooned with paintings. Robert turned full circle, examining the portraits of Camerons—men who had opposed his kin in battle.

Kennan gestured to a servant. "I must ask you to leave your arms with the footman."

"You're jesting."

"I am not."

"Bloody Christmas." Robert removed his sword belt, his dirk, and his musket and gave them to a man who looked nowhere near as polished as Lionel in Glasgow. "I'm trusting you to watch over these as if they were your own."

The man bowed. "Aye, sir."

Kennan clapped Robert on the back. "Make no bones about it, Grant has been given leave to visit with

Lochiel. Let us ensure we show him true Highland hospitality."

"Understood."

Robert watched the man retreat with his weapons—all but the daggers hidden in his hose. Was he doing the right thing by forging this alliance? His heart said yes, but his sense of reason wasn't as convinced. Reason told him to demand his weapons back, head for the stables, open the gate, and ride for freedom like a pillaging Highlander with Janet across his horse's withers.

But then there was the Jacobite cause. The succession. Camerons and Grants alike believed in the sovereignty of the Stuart line and, until the rightful king was once again on the throne, both clans could ill afford to bicker over grazing rights and petty cattle theft. Aye, during the time of his father, the Camerons had raided Grant lands, burning crofts and thieving cattle, and Robert's clan had repaid in kind. Was either clan right?

And what of the feud? The Camerons accused the Grant woman of seducing their laird, and the Grants declared the lady had been debauched. Most likely neither party was wholly innocent, and after centuries, how could they ever uncover the truth, even though Robert sided with the woman?

The question is, will a woman be the one who ends the feud once and for all?

Kennan led the way up the old wheeled stairwell and through a dim passageway. He stopped outside an enormous door of oak studded with blackened iron nails. "He's in the library. Are you ready?"

"Is Lochiel armed?"

"I've never seen him otherwise."

"Then let us pray we find him in good spirits."

As they entered, the old knight looked up from his ledger, which was spread before him on a writing table. "Ah, Laird Grant." Though he did not stand, he gestured to the seat across from him. "Please sit. Kennan, leave us."

The son bowed. "I'll attend you outside the door."

Sir Ewen of Lochiel needed no periwig; his wiry gray hair framed his face and curled just past his shoulders. His mouth was pinched, his nostrils were flared, and his eyes took on the color of coal. "I'll be the first to say this news brought by my son last eve was nothing short of disturbing."

"Was it?" Robert splayed his fingers at his sides to ensure he didn't have a slip in judgment and lash out with a fist. "Is there any truth to the rumor I heard in Inverlochy that the Robertsons stole four and twenty head of your prime beef only a fortnight ago?"

"They did, the backbiters. And they will pay. But Kennan tells me you desire a truce. You intend to make Clan Cameron and Clan Grant fast allies."

"I believe we would serve *the cause* far better as allies than as enemies. And word in Glasgow is that James is set to launch a rising if Queen Anne's Act of Succession is invoked upon her death."

"So 'tis true then." The chief of Lochiel tapped the quill in its stand. "He made an appearance at the Duke of Gordon's ball?"

"He did. And he looks well—in his prime. 'Tis a shame we have been forced to suffer the rule of the usurpers whilst our sovereign waits in exile."

Lochiel nodded and smirked, his guarded expression softening. "I believe those are the first words from a Grant I have ever agreed with." But his humor was short lived.

He leaned on his elbow and looked Robert in the eye. "Tell me, why the change of heart? It hasn't been long since we last faced each other in Glenmoriston."

Taking a deep breath, Robert collected his thoughts. This was the one question he'd rehearsed the most, and a careless reply could ruin his chances to woo Janet forever. True, at the time Cameron had continually interrupted him, but calling the man out would only serve to deepen their ill will.

"Even then I had planned to ask you for Janet's hand. Had I been able to convince you to come inside Moriston Hall, I would have professed as much. However, I am the first to admit that I let you take her away from me too easily. In the interest of avoiding a battle, and to keep Miss Janet from harm, I made a decision I have regretted to this day whilst I watched you take away the only woman I have ever loved."

"Hmm. Love. It is such an unwieldy emotion. One that grips men by the cods and turns them into simpering fools."

"I do not think I am being foolish, sir."

"Och, Grant, you are sitting across from your greatest adversary, in his lair, and you are wearing no weapons. In my eyes, that is the act of a foolish man—a man who would allow the woman he loves to ride away with her father simply to avoid a wee scuffle."

Saying nothing, Robert pursed his lips.

"Nonetheless." Lochiel sat back and tapped his fingers together. "My daughter is quite taken with you."

"She is an astounding young woman. I am honored to have her affection."

He smirked. "Did you ken my wife's mother was a Gordon? She thinks highly of you Grants as well...and now you've even tainted my firstborn son into thinking you're some sort of saint."

Pulling on his collar, Robert stretched his neck. "I assure you, I am a man just like any other."

"Oh, are you? Ye ken I was fast enemies with your father. I was there when he set fire to the rooftops of my crofters' cottages. I listened to women scream and bairns cry. You are arrogant, self-serving, combative, and ornery—"

"I've bloody heard enough." Robert pushed his chair back and stood. Towering over the knight, he jammed his knuckles into the table. "I love your daughter like I love the air I breathe, like I love the Highlands, my home, and the heather when it turns the mountains purple in late summer. But I have never cared a lick about you because I ken ye wouldn't think twice about setting my lands to fire and sword. You've done it afore—just as you accuse my father of doing. I ken your every evil deed. You may have stolen my cattle as well, but I'm prepared to forget and forgive, especially now I've killed the culprit who culled both our herds last year—"

Lochiel unsheathed his dirk and held it aloft. "You, sir, are—"

"I am not bloody finished is what I am!" Robert didn't care about the knife in his face. Besides, he was younger, bigger, and stronger than the knight across the board. "I *will* give your daughter a good home. I *will* put her on a pedestal and worship the very ground she walks each and every day for the rest of our time on this earth. And aye, I'm willing to resolve my differences with you for that privilege, but I will not sit idle and allow you to tread upon my honor as if I am nothing but a tinker thief." Breathing deeply, Robert glared across the table, refusing to blink, demanding respect.

After a seemingly infinite pause, Sir Ewen glanced away. "If I do not approve this union, my daughter will never speak to me again. My wife, who has just given me another son, will send me to the dogs. Christ, I will even be seen as weak in my own heir's eyes." He reached for a document and slid it across the desk. "I will approve this marriage. You will sign an agreement that no Grant clansmen will ever act out against Cameron of Lochiel, and in turn, I will grant to you my daughter's dowry of twenty thousand pounds."

Robert didn't budge. "And Cameron men will adhere to the same truce?"

"Aye."

Robert blinked. Had he heard right? The sum Lochiel quoted was a fortune. And yet he would pay that same sum just to marry his love. Rather than ask again, he scanned the parchment before him. Indeed, the lass's dowry was twenty thousand pounds. With a sure hand, he picked up the quill and dipped it into the ink. "I sign this with joy in my heart. May the union between our clans endure throughout the ages. And may we march side by side when the time of the succession is upon us."

Lochiel held out his hand. "I never thought I'd say this, but you have spirit, lad. Perhaps my daughter has chosen well. Nonetheless, if I ever hear of any mistreatment on your part, you will answer to me."

"I assure you . . ." Robert grinned. "There is no need to concern yourself with that, sir."

Chapter Thirty-Six

$\mathcal{J}$anet pressed her hands to her stomach. Her eyes welled with tears as Robert strode toward her, looking like a bold and powerful man. She dropped the lead line and whip and ran toward him while he unlatched the gate to the round pen. "You haven't been skewered!" she said, laughing and crying at once.

"Is that the first thing you say to your betrothed?"

Her jaw dropped as she drew her fingers to her lips. "Oh, oh, oh!"

He opened his arms, but she held up her palms. "If you check the windows, there are at least a half-dozen pairs of eyes watching us this moment."

"I care not, I—"

"Quickly. Fetch your horse." She dashed back to her gelding and checked the ties on her satchel. She'd packed cheese, oatcakes, and wine. "Come, ye beastie, we're going for the ride of our lives." Leading the horse to the mounting block, she climbed onto her sidesaddle just as

Robert exited the stable on his black steed, an enormous grin on his handsome face.

"Lead the way, *mo cridhe*."

Her stomach fluttered as she slapped the riding crop and demanded a canter. "The day is warm, and I will take you to a place of magic!"

More than once Janet had dreamed of taking Robert to the fairy glade that opened to the River Arkaig, and she rode there now. It was always pleasant in summer in the heat of the day when midges were less prolific. She took a trail into the wood, glancing over her shoulder to ensure no one followed. Thank heavens her family had left her alone. She would die if one of her brothers came galloping across the lea, demanding she have an escort.

"Tell me about your talk with Da," she said, slowing her horse to a walk.

"We engaged in bit of posturing, but he was amenable in the end. Evidently your stepmother can be quite persuasive with him."

"Aye, especially if it means I'll be out of her hair for good."

"I'd like to meet her."

"You will. We're all dressing for a formal evening meal where the main topic will be wedding plans."

"She is plotting already?" Robert chuckled. "Your father gave his approval but five minutes ago."

"Och, she'd plotted tonight's supper last eve."

"Had I known, I might have asserted myself sooner and saved myself from listening to your father's opinion of my kin."

"Oh dear, he didn't."

"He did. I expected it, though I finally told him one way or another I intended to marry you."

Janet threw her head back and laughed. When she was with Robert, no one would tell her how unladylike laughing was. "I still cannot believe it." Nearly to the glade, she cued her mount for a trot.

The trees opened to a grassy clearing just below the waterfall of a burn that emptied into the rushing river. Robert stopped his horse beside her and looked to the canopy of leaves above. "This is beautiful."

"I love it here. 'Tis my very own secret wilderness."

Reaching across, he took her hand and kissed it. "Then 'tis mine as well. Anywhere you are brings joy to my heart."

His words brought on a wave of warmth and tingling. "I brought food and wine."

"Brilliant. Who else kens we've sneaked away?" He hopped off his horse and moved around to help her dismount.

Janet placed her hands on his shoulders. "I've told no one. I even filched the food without anyone seeing."

With a low, rumbling chuckle, he grasped her waist and lifted her from the saddle. But rather than lowering her to the ground, he pulled her into his body. "Och, I've wanted to kiss you every moment since I carried you down the stairs at your auntie's house."

Grinning, Janet wrapped her arms around his neck and looked into the fathomless silver eyes she'd once thought menacing. "Then what are you waiting for, laddie?"

His long lashes lowered, while the dimples in his cheeks deepened. Ever so slowly he inclined his lips to hers, building Janet's anticipation. The first swipe of his tongue took her breath away, while her breasts swirled with longing. Closing her eyes, she reveled in his taste, the musky scent of man and leather, and the feel of honed muscles beneath her fingertips.

She trembled with need as he lowered her to her feet. She scraped her teeth over her bottom lip, boldly meeting his gaze. "I've brought a blanket as well."

Those blessed dimples grew deeper, the sparkle in his eyes more intense. "Och, you think of everything. But before another moment passes, there's something I must do. Since your brother ruined it the first time." The sunlight shimmered in the silvery glint of his eyes as he took a knee and held her hand before him. "Miss Janet, as I sat waiting for you in the alehouse, I thought about what I'd do if your father did not give us his blessing."

She couldn't imagine. "Dear me, you must have been on edge."

"Very much so. But I decided whatever your father's decision, I would do everything necessary to make you mine. I'm only thankful things didn't come to absolute anarchy."

"I am as well."

He pulled her closer and held her hand over his heart. "*Mo cridhe*, I ken we will be the brawest couple in all of Scotland, our children will be bonny and have strength of character, and right here in this moment, I want nothing more than for you to promise to be my wife as long as we both walk these blessed Highlands."

A tear slipped down her cheek as she nodded. "As I said before and will say over and over again, I will marry you, Robert Grant, and none other. I, too, worried about my father's reactions, and if I had to steal away and ride alone over the rocky braes, nothing would have prevented me from finding your arms."

She pulled him to his feet and kissed him again,

deeper, longer and every bit as passionately as the first time.

He swept kisses along her jaw until he reached her ear. "Let us drink wine and toast to our union," he whispered, releasing her and removing the satchel from Janet's saddle.

She removed the tartan blanket and spread it over the soft grass. Once they were seated atop, she carefully pulled out the leather-wrapped parcels of oatcakes so as not to break them and set them on a plate with a lump of cheese.

Robert found two goblets and the squat bottle of wine, which he skillfully uncorked with his knife. "This looks like a king's feast."

"'Tis but a wee morsel, but all we need to maintain our strength."

"It is amazing how little we actually need, given all the comforts available to mankind." He poured and handed her a glass. "To our love. May it stand the test of time."

She tapped her goblet to his. "It will. The two of us have already endured many tests and they have only made our bond stronger."

"*Sláinte.*"

Together they ate, staring into each other eyes, talking about their future together. They could have been eating straw and Janet wouldn't have minded. Robert plucked a daisy from the grass and skimmed it along her cheek. "Ye are the bonniest lass in all Christendom."

"I suppose it would be discordant if I said you were biased."

"I am biased, and I am right."

She handed him his goblet and took a sip from hers. "Then I wholly approve of your favoritism, as long as you accept that you are the brawest gentleman in all of Britain."

He grinned, looking as tasty as sugared plums. "Only Britain?"

"I haven't traveled anywhere else," she baited him, giggling at her antics.

"Then I must convince you there are no others like me."

"Och, I ken without a doubt ye are the only man for me, Robert Grant, and that tidbit of information you can lock in your heart until the ends of time."

"That's better." He returned the plate to the satchel, then set the goblets and the remaining wine aside. Watching her, he stretched out his long limbs, resting his head on his hand. Janet licked her lips. He looked entirely delicious in repose. Unable to stop herself, she cupped his cheek. "I feel like I am floating."

"We are floating." He captured a lock of her hair and drew it to his nose and inhaled. "Merely the scent of you turns me into a lovelorn savage." He laced his fingers behind her neck and pulled her lips to his, imparting a languid, bone-melting kiss. "Lie beside me, lass."

Before she complied, Janet pulled Robert's hazard dice from the basket. "Shall we have a wager?"

"If it pleases you, m'lady. It seems luck is with me this day."

"Nines as mains?"

"Agreed." He winked.

With her first roll, a five and a four turned up.

A knowing grin played upon his lip. "Nicks. How can I do your bidding, lass?"

Reclining beside him, Janet inched up the hem of her skirt until she exposed her calf. "It has been a long time since I last felt your heart beat in tandem with mine. But this day, I believe yours never will be able to race as fast as mine is thumping now."

"I wouldn't discount it." Robert glanced back to the satchel. "Are you no longer hungry, lass?"

She was about to say no when she caught the glint in his eyes. He stared at her with a hunger that had nothing to do with the need for food. The same need pulsing through her this very moment. Since they'd first met in Glasgow, every fiber of her body had been craving his touch, craving intimacy. Her tongue slipped to the corner of her mouth as she raked her gaze along his outstretched body. "Hungry for you."

A deep chuckle rumbled from his throat while the silver in his eyes grew dark. "Come here." He drew her flush against his body, his mouth covering hers with renewed wildness while his kisses imparted toe-curling urgency. As their caresses grew more impassioned, their bodies melded together like clay. With the past days of suppressed passion boiling to the surface, Janet matched his fervor swirl for swirl while his hands slid down her back and grasped her buttocks. A new rush of desire shot through her blood as she rubbed against the thickness pressing to her mons.

Robert's lips trailed down her neck and lingered, plying the tops of Janet's breasts. His finger circled her nipple. "I need to kiss you here."

Breathlessly Janet nodded while she released the bow on her kirtle. In the blink of an eye he spread the laces, untied her shift, and exposed her breasts. He moaned while he swirled his tongue in an erotic dance.

Janet arched her back, giving her breasts to him, while her need grew. "I've lain awake each night wanting you."

Kissing and tugging, he pulled her skirts higher up her

thighs. "I haven't stopped thinking of you since the day you stitched my cheek." His gaze dipped.

"Aye?"

"And I'm dying to see you completely naked. Right now."

She gulped. "You as well?"

"Aye, me as well."

It took only moments to unlace Janet's stays, then unpin and unbuckle Robert's kilt. In a flurry of woolens, in no time they lay in each other's arms with a westerly breeze caressing their skin. "Are you cold?" he asked.

"A bit."

He wrapped his arms around her. "I shall keep you warm."

As she inhaled his masculine scent, Janet's insides turned molten. "You're as warm as a brazier."

But her skin grew even hotter while he slid his fingers down her sides and slipped a hand between her legs. She parted slightly, and he teased her with his finger before he kneeled to untie her garters. His nose only an inch from her sex, he closed his eyes and took a deep breath. "Merely the scent of you can bring me undone."

Janet shuddered while his hard body slid up hers until he claimed her mouth. Wrapped in an embrace, skin to skin, he warmed her. Still, gooseflesh pebbled her skin as his manhood brushed her abdomen. Desperately needing him lower, Janet scooted up, wrapped her leg around his hips, and swirled into him.

Robert groaned, his chest heaving. "I can hold back no longer."

"Me also." Janet's breathless words came whispered and fast.

He rolled her to her back. "Part your legs for me."

Trusting him, she opened without a moment's trepidation. "Take me."

"It may hurt your first time."

She grasped his shoulders. "Join with me and together our love will overcome any pain."

He kneeled over her, and his kisses grew reverent while his member slid to her core.

A tiny gasp caught in Janet's throat as he slipped inside.

"Am I hurting you?"

"Nay." She shook her head, gazing into his handsome face.

Slowly he inched a bit farther, again stopping with her gasp.

Needing more, she grasped his buttocks and forced him deeper as a high-pitched moan slipped through her throat. "Please. Do not stop!"

"But—"

"Ride me like a stallion colt," she begged, steeling her mind against the sharp bite.

"By God, I love you." With a final thrust he filled her. Janet held in her urge to cry out, her need for him trumping the pain. Urging him farther, she tightened her grip and circled her hips around his enormous manhood.

"That's right, lass. Make your body grow accustomed to me." Slowly he moved with her until the rhythm changed to an insatiable rocking that took her higher than she'd ever soared before. And as the pain faded, their lovemaking grew. Faster and faster Janet rocked her hips, craving friction, the tension coiling tighter and tighter inside her body. A shrill cry caught in the back of her throat, and the heavens opened with blessed, shattering release.

Robert roared and drove his hips harder still, plunging into her as his eyes lost their focus until he stopped and held himself shuddering and buried to his root. "God's teeth, you were born to breed." He grinned down at her. "You have enraptured me mind, body, and soul. I never want to live another day without you in my arms."

"Your words are music to my heart."

He nuzzled into her neck, rolling to her side. "I want our wedding day to come as soon as practicable, for I would die if your father should have a change of heart."

Janet curled into his warmth. "Stepmother is already making the guest list. Perhaps we can set the date for a fortnight hence."

"All I need is time to fetch Emma. I want her to be here."

"Oh yes, and I want her to be my maid of honor."

"Truly?" He kissed her forehead. "She would be thrilled beyond belief."

"And she would be ideal."

"Then let us make it so. I'll agree on a date with your parents, then I'll ride for Glenmoriston."

"Will you take me?"

"Och, I'd love to have you come along, but aside from the foreseeable objections from your father, you'll have gown fittings and all that goes with preparing for the wedding day."

"Blast. Will you promise to return straightaway?"

"I give you my oath. A mob of angry dragoons couldn't keep me from you. I meant what I said about keeping you in my arms forever, and as soon as we are wed I will make it so."

Chapter Thirty-Seven

$\mathcal{J}$anet stood in front of the dressing table in her bed-chamber while tingles of anticipation made her feel as if she were in the midst of a dream.

"I believe you are the bonniest bride I have ever seen." Lady Jean, Janet's stepmother, primped the veil, her eyes moist.

Over the past few weeks, the woman had become more motherly as the wedding plans brought them closer. Perhaps she'd needed something like this to feel more a part of the family. Whatever the reason, Janet was grateful. "Thank you for all you've done to prepare for this day. I ken it will be perfect." But more than anything, Janet was grateful for the lass sitting on the overstuffed chair with an enormous grin on her face. "Emma, you look so bonny, I think you are prettier than the bride."

"Och," Her Ladyship began to protest, but Janet held up a finger and shook her head.

"And there will be a grand ceilidh this eve."

Clapping her hands, Emma stood. "Do you believe anyone aside from my brother will dance with me?"

"I ken it."

"Will they fear me?"

Janet grasped the lassie's hands and squeezed. "If they do, then they can go take a flying leap off the battlements."

"Janet!" Her Ladyship scolded.

Rolling her eyes, she huffed. "Well then, curses to the superstitious. I will stand for none of it."

"I thank you both for inviting me to Achnacarry. But I want to see you, lass." Emma raised her hands.

"Very well." Janet stood still while her future sister-in-law started at her veil and lightly swirled her fingers over Janet's eyes, nose, and lips and then along the collar of her wedding gown.

Lady Jean stepped in. "I think you should—"

"She ought to continue," Janet interrupted, guiding Emma's fingers to the neckline of her bodice. "The gown is of silk and trimmed with lace and pearls."

Emma whistled when her fingers brushed across the fine fabric. "'Tis exquisite."

Lena pushed through the servants' door. "The chapel is full, and there are people standing, and I think if you do not haste to the altar Grant will combust."

Her Ladyship chuckled. "We mustn't have that. Grooms are hard to come by in the Highlands." She primped the wedding gown one last time. "I do believe all is in order."

"And the bairn?" Her new brother had already won Janet's heart.

"The nurse already has him dressed and in the chapel."

"Then all is truly in order." Janet collected her hem,

then took Emma's elbow. "Let us walk side by side. Then, once we reach the chapel, Ciar MacDougal will escort you down the aisle and you'll stand beside me whilst Robert and I take our vows."

Emma sighed, and her smile grew radiant. "I still cannot believe you chose me as your maid of honor."

Janet kissed her dear almost-sister on the cheek. "I would have none other."

Funny; with Emma beside her, Janet felt no prewedding jitters. She was ready. Happiness filled her wholly, as if the ground beneath her feet were but clouds.

* * *

Pacing the vestibule of the Cameron family chapel, Robert clicked open his pocket watch and stared at the blasted thing, willing it to tick faster.

Kennan leaned over. "Has the bloody timepiece stopped working? By the way you keep pulling it out, I reckon 'tis on the verge of busting a spring."

Robert stuffed the damnable thing back in his waistcoat pocket. "You sound like my henchman."

Ciar gave him a slap on the back. "I cannot say I blame you. It must be exasperating to stand before God and pledge undying love to a single woman for the rest of your days."

"I agree there," said Kennan.

"I reckon that's on account of neither of you sops ever being in love afore."

"I've been in love plenty," said Ciar, thumping his chest. "'Tis just I fall out of love nearly as fast."

"God save the woman you marry."

"I'm with him." Kennan threw a thumb Ciar's way. "It

is as easy to fall out of love as it is into. Mayhap easier once you've met the lassie's kin."

Robert swiped a hand across his eyes. If the bride didn't make an appearance soon, he just might grab the cleric, make an insane dash across the grounds, barrel up the stairs, open every door until he found Janet, and marry her on the spot. To hell with the guests and his wayward groomsmen.

"Aye," Ciar continued. "It was not all that long ago you were a wandering buck yourself."

"Wheesht," Robert shushed them. True, he might have been a bit of a rogue, but that was before he fell in love with Janet. Since, he'd lived like a monk for the better part of a year. He'd be loyal to her until the end. He couldn't even think of looking at another woman—not ever again.

The door opened, thank God. Sucking in a sharp breath, Robert faced it. Lady Jean stepped inside with Emma on her arm. "Merciful Father," he mumbled, barely recognizing his sister. Not only was she dressed like a princess, she could be an angel, her face brighter than he'd ever seen it. "What have they done with my wee lassie?"

"She's no wee lass anymore," said Kennan, the rake.

"Do I look as bonny as they say, Robert?" Emma asked. "Tell me true, for I do not believe it."

Before he could answer, Ciar stepped in and took her arm. "Och, believe it, Miss Emma. You're so radiant this day, only a bride can compare. Are you ready?"

"I am."

A footman escorted Her Ladyship down the aisle and, on cue, the bagpipes began a march. Ciar took Emma next, which made Robert's hackles rise a bit.

After all, he was solely responsible for his sister and would tolerate no foolishness where she was concerned. Kennan followed, taking the arm of one of Janet's cousins, and then Robert proceeded forward, his kilt slapping the backs of his knees as he proudly took his place beside the priest and waited for his bride to make her grand entry.

The music slowed and grew statelier. Both doors to the chapel opened. Sir Ewen stepped forward with his daughter on his arm. Initially Robert saw only snippets of a blue gown and gossamer veil from behind the imposing form of her father. But when they turned to walk along the aisle, his knees turned to boneless mollusks.

The music faded.

The guests vanished.

Even Sir Ewen paled and blurred.

Robert somehow managed to breathe. His mind consumed with the beauty moving toward him, he could do little else but gaze upon his heart's desire. Happiness radiated from her smile. Her eyes shone like sapphires. Smooth skin, a slight blush to her cheeks, blonde curls peeking from beneath a sheer veil.

I cannot believe I am so lucky as to be marrying this woman.

As father and daughter stopped beside him, Robert clutched his hands behind his back to keep from taking her away from Lochiel before the priest asked, "Who gives this woman in holy matrimony?"

"I do," said Sir Ewen, making Robert's heart soar. The fierce chieftain of Lochiel uttered two wee words without argument, without bravado. And those two words opened the door for happily ever after.

Chanted in Latin, the Catholic service continued.

While Robert held Janet's hands, he gazed into the bonniest eyes he'd ever seen. While they stood together before God and their kin, Robert knew this was the most righteous, most holy, most honorable act of all his days.

At the end of the rite, he slid his mother's sapphire ring onto Janet's finger—the ring he'd retrieved when he'd ridden to Glenmoriston to fetch Emma. "To match your eyes, my love." And then he kissed her. Right there before a clan he'd never thought could be an ally, he kissed the woman who was now and would always be his wife.

Chapter Thirty-Eight

*E*njoying the wedding feast, Janet sat primly as a bride ought, though she held Robert's hand beneath the table. From the time she entered the chapel, everything had passed in a blur, but the one thing she would remember forever was the magnificent Highlander whose eyes did not stray from hers throughout the entire ceremony. Who knew she would fall in love with a man she'd once considered a rascal and a rogue? A man who'd accused her kin of cattle thievery, and whom she'd suspected of the same? A man who'd fought her brother in a deadly duel of swords?

Gooseflesh rose on her skin as she smiled at her husband.

No, he was none of the things she'd thought before. He was brave and honest and true. He'd ridden to her rescue, not once, but many times. Twice she would have died if it hadn't been for her hero. He'd cast aside his own preconceptions, his own inbred prejudice, and together they had hewn a bridge out of love.

Robert plucked a wild strawberry from the serving platter and held it to her lips. "For you, *mo crìdhe*."

The sweet tartness tantalized her tongue. "Heavenly."

"But not as delicious as you." He inclined his lips toward her ear. "How much longer must we endure these festivities? I want you to myself."

Covering her mouth, she almost laughed aloud, which would be most unladylike. "There are two more courses and then dancing. We mustn't be rude."

He swilled his wine. "If it pleases my bride, I will wait."

She winked. "As will I."

The meal was perfect.

"Will you be taking over the menu planning at Glenmoriston?" asked Emma from across the table, her expression a tad uncertain.

Robert squeezed Janet's hand, though he didn't try to answer on her behalf. Honestly, the wedding plans had been all-consuming, and there hadn't been much time to think beyond this day. Of course Emma would be anxious. Janet smiled. "You are so proficient at it, I do not see any reason to change."

The lass sighed. "I was hoping you'd be agreeable."

"Mayhap we can discuss the duties involved in running Moriston Hall on our ride home?" Janet suggested.

"I'd like that."

Da had hired a proper Highland orchestra with fiddle, pipes, drums, and flute for the dancing, and after the meal they took their places for a country dance.

Lochiel tapped his glass. "Afore the merriment begins, cheers to the bride and groom. May their lives be long, their children be braw and happy, and their coffers always be brimming with coin."

"*Sláinte!*" roared the crowd, but none louder than Uncle Broden, seated at the far end of the table.

He stood with his glass aloft. "I, too, toast the happy couple. I'm pleased to report that repairs to the town house are underway, thanks to Grant's generosity."

Gaping, Janet focused on her husband's face. "You are footing the bill?"

"It seemed the right thing to do."

"That was considerate of you indeed, though Sir Broden's coffers are quite healthy."

"Perhaps, but when one is building allies, it never hurts to spend a bit of coin. Besides, the man did write a missive on my behalf. It may have been the weight that tipped the scales in my favor."

Janet giggled behind her fan. "If that's the case, then we should build him an entire new town house."

"Let's not take things too far."

The music began. Robert stood and bowed. "May I have this dance, lady wife?"

At the sound of his deep brogue calling her "lady wife" for the first time, Janet could have melted. She placed her palm in his. "You may."

Across the table Ciar addressed Emma. "And would you do me the honor, miss?" he asked, placing a hand on her forearm.

The lass's lips formed an O. "Me?"

Rather than bow, which Emma wouldn't be able to see, Ciar took her hand and pulled her to her feet. "Aye, such a bonny gown mustn't remain hidden beneath the table all night."

As Robert led Janet to the dance floor, she inclined her head his way. "Has Ciar met your sister before?"

"Aye, he has been to the manse."

"I thought he might have. He seems to understand how to..."

"Hmm?"

"Well, he understands that for her touching is necessary— Ye ken." Together they strode to the dance floor. "If she were sighted, he would have bowed and offered his hand, but such a common gesture will not work with her."

As Robert escorted Janet to the women's line, he arched his brow at Ciar and Emma. His sister looked as happy as a lass on Christmas morn. "I only hope she doesn't end up turned around."

"She will not. I've practiced with her, and she's as sure-footed as anyone I know." The music demanded Janet curtsy. "Besides, Ciar will keep her on pace. You needn't be concerned."

Robert bowed, sashayed toward her, and grasped her hands. "Then I shan't. This night I have no worries." They joined elbows and promenaded in a circle, their gazes meeting in a smoldering exchange that made the other dancers fade into oblivion. "This night is ours and ours alone."

Author's Note

Thank you for joining me for *The Highland Renegade*. I've been ever so eager to write Robert and Janet's story. You may remember this pair from their cameo appearances in *The Highland Chieftain*, where I established the feuding between their clans. In truth, Clan Grant and Clan Cameron were allies during the Jacobite years, and I did use literary license in creating the rift between them. I based this love story on that of Iain-a-Chraggain Grant and Janet Cameron, who were actually married in 1698. To coincide with the time period of the Lords of the Highlands series, however, I chose to make the wedding occur in 1713.

Of note, Janet gave her husband six children and lived to the ripe age of eighty. She endeared herself to everyone she met. It is said that over two hundred relatives attended her funeral to pay respects to their beloved matriarch.

The record also reports that Robert was a staunch supporter of the Jacobite cause and raised the standard with the Earl of Mar in the 1715 rebellion. He forfeited his lands as a result, but never lost the deep love he harbored for his Janet.

About the Author

Award-winning and Amazon All-Star author Amy Jarecki likes to grab life, latch on, and reach for the stars. She's married to a mountain-biking pharmacist and has put four kids through college. She studies karate, ballet, yoga, and often you'll find her hiking Utah's Santa Clara hills. Reinventing herself a number of times, Amy sang and danced with the Follies, was a ballet dancer, a plant manager, and an accountant for Arnott's Biscuits in Australia. After earning her MBA from Heroit-Watt University in Scotland, she dove into the world of Scottish historical romance and hasn't returned. Become a part of her world and learn more about Amy's books on amyjarecki.com.

Social Media Links:

Facebook: https://www.facebook.com/amyjarecki/
Twitter: https://twitter.com/amyjarecki or
@amyjarecki
Instagram: jareckiamy
Book Bub: https://www.bookbub.com/authors
/amy-jarecki
Goodreads: https://www.goodreads.com/author
/show/5306959.Amy_Jarecki

Looking for more historical romance? Forever brings the heat with these sexy rogues.

MY ONE AND ONLY DUKE
By Grace Burrowes

When London banker Quinn Wentworth is saved from execution by the news he's the long-lost heir to a dukedom, there's just one problem: He's promised to marry Jane Winston, the widowed, pregnant daughter of a prison preacher.

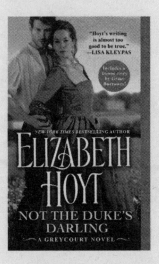

NOT THE DUKE'S DARLING
By Elizabeth Hoyt

When the Duke of Harlowe, the man who destroyed her brother, appears at the country house party Freya de Moray is attending, she does what any devoted sister would do: She starts planning her revenge.

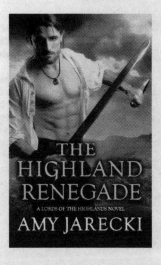

THE HIGHLAND RENEGADE
By Amy Jarecki

Famed for his fierceness, Laird Robert Grant is above all a loyal Highland clan chief. But when redcoats capture his rival's daughter, he sets aside their feud and races to her rescue. Aye, Janet Cameron is beautiful, cunning, and so very tempting, but a Cameron lass is the last woman he should ever desire.

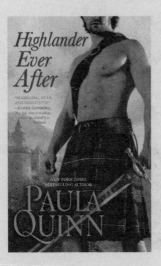

31901064011358